The Gates of the Sun

Luna
4th Archangel

The Gates of the Sun

Sharon Butala

HarperPerennial
HarperCollins*Publishers*Ltd

First published by Fifth House: 1986
First HarperPerennial edition: 1994

Canadian Cataloguing in Publication Data

Butala, Sharon, 1940–
The gates of the sun

"1st HarperPerennial ed."
ISBN 0-00-647535-3

I. Title.

PS8553.U6967G3 1994   C813'.54   C94-931586-9
PR9199.3.B87G3 1994

94 95 96 97 98 99 ❖ HC 10 9 8 7 6 5 4 3 2 1

Printed and bound in the United States

for my mother

The Gates of the Sun

PART ONE

CHAPTER ONE

He remembered a river, wide, flat, silver. It went on forever in every direction and far off from where he stood. People in miniature boats bobbed on its surface, without purpose or direction, like leaves on a puddle. Or rose and floated in the sky, above the water's surface, on a silver streak. Had he dreamt it, perhaps? No, somehow they had crossed a river and he had clung to his mother's black-gloved hand.

Before that there was the feel of a man's rough coat against his cheek, a man's deep voice and his heavy boots setting the air quivering, the jingling of bells on the milkwagon as it passed the window, the prickly silkiness of the horsehide sofa in the parlour, the fern that sat in front of the window so that when he tried to look out he saw only the lucent green, the underwater world of pale sunlight through fern fronds, the warm smell of milk heating for him on the tall black stove.

Then they were hurrying across a wooden platform and a fat man in a black uniform and a hat with a circle of red braid on it lifted him onto the monster that stood vibrating, humming, while whorls of steam gushed down its sides and a man ran shouting down the platform.

The journey, as time went on, tumbled out of a confusion of sensations to a series of clear and bright, but disconnected pictures: the long, jolting ride on the hard wooden wagonseat, the instant when his mother's hands were larger and reddened in the sun, the horses' flanks tightening and releasing. And the green of the Cypress Hills.

There had been a few log shacks with a handful of rough-looking men lounging in the shade and one man on a horse wearing a red jacket. Long after their wagon had passed he had stared backward over his shoulder trying to assimilate the mystery of that brilliant jacket.

All one night, or perhaps two, he had lain beside his mother under the sky. He had felt himself being drawn into the boundless, ringing space between the stars as though something in the complicated, secret interior of his body was a part of the night sky, yearned to break out of the hard prison of his bones, to go back to where it had come from.

But most of all there was the sun filling the sky. Molten light, thundering above them. For days they crossed the prairie under its blaze, until it came to him that he was in the sun's land now, that the sun was lord here, that the sun, perhaps, was the God he had heard of.

Through his dreams dimly he heard the thudding of horse's hooves. Lifting his head in the stuffy darkness of their homesteader's shack, he listened. Beyond the sound of his mother's steady breathing, he heard a faint whinny, the sound perhaps of wind, or a dream whinny from a herd of ghostly horses passing over the land. The sound lingered, growing louder, then softer, then louder again.

He pushed his blankets back, got up stealthily, and made his way by feel through their bedroom and the kitchen to the door of the shack. His heart had begun to thud in his chest and his mouth was dry with eagerness and a touch of fear. Using his fingertips, he found the latch and slowly, with infinite care, so as not to waken his mother, lifted it. The door swung open an inch or two with a muted creak. His mother turned over, the groan of the bedsprings drowning out the noise. He waited till her breathing grew even again.

This far the door creaked, then he had to lift it for a space where it wouldn't swing free over a warped floorboard. Another soft creak, and he was outside. He stood on the doorstep in his bare feet. The full moon struck him, froze him in its white light and he forgot for a second to close the door. When he turned to pull it shut he heard behind him the hoof-beats, the whispering of horseflesh against horseflesh, the snorting of horses mingling with his mother's heavy breathing. He closed out the dark, stifling world of the shack and turned tremulously to whatever the night held.

He wasn't cold, but goosebumps prickled his bare legs, his arms, the back of his neck. Under the thin cotton of his nightshirt, his chest felt enormous, full of awe. There was something miraculous here. He breathed deeply and waited.

They came into view. An endless herd, flowing past, through the unfenced, undefined yard, an immense herd of horses split in their flow by the house, the barn, the corral, so that they were in front of him and behind him, approaching on one hand and leaving on the other. Dust glittering silver in the moonlight rose in silent clouds around their chests, backs, rumps. Heads tossing, manes flowing, they ran silently by on a thousand flashing legs, not seeing him. It was as though they were not real. But in the small pole corral he and his mother had built, their team and two sad-dlehorses raced the fenceline, snorting and whinnying, tossing their heads, thudding to a stop, then racing again.

He watched. Sometimes the herd thinned to a stallion and his few mares and a colt or two, or it swelled in size till he was alone in a sea of horses that whispered in the moonlight, their bodies rubbing against each other, their hooves thudding, the silky sound of their manes and tails rustling in his ears.

After a long time he sat down on the crooked wooden step. He knew he had fallen asleep when the door behind him gave way and he tumbled backwards against his mother's legs. She looked down at him, then across the yard to the horses.

"Nobody could sleep in that racket," she said, turning to her corral where their horses were still stretching their necks over the railing and whinnying. "Go back inside, you'll catch your death of cold."

"I want to watch."

"Inside," she said.

But he lay awake on his cot and would have gone back outside if he hadn't known by her breathing that she was awake too. At dawn he slept for an hour. His dreams were of horses, black stallions, mares as white as the winter's snow that was beginning now to gleam in the coulees and draws of the distant hills. He dreamt of the stud he would conquer and ride to the ends of the flat, grassy earth. Together they would search out the secrets he felt whispering in the prairie breeze, in the harsh cry of the hawk and the nightly barking of the coyotes. He dreamt of being a man.

Andrew and his mother were heading south, bumping across the prairie in a buggy. A ground owl popped up from a deserted gopher hole, a buff-coloured miniature of the giant birds with glowing eyes that sat on the corral at night and woke him with their insistent, knowing call. At the sight of the horses' approaching feet, it vanished back down the hole. A light breeze, tangy with the scent of melting snow, of sprouting grasses and the promise of wildflowers, stirred the grass. A few horned larks swooped up gayly in unison, and down again. A rabbit, its winter white already turned to grey, startled up from a clump of sage and curved away from them with long, soaring bounds, nonchalantly, as though it knew it had nothing to fear.

Andrew imagined sighting down the barrel of his twenty-two, the crack, and . . . his mother bumped his arm roughly without speaking. Why did she never speak? He hated that about her. He looked up in time to guide the team around a three-foot wide burnout, the bottom still damp with the last of the melting snow. At the same instant he caught a glimpse of a few antelope skimming down a distant hillside, then melting away into a draw.

He could hardly contain himself, the slow, methodical pace of the horses irritated him so much. He slapped the reins angrily against their rumps and clicked his tongue.

"They're going fast enough," his mother said. He grunted. He wanted speed, he wanted to fly. He wanted to get down and run across the drying prairie, to roll in the matted, dun-coloured grass, to search with his fingers in it for the first sprouts of green. He wanted that morning back weeks ago when he had stumbled into the house, out of breath, forgetting even to pull off his boots.

"The coulees are running, Ma! The coulees are running," he had shouted, and even his silent mother had put down her broom and followed him outside into the winter brilliance; snow covering the land from horizon to horizon, the sunlight striking it and glancing off so that its shine was blinding. "Listen!" They had stood motionless, holding their breaths, straining to hear.

A faint rushing came to them across the undulating plain. It was the distant roar of cold, clear water running down the hillsides, burbling in rivulets, flooding down the rough, eroded sides of the snow-filled coulees, gathering to race down the coulees themselves. For months the sun had hung cool and white or the palest cream just above the horizon; involuntarily now they lifted their faces to its new warmth.

Andrew clucked his tongue again. They jolted over an anthill that, in his impatience, he hadn't seen. Ahead of them, along the horizon, a bump appeared. That would be the place they were looking for. The horses plodded on.

Soon the black spot opened into detail: a homesteader's house built of planed boards and shingled. Gradually the single spot divided, became two, the other a log barn with an unfinished roof. So it was somebody newly arrived, but they had already begun cultivating. On two sides of the buildings the greening prairie had been turned for a few rounds in long, brown furrows. He studied them, irritation rising again, because they spoiled the look of things.

They drew closer. Nobody came to the door, but a few puffs of pale smoke drifted lazily upward.

Hours earlier, in the first light, as Andrew had been dragging in a sackful of buffalo chips for his mother to burn in the cookstove, he had seen a rider approaching, picking his way slowly around the prickly-pears and the hidden badger and gopher holes, coming up from the south.

Somebody coming, he said into the open door, not taking his eyes off the figure. His mother hurried out and stood on the doorstep shading her eyes with her hand. Often a week went by without anyone even passing their homestead. They waited as the rider drew closer and finally pulled his horse up in front of where they stood on the doorstep. They stared at the trails of dried sweat that lay white against the bay's neck and flanks.

"Need a mid-wife south," the stranger said, jerking his head toward the pale blues and greens shimmering behind him in the direction from which he had come. They heard the soft sound of Montana in his voice. Andrew stared up at him. He was a tall man, wearing a long, stained canvas coat that split up the back and came down to his booted ankles on each side of his horse. In the morning stillness they could hear clearly Andrew's saddlehorse rubbing his head against a pole in the corral. A meadowlark called nearby. Andrew thought his heart might burst with the sound of it, with spring, with what this stranger made him feel.

"Come inside, I'll feed you," Andrew's mother spoke, then turned and stepped back into the darkness of the house. The rider set his felt hat back on his head, and Andrew stared up at his windburned face and at his long black moustache, the tips of which dripped below the line of his jaw on each side of his face. He dismounted wearily and his spurs, worn and blackened, jangled dully. Andrew took the reins from him and turned to lead the horse, a big, rough-looking gelding, toward the barn.

"Just tie him to the corral, Sonny," the man said. "I won't be stayin' long." Andrew obeyed, watching over his shoulder as the man stooped to enter their kitchen. Quickly he looped the reins over the fencepost in a halfhitch, taking a minute to examine the frayed bedroll tied to the back of the saddle, then hurried into the house.

His mother was at the stove frying steak. Then, wiping her hands on her apron, she began to slice fresh-made bread. The stranger was seated at the table, his hat beside him, his elbows making wrinkles in the shiny oilcloth. He seemed weary, half-asleep, and the light from the window behind him cast his face in shadow. He hadn't taken off his heavy coat.

"I hear Smith and Lambert are looking for men for spring work," his mother said, raising her voice over the sizzling of the steak in the blackened, cast-iron pan. Silently, not taking his eyes off the visitor, Andrew slid into a chair across from him. His mother set the sliced bread on the table and, turning back to the stove, broke two eggs on top of the meat. The man moved, the canvas of his coat protesting, and put one arm down so that his large hand dangled over the edge of the table.

"What makes you think I'm looking for work?" he asked, in a faintly amused tone. Andrew and his mother glanced at each other. The man laughed, a deep, quick chuckle, then stopped as if he were too tired to keep it up. The odour of horseflesh rose from him. Surreptitiously, Andrew drew it in. His mother set a plate of steaming meat and eggs in front of him. He began to eat at once.

"Big places always need men," he said, his mouth full. "Work you twenty hours a day, rain or shine, give you the ground to sleep on, and five minutes notice when they don't want you no more." The coffee had begun to boil. Andrew's mother took it off the stove, using a folded cloth for a potholder, filled a chipped blue granite mug and set it in front of their guest. "Thank you, Ma'am," he said. "The way settlers are coming in, soon won't be any range left anyway. Even up here. Be fences running this way and that all over the country Everything be plowed up. Where'll a man go then?" He turned his head to look over his shoulder toward the window as he said this. He didn't seem to expect an answer. He turned back, lifted his mug and sipped his coffee noisily.

"What's your name?" he asked Andrew.

"Andrew." He said it quickly, then held his breath.

"Andy, hmmm," the man said, and might have gone on, but Andrew's mother interrupted.

"She need me right away?" He didn't look up.

"They figured she was just getting started good." He cleared his throat, sighed. "Straight south, four miles, past that steep coulee. There's two hills over west behind the shack. Head for them." She nodded, her hands on her hips.

"The country's filling up," she said. "Soon be a homesteader on every quarter." She frowned, pursing her lips as if she were counting up all the babies she would be asked to deliver. Andrew tried to imagine opening the door of their house and seeing a steady stream of people walking past, riding past, wheeling past in wagons. The picture dismayed him, puzzled him, and he dismissed it. Impossible.

"It's all dry," the visitor went on, wiping his plate with a piece of bread. "You can cut straight south."

When he had finished the meal, he rose, took the sweatstained stetson Andrew handed him, and put it on his head, casting his lean face into further shadow. He was so tall he towered over them, and he bent his head a little from what seemed to be habit.

"Much obliged for the meal," he said. He turned and strode out of the house, the bare wooden floor complaining under his weight, his spurs clinking. Hastily Andrew shoved back his chair and followed. Outside, the man untied his horse and mounted him in one easy motion, then turned him north. When he had gone a few yards, he kicked him into a trot and turned in the saddle to give Andrew and his mother an indifferent wave and a faint, wry smile.

Andrew watched the figure growing smaller, his back rising and falling in a lazy, relaxed motion as he rode away across the grass. In the dim house, in that one gesture of lifting his arm to put on his hat, his coat had fallen away from his lean body, and Andrew had seen the glint of a revolver at his hip.

They drew closer to the two buildings. Andrew's mother reached inside her coat and straightened her blouse over her full bosom, then pulled down its long sleeves with a firm, authoritative tug. She patted the bun of dark hair that rested on the back of her neck and sat straighter. The door opened and a man came out and stood on the porch.

"Whoa." Andrew pulled up the team, putting his mother between himself and the doorway. She climbed down awkwardly, with dignity.

"How is she?" she asked, taking her knitted bag, which Andrew handed down to her.

"Close," the man said. He ground out a cigarette under his boot heel. As he bent, Andrew could see the beginning of a bald spot in his blonde hair. His skin was darkened from the sun and the wind and his face was lined and hard. He turned and opened the door into the house, waiting for Andrew's mother to enter.

"Unhitch the team," she said to him, then followed the husband inside. The door opened again at once and his mother called to him, "Then come inside." She shut the door again.

He sat for a moment, gazing out over the vast, bright prairie. That way was Montana, five miles to the south. The clear light poured evenly across the grassland, which seemed to him to float outward and upward to a thin line of hills on the other side of the invisible border. Above that, the Bear Paw mountains, a peaked, delicate, mauve shadow, sat for a short distance along the horizon. He thought how one day he would ride to those mountains, see them for himself.

To his right the view was much the same: miles of short yellow grass, faintly green, rippling out to meet the huge sky. West, it was no different, and if he could have seen behind him to the north, his own home would have been lost to view in the long miles of short yellow-green grass.

But now the wind was rising suddenly, whirling up dust-devils, making a loose red rag tied to a post by the barn slap, slap, against it. The wind blew cleanly, fiercely from the empty east, across the prairie, gathering strength, into the emptiness to the west. He sat in the middle of it and felt its sweep all around.

He slapped the reins, the horses started and he drove them to the barn. He climbed down from the buggy and, reaching in past the horses' rumps, unhooked the traces from the singletrees. The grassy scent of horse was strong in his nostrils and he savoured it. Bess swished her tail and caught him in the face.

11

"Don't," he said, conscious of his high-pitched boy's voice. It embarrassed him, when he was doing a man's job. He hooked the traces into the little hooks on the breaching and stepped back. Two children had appeared from nowhere, out of the barn, maybe, and were watching him. One was a boy his own age, in scuffed boots, wearing too-short pants that revealed his thin ankles, and a faded shirt under a torn jacket. The other was a little girl of about six, her washed-out cotton dress hanging limply around her bare knees and her jacket buttoned crookedly. She kept one finger in her mouth and stared at him.

Andrew nodded gravely at them as he walked to the front of the team. He copied the expression and the gesture from the men who hung around McNulty's store in town. To Belle and Bess, who were rubbing their heads together, he said, in as gruff a voice as he could summon, "Cut that out now!" Bess tossed her head again, then stood quietly. He stepped between them and lifted the neck yoke, undoing the snaps that held it to the harness, and let the yoke drop. When he stepped back, he was unable to resist a quick look at the other boy, hoping he had noticed what a good team they were, well-matched, their dappled grey sides smooth and fleshy, their chest muscles swelling under their shiny coats. The boy was watching silently, his hands in his jacket pockets, his expression alert, but noncommittal.

At the horses' heads again, Andrew unhooked the crosschecks. A few pigeons on the roof of the barn cooed noisily to each other. Behind the horses and the children, a door slammed, a thin sound in the miles of emptiness, in the wind. All three of them turned. The man had come out and was leaning on the porch rail smoking.

At the sight of him, Andrew began to work faster. He used half-hitches to secure the crosschecks over the hames, then unfastened the halter shanks which had been looped through the rings on the side of the hames, and let them fall to the ground. Immediately both horses lowered their heads. Andrew breathed an inward sigh of relief. He was still too small to reach their heads to take the bridles off as the men did. When they dropped their heads like that, Andrew knew they were tired, anxious to get them off, and he wouldn't have to fight them in front of his audience.

Rapidly he plaited first one line, then the other, and pushed each folded line through the rings where the halter shanks had been. When he finally slipped the bridles off, the horses shook their heads gratefully, then lifted them, and he led them, first Belle, then Bess, into stalls and tied them. When he came from the pungent dimness of the barn, the horses grinding on hay, their harnesses clinking dully now and then, the two children had disappeared.

Andrew lowered his eyes and started across the yard. The man straightened as he drew near, dropped his cigarette onto the porch floor, and ground it out under his boot heel. He nodded to Andrew. His hands, lying loose on the railing, were thick and brown and his jacket was stained and worn.

"I'll water them horses for you later, the man said. "She wants you inside." He tossed his head backwards, toward the door. Inside the house, someone walked across the floor and a woman's voice broke the silence. Andrew couldn't tell if it was his mother or someone else. Reluctantly he mounted the two crooked wooden steps onto the porch. He didn't want to go inside, but he could not avoid what his mother expected of him. He crossed the porch and reached for the doorknob. "I'll be in the barn," the man said.

For a moment till his eyes adjusted to the dimness of the light after the glare of out-of-doors, he could see nothing. Across the room his mother stood with her back to him at a cast-iron cookstove, its nickel trim gleaming dully, on which two grey granite kettles, one large, one small, were hissing and casting up clouds of steam. She turned to him, one strong, competent hand on her hip.

"Wash your hands." Using a folded towel, she lifted the larger of the two kettles and poured a little water into a white-enameled basin she had placed on the table which sat in the middle of the room between them. He set his hat on a wooden chair by the door, crossed the room and waited while his mother took a dipperful of cold water from a pail that sat on a stool by the stove and poured it into the basin of hot water. He put his hands into the water and she gave him a coarse bar of soap and a small towel made of floursacking. He tried not to think about what she might want him to do, concentrating on getting the dirt out from under his fingernails, sniffing his hands till he couldn't smell horse on them anymore.

As he dried his hands he looked curiously around the room. Now he saw an open door on his left and in that room, a woman lying on a double bed. The bed had an iron headboard and through the brown-painted posts of the footboard, although the room was even darker than the kitchen, he could see her mass of dark hair spread out on the pillow and her large, dark eyes gleaming in her white face. As he looked, she gave a long, grunting sigh that sounded as if it had been forced out of her by a giant hand pressing on her body. She tossed and the light sheet covering her raised up and twisted and then fell back. He couldn't take his eyes off her.

"Hurry up," his mother said, in a tense, low voice. She went into the bedroom and murmured to the woman, who had fallen silent. At her command, Andrew started, his heart speeding up a little, but he set the towel down and followed her.

It was a small, bare room with unpainted plaster walls thrown in shadow by the curtains drawn over the one window. Shards of light escaped from around the curtains and they stirred a little as the wind leaked in around the frame. His mother stood between the bed and a dresser, on which were laid out folded towels, rags, a basin and scissors. In the discoloured glass of the mirror above the dresser was a yellowish, floating image of the woman on the bed.

Supporting the woman's head with one hand, his mother pulled the two pillows out from under her, then threw back the sheet that covered her. The woman's nightdress was well above her bent and spread knees. Andrew was rooted to the floor with embarrassment and shock at her nakedness, and then his mother thrust the pillows into his arms. He walked around to the opposite side of the bed and set them on an armchair with a broken back that sat in the corner. The woman moaned again and thrashed heavily. Her face was distorted with some great effort, her eyes screwed shut, her face and neck shiny with sweat.

Heat seemed to rise and swirl about him as if there were a hot wind in the room. The iron bedstead vibrated with her struggle. Another moan escaped her, this one high-pitched, ending in an expulsion of breath. It was acute, despairing. Do something, he wanted to say, but he couldn't speak.

"Now, now," his mother said, her voice calm. She smoothed back the dark strand of hair that had fallen across the woman's face and neck. Andrew's hands were wet with sweat, sweat trickled down the back of his neck and his temples and into his eyes. His knees trembled. "Come around here," his mother said urgently, softly, and Andrew jerked as though his feet had been glued to the floor. When he passed the foot of the bed, he looked at the woman, unable to help himself, and saw between her spread legs what he knew must be the top of the baby's head. He stumbled as if there had been a hole in the floor and dizziness touched him, then left.

"It's coming," she said. "Get the kettle." The woman was grunting now—deep, involuntary grunts that seemed to have been wrenched loose by the baby's struggle to free itself. Andrew hurried into the kitchen. Wrapping the damp flour sack he had dried his hands on around the handle, he pulled the smaller kettle toward himself, too rapidly, so that water spilled over onto the stove, then bubbled and danced across the hot iron surface, burning his wrist. Carefully, holding the kettle with both hands out in front of his chest, blinking with the pain from his stinging wrist, taking short, jerky steps, he carried it to the bedroom.

"Sterilize those scissors," his mother said, tossing her head toward the basin that sat on a folded towel on the dresser behind her. She was bent over between the woman's legs and didn't look at him. He was glad of that. He didn't want her to see him now, how frightened he was, and how full of a sense of something wrong. The woman shrieked as if surprised, then her shriek trailed away into soft, puffy gasps. "The head's coming," his mother said, tense-voiced, but matter-of-fact. "Push harder." The woman moaned again and behind them Andrew gratefully rested the kettle on the towel and wiped the sweat and tears from his face. "Aaaah," his mother said, in a new voice.

There was the baby—slick, red, slimy, its arms flailing, its tiny fists balled. His mother held it in her hands and it was so small. He looked to the mother, but she had closed her eyes. Sweat gleamed on her face and neck. There were wet patches on her coarse, white gown. Alarmed, Andrew thought she might be dead. He tried to draw a breath to speak to his mother, but it wouldn't come. But then the woman drew a long, shaky breath and turned her head to one side.

Then he was working so fast, trying to do what his mother asked, that he hadn't time to wonder. He lifted the hot scissors out of the basin without burning himself again, handed them to his mother, waited while she cut the cord, saw the spurt of bright blood, took them back again, handed her a clean cloth to wipe the baby, found and gave her the new knitted blanket the mother must have made to wrap her baby in.

"It's a girl," Andrew's mother said in an absent-minded tone, as if this was of little interest. The woman had begun pushing again. His mother reached over to Andrew and handed him the baby. He was amazed at how light she was, no heavier than a puppy or a kitten, and how well she fit into the crook of his arm. She was silent, her eyes shut tight in her dusky face. He stared down at the wrinkled, ugly little face with the tuft of dark hair at its peak. She was alive. He could suddenly hardly credit it. How had this thing happened?

"Let me," the mother said in a weak voice, and he came back to the moment. She had raised her arm, opening it, and when he set the baby against her body, she drew her arm in around the child, folding it against her. She raised her head off the bed briefly, looked into the little face, and smiled. Then she lay back, not looking at the child again.

"Take this out and bury it somewhere." His mother's voice was sharp. She handed him a basin covered with a rag. He took it, not without reluctance, but his mother had already turned away to fuss with the bedclothes. He went slowly out of the bedroom, pausing at the door to put his hat on, while he balanced the basin with one arm. "And tell Mr. Royce he can come in now."

He stood for a second in the doorway, blinking in the blinding light of midafternoon. He could look only in flashes at the treeless, damp yard, the unpainted barn, the pale horizon a long, flat distance away.

He wanted to shift his hands under the basin so he wouldn't feel its warmth, but there was no other way to carry it. When he was almost at the barn the husband stepped abruptly out of the dark interior and stood blinking in the sun. His son and daughter slipped into the light beside him and waited as Andrew approached, staring at the bowl he held. The little girl had twigs of hay caught in her pale hair and she held onto her father's pantleg with one small fist. The boy stood motionless, his hands on his hips, imitating his father. Andrew fought back tears. He wanted to shout, my father's dead, but instead, he drew in his breath and spoke as gruffly as he could to the man.

"You can go inside."

The man's face quickened and he looked toward the house.

"Is there a shovel around?" Andrew asked.

Show the boy where there's a shovel, Nick," he said, without taking his eyes off the house. He brushed imaginary dirt off the seat of his pants with both palms and started toward the house, striding jerkily over the uneven ground, as if he couldn't be bothered to watch where he was going. They heard the porch boards creak under his boots, then the door shut behind him.

Nick disappeared inside the barn. In a moment he was back carrying a spade. They started around to the back of the barn, Nick still carrying the spade, Andrew with the basin, in the lead. He felt strong now, and in charge. The little girl was following them.

"She coming?" he asked Nick, halting abruptly. Nick stumbled over a gopher hole, looked first to Andrew, then to his sister. There was a long silence while they studied her. She had stopped walking, too, and looked back at them sullenly, her arms hanging by her sides. The wind lifted her fine, pale hair and set it down again. Andrew saw her mother, writhing, crying out. "She can't come," he said angrily to Nick. "Send her away."

"Go on, Emma," Nick said. She didn't move. "Go on to the house. I'll come in a minute." Still she didn't move. "Go on!" he shouted, taking a threatening step toward her. She stepped back then, turned away, and started for the house. In a second she was running.

They walked around to the back of the barn. Andrew set the basin on the ground, feeling as though he had been relieved of a great weight. The rag still covered it and he didn't lift it. Nick stared at it with frank curiosity, but made no move to look beneath the cloth either.

There was a long, melting bank of dirty snow pushed by the wind against the barn wall and in front of it the ground was wet.

"Easy digging, Nick said. He struck the ground experimentally with the tip of the spade. It dug into the yellow earth and pushed up a chunk of clay. They began to dig, taking turns. When the hole was deep enough, Andrew took the basin and without removing the cloth, slid the contents into the hole, and Nick, quickly, before they could see what was there, threw a shovelful of earth over it. Neither of them said anything. Far off behind them a hawk shrieked faintly, circling high above the earth, and a flock of crows swooped past. They ground the basin around in the snowbank till it was clean, and then scrubbed their hands till they ached, in the dirty, granular snow.

"Come on to the house," Nick said, and Andrew followed humbly, having been reduced, by the completion of this task, to a guest. They found Emma sitting at the table, swinging her short legs, eating a cookie, a half-full glass of milk on the oilcloth in front of her. Through the doorway they could see her mother propped up against pillows, holding her baby. Nick stood in the doorway silently, looking at his mother and his new sister. His father sat on one side of the bed and Andrew's mother on the other. They were drinking tea. Nick moved into the room and stood beside his father. Andrew sat down at the kitchen table across from Emma. She lifted her eyes from her cookie and studied him. Her stare disconcerted him, he didn't know how to respond to it.

Behind Emma's back, in the other room, Andrew's mother had finished her tea. She began to bustle around the room, tidying, picking up things from the dresser and the floor and putting them into her knitted bag. They would be going soon. Andrew wondered if he should go hitch up the team.

"You got a name for her?" his mother asked the parents. The man said nothing, as though all of this had nothing to do with him.

"Elizabeth," the woman said. Her reply floated through the shadowy, warm air to the kitchen where Andrew and Emma sat at the table.

"Elizabeth Ann." Abruptly Emma lowered her eyes from Andrew's face, and smiled at the tabletop, as if this were what she had been waiting for.

It had been daylight less than an hour when Andrew, sitting at the table eating his breakfast bowl of porridge, heard hoofbeats. He set down his spoon and hurried to the door. He was in time to see a rider disappear into the deep coulee that ran across the northeast corner of their land. He waited. Soon the rider appeared again; his hat, then his shoulders, then the fringed head of his horse, rising eerily out of the white morning fog that still floated in the low places.

Inside the shack his mother was banging pots and pans. He had just brought her home from three days nursing a sick homesteader's family to the south of them and she was tired and irritable. He watched the rider kick his horse into a trot as he neared the house. Andrew had lost his usual interest at the sight of an approaching rider. This fall there had been too many riders approaching, looking for his mother, full of tales of sickness and death. In a moment, the rider was at the doorstep, his horse's hooves ringing clearly on the hard-packed, frozen ground. It was Freddy du Chaler. His father raised the finest horses in the district, blood horses. Everyone was afraid of him, afraid of his contempt and his icy stare, of his sudden, unprovoked rages, especially when he was drunk. Freddy and Andrew went to school together, each coming from six miles in opposite directions to converge in the school barn at the last minute before the teacher rang the bell. Freddy hadn't been at school for at least a week the day the board chairman, nervous in his grease-stained workclothes, twisting his cap in his thick hands, came and told them all to go home.

"Ain't no use keeping it open for a handful of kids," he said to the prim young woman who was their teacher. "Doc says we're just spreading the influenza."

As soon as Freddy pulled up his horse, threw his leg over and slid off, Andrew knew there was sickness. He could tell by the way Freddy moved, by his failure to say hello, by the pinched look of his face and eyes.

"Your ma home?" he asked. He took small breaths between the words as if he couldn't quite get enough air. The heaviness in Andrew's chest tightened. He stepped back into the open doorway. "Come inside," Freddy knotted the reins around the post by the door and followed him inside. "Breakfast?" Andrew's mother asked without turning her head. She began to ladle left-over porridge into a bowl.

"My dad's sick," Freddy said, and the breathless way he said it also told them how sick he was. His mother's hand hesitated over the bread she was slicing, then it moved again, more quickly. They could hear Freddy's breath, quick and sharp. Andrew stood motionless at the door, waiting for his instructions.

"You sit down," she said to Freddy. "It's no help if you don't eat."

"Will you come?" He took a step toward the table, then stopped, as if whether he ate or not depended on her answer. In the shadowed room Andrew could see his faded, threadbare shirt quivering across his back, each heartbeat setting up a tremor.

"Maybe you need the doctor," she suggested in a flat voice, her back to him as she lifted the stove lid and poked at the fire.

"Doctor's way over west. Won't be back before tomorrow." He pulled out the chair and sat down, leaning hungrily over the food she had set out for him. He didn't lift the spoon, still waiting for her answer. "Mom don't feel too good either," he said. His voice caught. He breathed in rapidly, a rasping sound they could hear clearly over the crackling of the burning wood in the stove.

"Right after you eat," she said. "Hurry up." She was all action now, her tiredness had fallen away. "Hitch up the buggy," she said to Andrew, but he was only waiting to see Freddy take the first bite. Freddy dipped his spoon into the porridge with a gesture half-eager, half-reluctant.

Wordlessly, Andrew left them. He caught and harnessed the horses, and hitched them to the buggy. Before he had reached the house his mother came out wearing her good coat, her knitted bag under her arm. Freddy followed close behind. He untied his horse and mounted him, using the doorstep to reach, while Andrew's mother settled herself in the buggy beside Andrew. They set out north in the thin, late fall sunlight, moving slowly through the dissipating mist.

By noon they were at the du Chaler's. As soon as the place came in sight Freddy loped on ahead of them, dismounted and went inside. He didn't reappear until Andrew had dropped off his mother and was unhitching the team in front of the barn.

"Where's Hélène?" Andrew asked.

"Sick," Freddy said. They began to do chores, Freddy milking, and Andrew gathering the eggs. Then, carrying the milk and eggs, they went together to the house. His mother met them at the door. Freddy slipped past her, inside.

"There's no sense you staying," she said to Andrew. "You can eat some dinner, then go home and look after the stock. Come back tomorrow."

He was used to being alone. He had no companions, except when he was at school. He herded their cattle alone, he lay on his stomach behind greasewood alone and waited to snare gophers, or tried to see how close he could creep to a herd of grazing antelope. On foot, he ran alone from badgers that swelled themselves up and hissed at him, their long, sharp, digging claws extended, and often, he came upon coyotes who, like him, wandered in the lonely, windswept hills by themselves. And now, with sickness everywhere and his mother away more often than not, he, at ten years old, often stayed alone. But, in a country so huge that no matter how many settlers came it did not seem possible to fill it, and where so many men lived alone in shacks far from people, and where cowboys rode alone for weeks at a time—he often came upon one of them in the hills— it did not seem strange to be alone.

He ate the dinner she had prepared, ignoring the sick people in the bedroom and on the cot by the stove, put his hat on, and left. He drove home listening to the creaking of the harness, did the chores, made himself a cold supper, and went to bed. Hours later he found himself awake, as though he had been dreaming of something clean and bright and had slipped into wakefulness without noticing it. He lay motionless, puzzled. Then he saw that the interior of the house was brightly lit, as though from a full moon. But the full moon was past, more than a week. He lay still, listening. Outside the door, the dogs had set up a clamour. He threw back the covers, and padding on his bare feet on the cold floor, went outside.

The countryside was lit up like daylight. He could make out every knot on the poles of the corral, each shingle on the barn roof, the sculptured edge of the deep coulee to the north. But the clarity and hue of the light was not natural, it was like nothing he had seen before. It was blue-white, and sharp; it flooded the plain and cast no shadows. He saw this in a wondering second, and in the same instant he heard how the night was filled with noise. All the drifting cattle near and far on the plain before him and in the distant hills were bawling. Coyotes yipped and wailed from their perches on the distant rises. In the corral beside him the saddlehorses tossed their heads and whinnied in agitation.

He stood paralyzed with fear in the doorway, both hands on the doorknob, his feet like ice. The light held steady. He looked down at his hands, already calloused from work. He could see the veins on their backs raised and blue with blood. Fear made his heart pound, made sweat creep down his backbone and under his arms. He could find no explanation for this. He didn't know what to do.

Abruptly the light died. It happened so quickly that he could still see the lit-up buildings and hills against his eyelids when he blinked. A wind leapt up and he shivered. Now there was only the faint light of the few distant stars. Gradually the noises of the animals died, till there was only the night silence and the voice of the wind whispering through the cracks in the house and the barn.

Suddenly he stepped back inside the dark house, slamming the door shut, then dropping his hands as if the doorknob had been hot. He felt for and found the lamp standing where it always did in the centre of the table. He lit it while shivers ran up and down his spine and the hairs on the back of his neck bristled.

The lamplight flared, the walls drew in comfortingly as the light steadied. He lifted the lamp and held it chest high in front of him as he went into the new room they had built off the kitchen. There was no one there. He searched the bedroom but nothing had been disturbed anywhere in the house.

For a long time he stood holding the lamp, trying to absorb what he had seen. When the lamp grew heavy and he suddenly realized how very cold he was, he went back into the bedroom, set the lamp on the stand beside his bed and climbed into bed, covering himself up to his chin. He lay and shivered with the cold.

Was this something like whirlwinds in the desert and pillars of fire that his mother had told him about? A star losing its grip in the sky and crashing to the earth? But there had been no crash, no shower of light. After a while he fell asleep. He dreamt that he was walking in the light. He could feel the prickly, dry shortgrass under his bare feet and the cool night breeze on his thighs. All around him in the bright quick air, unseen creatures drifted, and he walked among them unafraid.

Again it was noon when he drove up to du Chaler's small frame house. There was nobody in the yard. Now it looked like all the other yards Andrew had driven into this fall, silent except for the scuffling of a few hens on the frozen ground, or the urgent mooing of an unmilked cow in the corral or the barn, and the house with a closed, dead look. He was suddenly too impatient to unhitch the team. He tied them to the corral and went straight to the house. As he put his hand on the doorknob the door gave inward and his mother was there, already speaking to him.

"Get some more firewood," she said as though he had only just walked out a minute before. He was taken aback, not so much by her tone as by the look on her face as she stood filling the doorway, the sunlight on her face. It was a look of fear, and perhaps even of a dark, smouldering anger kept in check all night. He stepped back, his eagerness gone. She turned away with a distracted gesture utterly unlike her and shut the door in his face.

The heaviness was on him again. He unhitched the team, working patiently, methodically, like the men did. Clumsily, the axe heavy and awkward in his grasp, he chopped a pile of firewood and carried an armload inside.

The outer door opened into the kitchen like all the houses did, and the bedroom off to the side was separated from it by a curtain hanging in the doorway which had been pushed aside and draped over a nail. The cookstove was on the other side of the kitchen and someone still lay on a small iron cot beside it.

He crossed the room, dumped his armload of wood into the almost empty woodbox by the stove, and opened the stove lid. When he turned back to the woodbox to get a stick for the fire, he saw that it was Freddy's father on the cot. He poked at the burning wood inside the stove and shoved in a fresh stick.

In the bedroom on his right, his mother was speaking softly to someone. It seemed to him that he had heard her speak in just that way a thousand times, that this moment had been repeated more times than he could count already in his short life. Someone sick, her soft murmuring, his listening, not wanting to hear.

Wearily he glanced over his shoulder into the bedroom and saw that Mrs. du Chaler and Helene, the oldest girl, were in the bed. His mother stood beside them. She came out of the room carrying a cup and a spoon. Where were the little kids? Where was Freddy?

He held the second stick above the fire, forgetting it momentarily as the rasping, too quick breathing of someone in the bedroom became audible. Involuntarily he glanced down at Mr. du Chaler beside him. He lay silently, not moving. As if in reply to Andrew's silent inquiry, he suddenly made a loose bubbling noise, which might have been a moan. It was so strange a noise that Andrew almost dropped the wood. Hastily he shoved it into the fire and replaced the lid.

His mother appeared noiselessly beside him and bent over the cot. She put her hand on the sick man's forehead, then straightened the ragged grey blanket that covered him. The fire crackled, the rasping breath came from the other room, his mother's red-knuckled hand pulled on the blanket. These sights and sounds seemed to Andrew to increase in clarity and intensity until he couldn't breathe; he was afraid everything would burst, simply burst and scatter.

"Freddy's gone for the doctor," his mother said, and it was a second before her words made sense to him. Everything tumbled slowly back into place. He cleared his thoat and it sounded normal. His mother patted her hair in the absent-minded way she had, smoothed down her dress collar, and then suddenly looking exhausted, sat down by the table. Andrew watched uncertainly. He looked again at the figure lying on the cot. His big, hooked nose looked pathetic now and with his straight black hair pushed back from his forehead it was possible to see the startlingly fine-grained, white upper half of his forehead which had been protected for years by his hat brim.

Freddy claimed his father was a Count and no number of schoolyard beatings would make him retract. Andrew's mother had said wearily, "Maybe he is, he wouldn't be the only one around here." Then she had laughed, a short, derisive sound. "A lot of good it does them." Andrew had asked her why a Count—he was not sure what a Count was other than it was something special—would choose to come here. "Probably got into some kind of trouble," she said. "Had to run away." Seeing how erratic and violent du Chaler was, Andrew had decided he must have committed a murder. He imagined a stone castle, darkness, the splash of oars in fog, and a tall ship looming darkly over a small rowboat rocking in the black water. He had seen it in a book their teacher had read to them.

But nothing the du Chalers had ever said or done gave a clue to their origin. Mrs. du Chaler was probably Indian, and all the children, boys and girls, were dark and slender and quick.

Mr. du Chaler's hair was straight and black without a hint of grey despite his lined face and wrinkled neck, which gave his age away. He had a large, hooked nose, which Freddy had inherited, and deep-set, very blue eyes. One long, thin leg was stiff sometimes, and he carried a cane which he didn't hesitate to use on anyone—his children, his wife—who got in his way or angered him.

Once, when Andrew had been out hunting and at noon had found himself near the du Chaler's, he had gone there in search of Freddy and been invited to stay for the noon meal. They had eaten in silence and as soon as the meal was over, Mr. du Chaler ordered his daughters with a look and a nod, to leave the table, which they did at once, quickly and wordlesssly. He lit his pipe then, and began to talk to Andrew and Freddy about hunting moose and elk in the north, which he had done when he first came to Canada. His small, silent brown wife worked around them. He ignored her. Andrew noticed she was wearing moccasins.

"Where did you come from, boy?" he had asked Andrew in a tone that was almost jovial.

"The United States," Andrew said. Mr. du Chaler fixed his sharp blue eyes on him.

"Everyone here comes from somewhere else," he said. "Even Frederic here, my uncivilized offspring, born in Québec, and my wife," he tossed his head toward her, "she comes from Ontario." Was there something peculiar about the way he said, "wife?" Was Andrew at last to find out about Mr. du Chaler's past? He gazed at his host, not daring to take his eyes off him. "But all these others," here he tossed his arm to indicate all the other settlers for miles around, "they come from everywhere. From Europe most of them, like me. Peasants. The scum of the earth." He stared hard at Andrew, his eyes deepening, growing fierce and full of scorn. Andrew couldn't look away.

"They come to the . . . new world," here he tossed his hand out again, ". . . the new world. And in this new world, each is lost. Lost. Each must make himself anew." Andrew and Freddy waited, afraid to move, sensing the emotion ready to flare in him. "To leave behind an old, a worn-out world, a world with too many people, teeming with people, for this emptiness." He was silent, then abruptly laughed a short, harsh laugh, too loud in the small room. "Perhaps it is easier to find God here." He looked at Andrew and then over to his son who looked exactly like him. "Do you think it is easier to find God here?" Andrew recalled suddenly another moment like this one in another settler's shack.

He had watched from a cot in the kitchen while the doctor and Sawa, the husband, drank a glass of home brew after the birth of the husband's seventh child. Andrew's mother sat with her in the bedroom, and outside, the morning's welcome rain had finally stopped.

"Ah, Mike," the doctor had said, "Why so many babies?" His thin spotted hand trembled as it reached across the space to the filled glass.

"A man has to have children," Mike replied. "God wants." He was a big, blonde middle-aged man, massive in the shoulders and chest. The doctor tipped back his head, emptied his glass.

"God doesn't have to buy them shoes," the doctor said, holding out the empty glass to have it refilled. Mike laughed loudly, throwing back his head, slapping the wooden table with the flat of his thick hand. The doctor tossed back the second drink. Mike stopped laughing and refilled the glass. Water dripped from the corners of the roof with a steady, cheerful murmur. The sun had begun to shine in the two small windows and now the flies, excited by the rain, buzzed noisily around the room.

"What they need shoes for? Except winter?" Mike asked. Two small girls watched the men from the corner by the stove. Their small feet were bare and dirty. "We plow the land, we grow wheat," he paused to drink, "and nobody tells me what to do. Nobody." He banged his glass on the table and sat back, his jaw thrust forward belligerently. The doctor watched him, his gold-rimmed glasses smudged and slightly askew. The unshaven stubble on his chin shone silver and his wrinkled eyelids drooped over his small eyes. His suit looked as if he had slept in it. It seemed too big for him, as if he might have shrunk since buying it.

"Another sip," he said, pushing his glass toward Mike, who filled it. "Somebody told you what to do in the old country?" Andrew had a sense that the doctor was talking only to keep Mike pouring drinks. He didn't take his eyes off the clear liquid pouring from bottle to glass. Mike made a large, disgusted sound. Andrew moved carefully. His back was aching from sitting so long in one spot, but he didn't want to call attention to his presence.

"Me, I have my own land—a few acres—not much, but I tell you . . . ." He leaned confidentially toward the doctor, who breathed noisily through his nose and blinked. Two spots of red had appeared high up on his flabby cheeks. "I tell you," Mike said, "the priests, they not leave you alone. They tell you who to marry, when to marry, you give them the best hen, the best fruit, grain . . . .They the boss!" He leaned back in his chair. "Here, I the boss!" The chatter of the birds on the roof grew louder. Andrew longed to be outside.

The doctor had drained his glass again.

"The boss of not much," he said, almost to himself. "This land won't grow a damn thing, and it's miles to school, more miles to church, and more again to a hospital. And look how far away your neighbours are. At least in your own village you had family and friends around you. Your wife wasn't lonesome. Nobody would let you starve." Mike grew louder as he drank.

"Schools! Churches!" His scorn was boundless. "I have enough churches in the old country to last forever." He slammed his fist on the wooden table so hard his empty glass fell over and the doctor's glass jumped. "I come for freedom," he said, whispering loudly to the doctor. The doctor, at the word "freedom" dropped his eyes. "Freedom from the priests, from the landlords. Here I have a hundred sixty acre and I get more, you'll see."

"Freedom," the doctor murmured, his head still down. He laughed, ever so gently. The more he drank, the steadier he became. His reddened eyes behind the dirty glasses gazed sharply at Mike, the shape of his mouth bitter. Mike was refilling their glasses. Andrew's mother appeared in the doorway to the bedroom, her hands on her hips, her lips pressed in a thin line. The children turned their heads in unison to look at her, then looked back at the men sitting at the table.

"Maybe you will," the doctor said. "Maybe you will, and we'll see how much good it does you." He turned to gaze speculatively at the two dirty little girls crouched on the chair in the corner, staring back at him with wide blue eyes. "Got to press on," he said at last. "Broken arm to set, sick children to tend to."

Andrew was suddenly afraid Mr. du Chaler might strike one of them with his cane.

"These settlers who come now by the thousands with their wives and babies and their puny belongings, they didn't come to find God! No!

What do they care about God? They came to find gold!" He leaned toward the two boys, his eyes pinpoints of light, fixed on them. He's crazy, Andrew thought, and was frightened. "Ha!" du Chaler shouted. "The only gold to be found here is in the pockets of the bankers, the grain buyers, and the land speculators back East! Gullible fools!" His face had grown very red, his nostrils dilated, he was breathing hard through them. "They come and pollute the place with their fences and their churches, their schools, their flower gardens, their filthy towns!"

Abruptly he stood up, and shoving back his chair so hard it tipped over, he strode across the room and out the door. There was no trace of a limp. Freddy's mother, still not speaking, closed the door, then, her face impassive, bent and set the chair in its place.

Now Mr. du Chaler sighed heavily and drew his knees up under the thin grey blanket in a stiff, unnatural way, then lowered them jerkily. Andrew and his mother watched him, Andrew from where he stood in front of the stove, his mother turning in her chair by the table.

He sighed again. This time the sigh ended in a chesty rumbling which went on and on. His mother leaned forward and as the noise continued without relief, she stood and went to him. Would it never stop? His body arched upward and Andrew's mother put her hands lightly on his shoulders as if to persuade him to lie back again, but Andrew could see that her hands on his shoulders had nothing to do with whatever was happening to him, that they didn't even reach him. Then, slowly, as if all of it were only a dream, he collapsed back onto the bed, the light blanket drifting down after him. He grew smaller, less substantial.

Slowly now, Andrew's mother took her hands away and straightened. She looked at Andrew, her eyes meeting his, her face held tight, her busy hands still for once.

"He's dead," she said. Andrew turned away from her and moving quickly, half-expecting her to call him back, went outside.

He stood at the door, staring at the cracked and blackened railway tie that served as a step. A red ant crawled across the top toward his boot. Du Chaler had come so far, all that way, to this. He moved his boot to crush the ant, then thought better of it. He watched it inch along and disappear into one of the cracks. Then he lifted his eyes. Clear, pure fall light poured relentlessly across the gradually lifting, subtle prairie, on and on to the distant horizon. Far off to the south a few cattle stood motionless against the flat sea of grass. All the rest was sky.

He stood this way for a long time until he saw a puff of dust rising faintly in the west. He watched it until he was sure it was coming toward the du Chaler place. Then he went back inside.

"Ma?" She stepped out of the bedroom. Behind her there was the sound of a child crying. "Somebody coming." She gave her firm, single nod, her lips tight, and went back into the bedroom.

Andrew went back outside, not looking at the cot. Squatting on his haunches, he dug holes in the dirt with a stick, and watched the buggy that carried Freddy and the doctor draw closer.

All the interminable night Andrew had clutched at a tattered blanket of sleep. At four he woke for the thousandth time with a jerk and, unable to contain himself any longer, crept out of bed and dressed quietly. He knew by something like the change in the texture of the air that his mother was awake, but she didn't speak to him, as if his going had already happened.

Outside it was still very dark and he made his way to the corral by memory and faint starlight. His feet recognized each bump and dip of the hard-packed but unseen ground under them. The air was frost-filled, sharp, and still, and he should have been cold, but the prospect of the day ahead kept him excited and warmed.

He had brought Punch into the corral the night before and fed him well; now all he had to do was catch him, saddle and bridle him, and ride out. Inside the corral he stood in the darkness and listened, but before he could call him, Punch came silently up to him and bumped the back of his head softly with his nose, his touch full of curiosity and willingness. Andrew led him outside the corral and, with much difficulty because he wasn't tall enough, bridled and then saddled him. Sometimes he still mounted by getting Punch to lower his head so that he could step into the halter with his left foot. Then, kicking him gently to get him to raise his head, he would swing his leg over and slide down the horse's neck to the saddle. This time he mounted quickly from the fence and turned Punch south in the October night, dawn still three hours off.

Low in the western horizon a darker mass rested, darker than the earth or sky: thunderclouds, or a shifting bank of fog, or a sleeping giant lying over the land. The darkness was resonant, retreating all around him, he was forever going toward it, never quite reaching it; he moved through it in perfect stillness. He couldn't see his horse's feet or the ground and the steady movement beneath him seemed suddenly unfamiliar and marvellous. His saddle creaked rhythmically. Far off in the hills coyotes barked their short, high-pitched bark, then began to wail. He could feel his horse's heat creeping through the stiff saddle leather, lapping against his legs. He sniffed the air. He smelled warmth, he smelled the approaching dawn. He felt that he carried inside himself the empty prairie that spread out to infinity around him. He leaned forward and buried his face in Punch's red mane, gasping with anticipation and joy, then abruptly pushed himself upright again.

Every once in a while he shifted impatiently in the saddle, wanting to lope, but resisting.

He breathed deeply again and inhaled the strong tang of horse, the delicate odour of sage, the powdery odour of old manure, and slough-water laden with the sour smell of alkali. He couldn't see them or hear them, but he sensed the presence of cattle as he passed them. For a while he listened to the whisper of his horse's hooves on the dry, frost-tipped grass, then kicked him into a trot and then a lope. They had gone only a few yards when Andrew pulled him up.

A few more miles to the south the cowboys would be throwing back their bedrolls, the stiff canvas scraping. They would be climbing awkwardly out of their blankets, their old breaks and sprains protesting, stumbling outside the big, empty barn where they had slept, urinating steamily into the chilly darkness. At the back of the grubwagon the cookstove would be already red with heat, and the Chinese cook, his string-tied pig-tail whipping, would be mumbling over his frying pans, his quick, fine-boned yellow hands making the cleaver flash through the grey and pink slabs of salt pork. Andrew could imagine the amber smell of coffee, how it would dispel the last of sleep, weaving its way through the chill, impersonal air, drawing the waking camp together with its warm, sociable odour.

With these images passing before him in the darkness, his stomach began to rumble and he almost spurred Punch again. But the men had warned him time and time again: save your horse, always save your horse. You never know what you might be needing him for. Andrew did this when he could, but just as often he would forget, would touch Punch's flank so that they ran for no reason across the sun-baked prairie like a pair of wild animals. But he didn't want to ride into camp with a lathered horse, which would give him away, so this time he managed to hold him back.

Now they would be pulling on creaking leather chaps over stiff, cold Levi's. He could hear the quick, not unmusical jingle of spurs being strapped onto boots, the hawking and spitting, the wisecracks, the laughter beginning to emerge out of the grim, lantern-lit, early morning reluctance.

He was still a couple of miles from the Willow Creek Post, but already he could hear the faint bellowing of cattle. Their cries lifted plaintively across the miles of silvered, still-night prairie: requests, declamations, narrations, long, sad questions. All around him above the dark rim of earth, the sky had begun to glow with light, the stars beyond this in the darkened sky were fading. He knew a pair of young coyotes were following him: he had seen their long, graceful silhouettes against the sky's silver edge as they trotted along the top of a rise that flanked him. He was glad of their company.

But almost before he realized it, he was approaching the camp on the creek bottom. Excitement flared up in him again and he descended the side of the coulee and rode at a trot in among the buildings: a big horse barn built for the Mounties' horses that was nearly always empty, and two smaller barns; three small wooden houses, one for the Post man, one for the Mountie, and the third for the government vet. He met and passed the wrangle-boy, this one a man of sixty, who was riding sleepily out to bring in the saddlehorses. As he approached the grubwagon, the smell of frying salt pork and boiling coffee grew stronger.

They were sitting on the ground, some leaning against their bedrolls, one or two using their saddles as backrests, eating off grey enamelled plates and drinking cofee from metal mugs. They looked up when he rode in, some of them smiling at him or calling "hello" or "morning, son," to him.

Andrew dismounted. He held the reins in his right hand and stroked Punch self-consciously with his left while he looked shyly at the twenty or so men who made up the roundup crew. Behind them, to the east and the south the sun was now a reddish glow along the horizon, and with its light, spirits were lifting.

The foreman, a tall, gaunt, middle-aged man named Ross, was eating standing up, holding his plate under his chin and forking in large mouthfuls, hardly bothering to chew them. While he ate he kept looking nervously toward the corrals, the outlines of which were clear now in the dawn, and inside of which the heavy, dark, moving mass of cattle could be seen.

"Eat," he said to Andrew, pointing with his fork to the food in the frying pan and then wiping his mouth with his sleeve, muffling the word. As soon as he had spoken he put the last forkful into his mouth, set his empty plate down hurriedly, almost tossing it, so that it rang out as it struck a stone in the grass by the stove, and turned away, striding on his long, thin legs toward the corrals. The jingle of his spurs grew fainter. The other men watched him go with mildly amused expressions, which puzzled Andrew.

Ross was the boss; to be foreman of so big an outfit was far beyond what Andrew could dream of for himself, whenever he tried to imagine himself as a man. These men, all these horses, as many as ten thousand head of cattle to be responsible for. Then, slowly, he understood why Ross ate standing up, without seeing his food, why he had an air of brusqueness and impersonality that set him apart from the other men, and as he saw this, some childhood core of certainty wavered, began to dissolve, so that everything around him, the men lounging on the grass laughing, the wrangle-boy bringing in the horses, the work that was laid out for them that day, seemed less natural and foreordained.

But, he realized, the work was still to be done, which surprised him, as if what he had just thought should change everything, and he turned with his horse and led him to the barn where he tied him in one of the empty stalls, hurriedly forked him some hay, and went back to the fire.

He got himself a plate from the stack at the back of the grubwagon, held it out while the cook in his flapping clothes filled it with meat and bread, then sat on the cold grass beside Shorty Marino and began to eat. The saddlehorses were pounding down the coulee now, the lead horses knowing to enter the rope corral the men had set up to hold their strings. Andrew found himself eating too fast, and his heart sped up, he kept feeling like he was swallowing it.

Dust rose and drifted silently down, the fire in the stove snapped and hissed, and the expressions on the faces of the men slowly changed, tightened, grew more alert, almost eager. One by one they tossed their empty plates onto the pile, wiped their hands on their pantlegs, and walked toward the improvised corral that held their milling horses.

The best roper was stationed inside the corral. The cowboys stood outside the rope barrier and studied the horses. As each one made his choice for the day, he would point it out to the roper, who would lasso it. Andrew stuffed the last of his bread into his mouth and set his empty tin plate on the stack on the grass. Already Mexican Pete was walking thoughtfully toward the horses. Andrew ran to catch up with him. Pete always let him ride one of his horses, since Punch wasn't fast enough for roundup work.

"Which one you gonna ride?" he asked Pete breathlessly. He and Mexican Pete liked each other. Often when Pete was out herding cattle or searching for strays, he would ride into Andrew's yard for a hot meal. Afterward, if Andrew's chores were done, he would go with Pete, would ride with him all day and come home alone by starlight, exhausted, halfasleep on his horse, but happy. He liked the Mexican's strange way of talking and the sound of the Spanish words he still sometimes used, even the cursing. Pete told him that he had drifted north from his homeland up through Texas, working for the big ranches, till he had drifted into Canada with a big herd some American was moving up to the more abundant grass and the still-open range.

His short, thick legs were bowed from riding and his smooth, dark skin got even darker with the wind and the sun, not red like the faces of the other men. And sometimes he sang Mexican songs while they were riding, in a soft, high tenor that ended nowhere and that seemed to Andrew the most beautiful songs he had ever heard. At home, when his mother wasn't around, he had tried to pick them out on the organ, but they never sounded the same, never captured that lamenting, sorrowful note they had when Pete sang them.

"Soon I go home," he told Andrew, time and time again, but he never did.

Pete didn't answer his question. Andrew followed his small, glittering black eyes, as the two of them stood by the rope, and saw that Pete was watching a tall black gelding with a tangled black mane. I could ride him, Andrew told himself confidently, but he knew he couldn't, not yet, and the knowledge made him lower his eyes. Some day, he told himself, when I'm bigger. Pete leaned across the rope, resting his small, thick hands on it, and pointed out the gelding to the roper, who cocked an ear toward him without taking his eyes off the horses. All the while he coiled and uncoiled the rope in his calloused hand.

It whirled, sang, and settled around the black's neck. Pete ducked under the rope, walked among the milling, racing horses, haltered the black and led him out, tying him to a nearby post. Then he went back to the corral and pointed out another horse, this one a big bay with a black mane and a white scar on his flank. When he was roped, Pete haltered him and led him out.

"Can you ride him?" he asked Andrew. The bay tossed his head and Pete jerked the haltershank and muttered at him in Spanish, then stroked his face. Andrew nodded gravely, trying to keep his face serious. Mexican Pete handed him the haltershank without speaking, their eyes meeting briefly, then he patted Andrew's shoulder absently and walked away to where the black was jerking and twisting at the rope that held him.

All around him cowboys were currying their horses, checking their feet, saddling horses or adjusting the saddles. Andrew led the bay to the barn, took his saddle and bridle off Punch and turned him out, and prepared to saddle the big bay. One of the other men in the barn, a big American called Al, who had been sent up by his outfit to pick up their strays, came over.

"Here," he said, and took the bridle from Andrew. Andrew wanted to say that he could do it himself, but he could already hear the sound outside of horses being mounted. He let Al bridle the horse and lift Andrew's saddle onto it. The bay kept tossing his head and stepping away from Al. When the saddle touched his back, the horse jerked. "You sure you can ride 'im?" Al asked.

"He's got to learn to handle these broncs sometime," Shorty Marino said, passing them. "Hell, at his age I thought nothin' of mountin' the toughest sonofabitch in the corral." Al grunted and glanced at Andrew. Andrew held his lips tight together and refused to look at either man.

"I can ride 'im," he said. Al bent and tightened the cinch.

"Hold him in," he said. "Keep a short rein." The wrangle-boy was extinguishing the lanterns in the barn, and the morning light shone in through the big, square doorway. Al handed him the reins and as the rough leather touched his hand the bay pulled back. Andrew thought of Punch, his willingness, his affection. His knees felt weak as he led the horse out of the barn, but he ignored the feeling. He would fight anybody who tried to stop him from riding this horse. And if he got bucked off, so what. He would just get up and get on him again. Hadn't he seen the men do that? Limping, cursing, eyeing the horse warily, they caught it, or somebody caught it for them, and they climbed back on and rode him. That was what cowboys did, that was what he would do.

Behind them, Shorty, who had been extracting his tobacco from his bedroll, straightened and followed them outside. The mounted men were circling here and there on their horses, pulling down their hats, shrugging more comfortably into their jackets, while others mounted from the shoulder, carefully, with a short inside rein. Here and there a horse bucked or spun and the rider rode him, cursing, till he settled down.

Al boosted Andrew onto the horse.

"Say your prayers, Sonny," he said, chuckling, and Andrew was on the bay, tense, waiting, feeling the horse under him, but there was no tensing in the horse, at least not yet.

"You and Shorty head east," Ross called to them, riding among them. "Jack, Ray, check that deep coulee south . . ." The men rode off in the directions Ross gave them. Andrew tagged along with Mexican Pete and Squint Jackson. They rode directly to the north, the direction from which Andrew had come. As the crew rode up the coulee in a bunch, the bay broke into a trot. Andrew held him back, and he tossed his head angrily, fighting the bit.

They broke the top of the coulee and with the open plain before him, the bay began to run. Andrew turned him in a tight circle. The horse slowed, but as soon as the circle was complete and he was allowed to go straight, he began to run again. Again Andrew turned him in another circle, crouching in the saddle, his legs tight, waiting for the bucking to begin. But the horse quieted, and Andrew felt a mixture of relief and disappointment.

"Did you see any cattle?" Mexican Pete asked Andrew, meaning when Andrew had come through in the dark.

"No, Andrew said. It was too dark, but there was some there." He pointed. The three of them spread out then, riding faster, and began to flush cattle out from behind rises, in draws and damp coulee bottoms. They were Mexican Longhorns, most of them, as big as horses and some of them faster, with long, dangerous-looking horns and mean dispositions. After a couple of hours they had gathered a small herd. They herded them back to camp, corralled them, and rode out again.

Clinging to the bay's back as they pounded across the prairie to head off a balking Longhorn, Andrew was no longer afraid. He knew in his bones and muscles that he could ride a horse. He told himself, dreaming on the bay's back, that one day he would be one of the legendary cowboys, one of those who could ride anything, who would be called in to break the unbreakable horses, and for whom there would always be a job waiting with any outfit.

Once the bay shied at a jackrabbit that popped up from behind a clump of sage, startling him. He reared, stepped sideways, then started to buck. Andrew rode him easily, full of confidence, till the bay settled down. When he caught up with Squint and Mexican Pete, he saw them grinning at him, saw the newly appraising look in their eyes. He said nothing, leaning forward to stroke the bay on his damp, silky neck. He breathed deeply, quivering with happiness.

At noon, as they were seated on the ground eating fried beef and beans, the corral behind them full of mooing, bellowing cattle, a team came down the coulee weaving between the buildings toward where they sat. It was a fancy team of matched bays, high stepping, well-fed and sleek, with fancy silver-studded harness. They pulled a democrat in which two men rode.

As soon as it arrived and came to a stop the wrangle-boy was on his feet holding the team at the head. Ross stood too, setting his plate down on the grass where he had been sitting. Flies immediately buzzed over it. The men were silent, watching.

The driver, who had pulled the team up near the grubwagon, was a short, stout man. A ring on the little finger of one hand flashed in the bright noon sun. Both men wore tailored, new-looking leather jackets and clean grey stetsons.

The second man, a taller, leaner version of the other, got down first. He walked slowly around behind the democrat, looking the crew over with small, dark eyes, his jacket pushed back and one hand resting on his shiny leather belt. His silver belt buckle blazed with light so Andrew couldn't look at it. He saw how the tall man's boots shone beside the dusty, worn boots of the men who sat on the ground looking up at him.

"Day," the tall man said to all of them, touching his hat. The men responded with grunts and nods, but the tall man wasn't looking at them. He extended his hand to Ross.

"Everything going all right?" he asked. Ross wiped his hand hastily on his pants before he took the one offered him. Now the driver of the team was climbing out, redfaced, stout and awkward.

"How's the cattle looking?" he asked Ross, glancing around the circle of men leaning against the grubwagon or seated on the ground. Ross gestured without speaking toward the corrals, then turned and began to walk toward them. The two men followed and walked with him, talking, while Ross lowered his head and listened.

"Who was that?" Andrew asked softly as soon as they were out of earshot.

"That's your bosses, Sonny," somebody said. "The skinny one's Lambert, and the big belly is Smith. They show up about once a week to look things over, give Ross his orders." Somebody else laughed quietly.

"As if Ross don't know what to do without them telling him." .

The men continued to eat, although there was less talking now. The Chinese cook silently refilled their mugs. Every once in a while they would glance over to the three who were leaning against the corrals. Lambert kept gesticulating toward the west as though he were trying to convince Smith of something. When Smith raised his arm to rest it against the railing, his ring flashed again and Andrew tried to imagine wearing such a ring on his own finger. Or even having a pair of shiny new boots like that. After a while the three men walked slowly back, the foreman still in his attitude of grave and silent listening.

Now Smith, as if to make up for his failure to acknowledge their presence before, said "Good day," to the men. He smiled then, took off his hat and wiped his forehead although it was not hot. Andrew saw that he was going grey in the temples and at the tips of his long sideburns. He gave off some slight scent, a keen, pleasant odour that was new to Andrew. "Good weather to round up in," Smith went on. Everybody agreed.

"Yup, sure is"

"Not bad." The men moved their feet and tapped their forks against their plate edges uncertainly.

Smith looked at the men one by one as if appraising them. His eyes reached Andrew, who was sitting across from him, balancing his half-empty plate of food on the triangle of his crossed legs. Their eyes met and Smith's expression changed, grew harder, his pale blue eyes beneath their thick, whitening eyebrows darkened and under his gaze everything in Andrew slowed and sobered.

"How old are you, boy?" Smith asked. Andrew swallowed, his fork half-way to his mouth.

"Almost thirteen," he said. Around him the men watched carefully as if he were a stranger and this was news to them. Andrew couldn't take his eyes from Smith's face.

"He earning his keep?" Smith turned to Ross. Ross nodded, his expression hadn't changed in the least since that first barely perceptible flicker when they had all seen the democrat rolling into their camp.

"He's all right." Lambert had turned to watch the cattle milling in the big corral, ignoring the exchange between his partner and Andrew.

"Cattle a little ganted up," he remarked to nobody in particular. He spoke to the crew in a false, hearty way. "Ross working you too hard?" The men's mumbled replies were indistinct, but this did not seem to bother Lambert, who stood with his hands on his hips smiling down on them. "Well, good to see everything going all right," he said. He slapped Ross on the shoulder affably and started toward the democrat. The men went back to their food.

"See you back at winter camp," Smith called to Ross. He was out of breath from the climb back into the democrat. He touched the brim of his hat, holding the reins with his other hand, as Lambert swung more easily up into the seat beside him. Then he slapped the reins and the team pulled out. The men watched it make its way down the trail among the buildings and up the far side of the coulee.

Andrew thought about the way Smith's face had changed as he looked at him. The faces of the men around him changed too, when they were riding a bronc or fighting cattle, but the change was neither unexpected, nor so complete, as if, like Smith, they had two faces. But then Smith was the boss of this entire crew, and of several other crews along the border to the west of them, he owned thousands of head of cattle and horses, he was rich. Was that what set rich men apart from poor men? That look? And if it was, did you learn that look, or did you always have it? Or did it just come to you after you got rich?

For the first time Andrew saw that he was not rich. He looked around and everywhere he saw cracked and scuffed half worn-out boots, patched and torn workpants, handmade cigarettes, tack held together with strips of leather or by the large, uncertain stitches of the owner. Would it be better to be rich like Smith and Lambert? The answer came at once, unbidden, forcefully, from deep inside him, where he hadn't even known an answer existed. No. All he wanted in this world was to be able to ride horses with these men, to be like them, free to go anywhere a good horse would take him, free on the open prairie, his own man. He knew this with every fibre of his being.

The men were rising now, brushing dust off the seat of their pants, tossing the dregs of their coffee onto the dusty yellow grass. Ross took a small notebook and a stub of a pencil from his shirt pocket. The men waited, stretching, then setting their hands loosely on their hips. Andrew waited with them, proudly.

"We got enough to start out," Ross said, tallying with his pencil, not lifting his head from the notebook which was dwarfed in the palm of his big hand. "I can spare five of you to take them out. This batch goes to the White Tail camp. I make it about a thousand head, but get a count on them as you take them out." He lifted his head now, and looked the men over in an impersonal way, pointing to the crew he wanted one by one. When he had chosen them, the men walked away toward the barn to pick up their bedrolls.

All that day they rode, bringing in bunches of cattle that the men had already spent weeks bringing in closer to the camp. They had been spread out as far north as the fence Lambert and Smith had built east and west for fifty miles in a line about twelve miles north of the Montana border. They roped calves that had been missed during the branding and sometimes slicks as old as two years that had been missed more than once. They stretched them out in the corral and branded them. Every once in a while a neighbour would ride up with a helper or two to pick up his strays that had gotten mixed in with the big rancher's herd.

When it grew dark and the horses were unsaddled and turned out and somebody had taken the first shift night-herding them, they lit a campfire by the grubwagon. Everybody brought out his bedroll or saddle to lounge against and made himself comfortable.

Andrew found a place to lie on the edge of the circle in the darkness where he was less likely to be noticed. He was silent, drifting in and out of sleep, content to be lying near his companions, watching the firelight flickering on their faces and hands.

Morton Plummer had begun to talk. He had shoved his bedroll up against a wagonwheel and sat with his back against it, one short, bowed leg extended in front of him, the other bent. He had tilted his hat to the back of his head so the firelight caught his long, grizzled moustache. His one wandering eye was barely noticeable in the dark and this made it easier to listen to him.

Once Morton had tried to farm, but his homestead quarter had turned out to be too poor and when he saw he would never get a crop off it, he gave up and went to work for a neighbouring rancher. He changed jobs at the beginning of every season and during the winter he rode the grubline. He had a regular circle of places he went to when the cold weather hit. He would reach Andrew and his mother's place about January, dig himself in, with some blankets from Andrew's mother, in the barn, and in return for a roof over his head and meals, make himself useful mending harnesses, helping Andrew work the cattle and do chores, trim horses' feet, chop wood, or fix things around the house. Andrew and his mother were always glad to see him coming. His arrival broke the monotony of the long, lonely winter. He brought their mail with him and all the news he'd spent the winter gathering. Then one morning he would ride off to the next place on his winter rounds.

He hawked and spit once, then began his story.

"One time me and old Shaky Wilson, we were out looking for some horses. We were fifty miles from home, out in that Manyberries country. My horse was playing out, he couldn't go any further, and there we were, fifty miles from home. So we rode up to Wild Horse Lake. You know, that big alkali flat about fifteen miles long over by—well, you know where I mean. Now you fellas may not know it, but there's thousands of horses out there, I mean thousands, running loose in that country, and they all hang around that lake for water. So we rode out to it and Shaky says, 'We'll hafta get you a horse from one of these.' Well, some of them horses belong to people, but most of them were mortgaged to banks, they're banks' horses. Hell, I knew I wasn't going to run into any bank managers out there so I said fine. So we looked through them all trying to find a saddlehorse. Finally, we saw one that we knew was a saddlehorse because he had a white gall on him, saddle marks on his back." He gestured suddenly with his hands, which flashed in and out of the firelight.

"So Shaky, he says, 'You run 'im against that fence there, and I'll rope 'im for you.' Shaky, he's real good with a rope. So I run 'im against the fence, and by God, Shaky, he roped 'im. He said to me, 'Boy, you'd better ride 'im 'cause once we let your horse go, it's a long walk home.'" Mort paused here both for effect, and to spit, and the fire hissed and spat back at him. Andrew rolled over onto his back, turning his other side to the heat. He looked up to the stars which gleamed silently down on him.

"Well, I knew I had to ride 'im. Shaky had a rope around his foot, so I took my saddle and bridle and let my horse go. I got on this horse, and by God! Buck! We were all over the place, down into the lake and out again, just a-buckin' and a-squealin'. But I rode 'im, and finally he settled down. So we set out for home and every once in a while he'd start buckin' again and we'd go round till he settled down."

"Finally, we rode into this yard. This man and his wife came out and stood on the steps. The man, he says, 'I see you found old Nugget.'"

There were a few guffaws around the fire.

"Well, Jesus!" Mort went on, not wanting to let his audience get ahead of him. "Here we'd rode into the yard of the fella that owned the horse! I said to Shaky, 'I thought you caught me a bank horse!' And he said, 'How the hell am I supposed to know whose horse it is?'" Some of the men were laughing now and Mort joined them. When they grew silent, he went on.

"Well, anyway, the rancher he says, 'You might as well ride him. Nobody around here can. That's why we turned him loose.' Turned out he got away on 'em wearing a saddle. Dragged that saddle for a week. That was how he got that gall, from that saddle. I took him and I rode him for a couple of years. Then the law, they got after me for riding an American horse, so I took him back." He sighed and leaned back against his bedroll, tipping his hat forward again. He would tell no more stories tonight, his posture said.

"Them Mounties keep that close an eye on you?" Al asked. "Down where I come from nobody'd even notice."

"Maybe," Rudy the wrangle-boy said, "But when I first come up here over twenty years ago, I was packin' my iron like I always did down home, and that Mountie, old . . . I forget his name . . . the one in Maple Creek? Made me turn in my gun. Said I wouldn't need it. Didn't neither, and that was a surprise."

"I remember," Andrew bent his head forward so he could figure out who at the foot of the circle was talking now. It was Jake McKenzie. "The first winter I came up here to work for the Matador, that was '06–'07, but you know that story. I came with my old man. I was just a kid, fourteen years old. That was the winter the weather finished off them big companies, the T Down, the 76." His voice trailed off. "They came up here 'cause the range was free, and big chunks of it hadn't even been grazed."

"No water on it," Rudy put in. "Only good for grazin' horses."

"The grass was tall. You could set down your mover and cut hay anyplace. And there was lots of it, I remember that for sure."

"Still is lots of grass," Ross said. There was a note of irritation in his voice.

"Not like when I come here," Jake said. "When I was a kid. It was stirrup-high in them days. Did the eyes good after that wore-out range I'd been ridin' on. Lots better range even than Montana. They'd been grazin' her for years and years there. Wasn't nothin' much left. But up here—hell! We all thought we'd died and gone to heaven."

"And fences," Al said. His voice drifted across the fire, his face in darkness. "Things are pretty well all fenced down south now. No more herding cattle, except inside fences. Still ain't no fences to speak of up here."

"Just wait," Jake said. "Them farmers'll fix that. Soon you won't be able to ride a half a mile without having to get off your horse and open a goddamn gate. A farmer can't stand to see a piece of ground without it's plowed up and got a fence around it. You'll see."

"Hell, no!" Ross said. "It'll never happen! This land's no good for farming. Those settlers coming in will be starved out and gone in five years."

At times like these Andrew didn't think of his mother and their life together on the homestead, even though he had no memory of a time without his mother. She had always been there in her heavy, dark clothes, never laughing, though she sometimes smiled in a silent, unreadable way. But increasingly now when he wasn't with her, he forgot her existence entirely. She was becoming for him something like a landmark he had passed by, imposing while he approached it and while it was close, but once behind him, forgotten.

The McGinnis boy, he was actually about eighteen, much older than Andrew, but the men still called him a boy, had his guitar out and was beginning to strum a few chords in a dreamy way. Slowly the voices died as the music picked up volume, fell into rhythm. The boy began to sing, humming at first, then, as he found the right chords, singing the words. A few others joined him, and Andrew sat up too, moved a little closer to the guitar player so he could watch how he made the music, and began to sing too.

He had started for school that early winter morning in the dark. It was twenty-five degrees below zero and at dawn, when he was two miles from home, the sun finally broke the horizon, casting a mauve light across the grey snow. As it rose higher it gradually turned the colour of fresh cream. He was following the path he had ridden for years across the prairie when, having reached a draw where the path curved between two hills, he simply turned his surprised horse around and started back the way he had come. The change in direction, although unplanned and unexpected even to Andrew, was irrevocable. In a month he would be thirteen. He was a man now and no amount of silent pressure from his mother would keep him in school another day.

When he reached home he saw through the thin covering of snow, the tracks of a car which had come and gone. He had been thinking so deeply that he hadn't heard it or seen it, although both, on that silent prairie and in the clear air, would have been possible. He unsaddled his horse, turned him out, and went straight into the house.

His mother was in the kitchen dipping water from the pail to fill the tea-kettle.

"You're back, eh," she said without surprise, recognizing and resigned to his decision. "Wash your hands and come into the parlour." He knew it was no use to ask more, but did as he was told, relieved that she had chosen to say nothing about his leaving school. She had known for a long time that it was coming. She set the kettle on the stove and waited in the doorway of the parlour for him to go in ahead of her.

Two women sat on the horsehide sofa, one at each end. They looked up at him silently.

"This is Mary Randall," she said, nodding to the younger of the two women, "and this is Anna King." Both women smiled politely at him and he mumbled a hello.

"Sit down," his mother said. "We want to talk to you." He hesitated, then sat down on the hard chair by the door, both apprehensive and annoyed. Hymns, he thought angrily, praying, or more sick people. But a sweet, clean odour rose from the younger woman on his right. He dropped his head and sniffed surreptitiously, risking a glance at her while his mother brought in a tray of teacups and a plate of cookies. She met his glance, her eyes were a soft brown fringed with thick black lashes and when she smiled at him, he felt something strange in his chest and had to look away quickly.

The other woman was older and had an air about her that was like his mother's, an air of being right, of expecting to be in charge. His mother had gone back to the kitchen and brought in the teapot, and set it on the small table in front of her chair. Miss or Mrs. King was talking in her clear, authoritative voice.

"We'll have to go back through town and pick up our supplies," she said. "They are supposed to be getting them ready at the store."

"It's on your way," his mother replied, without looking up from pouring the tea. Mary spoke.

"Have you thought of planting trees?" she asked, as though she hadn't been listening to them, had been dreaming of other things.

"Trees?" his mother asked, holding the teapot above a cup, as though Mary had suggested building a zoo in the parlour. "There's no water for trees. We'd never get them to grow. Our well just barely keeps us and our stock watered." She finished filling the cups and began to pass them. "Andy here hauls water to my garden all summer. It's a wonder anything grows." Mary nodded, her cheeks flushing.

"I see." She sipped from her teacup, then said, brightening, "Where we're going, there's a stream right behind the cabin."

"Battle Creek," Anna explained with a slight smile which showed her large, strong teeth. She said it with the air of a mother explaining a child's remark to another adult.

"Battle Creek?" Andrew asked. He looked from his mother to Anna and back again.

"These ladies," his mother said, sitting down heavily and pulling her teacup toward her, "need someone to drive them to that old shack that used to be Jackson Fish's on Battle Creek. You know the one." Andrew couldn't understand why they would want to go there at this time of the year.

"Why . . ." he began.

"I am writing a book," Anna said severely, "and Mary is coming to keep me company. We need an isolated place where nobody will bother us."

"Nobody'll bother you there," Andrew's mother said, a touch of sarcasm in her voice. "There is no road in and the nearest neighbour must be ten miles away. Maybe more."

"That is exactly what we're looking for," Anna said firmly. "Now, Andrew," she fixed her steady blue eyes on him, "your mother says you'll drive us there." For the first time he noticed her dark red hair and the pink cameo brooch at the neck of her dark blue dress. He glanced at Mary. Mary was watching, half-smiling, her lips parted in anticipation. He nodded quickly, looking away. It was a good twenty miles, he would never make it back before dark.

"Nobody's lived there in a long time," he brought out, looking at his mother. "Not since they found old Jackson frozen to death in that blizzard." He couldn't resist another quick look at Mary. She was following him eagerly, her eyes bright. All at once he felt that he would drive her forty miles if she asked.

"They're determined to go, Andrew," his mother said. Much to his surprise, it was so unlike her, she went on. "Nobody else will take them. So Mr. McNulty drove them out here." She laughed, a snort without humour, and she and Anna exchanged wry glances. "He seemed to think I'd talk them out of it," she said, then angrily, "well, he brought them to the wrong place for that!"

"We can look after ourselves," Mary said to him. "It's so foolish of them to try to tell us we can't go there." Anna set her teacup onto its saucer with a sharp click.

"We should be on our way. We still have to load our winter's supplies." Andrew rose and left the room. Behind him, his mother was offering to pack a lunch for them, refusing to listen to their protests.

When he came back into the house some time later, the women were standing at the door, wearing their coats, saying good-bye to his mother.

"I'll send Andrew out once during the winter to check on you, see if you need anything. If you want me to," his mother said.

"Maybe," Anna said, without elaboration, pulling on her black gloves with a smart, soldierly air. Mary stood straight and tall in a bright blue coat with a small red fox collar that touched her soft brown hair all the way around.

They climbed into the sleigh and Andrew went around to sit on the end of the seat, but Anna insisted he sit in the middle to drive. He changed places gladly. Now Mary was beside him. They set out for town, Andrew between the two women, trying to give all his attention to driving. The two passersby on the single street in the town stared at them as they passed. Andrew pulled up the team in front of the store, they climbed out and went inside.

The interior of the store was dark and smelled of spices, oranges, new leather, pickles and other unidentifiable but welcome fragrances. Andrew never got tired of it.

"Got your supplies ready," McNulty said from behind the counter. He said it gruffly, angrily. Anna pulled off her gloves finger by finger.

"How much is the total?" Mr. McNulty's expression tightened. "This boy will be driving us," she said, opening her purse. He turned to look at Andrew, who stood in the doorway.

"Mrs. Samson sent him, did she?" he asked. Anna raised her eyes from her open purse where she was rustling bills.

"Of course," she said. "Mrs. Samson," her tone was exasperated, "has managed on that homestead all by herself for years. Nobody knows better than she that Mary and I will be perfectly all right."

"You ain't even got a horse to get you out if one of you gets sick," he said. "Who's gonna shovel snow for you? Who's gonna cut your firewood?"

"How much is it?" she repeated, patiently. Mary stood quietly beside

Anna, watching Mr. McNulty. Andrew stepped to one side of the doorway and stood waiting. He had never doubted that they would go if they wanted to, and that nobody would persuade them otherwise. Hadn't he spent all these years with his mother? He knew a woman's determination. It was silly to argue with them.

Without replying, Mr. McNulty picked up a piece of paper from the counter and held it out to Anna. She took it from him, read it, set it back on the counter, and began to count money out on top of it. Andrew began to carry out the supplies which were in boxes stacked on the floor or in sacks leaning against the wall.

"Maybe the Mountie'll ride down now and then and check on you," the storekeeper mumbled as he put the money in the register. He came around the counter and began to help Andrew carry out the heavier items, the sacks of flour, sugar and potatoes. When everything was in the sleigh box and the items that might freeze covered with blankets, Mr. McNulty stood back with his hands on his hips.

"Hope you didn't forget nothing," he said.

"I doubt it very much," Anna replied, evenly. "We went over the list several times. I'll be surprised if we have." She climbed into the sleigh and motioned to Mary who was standing on the sidewalk. Obediently Mary got into the sleigh and sat down. Andrew swung up on his side and again moved into the middle position. Anna handed him the reins.

It was a clear, bright, windless day, but well below freezing. There had been several snowfalls, but the wind had swept away most of the snow, leaving only a thin covering on the level. In the coulees and draws the snow was a foot or more deep. After they had gone a little way Anna arranged the horsehide robes Andrew's mother had sent over their feet and legs.

They travelled a couple of miles down the main sleightrail out of town, then turned off the trail and headed out across the plain. The runners slid silently over the snow, the chains jingled, flocks of snowbirds swooped up at their passing and white jackrabbits leaped up from behind snow-covered sagebushes and bounded away from them in zig-zagging lines. Now and then the dull bronze remains of the summer's grass poked through the snow cover. They passed the occasional clump of weeds where the snow had been scratched aside down to the grass and rabbit tracks lay all around.

Ahead of them, the softly rolling white landscape faded into the grey-white sky, which gradually deepened to the palest blue, then, a little higher, to a brighter blue, and finally, high above them, deepened to a blue of such intensity and brilliance it hurt the eyes to look at it.

Behind them they left a trail, the only one to break the snow for miles in each direction. As they crawled across the prairie under the low mauve sun the day grew colder, not warmer, and they had to stamp their feet under the blankets to keep them warm. First Anna and then Mary took turns getting off and walking beside the sleigh until they had warmed themselves. Then Anna took the reins so Andrew could trot alongside till he could feel his toes again.

Mary exclaimed over the vast open distance, the sky, the hills, the animals, and Anna replied to her, sometimes turning to Andrew for more information. They grew easier with each other.

"Does your mother actually plow the fields herself?" Anna asked.

"Hire that done," Andrew said. "This year I'll be big enough to do it myself. But mostly we run cattle," he said. "When we get a little more secure," he went on, quoting his mother, "we'll let most of it go back to grass and just grow a little oats for feed. We're ranchers."

"It must have been very hard for her,' Mary said. "First to lose her husband and then to go so far away from her home."

"She wanted to," Andrew said, surprised. It had never occurred to him to ask himself why she had come here. Anna laughed, a quick, harsh laugh, as if something she had always known had just been confirmed.

"Women get sick of a regular life too," she said, and then nudged Mary so that Mary had to laugh, too. Her laugh was low and sweet.

Now and then they passed stray cattle, their backs snow-covered and humped against the cold, their noses blue-tinged .

"Poor things," Mary said, watching them. She shivered and huddled under the blankets.

"Look," Anna said, staring backwards over her shoulder. Andrew and Mary quickly looked back. Fifty yards behind the sleigh, a coyote was following them. He trotted a few yards, his long tail brushing the snow, then paused to sit on his haunches and wait till they were a little further away, then he followed them again.

"What does he want?" Mary asked, her voice low and tense. He could feel her fear in the rigidity of her body leaning close to him.

"They're just curious," he said, repeating the words of the cowboys. "They like company." Mary laughed again, the same bubbling laugh, and looked at him from under her thick lashes. Heat rose to his face.

Every now and then Mary's arm or thigh touched his as the sleigh rocked over bumps or swayed on the uneven ground. Once or twice her shoulder pressed briefly against his. When that happened an entirely new feeling came over him. It was as though her sweetness had slid down his throat, through his chest, into his stomach and hadn't stopped there, but kept on flowing into his thighs, which went weak every time she touched him.

The weakness he recognized. He had felt that before with Marta, who was his own age and who had allowed him to explore her body, in the dark behind the schoolhouse while a dance went on inside, and to enter her. So he understood part of what he was feeling, although he could hardly believe it, was embarrassed by it. But there was something more to this. He imagined the narrowness of Mary's waist under her heavy coat and tried not to look at the rounded softness of her breasts, which no coat could entirely hide.

Marta's body was straight and narrow, her breasts had hardly begun, and she smelled of strong, homemade soap and some other unpleasant odour which he thought had to do with what she and her family ate and the way they lived. He didn't like Marta, he didn't respect her. He had only been curious, then compelled. Now his hands in the heavy leather mitts were sweating, his face was burning. He almost wished the ride was over.

"Look, Mary cried suddenly and pointed to the southeast. Anna and Andrew followed her eyes. "What is it?" she asked, her voice tinged with awe. "It's so big!"

"An eagle," Andrew said, as surprised as she was. As he spoke, it rose from the hilltop, spread its massive wings and soared toward them. Mary gasped, and Andrew, conscious of his role as their protector, said quickly, "It won't hurt you. It just wants to have a look." But he could hardly believe his eyes, because the eagle kept coming. It was closer than any eagle he had ever seen, and as it approached them, it dropped down so that it was no more than twenty feet above them. Its wingspan was easily ten feet. When it was only a few feet from them it swooped even lower and passed over them in a planing curve so low that they saw the fine feathers under its wings, its scaly claws, and felt the wind it created in passing on their upturned faces. Then it was gone, disappearing into the sky, retreating till it was only a speck, which vanished.

Andrew dared to look at Mary. Her eyes shone, her soft lips were parted and her face so open that he felt embarrassed and dropped his eyes, confused.

"Golden Eagle," he said. Anna laughed.

"A strange thing," she said. "An omen, perhaps?"

"Oh, don't say that, Anna," Mary cried. Andrew felt her shiver.

They were approaching the hills now, shimmering white and blue in the frigid air.

"Is it much further?" Mary asked.

"A couple of miles, another hour," he said. He had wanted to stop some time back and rest the horses, but Anna had asked him not to.

"We promised your mother that you would be home before midnight," she said. "And it's so cold. They're probably better off moving. They can rest while we unload." The harness jingled, and in the increasing cold the sleigh-runners sang over the snow. Now and then one of the horses snorted.

"There it is," Andrew said, pointing. The frozen creek sat under its thick covering of snow between narrow, steeply-cut banks. Stunted grey willows, gnawed by wandering cattle, grew along its banks, where faded, stiff weeds and tall grasses emerged from the snow.

The cabin sat by a shallow crossing where the water had not yet frozen. It ran musically over rocks and disappeared under the ice. The shack itself was a low, one-room log building. Andrew halted the team, which stood gratefully, glad to rest. They began to unload supplies while

Andrew unhitched the horses, folded the lines, took off their bridles and watered them, then put some oat bundles he had brought along onto the snow in front of them.

"Good thing we brought poison," Mary remarked. "The mice have had a field day in here." There was no covering on the rough wooden floor, and the windows were bare of curtains, but all the furniture was still there. Four chairs around a rough wooden table, a tanned cowhide spread on the bed and wooden cupboards and shelves along one wall. An old stuffed easy chair with a small table beside it sat in a corner. The cookstove looked in good condition and there was no snow on the floor or the furniture, which meant that the cabin was still solid. But Anna gave them no time to look farther.

"Hurry up with the unloading," she said. "I won't feel comfortable till I know you're on your way home." It was three o'clock now, it would be dark in a couple of hours. Andrew had been about to offer to start a fire, but instead he went out to the sleigh and carried in more sacks.

When the sleighbox was empty except for a few oat bundles and the robes and blankets his mother had put in, and all the supplies had been stacked around the walls of the cabin, Anna paid him for his time, he re-hitched the team to the sleigh, and struck out toward home. He snuggled down in his mackinaw and clucked to the team urging them to walk faster. As the distance between him and Mary lengthened, he felt her receding from him, the warmth of her body which he could still feel against him became less real, and he began to dream about her as though he had only imagined her. Someday, he would like to have a woman like Mary.

It was growing dark. The moon had begun to shine. Its light lay upon the silver-blue prairie as far as he could see in every direction. The stars seemed very far away, cold pinpoints of light in a black sky. Now and then he dozed off, but never, even in his sleep, did he fail to hear the horses' hooves brushing softly through the snow, or the harness ringing with a tiny sound in the emptiness.

All that long winter he thought about Mary and Anna alone in the cabin by the frozen creek. Twice he almost set out to go to see them, but each time something else came up, once it was a storm, and once something his mother wanted him to do. Before he knew it, spring was near and he thought how they would be leaving the little shack and going back to where they had come from.

And then, just when the snow was beginning to melt, he found his first job. He had moved into the bunkhouse at Putmans along with a couple more men. At first he had been put to work at the most menial task of all—skinning cows that had died during the winter and been dragged out of the corral where they had lain frozen stiff until spring. It was a filthy, disgusting job, but he did it. He was the youngest, the greenest, and that was where you started. He was glad to have work, glad at last to be a man among men.

At night, exhausted, he sat with the men in the bunkhouse and listened to their talk, and watched closely if George Koestler played his guitar.

"Need me a new one," George said one night, his broad, dirty thumbnail plucking at the strings. "You want this one?" He turned to Andrew. Andrew sat up straight and stared at him to see if he meant it. "I'll teach you some chords," George said. "Alf McNulty's got a new one on order for me at the store."

"Lord I'm stiff," Mort Plummer said, working his knees. "I ain't rode so much for a long time."

"Just wait," George said. "We'll be doing a lot of riding soon, herding them sonsabitches."

"Not me," Mort said. "I'm hired to fence. I'll be doing the fencing." He had begun mending a saddle-leather and didn't look up.

The low wooden door creaked open. All of them looked up to see who was coming in. The Mountie, a tall man, was stooping to enter.

"Come on in, Corporal," George said. He pushed an empty chair toward him. The Mountie walked inside. The floor creaked under his boots.

"Hello, boys," he said. He took his time, ignoring the chair, and looked around the room at them, one by one. His eyes stopped and rested on Andrew. "You Andrew Samson?" he asked. Andrew resisted the urge to stand up, tried to be nonchalant like the others, but his first thought was that something had happened to his mother. "Your mother said I'd find you here."

"Something the matter?" Andrew managed to ask calmly. He sensed the other men watching him.

"Do you remember the two women you took out to Battle Creek?" the Mountie asked. He crossed the room and sat down on the chair George had pushed out for him. George got up and lit the kerosene lamp and hung it on a hook in the ceiling. They all watched him, waiting for him to finish. The lamp swayed, casting shadows across the room. George steadied it, then sat down again and picked up his guitar. "When did you take them there?" the Mountie asked Andrew, his voice sharper now. It was as clear to Andrew as if it had happened only yesterday: Mary's brown eyes under the thick lashes, the way she had looked up at the eagle, the softness of her breasts against his arm when the sleigh swayed and she fell against him.

"Early December," he said. "There was some snow," he added irrelevantly. The Mountie wrote something in a small notebook he had taken from his pocket.

"They seem okay?"

"Yes," Andrew said, puzzled, slowly becoming alarmed.

"How long did you stay?"

"Not long," Andrew said. "Just long enough to unload everything, then they sent me back. It was late." There was a short silence while the Mountie wrote again. "Are they sick?" Andrew asked, probing helplessly for some explanation. The other men were sitting motionless now, listening, one at the table, the other on his bunk. The Mountie lifted his head.

"They're dead." He paused with an air of waiting for their exclamations and questions. Andrew's chest was suddenly too tight. There was a strange buzzing in his ears. Mort spoke before he could get any words out.

"Dead! What happened?" He was giving the Mountie what he wanted so the Mountie would get on with it. George strummed his guitar thoughtfully once, then set it beside him on the bunk.

"Dead, eh," he said. He began to roll a cigarette.

"They froze to death," the Mountie said. He turned to Andrew. "You know that big order of groceries and supplies you helped them take down to Fish's cabin?" Andrew couldn't move, couldn't take his eyes off the big Mountie's face. "Well, they forgot something. Not the women," he put in quickly, "Alf and his helper. It was on the women's list that was still there in the cabin, but Alf didn't put it in." He paused to let this sink in. Nobody said anything.

"Matches," he said, and waited. There was a moment of perfect silence in the bunkhouse. Mort's hands had stopped in the middle of his cigarette-rolling, George had his hands on his knees as if he were about to rise and had been frozen in mid-action. Now the memory came flooding back over Andrew—how he had carried in sacks of groceries, how he had been about to make a fire when Anna had sent him away. He jumped awkwardly to his feet.

"I wanted to make a fire. I offered to make a fire, but she wouldn't let me. She told me to get home before dark. She said they . . . had everything." Abruptly he turned his back on all of them.

"Don't take it so hard, Sonny," the Mountie said. "It wasn't your fault."

"If I'd just looked back when I drove away. If I'd just looked back. Maybe they were running after me . . . maybe . . ." He wanted to say, she was so pretty, so pretty, but the words stuck inside him.

"One of them seems to have died within a week," the Mountie went on, ignoring Andrew. "She was in the bed. It was Jonas Walker found them. Went by with some strays and didn't see any smoke, so he stopped in. The other one, the younger one, she was sitting at the table when she died. She kept a notebook, wrote in it every day, that's what she was doing when she died. Just froze to death."

Andrew crossed the room through the men's heavy silence and went outside. He went around to the end of the bunkhouse where there were no windows, crouched there in the darkness and cried.

To think that she had died last. To think of her alone with Anna's body on the bed, freezing slowly, starving, writing in her notebook. He wondered what she had written, knew he would never see it, would never know what she had thought about when she was dying. He saw her lovely open face, her shining eyes. He had loved her. It was true, and the realization shocked the tears out of him. He had loved her, although he hadn't known it then and it had never occurred to him that she might love him. He had only seen her once.

Now there was only a pain in his chest, which was gradually subsiding to an ache, a penetrating heaviness, which he knew would stay there for a long time. Something had changed in him when the Mountie gave him that news; he was no longer the same as he had been before the door opened and the Mountie came in. He saw all the long years of his childhood spread out behind him like a trail fast-disappearing in a snowstorm. It was over now, and he could never go back to being what he had been.

After a while he heard the Mountie come outside, start his car and drive away. It was night now, but there was no moon, only the stars gleaming coldly far away. The wind began to move through the tops of the pines around the bunkhouse, making them moan, and far off the coyotes began their song. He leaned his shoulders against the rough log wall and abandoned himself to his anguish.

PART TWO

CHAPTER ONE

There was not enough light from the rows of red-shaded lamps that hung at intervals along each wall, so no image was clear, the dancers melted in and out of shadows, turning their faces upward or sideways momentarily so that the light caught them, then lost them to the shadows. Cigarette smoke, blue-grey and white, hung in a hazy cloud above their heads. It drifted upward from the smokers seated at the shiny, red-topped tables, or from the men leaning against the carved and gleaming mahogany bar that lined one side of the hall. The heat in the long, barnlike room was palpable; both the dry heat of the summer night and the steamier warmth of all the bodies packed inside it. Amber liquor in clear glasses caught the light and sparkled, the whiskey's urgent, harsh odour mixing with the penetrating smell of cigarette smoke and the musky, sometimes perfumed scent of the sweating bodies. The band played louder to make themselves heard over the shrieks of laughter and the shouted conversations.

Oliver set down his sax, wiped the sweat from his shiny black forehead with a crumpled, greying hanky, and leaned toward Andrew and William.

Behind them, at the piano, Charlie threw himself into his solo, paying no attention to the others. Sam, on the drums, was too far back to hear, and sat with his head thrown back, eyes half-closed, arms and hands moving lazily, rhythmically.

"Look at the bigshots!" Oliver said. They heard only, "bigshots," guessing the rest from the shape of his lips. He tossed his head toward the entrance at the far end of the hall. Andrew followed the toss, not breaking the steady rhythm his pick was working. He saw a fat man in a dark suit making his way through the crowd, which parted for him. A small blonde woman in a yellow dress clung to his huge arm with a hand the size of a child's. At the long bar and at the tables people turned their heads to watch their progress. Those closer to the bandstand stood and craned to see over the heads of the others who had come in.

Sitting on the raised platform Andrew could see them as clearly as he could see anyone in the room, but their faces meant nothing to him. He kept chording on his banjo, watching them move among the tables, the fat man shouting hello, slapping men on the back, the woman clinging to him, sometimes disappearing behind his massive body so that only her small, white hand showed. In the middle of the room a table had miraculously appeared for them, chairs were produced, and they sat down.

Oliver was working at his sax again, standing, sweat trickling down his cheeks. The room was an inferno of heat and noise. Andrew leaned forward and searched the indifferent faces of the dancers who swirled past him, vanishing and reappearing in the shadows and the smoke and the crush of bodies. He looked hard, eagerly. He would have welcomed louder noise, greater heat, more uproar. It was never enough. They ended their song but none of the dancers sat down. Now at the fat man's table, a waiter was pouring drinks.

He should have been tired. It was one o'clock and he had worked most of the day on the Parker ranch, ridden thirty miles south across the border to Havre and started playing at nine. But instead, he felt only the familiar urgency for some climax that never came, and that dissolved only when his exhaustion brought sleep. Sweat prickled along his backbone, under his arms, and he wiped quickly at his forehead with his pick hand to keep it from trickling into his eyes. He shifted his legs impatiently and felt the muscles tense.

A tall woman with long black hair left her partner, slid through the crowd on the dance floor and stopped at the stage by the box that sat between Andrew's feet and the edge of the stage.

"Play 'Dark-Town Strutters' Ball,'" she called up to Andrew, and then rested her eyes on his face, her expression bold and hard. Andrew met her eyes and let his face slowly relax into a smile. She wasn't a bad-looking woman, although from this close he could see the fine lines radiating out around her eyes and the wrinkles starting in her still-slender, dark-skinned neck. She was wearing a short, full, red skirt and a low-cut white blouse that swelled out tightly over her full breasts. She dropped her eyes, let some coins fall into the box, their tinkle swallowed up by the larger noise of the hall, and flashed him one quick look with her shiny black eyes before she turned away. He watched her walk back to her partner, swinging her hips so that the red skirt swayed back and forth. Andrew kept his eyes on the skirt and on her long, shapely legs until they disappeared from his view among the dancers.

"Okay, boys," William said, and struck a chord on his guitar. The rest of them joined in without thinking. It was dance music, they could play it in their sleep. The woman and her partner circled past the bandstand in front of him and Andrew studied her partner. He was a big cowboy with broad shoulders and a heavy, flat, wind-burned face. He swung her around and Andrew's eyes met hers over his shoulder. They smiled, she turned, and her partner was glaring up at Andrew, holding his eyes too long so Andrew knew it was no accident. Something fiery and insistent surged upward from his gut, but Andrew tried to ignore it. He kept grinning. When the cowboy turned away, Andrew reached under his chair, found his glass, raised it and swallowed. The whiskey burned and met the fire already in his gut. He felt like throwing down his banjo and leaping from the bandstand, hitting somebody just to feel the muscles in his arms, the power in his back and legs. Instead he took a deep breath and used it to dampen down the fire, anger or joy or whatever it was, and forced himself back to the music.

A fight had broken out in the back of the hall. The band kept on playing 'Baby Face.' A bouncer, who had been leaning against the corner of the stage, pulled himself upright and shouldered his way through the crowd, knocking smaller people out of his way, shoving aside empty chairs, and making the small tables teeter as he brushed past.

The crowd followed him or stood on chairs to see. Cowboys and their wives or girlfriends, in from the ranches for Saturday night after a hard week's work, townpeople, all kinds—from bank clerks to bootleggers—the district's best and the district's worst rubbed shoulders here, and all of them struggled to see what was happening. Near the door a woman screamed. There was no fear in the sound, delight maybe, but it cut through the boom of voices, the shouts, and the steady chink, chink, chink, of the band. A man shouted, the words indistinguishable in the general roar, there was a crash, or maybe two, and even they might have come from Sam, who sat behind them with his sticks and drums and cymbals. The back door opened wide onto the rich blackness of the summer night, there was a flash of white shirt, a face, and the door banged shut again. In a moment the bouncer emerged into view, coming gently through the crowd, righting chairs, patting men on the back, his expression calm, self-effacing. He stopped at the fat man's table, tossed back a proffered drink, handed back the empty glass and made his way across the dance floor to settle back into his station at the corner of the stage.

One of the prostitutes from the building that sat around the honky-tonk on three sides came and stood beside him. Tired of waiting for customers, she had come in for a drink and a look at the crowd. Or maybe she had heard there was a fight. Her blouse was pulled down as far as she dared to show the rounded tops of her dark breasts, shiny with sweat, and her short, bright skirt was wrinkled across the hips with tightness. She was called Mickey, although Andrew knew her name was Maria. Part Indian or part Mexican, or both.

Then, beyond the cacophony of the dance hall in front of him, he heard clearly the song of Mexican Pete echoing through his head, remembered the two of them riding together all day across the empty plain, the breeze playing around them, their horses' hooves whispering through the grass. It struck him in the heart, a pain as real as any. Astonishingly, tears sprang to his eyes and he dropped his head to hide them. He cursed himself and struck the strings of his banjo too hard, but nobody heard. Not even bothering to turn away from the crowd, he reached under his chair, found his glass, and drank, as if the whiskey were water. Mexican Pete, a long time dead.

He searched the faces below him for the black-haired woman and found her sitting at a table a row back from the dancing area, staring straight up at him. She was smiling at him, a challenge, and he smiled back, meeting it. She tossed her head so that her thick black hair swung out from her shoulders, then settled back and she pulled a strand of it over her shoulder and fingered it under her chin. A parody of flirtation. He didn't care, it was her body he wanted, or something else, harder and more fierce.

"Break boys," William said. They set down their instruments, stood, stretched, and sauntered off the stage, down the steps beside the side entrance into the hall, and went outside.

The temperature had hardly dropped since afternoon, but darkness had taken away the sun's burn and softened the heat. The sounds in the hall behind them faded to a murmur in the sudden opening of the night. The stars high above them sparkled distantly, their light not even reaching into the shadows under the hall's eaves, where the five men stood smoking their cigarettes. Across from where they stood, the prostitutes sat in the windows of the cribs, their dresses open to show most of their breasts, their legs crossed and raised high, their feet resting on the window ledges.

"Come on in boy," they called to the few men who passed down the board sidewalk that fronted the three walls of cribs. "Come on in, honey." They ignored the men in the band from experience, could hardly see them in the shadows. The black prostitutes were in another house on the other side of the honky-tonk. That was where the band, except for Andrew, would go if they had need of a prostitute. Andrew knew nothing of the other men's lives beyond the few hours in the dance hall on Saturday night. The prostitutes blew kisses with moistened lips and beckoned. Andrew and the others watched the sky or the ground, averting their eyes from them.

Oliver passed around a bottle and they each took a drink from it. The air had calmed Andrew, and he rested his back against the rough wooden wall. A couple more hours and he would see what the night would bring. A woman, he hoped, and he thought of the black-haired woman inside in the lights and the noise, imagined the heat of her body, her skin against his mouth. He shrugged in the darkness and pressed down the melancholy that came again, unbidden.

"You eyeing that black-haired woman?" William asked him, his voice deep and soft like music in the darkness. Andrew laughed.

She's got nice long legs, he said. The other men chuckled—a bass, a tenor, a baritone.

"And a nice big boyfriend," Oliver said. Again Andrew laughed, a harsh sound, almost a shout, its meaning not clear, and that surprised even him. He stretched and rotated his shoulders, feeling the ache leave them.

"How much money is there in the box?" he asked. "Are we working for nothing tonight?"

She's pretty full," William answered. "Pretty full. We're okay tonight." Andrew grunted, impatient. The others murmured and scraped their feet in the dirt. Someone sighed and leaned back against the building with a soft thump.

Out on the prairie, coyotes would be hunting. The wild horses would be still, the foxes running. There was a moon, he didn't know where. Behind them in the dance hall the noise grew louder.

"Time," William said. He ground his cigarette out in the dirt, wiped the sweat off his forehead and neck, and opened the door leading back into the hall. A square of light fell across them, noise spilled over them. Slowly they followed William back onto the stage.

As soon as they were settled on the bandstand, the black-haired woman came across the floor, her hips swinging. She dropped more coins into the box.

"Sing 'Mamie,'" she called to them, looking at Andrew. Andrew pushed his banjo aside and leaned forward.

"You be around when the place shuts down?" he asked. She had stopped smiling, ran her eyes down his body from the open "v" of his shirt collar to the "v" of his bent legs.

"I could be," she said, lifting her eyes to his again.

"Maybe I'll see you later," Andrew said, and looked away, over her head to the dancers coming now to crowd the floor. She turned and went back to her table. As she reached her chair, the man with her caught her roughly by the wrist and bent to speak into her ear.

Time passed, the crowd flashed through the smoke below him, all the noises blending into one roar of sound, the smell of smoke and whiskey and too many bodies weaving into one, not unpleasant, dance hall odour that he had grown used to and welcomed. It all meant something, he thought, or it meant nothing. Whatever, it answered some crying thing inside him, at least for now.

He played and sang without thinking what he was doing. He drank now and then, he stood and sang, he sat and played, switching from his banjo to a borrowed guitar and back again. The crowd began to thin, the noise diminished, the hall slowly emptied.

While an old black woman swept the floor and another polished tables the waiters had cleared before they left, Andrew, Oliver, Charlie, William and Sam put their instruments away, closed the piano lid, and had one last drink together. William poured the money from the box onto the piano top. Twelve dollars. They were surprised and pleased by the amount. William split it among them.

Andrew swept up his money, waved, and went out by the side door. She hadn't been hiding in the shadows at the rear of the hall. She might be waiting for him outside. He had seen her leave with her boyfriend an hour or so before, but he knew that if she wanted him she would find a way. It was his experience that women always did

To the west the sky along the black rim of earth was already beginning to glow with the day's first light. He lit a cigarette and leaned against the wall of the hall to wait. If she didn't come, what would he do? Down the boardwalk across from him the cribs were dark, the windows empty. The door beside him opened and Oliver and William came out carrying their instruments with Sam and Charlie trailing behind. They stopped under the eaves and, sighing, breathed in the cooling air.

"What you hanging around for, Andy?" William asked, chuckling softly.

"Looking for excitement," Charlie answered for him. They went on by, their blackness blending into the night, their laughter rising softly and floating out behind them.

"Good night. Good night," they called to him, their voices fading. He heard their old car start up, the headlights swept over him and then shifted onto the narrow dirt road. They drove away, the put-put-put of their car growing smaller, till the night was silent again. Andrew wondered where they went. Somewhere into the black section of town to sleep in shacks the inside of which he would never see. He drew on his cigarette and looked up at the sky that grew faintly paler as he watched. She's not coming, he thought.

He would go to the livery barn, sleep for a while in the hay, or maybe he would saddle his horse and head out for the Parker ranch. Or maybe he would go to the house of that small, blonde girl, Shirley. Her husband might be away again. There was still almost an hour of darkness left. She would be glad to see him, would give him a drink, and take him into her bed. He thought of her small, soft body.

Then he saw them. They were coming around the end of the hall toward him. Three of them, led by the big, flat-faced cowboy. He thought he caught a glimpse, but wasn't sure, of her white blouse and a flash of her red skirt behind them. He tossed his cigarette away and stepped out onto the boardwalk to face them.

"You come on alone," he called to the cowboy. The night had slowed, grown crystal sharp, he could see everything, could already feel the satisfaction of his fist against flesh, could feel the surge of power in his back and shoulders and arms. The cowboy kept coming, his companions following a step behind, one on each side of him. Andrew's breath was quick and shallow, he felt light and strong, his hands were fists already.

"Come on alone," he said, not calling now. The three of them kept coming. Andrew saw now that one of them was swinging a baseball bat, casually, at his side.

His fists fell open, he turned and ran, pounding down the boardwalk, the three of them close behind. It was still black under the deep overhang that fronted the row of cribs and was held up by narrow posts spaced at intervals down the sidewalk. He dodged into the shadows there, running, trying to find an open door. Behind the cribs was an open field and it was still dark enough that he might escape them if he could find his way back there. The men behind him had slowed, not sure where he was in the dark. Andrew paused. He would have to double back to escape unless he could find a door that was open, and could slip inside without them seeing or hearing him. He moved again cautiously, feeling doorknobs, calculating the chance of suddenly turning and escaping through his pursuers.

"Go around the other way," one of them shouted. "Cut him off." Andrew had begun to sweat. They were gaining on him, but where the buildings made a right angle, between the two corner cribs, there was an opening not more than a foot wide. He remembered it as he reached it, felt it in the darkness where the air swelled outward and he squeezed into it, tearing his shirt at the shoulder. He inched his way down the passageway, his back flat against one wall, smelling his own sweat, his head turned toward the end where the open field was.

One of them had found the opening and guessing this was the way he had gone, had bumped into the passage and was beginning to struggle down it in the dark. Andrew had reached the end of the passage, knew it by the feel of the air, and lunged out into the open field with the other man only a couple of feet behind. Right beside him there was one back door. He turned the knob and stepped inside, closing the door quickly and silently behind him.

"Who is it? What do you want?" It was a hoarse woman's voice.

"Shsh!" he hissed into the black, stuffy air.

Outside the door somebody shouted, "I can't see where the hell he is!"

"Ah, for fuck sake!" another voice yelled. He came closer, cursing only a few feet from the door behind which Andrew stood. The voice grew quieter as he moved away.

Andrew's fear left him, a weight that rose and disappeared into the shadows. A fight was one thing, a baseball bat another.

"You better get out the front door," the woman suggested in an emotionless whisper.

"Hell, no," Andrew said. "I'll wait a bit." He wanted to laugh, struggled to keep it down, his chest and throat hurting from the effort. He pressed his face against the rough wood of the door and closed his eyes, breathing raggedly against the pain, that felt like loss, that had struck again. Loss of what? After a moment he turned away from the door and struck a match. It flared and in the billowing orange light he saw a woman's face, dark and ravaged. He dropped the match.

"Let's get a look at you," she said. She struck her own match, reached up to a kerosene lamp that sat on the table beside her chair, lit it, turned the flame low, and replaced the chimney with care.

They stared at each other as the flame steadied. At first he thought she was old, but then he saw she was only in her late thirties, it was just that her skin had been coarsened by her life, her features were beginning to sag, her hair was dyed a brassy, unnatural yellow.

"You're a good-looking one," she said. She began to wheedle. "I've got a soft place for the good-looking ones." He couldn't tell if it was habit that made her say this, or some hope of profit. For a moment Andrew couldn't

"You've got a soft spot for any man," he said, adopting the bantering tone he saved for prostitutes. They didn't bother him anymore, knowing that nothing would induce him to go with one of them. He saw the men they went with—the ugly, the misshapen, the filthy, the crazy. He forced himself to grin at her.

"Come here," she said. She was sitting in a stuffed chair that had a torn cover. The lamp cast a soft yellow light across her face and arm. She lifted her skirt above her thighs. "Come on," she said.

"No time," he said, "but thanks." He turned again and pulled open the door slowly, checking the field that would soon be clearly visible in the dawn. "Thanks for letting me stay."

"You sonuvabitch!" she shouted. She drew in a deep breath, prepared to shout till he was out of earshot. Andrew reached quickly into his pocket and pulled out the money William had given him. She stopped, cut off in mid-word, her eyes fastening on the money in his hand. He tossed a dollar bill onto the table by the lamp. It whispered, then lay still. Her hand flipped out and covered it. He stepped outside, shutting the door softly behind him.

To give up now seemed possible, to lie down in the stiff, dry grass and weeds and wait for the morning light, the bright sun of the day. A night owl called, so close to town, he thought. He might have wandered off across the field onto the prairie and not ever come back. He stood a moment, feeling the clear air on his face, staring at nothing. Then it came back to him, that insistent, urgent desire, and he straightened, breathing deeply.

Shirley's house was less than five minutes away. There was still enough darkness that if he kept close to the buildings and moved fast he could easily get there without being seen. With any luck her husband would be away again, bootlegging Canadian whiskey further south. Maybe he would have left a bottle again. The last time Andrew had been there he had finished off the bottle and when Shirley realized that, she had begun to cry.

How can I explain it to Will?" she had asked "He'll know I had somebody here. He'll kill me! She had thrown back the covers and gotten out of bed, pushing her tangled blonde hair away from her face, and turned toward him. "You bastard!" she had said, trembling, in a low, furious voice. "You'd better do something about this, or you'll never get in here again!" She had pulled on a ragged, faded pink robe, knotted it at her waist, but it had fallen open at her chest, revealing her small, high breasts. In the shadowed room at that moment, he had not seen anything in that small, pale face of the woman who tempted him. Already she was taking on the worn, hard looks that women out on the ranches got from too much work, no money, a rough, drinking husband. He sighed and pushed himself up on his elbow, sat on the side of the bed with his back to her, reached for his pants.

"I'll get you some," he said, his voice flat.

"You better," she said fiercely, and then began to cry again. "Oh, Andy, it's just that he'll beat me black and blue. I'm scared to death of him." He reached into his boot, vaguely remembering that he had thrown what was left of his money in there before they fell into bed. He found a few coins in the bottom of one boot.

"Christ!" he said. "I must have spent every cent I made last night." He stood and turned to her. She faced him, clutching the robe together over her breasts, her fists tight and white-knuckled, as though it were freezing in the room. They stared at each other. He reached for his shirt, where it lay in a heap on the floor.

"I know where I can get a bottle," he said. "I'll be back." He stood at the window, buttoning his shirt and knotting his scarf around his throat. "It's plenty dark enough."

She had come up behind him without his hearing her and, putting both arms around his waist from the back, pressed herself against him. She was so small, so soft. He pulled her around, turning so they were face to face. He remembered her small body beneath his in the bed, saw the softness again in her face and kissed her, feeling her body grow weak and pliant against his. He lifted her away from him, set her down and, without speaking, left the room and the house.

It was no use trying to break into the honky-tonk. It was too well-protected by politicians and businessmen and he didn't want to think about what they would do to him if they caught him. The women in the cribs sometimes kept bottles, but he had no money and no amount of sweet-talking would work with them. That left only one of the other town women, somebody like Shirley. He thought them over. Madeleine always kept a bottle in the kitchen in the cupboard the wash basin sat on.

He reached her house within minutes and crept around to the back, passing her husband's Model T that was parked beside the house. He tried the back door. It wasn't locked, he had known it wouldn't be, and it swung noiselessly inward. He paused and listened. At first the place had seemed perfectly silent, heavy with the weight of the night, but slowly he made out the sound of regular, heavy breathing coming from one of the rooms. That would be her husband. He stood perfectly still, listening.

The breathing went on, rhythmically, evenly. He took a cautious step forward. The linoleum-covered floor creaked softly. In the bedroom, someone turned over; the bedclothes whispered, the bedsprings creaked. He concentrated on the instant, not thinking, conscious of his body tensed and waiting in the darkness, of his sweat, of the other man in the next room. He lifted one arm and wiped the sweat from his face. Jesus Christ, he thought. I can't stay this way forever, it isn't four feet from me. All I have to do is grab it and run. Sweat trickled into his eyes and angrily he wiped it away, he thought of the woman waiting for him, saw the prairie whispering beyond the town, and he crossed the four feet of space between him and the cupboard, no longer even bothering to keep quiet, pulled back the curtain that hung in front of the cupboard, felt for the bottle, grabbed it and was out the door, slamming it shut behind him as he heard a man shout, "Who's there?" and his feet hit the floor.

He was out the back door, vaulting the fence, dodging down the alley between the small wooden houses in seconds. Madeleine's husband was shouting now, standing on his back step. "Where the hell are you? Madeleine! Get me my boots! Get me my gun! Where the hell are you, you sonuvabitch!" Andrew looked back over his shoulder as he turned the corner and saw the light go on in the kitchen at the same moment as a shot rang out, and then another.

But he was gone. Two blocks away now, only a couple of houses from Shirley's and laughing so hard he could hardly run, the bottle cold inside his shirt against his sweating chest.

Shirley was in her kitchen, wide-eyed, staring at him.

"Was that shots?" she asked, incredulous. "Are you okay?" He sank onto a chair, laughing, still trying to catch his breath.

"Put the light out, quick," he managed to gasp through his laughter. She blew out the lamp. "Here," he said, into the sudden darkness. "I got you your bottle." He could feel her coming close to him, and he felt for her hand, found it, and wrapped it around the bottle. She was breathing quickly.

"Will he notice it's not the same bottle?"

"I'll pour the booze into the empty one," she said. He began to laugh again.

"You shoulda been there," he said. "The silly bastard firing into the air in the dark, screaming for her to get him his boots."

"Oh, Andy," she said, sinking down onto his knees, her mouth against his neck, his ear. "What do you do this for? Somebody's going to kill you some day. My old man, or somebody's." He grabbed her wrists, suddenly angry.

"I do it for this," he said, between clenched teeth, and kissed her hard, hurting her. "I do it for the . . . Christ! I can't stand it!" She had stood up, he could feel her surprise. "Every day, the same," he said. "Cattle, horses, work from sun-up to dark. The same men, the same jokes, the same grub, the same weather." She had put one small hand on his shoulder. He took it, pulled her down onto his knee. He felt like crying, wanted to bury his face in the soft place where her neck and shoulder joined, or in the comfort of her breasts. "I do it for this," he whispered, kissing her neck, her forehead, her cheeks, her mouth, his hands sliding down her thighs, curving under her hips. "For this."

Remembering that night, he started to laugh again, quietly. Her house was up ahead. There was a light on in one of the bedrooms. Maybe she was up, although it was only about four-thirty judging by the light. The kids maybe.

He opened the back gate and it stayed that way, propped open by the tall weeds that grew in the dirt and garbage at the back of the yard. He sidled up to the house next to the lighted window and listened. Inside, a child was crying sleepily. He heard Shirley's voice, weary, motherly.

"Quiet, Lily, quiet. You'll wake your dad." She hummed a few bars and the child's voice faded away into a whimper and then into silence. He looked in the window. The sheer curtains were pulled shut and all he could make out inside was a blonde head, its outline made hazy by the curtain. He tapped gently on the window with his fingernails. He saw her head lift, turn. After a second, she came to the window, pulled aside the curtain, and peered outside. When she saw him, a look of pleasure, quickly followed by fear, appeared on her small white face. He made motions with his head to indicate the back door. She shook her head violently no. But he would not let her go. He motioned toward the kitchen and the back door again. Again she shook her head no. He stared up at her and she looked back, then pulled her bathrobe tightly together. She glanced over her shoulder nervously. He tapped again, gently, and her eyes returned to his. Behind her the child moaned and then was quiet. She dropped the curtain, picked up the lamp, and went out the door of the bedroom.

He moved back to the kitchen door, keeping close to the house. The light had grown, forcing back the shadows till he knew he couldn't count on darkness for cover any longer. He crouched down by the back steps, as she opened the kitchen door.

"Shirley," he whispered. She jumped and then looked down at him in the weeds by the steps.

Go away," she whispered. "He'll kill me." Her face was pinched and white with fear, but a flush was rising to her cheeks. He motioned toward the outhouse at the end of the littered, grassless yard. She looked back over her shoulder, listening. But something seemed to change in her, that quickly, he saw it, and she pulled the door shut behind her. He ran, keeping low, over the bare patches of dirt and weeds to the outhouse, opened the door, and slid inside. She followed him, walking slowly, as if there was no one waiting for her. When she reached it, he pulled the door shut behind her.

"Jesus Christ, it stinks in here," he whispered.

"Shsh!" she said. Already she was holding him, pressing her body against his. He held her tightly, kissing her hair, her eyes, her mouth. She trembled against him, and he forgot the smell, didn't care about it, the hunger rising, swelling, filling him. He pulled open her bathrobe, pulled up her thin nightgown, while she fumbled at his belt, his pants. It was so cramped in the outhouse that he kept banging one arm against the door, and every time he did it she gasped and clung harder to him. He crouched, his knee banging against the wooden shelf of toilet seats.

"Lucky you got a two-seater," he whispered, laughing into her hair. "Wouldn't be enough room in a one-holer."

"Shsh," she breathed, but he was inside her, lifting her, she fell against him, gasping, clutching his shirt, holding it in her mouth to silence herself. In a minute, it was over.

"I've got to get back inside, she whispered, sliding away from him, pulling down her nightgown, straightening her robe, breathing quickly. "If he catches me, I'm dead. Dead, Andy. I mean it." She undid the hook that held the door shut from the inside, then hesitated, looking at him. He was bent over, his knees weak, trying to catch his breath, while all the things inside him slid and fell and grew quiet. "He'll kill you, too," she said. Her solemn face, her eyes, told him it was true.

The light was growing over the shabby town, the houses, the fences, the back yards now grey and dusty green in the dawn. She stepped outside, and Andy, fastening his belt, prepared to follow her. He heard her gasp and peering through a crack, he saw the back door standing open and her husband standing in his underwear on the step.

"There you are," he said, not even bothering to raise his voice in the early morning quiet. It carried easily to the two of them at the back of the yard. "Get in here."

She stepped the rest of the way outside, shoved the door shut, gave the wooden block that served as a latch a half-turn. He heard it squeaking over the wood. There was a small opening high on one side that served as ventilation, but he could barely get one arm through it. If her husband came this way there was nothing to do but burst out, hit him, and start running. And what about Shirley?

He could see her making her way up the path, taking short, wobbly steps, holding her bathrobe tightly closed. He cursed himself, watching through the crack. The stench was becoming unbearable. He tried not to breathe. Her husband watched her come, scratching his crotch. When she reached the back steps, he grabbed her by the upper arm and dragged her the rest of the way up the steps.

"Jesus Christ!." she said. "Can't I even go to the can?" The door shut behind them. Andrew waited, checking his fly, his belt. The smell was so bad he couldn't stand it any longer. Cautiously, he shoved against the door, knowing she had locked him in. Nothing happened. He shoved again, harder. The block of wood that held the door shut popped out with a squeak and the door opened an inch. He slid his fingers through the opening and worked the latch till he had pushed it aside. Then he opened the door, stepped outside, shut it, turned the wooden block into position, hit it once with his fist so that it popped back flush with the door, and turned away. He went back through the gate he had propped open, closing it carefully behind him, and started down the alley.

It worried him to see her treated like that. Her husband had dragged her up the steps as if she were a piece of meat. In the morning she would have bruises. But there was nothing he could do for her. And he wondered, sauntering down the deserted streets toward the livery barn, why women would risk so much for what little he had to offer. He thought of that moment between them when he felt her lost in the powerful secrets of her body, that moment he had brought her to, the moment when he surrendered himself. Sometimes it seemed enough to answer everything, but sometimes it didn't.

CHAPTER TWO

Andrew, on horseback, picked his way through the tall cottonwoods leading down to the Milk River, which flowed along the northern edge of the town. In summer it shrank to a shallow stream, the water a milky green, still cool now before the sun heated it. His horse moved easily, having rested from its run the day before. Following a draw, they climbed the steep cliffs on the north side that led up out of the dry, dusty town that would soon be sweltering in its valley bottom.

He broke the top of the cliff, ignoring the loud message his stomach was giving him. He had left town too early to get anything to eat. He picked his way through the short dry grass, around the cracked, orange and green lichen-covered rocks, his horse's hooves brushing over the greying club moss. He would stop at Eagleton's ten miles to the north, just this side of the border. He'd never tasted better biscuits than Eagleton's. Thinking of them, he pushed Steal to a trot.

More than an hour passed, the sun had begun to burn now, but he could see a lazy haze of white smoke over to the west rising against the pale blue of the sky. Judging by the sun it was about nine and old

Eagleton was cooking breakfast. He spurred his horse again, rode down a slope, crossed Lodge Creek, only ankle deep now in the height of the summer—he was surprised there was any water in it at all—and trotted into the yard.

Before him, under the sparse, dying cottonwoods, sat a small log house. Flies buzzed around the open door. Eagleton stepped outside, blinking in the bright light.

"Morning," Andrew said, not dismounting. He leaned on his saddle-horn and studied the sky. "Another hot one."

"Just in time for biscuits," Eagleton said. "You coming or going?" His white hair was shoulder-length, his white moustache long, he was tall and spare.

"Heading north," Andrew said. He dismounted.

"Tie your horse in the barn," Eagleton said. "It's still cool in there. He looks a mite the worse for wear."

"Ain't fed him yet this morning."

"Feed him," Eagleton said. He disappeared back inside the house. Andrew led Steal to the old barn, built of logs with a pole and sod roof, and forked him some hay. He took off the saddle and bridle, then went back across the hard-packed, dusty yellow yard to the house.

"You look a little the worse for wear yourself," Eagleton remarked, his small blue eyes on the rip in the shoulder of Andrew's shirt. He poured a mug of steaming black coffee and flipped some biscuits from a heavy frying pan onto Andrew's plate. He went back to the stove and returned with a pan of sizzling salt pork. "Don't see no bruises." He came back and sat down across from Andrew.

"Wasn't in a fight," Andrew said, his mouth full. "These sure as hell are good biscuits."

"You mean nobody caught you," Eagleton said, pressing his moustache away from the mug he sipped from.

"They don't get up early enough to catch me," Andrew boasted. The coffee was strong and hot, the steam moistened his nose and forehead. He felt suddenly how tired he was, last night's whiskey curdling in his veins, his chest and thighs suddenly aching. He sighed and leaned his arms on the rough wooden tabletop. Eagleton went to the stove and brought back the coffeepot.

"You burning the candle at both ends, boy," he said. "Better give it a rest." Andrew listened, too tired to protest. "Won't get you no place in the end," he said. "Believe me, I been there." He sat down heavily and tipped his chair back. "Get yourself a wife. Settle down."

"You're a helluva one to give me that advice," Andrew said, looking around the cluttered, dirty little room. There was only one other room in the shack. "Don't see no woman around here."

"You mind that border crossing," Eagleton said, ignoring Andrew's remark. "I hear they got a new man on there at the Willow Creek post, and he's swore to put a stop to all you borderhoppers."

"I heard that before," Andrew said.

"Brought in a horse 'specially to catch you with," Eagleton went on. "A big black stud, a blood stallion, a sonuvabitch of a horse." Andrew set his fork down and looked up at the old man.

"Just to catch me?"

"Don't get too goddamn cocky," the old man said. "You're good, but you ain't seen that horse. Big sonuvabitch, must be eighteen hands. Prime shape."

"There's nothing the matter with Steal," he said. Eagleton looked sharply at Andrew, his bright little eyes catching the light and glinting.

"I thought I seen that horse before!"

"He ain't one of yours," Andrew said.

"Didn't say he was. But I seen him with that bunch of Walters' last year during the fall roundup, didn't I?" He picked up his mug, sipped, set it down again. "I was looking for some of my strays and I'm sure I seen him in with Walters' bunch."

"You always did have some eye for horses," Andrew said, shaking his head. "I don't know anybody else can remember a horse the way you can. Only have to see him once and you don't forget him."

"It's the action," Eagleton explained. "It's the action that tells the tale." He leaned across the table to Andrew. "Always watch the action. Ain't no two horses alike." He sat back again. After a moment, he said, "How'd you get him?" Andrew grinned, remembering.

"I was riding south, and I seen from a distance all that dust, so I waited, figured Walters and his boys was rounding up their herd. I waited, and when I figured they had 'em all, I rode down into his place, just slow and easy, about an hour later. Walters and the boys was drinking beer in the houseyard, and I says, real calm, 'Say, I'm looking for strays. Missin' about four broncs. They're slicks. You see any strays?'"

"So we rode out to the pasture where the boys had driven them in and I rode around with Walters, just pretending to look 'em all over, looking for my own." He began to laugh. "Pretty soon I seen three slicks up against a fence, just standing there, and they looked pretty good, so I says to Walters, 'There, them three is mine.' So, old Walters and his boys helped me cut them out." Eagleton was laughing now too.

"I told him the fourth one must have gone the other way. I took them back across the border, east of the Willow Creek Post. Got through with no trouble. They didn't even see me cross." He sobered, thinking about the horses and the trip home with them in the night.

"So Walters helped you cut out his own horses," Eagleton said, grinning. "Wouldn't he be spittin' if he knew."

"I branded them, sold one, traded one for a new guitar a fellow had at the bunkhouse. And the other one is the one I'm riding, that you spotted." Eagleton shook his head slowly, looking across to the open door where the sun shone hard and white on the step.

"One of these days, boy," he said, "somebody's going to catch up with you, the law, maybe." Andrew looked past the rectangle of light. He could see the way he had come, far off across the faded prairie, lifting and falling gently in the heat. It hardly seemed real.

"I can't help that," he said, blinking and looking at the tabletop. Neither of them moved, sitting silently in the stuffy room. A hawk cried once, then again.

"I got a bronc in the corral. Need somebody to ride him." Eagleton began to roll a cigarette. "I'm too old," he said, "my bronc-riding days are over. I'd be glad if you'd get on him, ride him around a bit."

Andrew sighed, a shiver spreading down his back, across his shoulders.

"Could do," he said, as if it were nothing to him. "Let's have a look at the bastard."

The bay, a gelding, stood in the far corner of the pole corral. He lifted his head when he saw them and advanced on them, tossing his head, his tail arched. The two men leaned against the corral and studied the horse, not speaking to each other. The horse whinnied and reared, then kicked up its back legs once, and began to race up and down, turning so hard that the pale dust of the corral rose in clouds and hung in the air.

"Figure you can do it?" Eagleton asked, keeping his eyes on the horse.

"You want me to break my neck?" Andrew asked, watching the horse too. He could feel the muscles in his shoulders and his thighs tense and ready.

"Who could ride him?" Eagleton asked, pushing back from the railing and spreading his hands, surprising Andrew. "Look at the bastard! Look at that muscling! You could ride him all day and all night and he wouldn't even work up a sweat!" They turned back to the horse, which was watching them. Eagleton cleared his throat, spat. "A horse like that," he said. After a long moment, he said, "Tell you what. You ride him, you can have him."

Ahhh, Andrew thought, the sound a long sigh inside him. To ride that horse. That horse. He watched the gelding race up and down the corral, his flanks gleaming through the clouds of fine white dust.

"I don't know if anybody could ride him," he said.

"You ride him, he's yours," Eagleton repeated. Trickles of sweat were running down his sunken, ruddy cheeks. Dust had settled in the lines in his forehead, around his mouth, and in the creases of his faded shirt.

"How many has he put in the hospital already?"

"Broke Buck Anderson's leg," Eagleton said.

"Shit," Andrew said. "Buck Anderson can't ride. Likes to show off. He's one of them rodeo riders. Can only ride if he's got an audience and a pick-up man and a ten-second whistle."

"Broke it pretty good," Eagleton said. They were both silent again, watching the horse. After a while Andrew climbed the corral, went into the barn and came back with his rope. Nobody to help him. He would have to forefoot the horse. He caught him on the first throw, bringing him up short, almost dumping him.

"Bust him!" Eagleton yelled. He was sitting on the railing now. Andrew shook his head. He worked his way up to the horse and, using the end of his catch rope, made a half-hitch, tying the bronc's front feet together. He left the horse standing while he hurried to the barn and came back with one of Eagleton's hackamores. The horse kept hopping forward. It was a wonder he hadn't fallen yet, and Andrew didn't want him down.

He paused, thinking. The best way, what was it? When he was alone, and had to be back in the bunkhouse by nightfall or he'd lose his job. The gelding was trying to hop away again, and a lather was breaking out on his now dusty flanks and chest. He watched Andrew out of wild fathomless eyes. But he would ride this horse, would break him, would call him his own.

He worked his way close to the horse, keeping the hackamore by his side. The horse pulled away, lifted his head, jerked it from one side to the other, trying to avoid being bridled, but hobbled as he was, he couldn't escape it. That done, Andrew stood a moment in the dust in the shadowless corral, the sun's rays burning his back through his shirt. He wiped the sweat off his face and neck with his arm. He would teach him to lead when he set out for home with him. There wasn't time now.

He glanced over to the old man. Eagleton was rolling another cigarette, concentrating on it, Andrew saw how thin his legs were in his faded, worn Levi's, how his flesh sat thinly on the bones that pushed out awkwardly under the cloth of his old shirt. His hands trembled a little as he rolled his cigarette, and Andrew, standing motionless in the baking heat between the frightened, struggling horse and the old man, thought, a man's life is a funny thing. He looked from the horse to the old man again.

A funny thing.

He could feel the waves of dry heat rolling up from the hard-packed dirt beneath his boots, could smell its dry, familiar odour. The cottonwoods stood motionless behind them, their leaves glistening in the sun, and above them the sky soared, too bright to look at, even from under the wide brim of his hat. A man's life, he thought again, and then did not know what he meant.

"There's a gunnysack in the barn," Eagleton called to him. Slowly Andrew raised his eyes from the dry white dirt across to the old man. "If you're ready to sack him out."

"I'm ready," Andrew said. "Need another rope, too."

"In the barn," Eagleton said.

He caught up the gelding's back foot with Eagleton's rope, and tied it in a sling which he fastened to the saddle horn. The horse was helpless now. He picked up the gunnysack and let the horse smell it. He rubbed it down the horse's neck, he passed it in front of the horse's face again and again, and under his belly, down his legs, past his flanks, and over his back. He kept this up for a long time, he didn't know how long. A horse with that much spirit. He didn't want to lose it, didn't want to turn him into an outlaw, either. When at last the horse had stopped flinching and fighting, he tossed the sack onto the ground and began to think about riding him.

"Want to take a break first?" Eagleton called.

"Nope," Andrew said, not bothering to look over at him. He went to the barn and brought out his saddle blanket and saddle, dropped them onto the ground near the horse.

Sweat was running down his spine, the sun was diamond-hard and high, the corral like an oven. He began to work the saddle blanket, getting the bay used to it by putting it on him and taking it off, over and over again till the bay accepted it.

Then he approached the horse with the saddle, set it on his back, lifted it off, set it on again. When finally the horse had stopped flinching, he left it on him, went in and did up the cinches. The horse quivered and Andrew backed out of his reach. The horse tried to buck, and fell, then struggled to his feet. Andrew left him and walked over to where Eagleton was perched on the rail. He wiped the sweat off his face and neck again.

"Sure as hell is hot," he said. Eagleton studied him.

"Yeah," he said. Andrew lifted his head and grinned up at the old man, shrugging his shoulders under the sweat-stained, torn shirt. "You changed your mind?" Eagleton asked. Andrew laughed once, a sort of 'ha,' as though the question were both surprising and yet half-expected. He went back to the horse.

He murmured to the horse for a second, then put a foot in the stirrup, hanging with his full weight in it. Then he stepped down. The horse shuddered. Andrew put his foot back in the stirrup and hung there, then leaned across the saddle, allowing his weight to fall on the horse.

He stood back, looking at the horse. The dust slowly settled around them, behind him a few crows flapped by, making their sore-throated, 'caw,' 'caw,' 'caw.'

He let down the horse's back leg. The bay backed away, fighting as soon as he thought he was freed, but his front legs were still tied. Andrew held the hackamore shank and talked to him. Then he stooped cautiously, and untied the horse's front feet. Quickly, before the bay could strike, he leaped into the saddle.

For a moment the horse stood quietly, shivering. Then he moved, found his front legs free, threw back his head and leaped twisting, into the air.

"Yahoo!" Eagleton shouted. "Ride him there, boy!" Andrew had stopped thinking. The mass of power beneath him leaped and twisted. The dust rose so thickly that they churned together inside a cloud that shut out the fenceposts, the rough pole railings, the shacks, the cattle grazing nearby, the willows and the cottonwoods.

Sometime, he didn't know when, the horse stopped rearing, stopped kicking out his back legs, stopped trying to rub Andrew off against the corral rails. Then he ran in huge circles around and around the corral, until even that ancient urge to run and run and run was, for the time being, worn out. Andrew sat on the horse's back while the dust slowly settled around them. Another horse. He had ridden another horse.

"By God, you rode him, boy!" Eagleton shouted. "He's yours! Andrew pulled with the inside rein to get the bay's head near him, reached over and grabbed the headstall, then dismounted, fast. He hobbled the horse and tied the hackamore reins to the hobbles.

He walked toward Eagleton. The hard-packed dirt puffing up behind his boots felt strange, as though it might tilt. He felt the sun now, it burned like a heated iron on his head and he realized he had lost his hat. He wiped away the sweat again with his shirt sleeve and the warm cloth smelled like horse and sweat and dirt. In that second, his eyes hidden from the light, he wanted to stay there in the darkness, but then his arm was down, the light striking hard all around him. He saw the railings in front of him, Eagleton's worn, dirty boots, the heels caught on the rail. He lifted his eyes, squinting. Behind Eagleton the old shack still sat, leaning a little, worn out too. He took a deep breath, expanding his chest, smelling the dusty air, pungent with sage and manure. He realized then that he had hardly been breathing.

"Try this," Eagleton said, holding out a clear glass bottle, half-full of a colourless liquid. Andrew blinked, then accepted it, took a long pull. Then he squatted and leaned back against the corral. He closed his eyes and handed the bottle back over his head to the old man.

"I didn't think you could do it," Eagleton said. He tipped the bottle and drank, then handed it back to Andrew.

Andrew squatted in the dirt, his back against the rough, unpeeled poles. He noticed that his hand was stinging and when he glanced down he saw that he had lost the skin off the knuckles of one hand.

"Still got to teach him to lead," he said.

In another hour he was mounted on Steal and leading the twisting, balking gelding, leaving the Lodge Creek camp out of sight behind him. Steal picked his way carefully through the sagebrush, around the greasewood bushes and the gopher and badger holes. They scared up a few mule deer out of a shallow coulee full of wild rosebushes and the deer's alarm was so sudden that Steal shied and the bay reared. East of them a herd of antelope raced across the prairie and disappeared around a low hill.

He reached the last half mile before the border and chose to cross where it was roughest, thinking of the day, coming soon, when he would challenge the Mountie and his horse. Here there were deep, wide burnouts in the yellow clay, huge patches of prickly pears that Steal skirted, soft, crumbling yellow rocks and steep, shallow cutbanks where the rapid spring runoffs had gouged the beginnings of what would one day be coulees. Andrew rode cautiously, studying the terrain, making a mental note of rocks and holes as he passed them. The sun poured down. Here among the hills there was no tree, no shade of any kind. He kept low, riding through draws and coulees, mindful that on the line of the hills his silhouette could be seen for miles in the clear air.

To the west a hawk circled, then dove, screaming. Andrew began to angle in that direction. Dun-coloured rocks streaked with ochre lay scattered down the yellow, powdery hillsides. Here the land was so barren even the sage and cactus had a hard time surviving. Ahead of him, at the base of a steep draw, there was a basin that sometimes caught runoff or rainwater. Usually the water was too brackish for even stock to drink, but sometimes, if he was lucky, he found drinkable water there. He approached slowly, his back and legs aching, his mouth and lips dry from the heat, a dull headache thudding at the back of his neck.

Steal's ears suddenly prickled and the bay jerked back, pulling the slack haltershank taut. He paused, listened. Male voices drifted upward toward him on the afternoon heat waves. Quickly he dismounted and led the two horses upward a few more feet. From there he could see below him, maybe a hundred feet from where he stood, a cluster of men and horses. Instantly, still leading the horses, he backed away, down, below their horizon. He paused again, thinking.

After a moment, he hobbled both horses, using his lasso rope and a short length he carried in his saddlebag. There had been something familiar about the squatting man, not so much anything Andrew had seen, as a feeling he had had at once, an instinct, as though he might somewhere have seen this very scene before. Andrew walked upward again, toward them, then fell onto his stomach and inched forward, leaving his hat behind in the dirt.

Two of the men wore holstered guns and one carried a rifle. American police. They stood looking down at the squatting man. Between them there was a dead, blackened campfire and to one side, three saddlehorses, two with saddles, one without. The third saddle lay on the ground beside the squatting man. The prisoner wore a faded blue shirt like the one Andrew was wearing and a big, stained stetson. As Andrew watched, he stood up slowly, seemed almost to unfold, until he towered over the two policemen.

It was the outlaw, the one who had come to their homestead years before. Twice more Andrew had seen him, once on the street in Havre only a couple of years ago, and once long ago when he had been rounding up with the Lambert and Smith crew. Andrew had topped a rise and come upon him riding down below. The outlaw had tipped his hat to Andrew, then spurred his horse and headed south.

His arms were handcuffed behind his back. One of the policemen had begun to saddle the outlaw's horse, while the other one held their horses and trained a handgun on their big prisoner.

Andrew watched them, a strange, uneasy feeling quivering in his gut. The outlaw was a horse thief, that much was common knowledge, and it was said he rustled cattle. He had never killed anybody as far as Andrew had ever heard, wasn't even known for fighting. He had never done anything more than Andrew himself had done, although he had been doing it years longer, but here he was handcuffed, a prisoner, on his way to jail.

Andrew thought of trying to help the outlaw, but he couldn't see how, and anyway, they were mounting, one policeman ahead leading the outlaw's horse, one behind with the rifle trained on his back. Sweat trickled down Andrew's forehead. His hair was soaked. He felt exhausted suddenly, worn out from the long night and the struggle with the bay. When the outlaw was free again, he would be an old man.

Andrew crawled backward, picked up his hat and jammed it on his head, removed the hobbles from the two horses, mounted, and rode north at a trot, forgetting about the water. Christ! he thought. Christ! He shuddered, breathing hard as though he had been running, the saddle creaking beneath him, the bay pulling now and then against the lead rope. Suddenly Andrew urged Steal into a lope, pulling hard on the hackamore shank so that his skinned knuckles stung again. He rode fast through the rest of the badland, slowing only when he saw the gently rolling Saskatchewan prairie stretching out before him.

CHAPTER THREE

A mile or so ahead of him he could see the Connolly's farmstead looking spruce and trim even from this distance. He had been to this farmstead for the first time years ago helping his mother deliver a child.
Elizabeth Ann. He would never forget the baby's name even though
he had long since forgotten the last name of the family who had lived
there then. They'd been gone for years. Starved out. Nothing would
grow for them.

Wherever Andrew rode on the prairie he found abandoned home-
steads, nothing left but the crumbling hole that had been the cellar, a
cement step maybe, a few flattened, rusted blue granite pots, a pile of
bricks where there had been a chimney, an uneven row of stunted, dying
carraganas, and a plot of farmland gone back to weeds and wild grasses.

There was never enough rain. All summer long the sky was an endless,
clear blue, high, empty of clouds, and from its quarter in the sky, the sun
burnt down, turning all growth to yellow, then to brown, and finally to a
dead grey. That's how it is in this country, Andrew thought, not without

affection. But then, he didn't try to make it do things it was never meant to do.

He thought of the new wave of settlers that was flooding the district, reclaiming the abandoned farmsteads, adding buildings, fences, and re-breaking the land. The country is filling up again, he thought, and then predicted grimly, they'll starve out too.

He rode slowly across a field of summerfallow, the bay leading quietly now, and entered the house yard. There was nobody around, but the door opened suddenly, and Jack Connolly came out and stood on the step.

"Put your horses in the barn and feed them," he called, grinning, before Andrew had even come to a stop. "Then come on in and have some supper." He waited on the step while Andrew went to the barn with the horses, put them in stalls, hobbled the bay with the hobbles he had made from a length of rope, forked both of them some hay, and came back to the house, hopping the new rail corral.

"Haven't seen you in a dog's age," Jack said, throwing an arm across Andrew's shoulders. He wasn't a tall man and he had to reach up to do it. "What brings you by?"

"I'm on my way up to see my mother," Andrew replied. "Have to be at work at Parker's tonight."

In the kitchen Mrs. Connolly was busy at the stove, dishing up bowls of food. Andrew counted seven children sitting around the table, watching him as he followed Jack into the big room. It was steamy with the heat from the stove and from the baking summer heat outside. A few flies, inevitable on the prairie, buzzed around but otherwise the room was spotless. A little boy of four or so, with a mass of curly blonde hair, held his spoon in front of his face, waved it, and asked nobody in particular, "Who dat?" When nobody answered him, he repeated his question, letting it degenerate into a little song which he sang, waving his spoon in the air. The baby, sitting in a high wooden chair at the corner of the table, began to cry and Mrs. Connolly, a big, robust-looking woman with pale blonde hair pulled back from her face, without turning or stopping her work, called, "See what he wants, Jeannie, hurry up." One of the girls, a child of ten or so with hair just like her mother's, obediently pushed back her chair and went to the child.

"Why, Andy," Mrs. Connolly said, having just noticed that somebody had come in with her husband, "It's good to see you again. Sit down, sit down. You're just in time for supper."

"Mrs. Connolly," Andrew said, removing his hat. "Quite a houseful you got here." Jack laughed, a little embarrassed.

"Never a dull moment," he said. He pulled out a chair and pointed to it. "Sit down, sit down." He went on down the table to his place at the end near the curly-headed little boy. The other children watched the two of them silently, their eyes lively and curious, their cheeks rosy from the heat. Andrew winked at the little girl, who had returned to her place. She smiled and dropped her head. "It's a helluva job to keep them all fed," Jack remarked. "Work never stops." At this, his jocularity left him and he looked away, out the window above the washing-up basin, and he grew silent. Andrew saw then that he wasn't as old as he had thought. There was youth still in his clear brown eyes, although his once thick dark hair was thinning, and his shoulders, arms and hands were thick and heavy from work. Andrew noticed then that his body was like Jack's. He thought, not without disdain, that he would not wind up like Jack, with that look on his face. "Soon, the boys'll be big enough to do their share," Jack said, his good humour returning. "Right, Kenny?" He looked down the table to the oldest boy, a blend of his mother and father, with dark hair and blue eyes. The boy nodded, grinning with pleasure. At his age, Andrew thought, I was delivering babies and riding in Lambert and Smith roundups.

Mrs. Connolly set a big bowl of steaming mashed potatoes on the table in front of him.

"Help yourself, now," she said. "Don't be shy. There's lots more."

"Mountie was here looking for you," Jack said. Andrew took his time, accepting a piece of bread from the plate one of the kids silently handed him. His eyes suddenly felt gritty from lack of sleep and he remembered he hadn't been to bed for almost two days now. The Mounties.

"You don't say." He buttered his bread thoughtfully. "Did he say what he wanted?" Jack laughed again so that Andrew had to look at him.

"Didn't say," Jack replied, "but he looked a little put out. Been riding hard, too. His horse was all sweated up." Andrew didn't say anything to this. After a moment, Jack went on. "About two, three weeks ago."

"Three," his wife said. A strand of fine, pale hair had slipped out of the bun on the back of her head and was plastered with sweat to her plump, white neck. She lifted it and smoothed it back into place.

"When I seen him coming," Jack said, "I figured he was after them rum-runners that come down this way from Consul."

"They come right through the yard!" Mrs. Connolly said, indignation reddening her already red cheeks. She pulled out a chair and sat down by the baby, who was happily sucking on a crust of bread.

"They come in the dead of the night," Jack went on. "We hear their motor."

"Sometimes I get up too," the oldest boy suddenly announced. When everybody turned to look at him, he looked embarrassed and dropped his eyes.

"I keep a damn close eye on them," Jack said. "You can't trust 'em. They come right through the goddamn yard!" He stared indignantly at Andrew. "I get my rifle, stand there," he nodded toward the window that faced the yard. "I aim it at them and I don't take it off till they're gone."

"When I was a kid," Andrew put in, "I used to see their lights at night way out on the prairie, circling around. They'd be lost, trying to find the border crossing. So I'd saddle my pony and go out and show them the way."

"You got nerve," Jack said.

"My mother never knew," Andrew said. "I was careful. I'd ride way out in front of them so they could see me coming. Always figured they'd shoot first and ask questions later." He smiled, remembering. "They used to give me a silver dollar for my trouble." The boy was watching him with admiring eyes.

"Some fellow was telling me there's talk about ending Prohibition," Jack said.

"What's Prohibition?" one of the girls asked, struggling with the word.

"How's your mother?" Mrs. Connolly asked Andrew. "I keep meaning to drive up and see her, but I'm kept so darn busy around here . . ."

She began to set servings of pie at each place. "Saw her about a month ago in town."

"She's fine," Andrew said. "Looks like a good crop this year," he remarked to Jack.

"So far so good," Jack said. "Christ! I never thought I'd get all that land broke, and now it's done and it ain't enough. I need more if I'm going to keep this crew fed." He looked to the window again, sighing. "They told us you couldn't farm here, you know?" Andrew nodded. "Said it was too dry, said we'd starve out like the people who home-steaded here before us. Hell! If it don't hail, I got twenty bushels to the acre out there." Andrew said nothing. "I figure it was just them cattle-men, them Americans, wanted the land for themselves, for grazing, did-n't want no farmers, so they tried to talk us out of coming. Didn't want anybody plowing up their cheap grazing land." He snorted, then glanced at Andrew. "No offence intended," he said.

"No offence," Andrew said, not looking at Jack. To Mrs. Connolly, he said, "Darn good meal. I want to thank you for it." She cast him a shy smile and he saw that she too was younger than he had thought. She might even have been pretty once, before she had all her babies.

When he had finished eating, Andrew went out to the barn with Jack and untied Steal, took the hobbles off the bay, led them out of the barn, and mounted.

"Listen, Andy," Jack said. "That Mountie looked a little put out. I'd take it easy for a while if I was you." He shaded his eyes with his hand, looking up at Andrew. "Where are you working now?"

"Still at Parker's," Andrew said. "I'm halter-breaking all his young stuff. I expect I'll be there this winter too."

"Why don't you get your own place? A fellow like you must get tired of working for somebody else. It'd keep you out of trouble, too."

"I been thinking about it. I got my own shack now, an old bachelor's shack nobody lives in, west of here. I spend a little time there now and then."

"You file on it?"

"Nope, just squatting." He settled into the saddle and looked out to the west, where the land lay flat and silent.

"I been thinking about leaving, seeing a little of the country." Jack lowered his head and stared at the pale, dry ground. A couple of chickens bobbed by and a calf in a nearby pen began to bawl. Jack sighed, and lifted his head again to look at Andrew. Their eyes met. Then Jack looked away and cleared his throat.

"Well, say hello to your mother for us," he said.

Andrew rode slowly away, leading the bay. There were big stonepiles in the corners of the wheatfield he was skirting, but he could also see stones lying in the crop. As soon as it stops raining, he thought, and it will, old Connolly's going to be in for a surprise.

A couple of miles ahead of him, just below the horizon, he could see a few black strokes against the backdrop of low hills. Horses. Unless they were strays, they might be his mother's horses. He drew closer to them, waiting for the moment when they would reveal themselves. They took shape, took on colour: two bays, two sorrels, a black. Not horses he knew.

He approached them cautiously. They lifted their heads, their ears up, watching him approach. He rode parallel to them, keeping a good distance away, and they came a little closer to him. Tame horses, he thought. Maybe broke horses. They came to a stop again and he rode slowly up to them and paused. One had the Lambert and Smith brand. The other four were young horses, unbranded, but it was a good bet they were Lambert and Smith horses too. The land he was riding on had once been Lambert and Smith grazing lease, but most of it had been taken back by the government to give to settlers as either homestead or grazing lease.

He debated. That big coulee on his mother's place was only a few miles to the northeast. He could run the unbranded ones in there leave them while he visited his mother, then chase them to his own place tonight and brand them. He'd have to be damn careful his mother didn't see him when he rode past the house. A picture of the outlaw, rising and unfurling below him in front of the American police, flashed through his mind. He hesitated, then thought of the herd he hoped to start or the money they would bring if he sold them.

His mother was playing the organ when he rode in, still leading the bay gelding. The sound of the organ reached him across the yard, bringing back his childhood, the smell of her bread, the look in her eyes.

"It's me, Ma." He heard her close the lid of the organ, heard the squeak of the stool as she turned and stood and then she was in the doorway looking at him with those blue eyes that seemed to grow more piercing with each year. She gave him a long, searching look.

"I'm glad to see you," she said. "You don't come by often enough." She went to the pail of water and began to fill the kettle. He crossed the room to her, and bent to kiss her cheek while she stood at the stove. She didn't respond, but then she never had, and this embarrassed him. He stepped back and pulled out a kitchen chair to sit facing her. When she was satisfied that the kettle was in the right place on the stove top, she sat down in the rocking chair beside it.

"How you been?" he asked. She didn't reply. Her hands were still on her lap. They seemed whiter and more fragile and he was surprised at their femininity.

"How long are you staying?"

"Just a while," he said. "I have to be back at Parker's tonight."

"How you burn the candle at both ends," she said. She stood again, and went to the cupboard to take down teacups. He noticed she had lost weight since the last time he had seen her.

"You all right?" he asked again. She set the teacups on the table.

"Had supper?" she asked.

"At Connolly's," he said. "They got quite a houseful." She measured tea into the teapot slowly. "Everything okay here?"

"That means you come up across the border the wrong way." He didn't say anything. With her he never had gotten away with a thing. He wanted to laugh, but managed not to. "I wouldn't want to be you when they catch you," she said, heavily. He opened his mouth to tell her about the outlaw, but thought better of it.

"Feel like singing a few hymns?" he asked her, teasing. She snorted, and glanced over her shoulder at him. The kettle had begun to boil. Their eyes met and they seemed to see one another again, mother and son. She made the tea and they sat silently across from each other sipping it.

She was what? fifty-three, fifty-five? She looked older, especially now since her hair had gone completely grey. He remembered the four horses grazing in the coulee to the north. He hoped he could get them to his own place and get them branded before anybody saw him.

"Andrew," his mother said. He lifted his head and looked at her, surprised to hear her calling him by his name. She was not looking at him, but instead sat holding her cup and saucer chest high, while she stared into the air just past his shoulder. "I have something to tell you."

Neither of them moved. He thought again of the horses waiting in the coulee. "I have cancer," she said. He had been sitting squarely at the table with his hands around his cup. Now he half-turned toward her, and opened his mouth to speak although he had nothing to say.

"No," she said, "It's cancer and I'm going to die pretty soon." She kept looking at that spot in front of her and her voice didn't waver or break.

"Mom," he said. He rose, bent, and kissed her forehead. A wisp of her tightly controlled hair pulled itself loose and fell down her cheek as if in protest. He smoothed it back, smelling her dry, powdery scent. He wanted to hold her and cry.

"Sit down," she said. "Sit down. It's time to talk." He obeyed, wondering what there was to say. Had she waited for this moment since his birth to finally talk? He was angry suddenly, and bent his head to hide it. "I've got this quarter, my homestead quarter, and I got the preemption. You know that. And I got the grazing lease. You'll be able to get that if you apply. But listen." She set her cup and saucer down and leaned toward him, her eyes fastened on him again with an intensity he had never seen in her. "I only farmed that homestead quarter so I could get the preemption. I don't have to tell you this ain't farming country. Don't try to farm. You and me, we're ranchers," she said, and he could have cried again. Suddenly she touched his hand, let hers rest on his. He seized it and wouldn't let her pull it away. He thought he could feel her blood rushing through the veins. He wanted to say, don't die, as if she could stop it if she tried hard enough. He was having trouble breathing and he averted his face so she wouldn't see. She pulled away her hand.

"Do you want me to stay?" he asked. "I'd better stay."

"No," she said.

"Of course, I'll stay."

"I don't want you to," she said, her voice even. "I'm used to being alone. I like it. I got a man comes over to do what work there is. When I'm sick enough, I'll send for you." She began to rock slowly, the chair creaking softly. He turned from her and sat squarely at the table again with his arms resting on it. He studied his hands. Swollen knuckles, rough-skinned, scarred. His hands were shaped like hers.

"One more thing." He waited. "I can't stop you from getting into trouble." She drew a long breath, seemed not to know how to say what she wanted to. "I don't want you in jail." Her voice strengthened. "Stay out of jail, Andrew, for my sake."

The blood rushed to his head as she said this. It pounded so hard he could hardly hear her. She had never asked anything of him. He shoved his chair back hard, stood, and pushed it out of the way angrily, was half-way across the room before he stopped and came back to her. He wanted to speak to her, but could think of nothing to say.

"I'm sorry," he said, finally. He thought about her all the way to his shack, as he led the bay and chased the four slicks ahead. In all these years his mother had never changed, only grown older and keener somehow, as though with every year that passed she had understood life better and read more meaning into every movement and sound. He thought she must be wise and he regretted that he did not know what her wisdom was because she would never tell him.

For the first time he tried to imagine his life without her there, always there, as inexorably as the prairie itself. Once she was gone, who would take her place? Loneliness swept over him, as if she were already dead. There was no one, no one else to care about him. Then he thought about what lay ahead for her and pity bent him over in the saddle. The four horses ran ahead of him, their silhouettes black against the moonlit sky, and the bay let the rope between them slacken as he trotted up beside Steal and whinnied to him.

His back ached between his shoulders and at the bottom of the spine, his shoulders ached, even his feet in the stirrups ached with an indefinable, hopeless pain. Inside his chest there was only an infinitely large and empty blackness.

Why had she come here all alone, with only him, a small child? What had she hoped to find here? To do with her life? Had she succeeded? Had she been happy? Did she find what she came for? He wanted to forget the horses, turn Steal around, gallop back and put these questions to her. He wanted answers. He wanted to know. "Mom!" he cried out loud. "Mother." But he did not turn around. Our lives are separate, he thought. Even if she told me, I wouldn't know.

He was nearing his own place now. When he branded the horses he would turn them out, and ride the last ten miles back to the Parker ranch.

It struck him suddenly that he was doing what she had asked him not to do. He almost pulled Steal to a stop and let the horses go. He debated with a measure of sincerity, even as he closed the corral gate behind them, wondering at himself. It wasn't that someone else would steal them as he was about to do, or even that he would lose the money their sale would bring, or even that he loved horses and wanted to possess all of them, although all these arguments came to him. It was instead, that his mother was a woman, after all, and women couldn't know what a man's life was. It's not that she's wrong, he thought, but only that she doesn't understand.

He wondered if he understood himself, leaning against the corral rail in the moonlight, and he pondered while the horses raced in front of him sending up dust that fell again, glittering. He would do it because he needed to, that was all, and the old rage rose again, pushing out the sorrow, pushing out the guilt, and all his reasons. He was a man, he wanted to live.

He was riding south, his eyes on the distant horizon that was lifting and falling slowly with the waves of heat. The landscape grew paler and paler, washed out by the sun to faded blue-greys and mauves. He thought that if he could ride into the shimmering haze that floated above the horizon, that lifted the prairie and made it dance, if he could ride far enough till he had reached it, ridden through it, he might come out into another world on the other side. A world that would be cooler, he thought, clearer and sharper, like the winter sky at night. He was surprised and amused by this thought, and shifted in his saddle, then spurred his horse.

He had come on the big bay to challenge the stallion the Mounties had brought in to catch him with. All this past week he had been working with his horse, riding him to herd cattle and to chase in the horses. The bay was ready now, still half-wild, but controllable.

He stopped on the rim of the coulee and looked down to the post buildings below. He waited, silhouetted against the high, hot afternoon sky and looked at the barns and corrals, remembering when they used to be full of cattle and horses, cowboys everywhere.

After a while the Mountie's house door opened and a man in an undershirt and trousers came out carrying a basin. He stood on the steps and made a throwing motion with the basin and Andrew heard the splash of water and saw the flash of silver as it flew and struck the ground.

The basin flashed again as the man lowered it, then turned to go in, but something must have caught the corner of his eye, because he turned quickly back again to look up at where Andrew sat on horseback at the edge of the coulee.

The Mountie, a stranger, Andrew wondered where he had come from, shaded his eyes with his hand and studied Andrew. Andrew saluted him once, a clean exaggerated gesture, holding the reins in his other hand. Then he turned his horse and headed south, riding slowly, in full view, toward the border.

He was grinning to himself. He could imagine the Mountie running for the barn, pausing to strap on his spurs, throwing the saddle on the black. He decided to lead the Mountie across the border, keeping in full view, and then loop back again through the roughest crossing he could find. After a while he pulled his horse up and listened. In the afternoon stillness he could hear a horse coming at a gallop.

He spurred the bay and they flew over the sparse, dry grass. When he judged the Mountie would be in view, he slowed, checking over his shoulder and saw the Mountie coming a half mile back. He waited, turning the bay in circle after circle, barely managing to hold him in. He wanted to see the black. When there was barely a quarter of a mile between them, he got a good look at the horse.

Such a horse. A big stallion, his coat black and shiny as coal from constant currying and good feed. His slick black sides shone, the muscles richly defined under his gleaming coat. For a moment Andrew forgot the race, he was so overcome by the sight. But the Mountie was gaining on him, the bay was prancing, would be bucking in a second, so he spurred him, let him go, and the Mountie pounded up behind.

When he was through no-man's-land and on the American side, he started a slow loop to the east, gradually heading back north. The Mountie was still coming, the horse gaining.

The terrain was rougher now, as they approached the edge of the worst land, and the Mountie wasn't a hundred yards behind him, the gap closing. He spurred the bay again and they flew over the hard, dry round. The bay leaped a burnout without even slowing his pace.

Rocketing over the rough land, crouching over the bay's mane, Andrew saw the ground lurching by in a blur of rocks, badger holes, patches of cactus and sage. The horse didn't care, he was a wild thing, he leaped, he dodged, he flew over and around obstacles as if there was no such thing as a fall, a broken leg, another day. And Andrew clung to him, rode with him, his spirit shared, never thought of checking him. He looked over his shoulder and was surprised to see that the black had fallen behind. He watched, trying to see what had happened.

And then, watching over his shoulder like that, he saw that it was the Mountie. At every burnout or rocky patch the Mountie pulled the black up, checked him, slowed his pace. The Mountie was afraid. The horse was straining against the bridle, burning to go, but the Mountie wouldn't let him. The black could have caught Andrew easily if the Mountie would have let him go.

Such contempt welled up in him at the Mountie's fear that he once again let the bay go completely and in seconds they had put the short, rugged patch of hills behind them and the Mountie was left out of sight, far behind. When he was well back on the Canadian side, he waited till he could see the Mountie coming slowly through the hills. He turned the bay parallel to the border and when he was a hundred feet from the Mountie, he rode parallel to him, heading toward the post buildings. Andrew tipped his hat ostentatiously. "Evening," he called. The Mountie didn't reply, casting him a sullen glance from under the brim of his hat. Andrew grinned, not even bothering to hide his scorn. "Looking for something?" he taunted. Again the Mountie didn't reply. They rode silently side by side a hundred feet apart until they reached the coulee where the buildings were, then the Mountie disappeared down the trail still without having spoken.

So they had brought in a Mountie from Regina, or maybe even from the East, to ride the black and catch him, and the Mountie had been afraid to ride full out on the rough terrain Andrew had led him through. A city man. No wonder. There wasn't another border guard, American or Canadian, who would have pulled that horse up. Andrew turned the bay north, riding slowly now, musing on this, as he headed back to the Parker ranch.

The light was changing as the bright day wore into night. It grew more intense as it darkened. Above him, the zenith of the sky was a deep blue which, as it curved to the east, grew gradually clearer. There the light-filled blue had such a depth to it that it seemed almost palpable. It was at once translucent and textural, a clear, magical blue-green which, as his eyes descended further, lost all colour, became a clear, colourless nothing that changed gradually to shades of apricot increasing in intensity till it slid below the horizon.

The grassland all around had turned to gold, shaded with tones of brass and copper. It made the grass glow, and to the west the sky burned with a clear, pure light. He rode on, no longer thinking, into that burning, golden world, his eyes straining ahead. There were no shadows, only a lifting, gleaming, yellow-gold world.

CHAPTER FOUR

Andrew threw back the canvas cover of his bedroll. Hank was already up and had lit the lantern. Its light showed the snow that had sifted onto the bedroll during the night lifting in a fine white cloud, then sliding down the tent wall. Beside Andrew, Morton was moving too, the snow on his bedroll sliding gently down the canvas onto the tent floor. His breath rose in icy white shreds above the mound of canvas that covered him, and his beard, as his head emerged, was white with frost.

"Jesus goddamn fucking Christ," Hank muttered. The lantern swayed, making his shadow veer crazily across the tent wall. Outside they could hear their saddlehorses' hooves crunching on the hard-packed snow as they moved about restlessly, anxious to be going after standing all night blanketed and tied to the wagon. "What a goddamn fucking way to make a living," Hank went on in the same despairing undertone.

"Who's gonna make the fire?" Andrew asked, raising his voice over Hank's lament, which promised to go on and on and on.

102

"Not me," Morton said. "I made it yesterday." He began to cough, drowning out Hank's groans. Between coughs he managed to say to Andrew in short, breathy bursts, "It's your turn."

While Hank continued to curse to himself, Andrew silently reached inside his bedroll, found his mackinaw, and pulled it on. He thrust his arm through the tangled blankets to the bottom of the bedroll feeling for his boots, and struggled into them, trying at the same time to keep the blankets up around his chest. When he had his boots on, he clenched his jaw, took a deep breath of the cold, steamy air, threw back his covers and stood up. Rapidly he shook the snow off his cap and put it on, pulling down the earflaps, turned his overshoes upside down and banged them till all the snow fell out, pulled them on over his boots, and thrust his hands into the stiff leather mitts that he took out of his mackinaw pockets. Ready, he threw back the tent flap and crawled outside.

It was still well before dawn and the winter night sat heavily on the snow-covered prairie. On each side of him the two remaining tents glowed faintly with the light from the lanterns that had just been lit and that hung inside them. Routledge, the camp cook, had hung a lantern on the wagon box. It sent a yellow light spilling across the snow. In the distance coyotes yipped and howled eerily. The cold air bit at Andrew's nose and forehead. He blinked, his eyes watering from the cold, and set his mind doggedly on the task before him.

The stove sat on the ground at the back of the wagonbox, where they had left it the night before. Andrew threw off its cover, got some wood from the wagonbox, and without taking off his mitts, struck a match and held it to the kindling and paper he had pushed inside the stove. They ignited at once, the stove drawing easily, and he was grateful. Some mornings the atmosphere was strange and fires either wouldn't start at all, or once started, kept going out.

As soon as it was blazing well, old Routledge, using snow which he packed into the pot, made the coffee and set it on the stove. He took a small axe and began to chop beef off the side that lay frozen solid in the bottom of the wagon while Andrew held the lantern high for him to see.

"Thirty below if she's anything," Routledge said to Andrew, pausing to catch his breath. His nose was running a thin silver stream and he wiped it roughly on his frozen leather mitt. Andrew grunted. The blows of the axe on the iron-hard meat made a thin, high-pitched sound in the still, frigid air.

One by one the men emerged from the tents into the darkness, cursing, their heavy clothes creaking in the cold, their ghostly breaths, visible in the lantern light, preceding every movement. One of the men took the last of the oat bundles from the wagon and fed them to the saddlehorses and the cook's team. While he was doing this the others began slowly and silently to dismantle the camp, folding their cumbersome bedrolls, tying them and placing them in the bottom of the wagonbox. Then they took down the ragged tents, packed them and stowed them away in the wagon too. By this time the team had finished eating their meagre breakfast, and while Routledge cooked, Andrew and Hank harnessed the horses and hitched them to the wagon.

At last the coffee was boiling, its welcome smell drifting through the frozen, dark camp. On the stovetop the beef sizzled in the pan and the bread, placed on the stove too, had long since thawed. The crew ate quickly, hardly waiting for the steaming coffee to cool, downing it gratefully, their hands tight around the tin mugs for warmth. They chewed on the bread and beef, saying little, listening to the coyotes yelping nearer now.

By the time they had finished eating, the first hint of dawn was playing at the horizon. Two of them helped the cook dump the fire out of the stove, then lift it into the wagonbox. There had been no place to put the saddles so they had all left them out overnight and now the leather was frozen, the rings covered with frost. Each of them carried his saddle to his horse, pulled off the horse's blanket, threw on the saddle blanket, and set the saddle in place. As soon as the cold leather touched each horse's back, the horse jerked away and reared, protesting. All over the camp, saddles slid off into the snow and saddle blankets fell or were kicked away.

By the time they were ready to go, the sun was just climbing above the horizon, colouring the sky above them the palest, saddest yellow. They had camped beside a deep coulee and in the bluish, frozen morning the breaths of the horses sheltered in the coulee bottom had risen to form a motionless cloud of frost that hung in the still air above them. The hills to the west stood out sharply, still blue-shadowed, so that every ridge was clearly delineated.

The horses were beginning to emerge from the coulee, their fringed heads rising awkwardly above its edge. They began pawing at the thin cover of hard, dry snow, looking for something to eat.

"They musta chewed up all the grass in that coulee bottom," Hank said.

"There was hardly anything there," Morton pointed out. "Look at the poor buggers. They get any thinner, they'll die. They're just about starved." He began coughing again, softly, no louder than the men's voices that barely broke the vast, snowy silence. They stared at the herd morosely. A couple of hundred head of mustangs—mares, colts, a few stallions, geldings that some of the men recognized from having driven them in and castrated them when they were still yearlings. In the bluish light, they were a spiritless bunch, sickly, half-frozen, their ribs showing.

The foreman, Jerry Lozinski, murmured as if to himself, "They're gonna move pretty slow. They're weak."

"Don't worry, boys," Old Routledge called to the horses from his perch on the wagon seat, "by tonight you'll have a little grass." The horses milled slowly about the handful of men on horseback, the snow on their backs blue-tinted.

"A helluva little," Charlie Butler said, and spat, making a long, brown stain in the snow. Lozinski hawked and spat too, angrily. When he spoke, his voice was too loud, so that the horses nearby jerked their heads up and stepped away nervously.

"Let's get moving before we lose the bastards. I don't want to be out here any longer than I have to."

"Freezing your goddamn ass in a goddamn fucking saddle," Hank muttered. Andrew worked his shoulders irritably under his heavy mackinaw. Shut up, he wanted to tell them. Shut up and let's get it done.

"Meet us at the Wilson shack about noon," the foreman called to Routledge. "We can get warmed up there. If the stove is still inside, use it." The team pulled out slowly, the iron rims squeaking in the hard, crusted snow.

The sun was a little higher now, but it gave out no warmth and even its light was thin and sickly, colouring the long, empty prairie a dismal, but not unbeautiful, blue-grey. The riders spread out and began to bunch the herd, slowly directing it southeast toward the Gillespie ranch head-quarters and the field of untouched grass waiting there. The herd moved slowly, reluctantly, the men watching the sky as it grew lighter, on the lookout for signs of sudden blizzards.

As far as they could see in each direction now that the sun was truly up, the grey-white prairie melted into the low, grey-white sky so that they couldn't tell where the land ended and the sky began. A few tufts of faded yellow prairie grass rose here and there above the snow cover, along with the occasional weed that had cured to a dull bronze. In the hollows where water gathered after a rain, a few spindly rose bushes or badger bushes stood, stripped of their leaves, their flimsy branches frozen to charcoal tinged with orange. Rabbit tracks crisscrossed the snow and in spots there were patches where they had scratched it up, revealing dead grey grass. The men rode past cattle, their backs humped and covered with crusted snow, their noses blue.

Every once in a while as he rode, Andrew switched hands, keeping the one that wasn't holding the reins in his pocket till it was warm, then switching again. His feet ached with the cold and twice, when he could stand it no longer, he got off and walked, leading his horse, till his feet warmed. He made no attempt to keep the frost from forming on his beard and moustache.

The other men rode companionably in twos or threes, talking to each other. Andrew rode alone. The colder it got, the harder the job, the more silent he became, burrowing into his mackinaw, into himself, his deter-mination focused on details, answering the others, when they spoke to him, with grunts or silence. His cheeks were numb, frostbitten that meant, so they would be tender all winter. He settled further into his mackinaw and switched hands again, flexing his toes inside his boots. Riding into that bitter day, from out of the bitter night, one small part of him frozen, he caught a glimpse of his own fragility, how at every second, he teetered into death. And nothing to save me, he thought, and no reason why.

At noon, as they approached the Wilson place, the sun was a mauve smear that hung not more than a handsbreadth above the southern horizon. A thin stream of smoke rose from the old grey house that sat next to greying, tumble-down corrals. The wagon was pulled up in front of the house, the team unhitched and blanketed and tied to the wagonbox. Spirits rose palpably.

Andrew never took the first shift to eat. He offered no explanation for this, and the others, looking impassively at him, betrayed their uncertainty about his refusal only by the fact of their looking. They asked him no questions. He couldn't have answered them anyway. It was only that he had gotten this far, that stopping to eat and getting warm, required a letting go that he saw no reason for, that he felt contempt for. He could go further, often wondered in fact, how far he could go, often fought the temptation to find out.

By late afternoon, as the sky passed from pearl to a deeper grey, they drove the herd into Gillespie's field on the other side of the ranch buildings. They left them there, pawing in the snow, and rode back to the barns, where they unsaddled their horses and turned them out with a little of the sparse supply of feed.

Soon they sat at the long wooden table in the kitchen cracking jokes, letting the warmth seep into their bones, waiting while Thelma Gillespie and her daughter Nettie dished up the bowls of mashed potatoes and vegetables, the platters of roast beef, the stacks of homemade bread. It was as if the last few long, cold days on horseback had never happened. Andrew was reminded only by the burning in his cheeks, a souvenir he would have with him all winter.

Nettie was pouring coffee and instead of going around the table to fill the cups of the men on the other side she stood by Andrew and reached across the table, her thigh pressed against the arm of his chair, so that he had to lower his arm onto his lap. He hardly noticed this, but the second time, when she came up behind him to serve dessert to the man next to

107

him, she bent over, staying close to Andrew's back so that her warm hip pressed against his arm, and he realized she was doing it on purpose. He lowered his eyes, hoping the other men hadn't noticed.

So, he thought. She would come to him. He allowed himself to savour the feeling she was working to arouse in him. He could feel her warmth radiating between the rungs of the chair as she stood behind him talking to her mother.

When supper was over Andrew went straight to the old log shack he lived in, since the bunkhouse was full, stoked the fire, stripped to his underwear, and fell into his bed. He had meant to stay awake to wait for her, but after the long day in the cold, his frostbitten cheeks burning, his limbs stretched out comfortably, basking in the heat from the stove, he couldn't keep his eyes open.

He wakened to the sound of the door creaking open. For a moment he didn't know what it was. He felt a wave of frigid air sweeping across him, heard the brush of clothing as someone came toward him. The boards creaked and in the light that escaped through the cracks in the stove door, he caught a glimpse of a man's coat.

"Andy?" she whispered. He raised himself on one elbow, surprised. It wasn't Nettie's high-pitched, girl's voice.

"What is it?" he asked, confused. The coat fell to the floor with a soft thump, a woman bent toward him and he saw in the firelight that it was Thelma. Her body heat, captured and held inside the sheepskin coat, rushed out and engulfed him, the smell of woman, and without thinking, he reached for her.

She fell onto the cot half beside him, half over him. He moved back awkwardly, holding her onto the cot and, pulling his blankets out from under him, threw them over her. She was wearing a long flannel nightgown. She shivered, and as she lifted up to let him pull the covers out from under her, he felt both her breasts, loose, brush against his face.

He was afraid of Gillespie, afraid of getting caught, bewildered by her presence, but at the same time his hands were sliding up her nightgown as she lifted, her legs around him, her mouth on his. He let go of his last scruple.

Afterwards, before she left, he said, "Your old man isn't going to like this if he finds out."

"You planning to tell him?" she asked. He didn't answer. "Well, don't worry," she said, "cause I'm not going to tell him." She fell back beside him, sighing softly. "He's away too much, and anyway, he isn't interested anymore" She got up, pulled the coat on, and crossed the small room. When her hand was on the doorknob, she said to him, "Okay if I come back?" He was drowsy again, couldn't remember later if he had answered 'sure' or not. He felt the surge of cold air again, and was asleep.

Hours later the door opened again, Andrew heard it creak, felt the wave of cold air, thought he must be dreaming. He turned over and was asleep again.

"Andy?" He pulled back up from the dream, trying to remember something. "Andy, it's me." He turned onto his back, coming awake slowly. "Andy," she said. It was Nettie. He sat up, bewildered again, not sure now what she wanted.

"You knew I was coming," she said, pouting, and sat down on the edge of the cot. She was even wearing the same man's coat her mother had worn.

"What do you want?" he asked, stalling for time. Did her mother know she had come? Had she sent her? She giggled.

"Guess," she said, and put her hand on his chest. Paul Sawa had told him how she had met him at midnight out behind the ranchhouse in the trees when she was barely sixteen. She bent over him and he felt her body against his. She began kissing his neck, then lifted her head and put her mouth on his. He was kissing her back before he had thought about it.

"Wait a minute," she said. She pulled away, threw off the heavy coat onto the cold wooden floor, rose to her knees and pulled the night-gown off over her head. The light from the fire, now burned down to a red glow, glinted on her ample white breasts, on her soft, rounded white belly.

"You'll freeze," he said, pulling her toward him. Such flesh. Already he was running his hands over her lush body, his palms and fingertips erasing the sharper contours and the silkiness of the other woman's body.

When she left him, the bed felt empty. He fell into a dream as though he had never wakened at her coming. He dreamt he was walking in a field of white flowers that grew up taller than he was. They bent and swayed, their cool white petals ignited a sweet fire when they touched him. Below the thin crust of earth on which he walked was an infinite blackness, and he was torn between the ecstasy of the petals' touch and the terror of the blackness below.

They came after that, alternating nights, as if each knew that the other was coming to him in the darkness, and had mutely agreed their paths wouldn't cross. He wondered if one of them, creeping down the stairs in the night, reaching for the old sheepskin coat, and finding it missing from its peg on the wall, merely turned around and went back upstairs, knowing that the coat lay in a heap on the cold floor beside his cot. Didn't they care, he wondered? How could Thelma not care about what Nettie was doing?

Whenever Lloyd came home, their visits stopped, and Andrew was glad to get a few nights of unbroken sleep. He was beginning to think that he might have to quit and find another job if their bewildering persistence didn't fade. But he wouldn't ask either of them to stay away. When he asked Thelma why, she said what he might have said himself. Because I'm not old yet. My life isn't over yet. Because I don't want to be dead on my feet while I'm still breathing. He had wanted to ask, does it help? Is it enough? But when he touched her with his hands and her body heat radiated against him and into him, burning inside him, he knew, yes, it helps. Yes, it makes a kind of sense that nothing else does. With his mouth against hers, their bodies joined, he felt solid and real, in a way he never did otherwise. He didn't question Nettie, knowing, because she was young, her reasons without asking. He even understood sometimes why Thelma didn't stop her daughter from coming to him.

The winter wore on, alternating blizzards with hard bright days, the rare chinook blowing through to give them a little respite. Lloyd left to sell or buy horses or cattle, stayed away a week or so, then returned. When he was home he rode all day with his men looking his herd over, helping round up strays, or doctoring sick cattle or horses. Andrew watched him, looking for signs that he knew about his wife and daughter.

110

One day, as Andrew was riding up from a coulee bottom, chasing ahead of him a few head of cows that had strayed from the main herd, he found Lloyd Gillespie waiting for him at the top.

"Saw the Jorgenson's boy in town yesterday," Lloyd said. He sat, his heavy body comfortable in his saddle, smoking a roll-your-own. The smoke rose straight up, a wisp in the still bright day. Andrew kept his face expressionless, drew his horse up beside his boss's. "He tells me he saw five or six head of mine over by his place not two days ago. I want you to find 'em, bring 'em back."

"Sure," Andrew said, as though he had not been tensed for a fight. He took out his own makings, and began to roll a cigarette, concentrating on it.

"Might as well go now," Lloyd said. "The boys can finish up here. It might take you a couple of days to find 'em, so you'd better get Thelma to feed you before you go, pack you something to eat." Andrew waited, expecting more, hearing something in Gillespie's voice. Instead, Gillespie turned his horse and started to ride toward the ranchhouse. Andrew caught up with him and they rode in silence for a quarter of a mile or so.

"You know," Gillespie remarked, glancing up at the sky and then turning his head away from Andrew so that he was studying the horizon far to the east, "I don't worry about what Thelma does when I'm away." Andrew said nothing. They rode another few yards. "No, what Thelma does, don't worry me none. She can do what she likes." He leaned over and spat his butt out into the snow. "I ain't saying anything about you or anybody else," Gillespie went on. He lifted his head and grinned suddenly at Andrew, then looked away again. "I got my own life, as far as that goes." It was Andrew's turn to look quickly at the other man. "It's Nettie." Again they rode in silence, this time for a good half mile, while Andrew's mind raced, thinking a fight, he'll fire me, can he make me marry her? Till finally it slowed, calm returned, the familiar determination settled into his bones and gut. He waited, knowing he could outwait Gillespie if it took forever, remembering in a flash which he instantly dispelled, the fullness of Nettie's breasts and hips, and her way of surrendering.

"I'll shoot any man who messes with Nettie. She's a virgin and I'm gonna keep her that way till I find her a husband." Gillespie's voice

111

deepened as he said this, till it was a thick, tight growl deep in his throat. Andrew was tempted to say something, a denial, an agreement, anything. But he could not imagine why a man would want to shoot someone for such a thing. He rode, pondering knowing now that Gillespie didn't know. Christ! he thought. What the hell's the matter with him? "Wait till you're a father, you'll find out," Gillespie said, his voice almost back to normal.

It was a long ride to Jorgenson's place on Battle Creek, just south of Fort Walsh, but the sky was clear and a burning blue, the cold air still and crackling with frost crystals that cast a halo above the low hills and rises. There would be a lot of snow to plow through when he got close to the Fort, he knew, there always was, and he found himself looking forward to it as a change from the sparse, dry snow he was used to.

It was late morning. If he kept up a steady pace he would reach Jorgenson's by mid-afternoon, and if he was lucky, he might locate the cattle today and be able to start back with them in the morning. He smoked as he rode, his horse's hooves crunching on the thin, hard snow and his breath making white plumes ahead of them. The inevitable network of rabbit tracks lay all around them and to the west there was the familiar sound of a coyote yipping in a cheerful, neighbourly way. Andrew turned his head at the sound, noticing that a light snowfall had begun, and was in time to see a grey shadow vanish out of sight over the crest of a hill a hundred yards from where he rode. You'd wonder what was wrong if you didn't see a coyote trailing you, he thought, amused.

In a couple of hours he was riding into wooded country, mostly pine and spruce, the land beginning to climb, and he knew he was halfway to Jorgenson's. He crossed Battle Creek, frozen hard with a skiff of snow covering it, and climbed up the bank on the far side through the low willows and rosebushes. As he settled into the trail on the other side it began to snow harder and the white snow and white sky were beginning to blend, blotting out the detail of the trees on each side of him, muffling sounds and blurring the distances, making them hard to judge. He tugged his earflaps down, shrugged more deeply into his mackinaw. The higher he climbed into the Cypress Hills, the deeper the snow became.

He guessed it to be about four feet deep in the coulees and wherever there was something for it to drift up against it was anywhere from two to eight feet deep. It was coming down harder now, too, worsening the visibility, but he kept moving at a steady pace, sure of his direction.

It was the sound he noticed first. He became aware of a distant whine, a moaning, and knew that the wind had come up. Where it broke through spaces between the trees it lifted the light, fresh snow, whirled it around, and dropped it again. For the first time, Andrew began to worry a little. This could whip up into a full-scale blizzard and if it did, he'd be lucky to make it. Mentally he reviewed the way to the Jorgenson ranch-house. He would keep to the treeline along his left side until he came to a fence running east and west. Not far down it there was a gate which he would go through. Then he would turn right and follow a fence that ran north and south to another gate a mile up it. That far he would be all right no matter whether it stormed or not because he would have a fence-line to follow and wouldn't have to risk getting lost by crossing an open field. But beyond that point he would be hard-pressed to find the rest of the way in blowing snow since the Jorgensons had built new fences since his last visit, and the Jorgenson ranchhouse was high up in the trees out of sight from below.

He buried his face further into his upturned collar and felt the ice on his beard crumble against the canvas of his coat. When he lifted his head to check his position again, the trees on his left had faded to a pale grey shadow that he saw only in snatches through the gusting snow. This was bad. This was serious. Even the snow on the level was much deeper here.

His fingers felt like ice inside his mitts and his feet were numb. He tried to work his toes inside his boots to bring feeling back into them. Even his thighs were growing numb and he realized he would soon have to get off his horse and walk before he froze, but he kept putting it off, thinking he would be all right a little longer.

Snow whipped up around him so that he could barely see beyond his horse's head. Now he was urging the horse forward, forcing him to lunge through the snowbanks in his path, pausing, lunging again. Andrew's pants were plastered with snow, there was snow pressed into the creases of his coat and his mitts, and no matter how tightly he pulled his collar around his neck, the wind found a way to force snow down it. He would have to walk before he froze to death.

When he rose to lift his right leg over the saddle, his left leg, taking his full weight in the stirrup, almost buckled, and he had to wait till he had it better braced. He got his right leg over the horse's back and managed to free his left foot from the stirrup. Surprised by his weakness when he first tried to dismount, he had held onto the saddlehorn as he struggled clumsily off the horse. It was a good thing, because when both his feet hit the deep snow, his knees buckled and refused to straighten no matter how hard he tried to make them work.

I can't walk, he said to himself. He had stayed on the horse too long, till his legs were so cold they had lost all feeling. He couldn't walk, but neither could he remount. He clung with both hands to the reins and the saddlehorn, trying frantically to get his legs working again, while his horse pulled him along, Andrew clinging to his side.

He stayed this way for what seemed a very long time, trying to move his legs, bouncing against the side of his horse, his arms beginning to ache from the weight of his body and from his efforts to lift himself. At last the strength began to return in his knees and thighs and the muscles responded better when he tried to flex them. After a few more feet, his shoulders straining, his hands aching from the cold so that he could barely hang onto the saddlehorn, blinded by the blowing snow, he managed to get his foot back into the stirrup. The rest was easier, but when he lifted his right leg, it dragged across the horse's back and for a long time he didn't even try to find the other stirrup. During all of this his horse had kept moving, refusing to stop.

He had no idea any more where he was. His mitts were crusted to the reins which he couldn't feel anyway. He slackened them and gave the horse his head, hoping that the animal would find the shelter he was unable to. He couldn't feel his feet any more and the two spots on his cheeks that he had frozen earlier in the winter had been numb now for a long time, as had his nose and chin. The horse plunged on through the howling white world.

It came to him that he did not want to die. In his desperation he thought of all the things he had not had enough of—women, the sound of hoofbeats, the prairie, the sun. They came to him wordlessly, whole and bright, and he was filled with longing for them as they vanished. He wanted, and this surprised him because he hadn't known it before, he wanted a home, a wife, and a child. He wanted a child someday.

He urged his horse on, Clue, this one was, another big, powerful gelding, chosen for his strength, not his beauty, a strength Andrew was glad to depend on. He kicked the horse feebly, more by accident than choice, trying to squeeze his own numb legs, working his hands inside his frozen mitts. Clue faltered, stumbled, righted himself, paused, and plunged on.

Time had stopped. Andrew rocked onward, the wind working its way inside him, filling his head and his chest with its malignant howl. He tried to shut it out but his own sweet warmth had left him. It was as though he rode naked, the weather a part of him and he of it. He fought it, but he could feel himself being transformed into the storm, feel it hugging him, poking through him, chilling his brain and his heart. What was it that ticked inside him, so soft as to be almost drowned out in the cataclysm? Something, he felt it whispering steadily, solidly, without fear. He saw himself lifted from his horse, swept away in the white wind, a shroud for his frozen flesh. But the steady whisper went on and on and on.

Suddenly his horse stopped. He tried to urge him forward but the animal wouldn't move. So this is it, he thought, and was surprised that, facing death, no new words came to him. He wiped his mitt against his face, knowing he was pushing away ice that he couldn't feel. He tried to straighten, wondering if he should try to dismount. Poor Clue, he thought, at least we'll die toether. He felt so close to the horse, like a lover. He lifted his head and opened his eyes into the storm, he could stand it for only a second, but in that second he saw a dark shadow in front of them. At first he was merely bewildered, then, through his cold-dulled brain, he realized that Clue had found a cabin.

Was that a light? In the blasts of swirling snow, he couldn't be sure, but he thought there might be a light, a lamp maybe, that someone had set in a window. He tried to call, but his face wouldn't move. He tried again, "Anybody home?" but knew, even through the roaring of the wind, that he had made only a meaningless jumble of sound. He shouted again, "Hey! Hey!" then tried to get off the horse. He fell forward against the horn, slowly lifted his right leg till it lay against the horse's back. Then he simply let go and fell off, in slow motion, his other foot falling out of the stirrup. And then he was on his back in deep snow, snow in his mouth and eyes, and he was fumbling, trying to find the stirrup to pull himself upright.

"Hey!" he shouted again. Suddenly he could feel light on him, and he thrashed harder and called again. "Hey!" Then someone was helping him and he was upright in the snow, lurching toward an open door through which yellow light fought against the storm.

"There'll be lots of dead cattle after this one," Jim said, standing with his back to them. Fed on biscuits and beef, whiskey burning in his belly, the pain gone from his face, hands and feet, Andrew could hardly care. Jim's wife sighed, resting her head on her arm on the table in front of her. Her husband was staring into the stove, poking at the burning wood. The wind howled in reply. Andrew shivered, then glanced at Jim's wife. She was slim and small with large, dark eyes and soft brown hair that curled sweetly around her small face. He imagined holding her in his arms, it happened before he could stop himself, feeling the long, delicate ridge of her backbone against his palm. He wrenched his eyes away to Jim, who still stood aimlessly poking at the fire.

"Let's hope it's only cattle out there," Andrew said.

"Didn't look good up here all day," Jim said, turning and sitting down across the table from Beth. "The boys would have had sense enough to stay home, I think." "Jesus! Listen to that!" Andrew said, without meaning to. They paused, listening attentively, as if it were talking to them. The cabin shook with its violence. There was a wrenching noise on the roof. "There go the last of the shingles," Beth said sleepily, smiling. The two men studied her, glad she was there. Then Jim looked up to the ceiling as if he thought he might see the shingles go flying away, end over end. Beth raised her eyes to Andrew's and smiled at him. Andrew's cheeks were burning from the frost and then the heat inside the cabin and he concentrated on the sensation, trying to make his desire for her subside.

After a while they went to bed, the young couple in the bedroom, which was separated from the main room by a curtain, and Andrew on the couch by the fire. Jim put the lamp out, then opened the curtain separating the two rooms to let the heat into the bedroom.

Andrew lay sleepily, warm and safe, listening to the crackling of the fire and the creaking in the walls from the wind, and thought about how it was outside. It would be pitch black now, the storm not allowing a glimmer of light to penetrate it. But surely, high above it, the moon and stars were still shining? Gradually the fire died to a red glow, the coal radiating silent heat. The air in the cabin grew very still.

A light appeared on the wall above the door, a small, white light. After a moment it moved, and it occurred to Andrew to wonder what it was. The light moved slowly around the walls, near the ceiling, crossing one wall, sliding around the corner onto the next wall, and then the next. A long shiver spread down Andrew's backbone, and then another, and another. When the light had travelled the full circumference of the room, it disappeared through the doorway into the bedroom.

Andrew could tell by the sudden tension in the air that in the other room the young couple were watching it too.

"What is it?" he whispered, then said it again louder, to be heard over the wind. Jim's voice came back, softly, full of awe.

"Somebody's in trouble somewhere out there." There was no help for it, nothing they could do.

The light came slowly into the main room, flickered a few times, then vanished. Andrew drew a long, sighing breath. There was the sound of the bedsprings giving suddenly in the other room and Andrew knew Beth was clinging to her husband.

It stormed all the next day, too, and Andrew, Beth and Jim spent the day playing cards. Beth was endlessly lucky and beat them both at game after game of rummy and then poker played for matchsticks.

By evening it was quiet outside again, although bitterly cold, and Andrew said he would set out the next day for Jorgenson's. His mitts and boots were dry, his jacket warm from hanging inside, and his horse rested.

In the morning Jim dressed to go riding at the same time as Andrew did.

"Got to find my cows," he said grimly, "what's left of them." Beth stood behind them, near the stove, shivering, her hands clasped in front of her, her eyes deep and darkened with worry.

"I'd pick up a few of Jorgenson's slicks," Andrew said, buckling his over-shoes. "He'll never know." He lifted his head, his eyes meeting Jim's. "Brand them quick," he said softly, directly to Jim. He put on his cap and pulled down the earflaps. Jim still hadn't moved or spoken, his eyes on Andrew's.

"He's got so many cattle, he don't even know how many he got," Jim said, a bitter twist to his mouth.

"I'll help you," Andrew said. Jim started to say something, but Andrew interrupted. "Hell! You saved my life!" He had only just realized this, and it felt good to say it. "He ain't gonna starve," he added, laughing without mirth. 'But you will,' was unspoken, and hung in the air between them.

"If anything's alive out there," Jim said, turning away.

"Jim," Beth said, turning her dark eyes on him, then stopped. Jim turned on her impatiently.

"How do you think he got that big herd of his?" he asked her harshly. "American cattle that drifted over the line, took the calves, and branded them for his own! Took the slicks!" Beth came forward and put her hand out in a meek gesture toward him. Jim took it and smiled. "Don't worry," he said.

Andrew watched. She had such little hands, wrists like a bird's, a small, sweet mouth. He thought of coming back some day when Jim was away, then, ashamed, lowered his eyes and followed Jim outside into the cold, bright air.

CHAPTER FIVE

In February his mother sent a message with one of her neighbours. One of Gillespie's hands saw the car drive into the yard, and after talking to the driver, went to the bunkhouse to call Andrew out.

"She says you should come and see her," Milne said to Andrew. "My wife's with her. She should be in the hospital but she won't go. She wants you." Andrew had a hard time hearing him because he hadn't shut the motor off nor gotten out of his car and he looked straight ahead when he spoke, as though his disapproval of Andrew prevented him from meeting Andrew's eyes. Andrew couldn't think what to say, but he had the feeling Milne expected more from him than a simple yes. He shoved his hands into his pockets and stared at the ground.

It wasn't that he had forgotten what she said. But somehow he couldn't believe it, or grasp what it meant, so he had been able to thrust it to the back of his mind. Nettie came out the front door of the ranch-house, flapped a rug a few times in the air and went back inside. Milne let the clutch out slowly.

"She says it's in her bones," he said. The car began to inch away, its rattle speeding up.

"I'll be there by tonight," Andrew said belatedly, startled out of his reverie by Milne's abrupt departure. Milne waved his arm out the window without turning his head, the car rattled down the road and went out of sight behind some buildings. Andrew stood watching it without really seeing it. Then, shivering, he hurried back into the bunkhouse where he'd been mending harness, picked up his jacket and strode across the yard to his shack.

He tried not to think. He concentrated on folding his bedroll, tucking it neatly, gathering his few clothes, his good boots, the new halter he had bought in Havre on the weekend. When he had everything in a pile on the cot, he paused. He couldn't carry any of it on horseback. He'd have to come back for it with a team and wagon or a borrowed car. He moved it from the cot to the back room which he never used and stowed it in a corner.

He wondered where Gillespie was. In the house? In the barn? Would Gillespie keep his job for him if he wasn't gone too long? Should he say good-bye to Thelma and Nettie or should he simply leave? He stood on the bare wooden floor in the middle of the small room and stared straight ahead.

She's dying, he thought. In her bones. Abruptly he sat down on the stained, lumpy mattress. The cot springs groaned and creaked rustily under him. After all she had done, the babies she had brought into the world, the sick people she had nursed back to health, all the hymns she had sung, had made him sing. None of it would help her now. Curses came into his head and faded away unspoken. She would suffer. He had heard about cancer in the bones.

He put his head in his hands. How could her god do this to her? Her, of all people? She was only in her fifties. It was not fair. He was breathing heavily now, he could feel heat in his face and neck and all his muscles had grown tense and hard. He remained motionless. His eyes focused, he saw the dim, bare room, the cold iron stove, the cracked and splintered wooden floor. He became aware that he was cold, bitterly cold, but still he didn't move.

Mother, he thought. Mother. It was not her he was seeing. He could hardly remember what she looked like, as though it had been years since he had seen her. It was her presence, her bodiless being he felt around him.

He began to cry. He was ashamed of himself for crying because his tears were so useless and womanly besides. Why should I cry, he asked himself. She's the one who's dying. But he couldn't stop. All the things he had forgotten about their life together came back to him. Her nursing him when he was sick, carrying him when he had sprained his ankle in the corral tripping over a frozen cowpie. Kissing him. Once. He remembered that from somewhere, from some long-forgotten time before he had declared himself a man. She had kissed him, had been his real mother. His only mother.

He forced himself to stop crying, he rose, buttoned his jacket, put on his cap and strode across the room. All right, he thought, she would die, but she wouldn't die without him. He banged the door shut behind him, and shading his eyes from the brilliance of sun on snow, went toward the ranchhouse.

Gillespie was drinking coffee at the long kitchen table. Thelma was at the stove stirring something in a big pot. He had entered noisily, without knocking. Both of them turned to stare at him. He stared back, not speaking.

In this well-lit room he suddenly saw Thelma as the woman he made love to at night. He saw in the bones of her thin face, in the slight curve of her hips, in the way her small earlobes showed under her short, dark hair the woman who touched him and whom he touched in the darkness. It was the first time the middle-aged, daytime woman, Gillespie's wife, the cook and housekeeper, had ever come together for him with the soft and passionate, unseen woman in the night. He wanted to go to her, to kiss her, to hold her, to tell her about his mother. She saw him looking at her and turned nervously back to the stove.

"Andy," Gillespie said. He turned to where Gillespie sat at the table. He saw the man's cold, narrow eyes, the wind-burned edge to his cheekbones, his too-large mouth.

"I have to leave," Andrew said. "My mother . . ." Thelma turned toward him again. "I just got a message that my mother's . . . dying. She wants me." He stopped. Nettie came quietly into the room and sat down at the far end of the table, a long way from the three of them.

"That's terrible," Thelma said. "What's the matter?"

121

"Cancer," Andrew said. He clenched his jaw to keep from saying more.

"I'll be sorry to see you go," Gillespie said. "You're one of my best men." Nettie sat motionless at her end of the table. Out of the corner of his eye he saw that she was wearing a pink sweater and knew that if he looked at her she would be soft and rounded, sweetly feminine, and he was ashamed of himself for thinking this at this moment. He wished he had never made love with her. Or that he had not known Thelma. He didn't know which.

"Nettie, get my book," Gillespie said. She rose and went out of the room. There was a silence. "So, you're leaving right away," Gillespie said. He tapped his fingers on the table. Nettie returned, came down the room past her mother and reached the account book across the table to her father. "Goddamnit!" he said. "That's the wrong one." He took it from her. "I'll get it myself." Ponderously he pushed himself away from the table, brushed past Andrew who stood beside him, near the door, and went out of the room.

"Sit down, Andy," Thelma said. She was still nervous. He shook his head, no.

"Are you coming back?" Nettie asked him. He shrugged.

"I don't know." Thelma suddenly set the spoon she'd been stirring with onto the counter noisily.

"Nettie, go and make the beds," she said angrily. A spot of colour had risen in each cheek. Nettie turned her head, surprised, was about to refuse, thought better of it, and walked out of the room in the direction her father had gone. She glanced back once at Andrew, gave him a little wave over her shoulder. He didn't respond. Then she was gone.

"She'll get over it," Thelma said, bitterly, watching her daughter retreat.

"I'm sorry," Andrew said suddenly, meaning about Nettie. He had not understood any of this, holding each of them blindly in their nocturnal world. Thelma seemed to understand him. She shrugged, then sadness crept into her face and her dark eyes.

"I'm not much of a mother," she said, looking up at him, asking him something with her eyes. After a moment, he said, "You're some woman," meaning it. His heart felt as if it might crack in his chest.

In that second he understood why there had to be a woman. He had never known that there had to be a woman. He had been ashamed of his need, had been bold, reckless, and arrogant about it and about them, because he had believed somehow, though when he looked at it it made no sense, men did not need women for their real lives. Now, as she looked up at him and he saw through her eyes the rich darkness inside her, and saw all the things she was—housekeeper, wife, mother, lover, friend, and something else bigger than all of this, something deeply mysterious—he understood that there *had* to be a woman and it was right, not wrong. Dumbly, he put out his hand as if daring to touch her.

"Here," Gillespie said, entering the room. They saw by the glitter in his eyes that he had seen that second when they had almost touched, but he held his face steady, showing nothing except in his small, hard eyes. He held out a cheque to Andrew. "And a bonus," he said. "I like your work." Was there humour there? Gillespie hesitated as if he wanted to say something more, each of them holding one corner of the cheque. Then he let it go. "Sure sorry about your mother," he said brusquely. He turned away, pulled out the chair where he had been sitting when Andrew came in, and sat down. Thelma glanced at Andrew over her husband's head.

"Drop by and see us now and then," she said evenly.

"I'll come back for my things later," Andrew said. They stood for a second looking at each other over Gillespie's head.

"Take good care of her," she said, her voice low. Then she drew back, no longer seemed to be connected to him with her eyes, and he, seeing this, relinquished her. He turned away, opened the inner door, then the storm door, shut them carefully behind him, and was outside again in the sharp, bright winter day.

It was almost dusk as he rode into his mother's yard.

The house would need paint again when spring came and there were as usual a few shingles missing from the roof. Always the wind working at everything, destroying every construction as man built it. Milne's car was

123

parked in front of the door. Andrew rode to the barn, unsaddled his horse, fed and watered him, then turned him out into the corral and walked over the thin, hard-packed snow to the house.

Inside he found Milne sitting at the kitchen table, an empty teacup in front of him. There was a strange, unpleasant odour in the house. Andrew couldn't place it. Although the room was small and there were two of them in it, it seemed empty.

Milne stood up. He was a small man, greying already, and after a moment he put out his hand to Andrew nervously. Confused, Andrew shook it. Then, as the man remained standing, Andrew said, "Sit down. Thanks for being here." He was used to the disapproval of hard-working family men like Carson Milne. He paid it little mind because they had nothing he wanted, and he knew that most of them secretly envied him.

"She's in there," Milne said, apparently for something to say, and nodded toward the room that had once been Andrew's. Andrew hung his hat where he had always hung it, on the peg by the door, took off his jacket and hung it up too, then pulled off his overshoes. He did all this slowly, deliberately, dreading the moment when he would have to see her.

Mrs. Milne came and stood in the doorway. She was small, too, with a slight figure and greying hair. When she saw him, she smiled over her shoulder and said into the darkened room behind her, "It's him." There was a rustling in the bedroom. "Come" she said to Andrew urgently, "or she'll insist on getting up." Behind him Milne said, "You can't keep her down," then cleared his throat. Andrew followed Mrs. Milne into the room.

His mother was propped up with pillows on the bed. She was wearing a long dark robe and her hair, grey now, was pinned neatly back from her face. He was sure her hair had not been so grey in the fall. He drew closer. Her skin was pale, had a yellowish cast, he saw the shape of her strong bones clearly through the thin flesh of her face. But her eyes were as penetrating as ever.

"You can go home now, Margaret," she said to Mrs. Milne. "You've got a family to take care of, and my son is home." He bent and kissed her forehead. He could hear Mrs. Milne leave the room. In the kitchen she and her husband were murmuring to each other.

Andrew sat down in the chair by her head and took her hand. She let him hold it.

"How are you?" he asked at last.

"Well enough," she said.

"Is the pain . . ."

"Very bad," she said.

"Did the doctor . . ."

"On the table beside you." She drew a long breath. "You'll have to get up in the night to give me medicine."

"Yes," he said softly.

"I'm sorry," she said stiffly, as though it cost her something to say this. He laughed.

"So am I," he said, and took a firmer grip on her hand. She gasped, then seemed to hold her breath, her eyes closed. Horrified, he let go of her hand. When the pain had passed she said, "Go and tell Mrs. Milne to go home."

In the kitchen he found Mrs. Milne bending to look at something in the oven. Carson Milne stood looking out the kitchen window with his back to the room. Andrew waited till they were both facing him. He felt their uncertainty, their reluctance to leave things to him. They didn't know him at all. They were still farming in Ontario when he and his mother were here building up this place together. All they knew about him would be the stories, which he didn't know but could guess—about his women, his wildness, his border-hopping and drinking, his suspected horse and cattle thefts. They seemed almost afraid of him.

"I've made some supper for you," Mrs. Milne broke the silence. "I thought you'd be hungry. Your mother doesn't eat much."

"I appreciate that," he said. "I want to thank you for everything you've done for her."

"Anybody would . . ." Carson Milne began. His wife interrupted.

"The doctor said he'd be back tomorrow." She lowered her voice. "He wants her to go to the hospital where he can take better care of her, but she won't go."

"She said she was waiting for you," her husband broke in. Andrew smiled, thinking of his mother's iron will.

125

"She pretty well does what she wants to do," he said. "Always has."

"There's medicine for the pain . . ."

"I know," Andrew said.

"Well then," Mrs. Milne looked about uncertainly, then began to gather her few things from around the room. The two men watched her, Andrew patient, the other man nervous. When she was ready she said, "Call me if you need help."

"We'll drop by tomorrow or the next day," Milne said, "see if you need anything."

"Thanks," Andrew said. They went outside, soon their car started and finally its noise receded down the road.

When they were gone he went back into the bedroom and sat again beside his mother. Her eyes were closed and he didn't speak to her.

"Are you going to send me to the hospital?" she asked at last. Her question made him look down at her. Her eyes were open wide, her expression vulnerable, fearful, like a child's. He had to turn his head to hide the tears that sprang to his eyes.

"Not if you don't want to go."

"I want to die here," she said slowly, spacing her words.

"All right," he said, looking at her again.

"I looked after your father till he died," she said. "I was only a young woman. I hoped you would do that for me."

"I will," he said.

"You'll have to do everything for me," she warned him. He tried to think of all the things she meant. "Everything," she said.

"You're my mother," he replied, after a silence.

"Get Mrs. Milne to bathe me," she said, planning now.

"How dirty can you get?" he asked, joking.

"I smell bad, Andrew," she said. "It will get worse. I can't bear to be dirty too."

"I'll get Mrs. Milne in," he said gently. "And anything else you want." She was silent, but her eyes were restless, searching the room, not seeing it.

"Can you give me . . . the bedpan?" she asked. Her voice was fierce.

"I can," he said, keeping his voice steady.

"And change my clothes?"

"Sure," he said. "You were never one to worry much about clothes. If I get them on upside down and backwards, will you care?" She snorted, then almost simultaneously winced and lay still.

"It doesn't hurt if I just breathe," she said, and smiled briefly. It was the closest thing to a joke she had ever made. It touched him almost more than her pain.

"Don't worry about it," he told her. "You taught me what to do a long time ago." He paused. "When did you . . . go to bed?" She stirred angrily.

"I haven't gone yet!" she said. "Tomorrow I'm going to get up. The Milnes aren't as strong as you are. You'll help me."

"All right," he said. What did it matter if she died sitting up or lying down?

"You get me some tea," she told him. "Not too strong. Then eat your supper. You must be hungry."

"Just as bossy as ever," he remarked, but her face had gone taut again, her eyes had closed. She hadn't heard him.

The doctor came at noon the next day. He was a small, square man approaching sixty, and at this time of day always had an excessive neatness about him. That, combined with the pale, papery skin of his face and his unsteady hands, told the story of the frailties that had reduced him to doctoring in the wilderness.

Andrew met him in the doorway as he and his mother had always done for guests. It was another bright February day, the hard mid-winter snow shining so that he had to shade his eyes with his hand. It was cold but not more than ten or so below. At this time of year the sun's rays were still weak but when they struck in sheltered places they held enough warmth to melt a little snow.

The doctor stumbled climbing out of his car, almost dropping his bag, then righted himself and hurried the few paces to the open door.

"Good morning," he said. He was an alcoholic or possibly addicted to one of the drugs he carried in his bag, and his greeting sounded false. He came into the kitchen, stamping his feet and shivering. Andrew took his coat and hung it up, waited while he removed his overshoes and straightened his suit jacket, patting it carefully into place, then led him into the bedroom where his mother was lying back against the pillows. The curtains at the small window to the left of her bed were open and light fell across her legs. She had insisted that Andrew open the curtains and it struck him that for the first time in her life she wanted light.

"Good morning, Mrs. Samson," the doctor said. "How are you today? Ready to come to the hospital?" She didn't answer, her fingers plucking—an odd gesture for her—at the bedclothes.

"No," she said faintly, then in a louder voice, "My son is going to take care of me. I'll be staying here." The doctor paused, reaching inside his bag, and stared up at Andrew with pale, greenish eyes. Andrew, moved by his mother's trust in him, said, "That's right," then without waiting for a reply, left the room, shutting the door behind him.

After a while the doctor came out, shutting the door again.

"If you two insist, there's nothing I can do about it," he said without preliminaries.

"Have some coffee," Andrew offered, ignoring the remark. The doctor pulled out a chair and sat down at the table across from Andrew.

"But I can't get way out here more than once a week unless there's an emergency."

"Just leave us some pain-killers and tell me what to do," Andrew said, feigning confidence. He filled a cup from the coffee pot and gave it to the doctor. They sat across from each other, their antagonism filling the room. Andrew longed to be outside in the chilly, sunlight-filled air.

"If she insists on getting up, hold onto her." Andrew nodded, holding his face still and blank. "Because if she falls her bones will crumble like chalk." He could sense the doctor's urge to hammer home to him what he had already seen in his mother's face the moment he walked into her room. He nodded again. "Is she eating anything?"

"Not much."

"Try to get her to eat, and to drink." What for? he wanted to ask.

"All right," he said mildly.

"Is she vomiting?" The doctor's coldness was increasing.

"Some, not much."

"It may be moving into her liver."

"What does that mean?"

"It will kill her sooner." He said this fiercely, as if it were Andrew's doing.

"She will suffer more here than in the hospital." Andrew reflected. He would send her to the hospital if it would spare her one thing, but she chose not to be spared anything, although he could not in all honesty see why. He lifted his hands, open, and let them fall against the table top. He tried to be reasonable in the face of the doctor's anger.

"She knows all that," he said. "She knows it as well as you do. I have to do what she asks," Andrew said, finally. He wanted to go on, to explain this, but no satisfactory words came to mind. It was not even that he owed her this. It was something about her rights. She could die the way she wanted to, she could suffer if she chose to. In his confusion even this made little sense to him. Yet he was united with his mother against the whole range of things the doctor stood for. Her illness is ours, he thought, her suffering is ours, not yours, and we claim it. He wanted to tell him to leave, not to come back, but he restrained himself. His mother needed the things the doctor carried in his bag.

"She's weakening" the doctor said. "That kind of pain, aside from everything else, takes an immense toll on the body."

"How long?" Andrew was angry with himself for asking this. The doctor shrugged. He sipped the last of his coffee.

"It's impossible to say. But I don't think it will be long. A few weeks." Andrew didn't move. The doctor stood up and reached for his jacket. "This is nothing," he said angrily, throwing one hand out toward the bedroom. "It will get much worse."

Abruptly Andrew pushed his chair back and stood. He wanted to hit the doctor, but already the doctor was opening the door and stepping out into the light. Andrew followed him.

"Wait a minute," he said, his voice full now and strong. "Is there something I should be doing?"

After the doctor had driven away, Andrew opened the bedroom door. His mother was sitting up, alert, as if she had been waiting impatiently for him to open the door, anticipating his protest at her request.

"I'm going to get up and sit in my rocking chair," she said. "Come and help me."

Each day he helped her to the kitchen. He couldn't carry her because she couldn't stand to be touched. It was easier for her if she held her body upright, away from his, and he supported her by the arms while she placed one foot slowly, waveringly, in front of the other. The walk was growing more difficult for both of them, the times when she would be seized by a pain so appalling that she would have sunk to her knees if he had not been there to hold her up were increasing. They were on their way back to her bedroom.

"Wait," she gasped. She began to fall. He grasped her arms more tightly and as she still fell, he shifted his grip to her waist with one arm. She cried out. It was not a loud cry, but it was the first time a sound had escaped her. He got her the last few steps into her bed, half-dragging her. All the way, short, sharp, moaning sounds bubbled rhythmically from her with each breath. When he had her lying down and covered, the noise ceased and she lay very still. He thought she had died. He stood motionless above her, blinded by his sweat.

"Mother?" he said. He wiped his face with his sleeve. Her eyes opened suddenly. He was disconcerted to see how dark and powerful they were, as though she drew strength from her pain. He almost took a step backwards. She seemed to be looking straight into his soul.

"Call me Adele," she said, in a clear voice. Adele? He had not even remembered that that was her name.

"Adele," he said, humbly.

Evenings, after Mrs. Milne had come and gone, she was better. He sat by her then and sometimes she talked to him.

"I want to tell you about your father," she said to him one evening. He raised his head but didn't look at her. He studied the bureau on the opposite wall. He rarely thought about his father, had no mental picture of him. At this moment it seemed even less important to him. But she went on.

"He was a blacksmith. You got your size from him. But you don't look like him. He had dark brown hair, deep green eyes."

"Green?" Andrew said, although he had hardly heard what she said. It meant nothing to him. She sighed, uncharacteristically.

"I hardly remember him myself," she said. "We got married, you were born. He started to spit blood, in the mornings especially." An owl perched on the barn across the yard began to call, "Hoo-hoo, hoo-hoo, hoo-hoo." Its voice carried clearly through the still, cold air, as if it were nearer.

"He got so weak. It was sad to see such a big man as weak as a baby. Then he hemorrhaged and died." Still Andrew didn't say anything. So what? he wanted to ask. For some puzzling reason he felt angry. She said, "Why did you never ask me about him?" With an effort he held his voice steady.

"You never said his name, never talked about him. I thought he didn't matter." There was a long silence. He wanted to say, what did I need a father for? but it came swelling over him how he had worked when he was still a child, how she had worked, how they had each been alone.

"Why did you come here?" This he had wanted to know. She didn't answer, collecting her strength, or her thoughts.

"I was born on a farm. I hated the city. After he died I had so little money, not enough to buy a farm. I knew how we would have to live in the city." She moved restlessly, then stopped. He could tell by the tense silence that she was gripped by pain. He waited. "I wanted . . ." She had wanted something? His heart speeded up. ". . . freedom," she said.

He could not imagine what she meant, although he knew at least that it was not precisely what she had said.

"Someday you'll find out," she said, her voice distant, without hope. Again Andrew refrained from speaking. "Do something with your life,

Andrew," she said. At this he turned slowly to meet her eyes. Emotion rose in him, to cry, to shout, to get up and go outside.

"Hm," he said, a grunt. After a moment she smiled sadly.

"There must be something that should be done with life," she was staring at the ceiling. His anger left him. Didn't she know what it was? She had come all this way and she didn't know? All these years he had thought she knew. Thinking that she at least knew why each of them had been born had given him the courage to do all the things he did. He could not believe she didn't know. He was appalled to think that she would not understand her dying either. He turned his body fully toward her and took her hand gently. Tenderness for her, that she was only flesh and blood, welled up in him.

"I'm not afraid to die," she said, fierce again. "Don't you think that."

"No," he said. "I don't think that."

She woke him in the night, crying out in her sleep. He stumbled into her room from the cot he had set up by the stove in the kitchen. The lamp was still lit, burning low. When he saw her eyes in the flickering light from the smoking lamp he knew there was no longer any difference for her between sleep and wakefulness.

"Andrew, Andrew," she cried, and he was amazed at the strength she had found to call his name. He leaned over her and held her to him as gently as he could. Every touch caused her agony. Was it worse now for her to be touched or not to be touched? She was gasping for breath, her nightgown was soaked with her sweat. Her body was tensed against the pain, she rose with it as if to meet something, then slumped suddenly, unconscious.

She died a few days after that and he was grateful for her death. He went outside into the cold winter morning, the snow still tinged blue, here and there tinted rose from the rising sun. Their cattle were mooing sadly in the hills nearby. A few horses that had come in for shelter stood quietly against the side of one of the sheds. They picked up their ears and turned their dark, beautiful heads toward him. Their hooves crunched on the cold, crystalline snow.

In the night he had dreamt of a coyote. A white coyote limping past their cabin in the full moonlight, through deep snow, one paw lame and held against its breast. An omen, he supposed. It had turned its head to look at him, its eyes were dark and slitted, recognition of him there, but no message.

We're like coyotes, he thought. Adele and me, and he laughed.

He shivered in the cold without his jacket, his hands thrust deep into his trouser pockets. Soon the sun would be up and when the Milnes came they would find her dead, her crumbled bones lying on the bed. Then for a few days, as his mother would have asked, he would obey all the conventions. Then it would be over.

CHAPTER SIX

Andrew stopped the horses, wiped the sweat out of his eyes and took a swig of warm, tasteless water from the bottle he kept beside him on the triple plow. He balanced the bottle on the seat of the plow, breathed deeply, and using his handkerchief, wiped the dirt out of the creases of his face. It was unbearably hot, but the strong wind made it possible to stay in the field even at the height of the heat. He lifted the bottle and drank again, his face tipped up toward the sun, which was white, small and very high.

The prairie grass alongside the summerfallow he was almost finished working was only a few inches high. The tips had been burned white by the sun and nearer the ground, it was grey with a touch of dun. The earth, hard-packed from the wind and sun, was white too, and continuously blowing in the air so that he saw everything, the hills in the distance, the grassland stretching out around him, the sky, muted by a white haze. He drank again and thought of the sun burning down on them scrabbling in the dirt below.

How could the sun be so small and high and yet more fierce than he had ever known it? Cattle and horses were dying every day from lack of feed and water. If it burned any harder, they would all die.

He screwed the top back on the bottle and rubbed his hands on his pants, preparing to take up the reins again. Six in each hand. His arms and shoulders ached from the weeks he had spent on this job wrestling a dozen horses all day, with the taste of dirt in his mouth, dirt in his eyes and hair, ground into all the creases of his skin, even under his clothes. He felt as though he would carry the traces of this despicable work with him to the grave.

Plowing up the land. Plowing it up so it could dry up and blow away. He hated himself for doing it. But he needed work and Zbignew paid well. He knew he'd be a long time finding somebody else who could handle a twelve-horse hitch like this, break broncs at the same time, and have the endurance to keep at it till the job was done. Andrew spat in the dirt contemptuously. But he'd be done tonight, would go home to his mother's place, now his, sleep the clock around and then what? he asked himself.

A few small thunderclouds had been drifting up from the southwest for an hour or so, but he had ignored them. For what seemed like years now, rain-filled clouds would drift toward them, they would look hopefully at the sky as the clouds came closer. But either they drifted on by or paused, let a few drops fall, then moved on. Thunder boomed in the far distance, but that, too, meant nothing.

Now he glanced over his shoulder toward the southwest, squinting to see through the blowing dust. He was surprised to see that the sky had changed, that the thunderclouds had massed and grown purple-blue, and were moving fast toward him and his horses. Thunder cracked again, closer now. It was impossible to tell if what was coming was only another windstorm or a rainstorm, but he didn't like the looks of the sky, had no desire to be caught out in the field in a twister or a hailstorm.

More thunder split the sky, the wind picked up and the sky was rapidly darkening. The horses were moving restlessly as he tried to undo the twenty-four traces, and he had to keep shouting at them. When the last trace was undone, he turned the team toward the trail and the farmyard a mile away. The three broncs in the centre of the hitch began to rear and kick, and soon he was running, leaning back on the reins, struggling to keep the horses from bolting.

When he made it into the yard, Zbignew appearing on the run from somewhere to help him, Andrew was panting, sweat running down his face mingling with the dirt, and his hat had blown off.

"It's just another goddamn dust storm!" Zbignew shouted to him as they folded the lines, unsnapped the horses from each other, began to take off their bridles and led them one by one into the barn. A few fat, cold drops splattered onto their shoulders and backs, landing with such force that they stung. The men worked faster, anxious to get the horses stabled before the full force of the storm was on them.

The air had turned an even, light-filled brown, so thick that they couldn't see the barn a few feet from them, couldn't see the corral railings or the hills beyond. The wind roared above them with a terrifying, hollow sound, but for an instant in the yard the air was perfectly still. Andrew and Zbignew led the last two horses into their stalls in the barn, then, both of them pushing against the wind which had struck again, managed to close the barn door. They sat down in the corner where the saddles had once been kept, lit cigarettes, and listened.

The barn walls vibrated, loose boards banged, shingles tore off the roof with a ripping sound, and clattered as they skittered away. A tin pail somebody had left in the yard hit the side of the barn with a clang and then rattled to the ground. Zbignew and Andrew smoked silently, crouched in the corner, listening.

In ten minutes the storm had blown past. They pulled back the barn door and stood looking out. A heavy, hard rain was slanting into the dirt, kicking it up and filling the air with the smell of dirt-filled water. It lasted a moment, then it passed too. The clouds whipped by, leaving behind a clear, bright sky, with a faint haze of dirt hanging low in the air.

Andrew set out for home early the next morning and by late afternoon, with the sun high and to the south and the land shadowless and hazy with wind-blown dust, faded and white with the heat, he was near home. He hadn't eaten since breakfast before dawn in the Zbignew's kitchen, and he was aching with hunger. At his own place, he knew, he'd be lucky to find a can of beans, but for hours now, each place he rode up to was deserted, abandoned to the wind and sun, the house usually not even boarded up, just turned over to the pigeons and the swallows and the mice. The corrals would be falling down, the barn door opened onto emptiness, the fields turned to dust, piles of sand banked up against the buildings, fences pulled down by the masses of tumbling mustard and Russian thistle. His spirits sank further at each place.

Then he remembered the Connollys south of his own place. They would feed him, if they were still there. He looped south, riding faster, his stomach contracting and growling. At their house, he almost didn't stop, it looked so deserted, but there was a thin thread of smoke drifting upward from the chimney into the hot, pale sky, and a boy came and stood in the barn door, then disappeared inside again. Andrew dismounted, tied his horse in the shade of the barn, and knocked on the door.

For a long moment nobody answered. Then the door opened and a woman stood blinking out into the harsh, white light.

"Andy!" she said, and Andrew saw then that it was Mrs. Connolly. "Jack," she called over her shoulder to someone in the dark interior, "it's Andy." For a second it was like it had been before when he had come to see them. "Come in, come in," she said. "I bet you're hungry." But here her voice faltered, as though she had just thought of something else. Andrew stepped inside and closed the door behind him.

He waited for his eyes to adjust to the dimness in the big kitchen, then saw the children sitting, big-eyed and silent, around the table. Flies zoomed around their heads and banged against the dusty window, buzzing as they fell. At the end of the table, Jack was rising, coming to meet Andrew, his hand out.

"Damn glad to see you, Andy," he said. "We don't get too many visitors these days. Nobody can afford to run their vehicles anymore, and nobody's got any feed left for their horses." At this Andrew thought of his saddlehorse, standing hungry in the shade, and knew he would have to go without feed.

"Make a place for Andy, there," Jack said, too loudly to his wife. Andrew heard the falsity in his hearty tone and was puzzled and embarrassed by it.

The children sat, still and silent, and watched their father and Andrew. Mrs. Connolly set another plate on the table and Jack brought a chair from a corner and set it at that place.

Andrew sat down and Jack went back to his place at the end of the table.

"I didn't even seed this year," Jack said, although Andrew hadn't asked, was speechless, in fact, by what he was seeing. "You been working away, I hear."

"Yeah," Andrew said, finding his voice. "Northeast of here sixty miles or so. Been breaking land and doing the summerfallow for a couple of farmers."

"Didn't have any seed wheat left," Jack went on, as though Andrew hadn't spoken. "Not that anything would have grown." He made a noise like laughing, but his expression remained the same, grim, and sad. Andrew glanced down the length of the table, suddenly noticing that there was no appetizing smell of food cooking, no sizzling sound from the stove, no cheerful prattle from the children. A bowl of potatoes sat growing cold in the centre of the table, a slice of salt pork lay on each plate and one piece of bread lay beside it. There was nothing else on the table.

Mrs. Connolly pulled out her chair and sat down.

"Eat, you kids," she said, "then go outside." Obediently the children bent over their food. There were only five of them. The other two must be grown and gone, Andrew thought, and the babies had been transformed into skinny, solemn children. He turned to say something to Mrs. Connolly, and saw then that she had no plate in front of her. The children were eating rapidly, their faces close to their plates.

"Somebody pass them potatoes down to Andy," Jack commanded, the false heartiness back in his voice. "Get him some of that salt pork," he said to his wife. "It ain't much," Jack said, and then made that same, harsh, laughing sound, "but it keeps body and soul together."

"Oh, I ain't hungry," Andrew said quickly. "Mrs. Zbignew made me a big lunch and I been chewing on it all the way down here. I really only stopped for a visit."

As the children began to leave the table, Andrew saw how thin they were, was shocked by their ragged clothing and their bare feet. They've been sick too, he thought. He looked down the table to Jack. Jack's eyes met his, then a veil seemed to come between them and Jack said, "Going to hear the speaker tonight?" Andrew said carefully, "What speaker is that?"

"I forgot you've been away," Jack said. "We been getting speakers down to the schoolhouse fairly regular on Saturday nights. Everybody goes. We can just walk over it's so close."

"Politicians?" Andrew asked.

"Mostly," Jack said.

"I ain't interested in politics," Andrew said.

"It's something to do," Jack said. "Lots of people there, and it don't cost nothing. You can donate for lunch if you want to."

Their conversation went on, halting, jagged, neither of them giving it their full attention. Flies buzzed around their heads and the children came and left again silently, as if they hadn't the energy to fight or yell. Mrs. Connolly sat silently at her end of the table.

Later, as Andrew untied his horse and prepared to mount, with Jack standing behind him, he had to lean against the saddle for a second, fighting the nausea at what he had seen. Then he straightened, backed his horse up, turned the stirrup, and put his foot into it.

"Andy."

"I want to help," Andrew said quickly, before Jack could go on. Andrew took his foot out of the stirrup and turned to face him. "Got no feed left, but then, I got only one horse left," Jack said. He didn't bother to try to laugh. "But Andy," he said, and stopped. Andrew waited, watching him. "We're out of grub," Jack said, lifting his eyes from the dust between them to fasten them on Andrew's. "Just a few spuds."

Andrew raised his eyes beyond Jack's head to the sagging house behind them, saw the peeling paint, the missing shingles. Anger swelled in him, and he turned from Jack to mount, almost leaping into the saddle. He pulled hard on the reins and the horse lifted his head and pranced in surprise. Andrew turned him south, toward the border.

"I'll be back tonight," he shouted as though he and Jack had quarrelled. He rode away without looking back.

The sun poured down. There was nowhere to go to escape it, no shade, no trees, no shelter from it. It burned into his back, and he rode into it, through the drifting sand and the dried short grass that crumbled to powder under his horse's hooves.

He would butcher a beef for them, but not one of his own. He was a poor man himself. What right had anybody to expect that a poor man should give what little he had to another poor man, when there were rich around? Let the goddamn rich do something for the Connollys. He would find a Lambert and Smith steer, one of the goddamn very best in the herd, haze it home after dark, and butcher it for them. He kicked his horse into a lope.

Andrew sat in his mother's old rocking chair in the kitchen of their homestead. Outside, the wind blew lazily, whistling through the cracks in the windowframes. Home a week and not one person had stopped by. He hadn't seen anybody since he and Jack had hung the two halves of the steer in the well. If he didn't talk to somebody soon he'd go nuts.

He stood and went to the window, the chair rocking behind him, his boots gritting on the sand on the floor that no amount of sweeping could get rid of. Every surface in the house was covered with a layer of fine sand. He rubbed at the window with his sleeve, trying to see out, but succeeded only in making his sleeve dirty. A grasshopper leaped across the counter in front of him. He didn't bother to catch it.

They were getting worse and worse, too, although what they ate was a mystery to him. Wherever he walked in the yard or the fields, they rose in a whirlwind away from him, clicking and whirring. They landed on his arms, his chest, his thighs, and sprang away again. They came into the house on his clothes. In the mornings he found them in his boots, and when he combed his hair, he combed out grasshoppers. They were in the corners of the windowsills, under the bed, on the table, in the frying pan when he went to cook breakfast.

A good thing mother didn't live to see, he told himself, then had to laugh, remembering her expression that nothing seemed to change.

He went back to the chair, which had finally stopped rocking, and kicked at it irritably. He felt as if he hadn't seen another human in months, hadn't touched a woman in years. It was Saturday night and Jack Connolly had said everybody would be over at the schoolhouse. He would gladly suffer through a politician's speech if it meant that afterward he could hold a woman in his arms. He put on clean clothes, saddled his horse, and rode out.

He was one of the last to arrive, coming on horseback through the rare, quiet evening. The small school was packed with people who had come on foot, by saddlehorse, with a team and wagon, and even in Bennett buggies. The women occupied the desks, and the men stood three deep along the walls and across the back. The room buzzed with noise, and on the teacher's desk at the front two gas lamps sat, waiting to be lit when the evening grew darker.

Andrew found a place to stand along the wall to the right of the speaker's place at the front. McNulty, now well into his sixties, but still vigorous and strong, pushed himself away from the blackboard where he had been leaning, and went to stand behind the teacher's desk. He rapped on the desk top for silence and gradually the room quieted.

"Our speaker'll be here in a minute," he said, and they could all hear in the silence, the rumble of a Model T as it drew closer. "I'd ask all of you along the back to make room for them to get through." He stood waiting, tall, his eyes bright, his hair silver now, and gradually the buzz of voices rose again. Andrew took this moment to look around the room. There were people here he hadn't seen for years, many of them had come from more than twenty miles away. He was surprised at this, wondering that anybody would care so much about politics. As if the government could stop the wind from blowing and the sun from shining, he thought.

He studied the women sitting in the rows of desks. Mrs. Connolly was there, a spot of colour shining in each cheek. She sat near the back in one of the big desks kept for the big boys. Mrs. McNulty, a tiny, grey-haired lady, sat in the front row. She was wearing the only hat in the room. His eyes swept up and down the rows, recognizing most of the faces. In the fading evening light most of them looked middle-aged, whether they were or not. He knew them to be married and he felt irritation growing that he had ridden over for nothing.

Then he noticed her. She sat almost in the centre of the room directly across from where he was leaning against the wall. He liked her small, neat nose, and the way her hands were folded neatly on the desktop in front of her, her eyes on McNulty, who still stood at the front, waiting. She had short dark hair held back on the side next to him with a shiny clasp of some kind, and even from the side he could tell that she had a full mouth and dark eyes. He shifted position so he could see her better, and was touched by the way her slender but rounded arm emerged from the short sleeve of her dress. He felt an elbow in his ribs.

"Her name's Karen Turnberry. She's the new teacher," the farmer standing next to him said, grinning up at him. Andrew grinned back and looked back at her. "She's single," the man said, and laughed. Andrew ignored the other men who were turning to look at him.

There was a commotion at the back of the room, people moving and squeezing against one another, and two strangers came through the crowd and up the aisle to the front of the room. The crowd grew silent, watching the two as McNulty extended his large, white hand to each of them. Andrew glanced at the teacher quickly and saw how she sat motionless, her eyes on the men at the front, her expression expectant, yet still. He found himself wanting to put a hand on her shoulder.

"Ladies and Gentlemen," McNulty began. One of the two men was to be the speaker. He stood silently, looking the crowd over with piercing blue eyes. His suit hung baggily over his long, thin frame. It looked as though he hadn't taken it off in days, and there was a thin film of dust all over it. His tie was crooked too, but he seemed, in the way he stood and watched the crowd with his chin lifted, not to notice or care how he looked. Andrew turned his head casually and looked toward Karen Turnberry again. She moved slightly and lifted one arm to rest her hand under her chin, placing her elbow on the desk in front of her. Her hand was small and dainty.

"I hear things are so bad here," the speaker began unexpectedly as if there were no time to waste, so that the room grew even quieter, and the crowd seemed to hold its collective breath, "that the provincial government is actually moving some of you out. Is that right?" For a moment nobody moved, then a few heads bobbed affirmatively, and a male voice or two broke the silence to tell him he was right. "They tell me the idea is to put you on better land north of here, somewhere where there's more rain, maybe." His knuckles rested on the desk in front of him, he bent forward from the waist like a runner, his eyes scanning his audience. "I been from one end of this province to the other," he said. "I been all through southern Alberta, too, and let me tell you, moving you out of the places where you homesteaded, the places where you've put in years of hard labour, isn't the answer. There isn't any more rain north or south or east or west of here. There aren't any crops anywhere." He paused, a long wait, while the crowd hung breathlessly, waiting for him to go on. "Things are so tough in this country under Bennett's hunger government that people are starving. Well, I don't have to tell you that!" He paused again and looked deliberately from face to face in the crowded schoolroom. The people moved restlessly under his stare. It was too personal, he seemed to read each one of them.

"I spent a lot of time this year in British Columbia," the speaker said, dropping his voice so they had to strain to hear him. "Things are no better there. In British Columbia, that beautiful, wealthy province, I visited the slave camps Bennett's government has set up. You didn't know about that, did you. You've got no power, no newspapers, no radios." He paused again, holding his audience. Andrew caught a glimpse of movement from Karen and his eyes went at once to her. She rubbed a hand across her forehead, frowning, and pursed her lips. Then she turned her head and looked directly at Andrew. Their eyes met and he smiled at her. At first she only looked as though she hadn't seen him, but then she blinked, started to return his smile, seemed to think better of it, and turned back to the speaker.

She was beautiful. She was so goddamn beautiful he could hardly breathe. He wanted to shove his way through the desks to her, he wanted to grab her up, carry her away, make love to her somewhere out in the night. The small man beside him who had told him her name shouted out, "Why don't they leave? Get the hell out?" and Andrew was brought back to the moment, to the meeting, to the packed and stuffy little room. He straightened, shifting his legs, and tried not to look at the girl again.

"They don't leave because in this country where everybody is starving under Bennett's hunger government, twenty cents a day and mush to eat is better than nothing at all! It's better than starving in city gutters!"

"Some of the men in the camps have tried to organize strikes for better pay and better living conditions. In one camp I visited the men had cut down the top bunks. They refused to sleep three deep! The men who slept in the top bunks were getting sick from the stuffy air up there. But what does this government do when the men agitate?" The room was growing hotter although the door was open, as well as most of the windows. McNulty had lit both lamps and passed one to the back of the room. Moths had flown in the open doors and windows and were bumping against the lamps. Every once in a while a woman would duck her head and brush away a miller with an irritated gesture.

"They call in their cossacks and they expel them from the camps. Then they refuse them admittance to any other camp and they blacklist them so that when they return to wherever they came from they can't get Relief."

"You say this is going on all over the country?" McNulty asked.

"Outside the big cities," the man answered. "In Soviet Russia there is a depression too, but the people aren't starving, they aren't being shoved into concentration camps for being hungry. They have a political system there that says no man is entitled to be rich while another is starving!"

"Are you a Communist?" a stout woman in the front row demanded. Several other voices said, "So what?" and, "What if he is?"

"You bet I'm a Communist," the speaker said, not looking at her, his restless eyes still roving over his audience. "I been a Communist since 1926. But what is a Communist?"

Andrew was watching the girl again, unable to stop himself. Her cheeks were flushed, and she was leaning forward, her hand still resting under her jaw, and she pushed her hair back and rubbed her neck slowly. He could see how white her jaw and throat were. He imagined himself putting his face against her neck, smelling her skin, tasting its whiteness with his tongue.

"Work and wages!" the speaker shouted suddenly, jerking Andrew's attention back to him. "That's all any of us want! Work and wages!" Farmers had turned to their neighbours, mumbling agreement or criticism, their arms crossed over their thick chests, their feet moving restlessly. They turned their faces back to the speaker.

"What has brought this nation to such a sorry state?" the speaker asked. Outside, the wind had begun to blow again sending a gust in through the window that sent McNulty scrambling to catch a few papers that flew off the desk. The speaker seemed not to notice. "What has plunged us into this nightmare? Let me tell you a little history. Oh, I know you don't want to hear history, but bear with me for just a minute."

"Each one of you owns a little land. The government has let you have a little piece of land to call your own. Why do you suppose they did that? What does the ruling class care if you have land or not?" The wind whistled around the building and the speaker raised his voice. "They let you have it because settlement out here in the West means money in the pockets of the bankers and the other bloated capitalists in the East. This land was no good to them empty! How could they make money off the West if there was nobody in it? So they built the railway, and they opened the country for farming, they brought in you settlers from Europe and the United States and the East by promising you free land!"

"And when you got here, you formed a ready-made market for farm implements, wagons, plows, axes, threshing machines. But what did you do most of all? You borrowed money! You went to the banks for money for seed wheat and equipment and to buy more land. And when times got tough, you mortgaged your farms, and where did you go to do that but to the same bankers and businessmen who brought you out here to this desolate country in the first place! The people who lured you out here from your snug homes around the world with false promises of plenty and streets paved with gold!"

Andrew thought of all the cowboys he had ridden with when he was a boy, of Lambert and Smith's shrunken spread, of all the farmers he had seen come and go. His mind wouldn't work clearly, he couldn't concentrate on the argument, he was anxious for the meeting to be over so he could approach the dark-haired young teacher. He shuffled his feet, shoved his fists into his pockets, tried to listen. At last the speaker was winding up his talk.

"What we have here today is starvation in the midst of plenty. Ladies and gentlemen, hard-working men and women, we have to know the enemy, and the enemy is capitalism." He said a few more words and then McNulty asked for a collection, but Andrew had stopped even trying to listen.

The men standing at the back had begun to move outside where it was cooler and where they could smoke in the lee of the building, out of the wind. The women were carrying packages and pans to the desk at the front and were opening them, arranging sandwiches on plates and pouring coffee from jars. In one corner the speaker stood surrounded by men who were asking him questions or arguing with him.

Karen had gone to the desk with the other women and was helping them set out the lunch. She took a tray of sandwiches and began moving slowly around the room, offering them to the people who sat or stood in small bunches chatting. Andrew stayed where he was, not talking to anybody, waiting.

In a moment she was standing in front of him. Her dark red dress was buttoned up to the blue-shadowed hollow at the base of her throat. Her eyes were dark, the delicate, clearly defined black brows drawn straight across her brow. She smiled at him.

"Sandwich?" she asked. Her gaze was direct, she wasn't shy, and her eyes met his frankly. He reached out slowly, and took one from the plate, wanting to speak to her, but silenced by her loveliness. Finally he said, "You new here?"

"Not so new," she said. Her voice was soft and husky. "I taught here last year, too, but I don't know how much longer they'll be able to keep me." She made a little face, wrinkling her nose. "I don't know where I'll go then."

"Come and stay with me," he said. "I'll keep you." She looked surprised, then flushed ever so slightly.

"Wouldn't you die if I took you up on that," she said. She turned her back on him in a slow, graceful movement, and moved on with the plate of sandwiches.

He didn't make any attempt to speak to her again as he waited for the crowd to grow smaller. He watched her though, to make sure that he left at the same time she did.

In half an hour the speaker was at the door, his suit even more rumpled than when he had arrived, saying his last few words to the men standing there, his driver yawning and waiting impatiently. There were only a few people left in the schoolroom, women wrapping leftover sandwiches and cake, while their husbands waited.

When the speaker left the schoolroom, Andrew went out behind him and stood in the shadows by the steps as the Model T was cranked and then chugged away down the dusty road in the moonlight.

Karen was the last person out. She shut the door behind her, pulling it against the wind, and locked it. She stood for a second on the steps, not seeing him in the shadows beside her.

Andrew stepped out of the darkness and spoke to her. She turned slowly toward him, as if she had been expecting to hear his voice. They stood close to each other in the moonlit night.

"Where are you staying?" he asked.

"I'm at Anderson's this month," she said, indicating the direction with a nod. "It's about a mile."

"I know where it is," he said. "Can I walk you home?"

"I've only got my saddlehorse or I'd offer a ride"

"Yes," she said. "Please do."

He untied his horse from the fence and led him. They set out across a field in the windy darkness. After a moment he took her hand. She didn't resist, letting it rest warmly inside his.

"My name . . ." he began.

"I know your name," she said. "I asked as soon as I saw you looking at me. Everybody's talking about us already." They both laughed. He moved closer to her and put his arm across her shoulders. Her soft hip and thigh bumped against his leg now and then as they crossed the uneven ground. Tumbleweeds blew across their path and he had to lean close to her to speak or to hear what she said above the wind. She reached up and placed her hand lightly on top of his shoulder.

The full moon, round and orange, sat above the hilltops ahead of them spilling its light onto them. Wisps of cloud, purple and blue, sped across its face, vanished, and were replaced by others. It was a violent night, full of the promise of the impending storm that never came. He pulled her closer to him, dropping his hand to her hip, his chest so full of longing that he felt it might burst.

They made love in a patch of sparse grass in the shadow of a few carraganas still standing in an abandoned farmstead where they had stopped to talk. She lifted her body up to him eagerly, as though she had been waiting as long as he had. She held her mouth to his with tenderness and passion. Later she told him that she had been married, that she had left her husband and wouldn't go back.

"I got nothing," he said to her. "Some land, a hundred head of starving cows, forty head of horses." She lay beside him with her head on his shoulder next to the carraganas, sheltered from the wind. "Will you get a divorce?" he asked her.

"As soon as I have enough money saved," she said.

"I'll try to help you get the money together," he said.

She did not disagree, only caressed his face with her small hand.

"I'll have to find another job soon," she said. "Everybody's too poor to keep the schoolteacher when it's their turn, and anyway, the board will soon have to close the school. They can't even find my wages this month."

"Where will you go?" he asked, holding her tightly, as if she might leave him that moment.

"I don't know yet," she was whispering into his ear. "Maybe into Alberta. There's jobs around Calgary, maybe."

He wanted to say don't go, stay with me, but he held back, afraid of what he felt for her, a woman he had seen for the first time this very night. Besides, she still had a divorce to get, and he could barely support himself, never mind a second person. She lay pressed against him, one hand on his neck, the other against his ribs. Her soft hair brushed his nose. He didn't want to let her go.

"Winter's coming," he said, suddenly saddened, afraid of something nameless. Clouds covered the moon, he couldn't see her anymore. She didn't answer him, only lifted her face to his, raising herself so that she lay over him, her mouth open on his.

In December, as she had predicted, the school was closed. By early January she had found work in a small school south of Medicine Hat. She wrote weekly letters to him and he replied, short notes telling her he loved her, that he would see her in the spring.

He was drinking in the beer parlour in town when a stranger came in. He was a big man, with blonde hair and pale blue eyes. He walked with a barely perceptible limp and he came straight across the bare wooden floor to where Andrew sat alone.

"She's still married to me," he said. "Leave her alone."

They went outside to the dark alley behind the beer parlour and stood facing each other.

"She says she don't want you," Andrew told him, without menace. "Why don't you just leave her alone?" They fought then, in the dirt and the darkness, falling, missing each other, banging up against the wooden walls of the old buildings, till finally, both winded and hurt, they stopped.

"It's no use," Andrew said to him. "She don't want you anymore, and this won't change anything." Her husband leaned against the beer parlour steps, panting. He drew in his breath shakily and Andrew realized that he was crying. For a moment he stood there listening to the other man's sobs, then he walked down the alley to the livery barn, saddled his horse, and rode home at a gallop through the dust-laden, howling night.

At last spring approached. He had been out checking his herd of horses, looking for a way to make a little money, when he saw with some surprise that smoke was rising from his chimney. He had been gone since early morning and the fire should have been out. He turned his horse and headed for the house. Now he could see a car drawn up in front of it, and as he drew closer, he recognized it as the Mountie's.

The Mountie was sitting at his kitchen table when Andrew walked in. He was drinking a cup of coffee and the pot was steaming on the stove. His feet were up on Andrew's mother's table. As Andrew walked in, he lowered them to the floor and turned to Andrew without getting up.

"Helped myself to your coffee while I waited," he said, grinning at Andrew. "Hope you don't mind." His smile was insolent. Andrew crossed the room without speaking, got down a cup, and filled it.

"Sure," he said, his back to the Mountie. "What can I do for you?" He sat down across from him.

"Know anything about some horses?" the Mountie asked. "Horses that belong to the Lambert and Smith outfit?" He was not smiling now. Andrew took his time answering.

"What horses is that?" he asked. "I been busy most of the winter," he went on. "I ain't seen any horses but my own. Anyway, you must know the Mountie north of here drove 'em all in a couple of months ago and checked all the brands. Didn't find nothing."

"Funny," the Mountie said, grinning again. "I heard you knew all there was to know about stray horses and cattle around here." Andrew didn't reply. He drank from his mug and waited. The Mountie said nothing more. Andrew set his mug down. He could feel his cheeks and forehead hot with blood.

"Listen, you sonofabitch," Andrew said. "If you've got something on me, let's hear it. If you don't, you get the hell out of my house." They stared at one another until finally the Mountie reached for his hat and put it on. He rose and went to the door.

"You can expect me back, he said as he went out, slamming the door behind him. The car started up and Andrew listened until its noise receded down the trail.

Andrew rode again the next day, bent on chasing his horses in and cutting some out to start breaking them. He rode northeast into the big coulee where they often grazed. When he started up the coulee again, intending to head further north into the hills, he saw a car approaching, picking its way slowly around the patches of snow, the badger holes, and the rocks. He waited. As it drew closer, he saw that it was the same car as the day before, but this time, there were three men in it.

It drew up beside him and stopped. The man sitting beside the driver opened the door and got out. As soon as he straightened and looked up at Andrew with an expression both surly and self-righteous, Andrew knew what they had come for. He held his expression steady. Suddenly his horse back-stepped and pranced, and even as he calmed him, Andrew thought of letting him go, heading out south through no-man's-land into Montana. They'd never catch him. But a deeper, stronger voice was flowing there behind the frantic, captured one and it said, steady steady. You'd never be able to stop running. In the end, there's nowhere to go.

"I'm arresting you, Andrew Samson," the man said, savouring his words. Andrew looked out toward the pale peaks of the Bear Paws rising low in the sky to the south. After a moment he looked back to the man who had spoken to him.

"What would that be for?" he asked, his voice mild. The back door opened and a second man climbed out of the car.

"Horse-rustling," the first man said.

"You'll have to come with us," the second man said. Andrew looked around again. They were far out on the prairie, no buildings in sight. The second man said, "You can ride to your place, turn your horse out, get your things. Let's get moving." He got back in the car.

They followed Andrew to his house and waited while he unsaddled his horse and turned him out. They even let him put on a clean shirt before they drove him away. All the time he refused to think, or couldn't think, beyond whom he would ask to look after his stock and what he would tell Karen. Below his inner silence as he unbuttoned his dirty shirt, put on a clean one and packed his shaving kit, was his inability to believe in his guilt.

He had done what he was accused of, and more besides, but he could not feel guilty. Still, he knew as clearly as the Mounties who had arrested him knew, that he was going to jail.

CHAPTER SEVEN

He was forking hay to the horses in the early morning sun shining in the open barn door. Postnikoff and Sawrenko were working silently on each side of him. He forked automatically, not thinking about what he was doing, concentrating on the feel of the pitchfork's smooth handle, on the forkful of sweet-smelling, green hay mingling with the odour of horses and manure, and on the pull and power in his shoulders and arms.

"Christ, we should have had hay like this at home," Sawrenko said. "My horses wouldn't be starving already."

"They call this hard labour, eh?" Postnikoff said, laughing. "I work a helluva lot harder on the old man's place." Andrew laughed at that, knowing it was true. The routine wasn't easy, but all of them were used to much harder work and longer hours than this.

"Okay, boys," the guard said, coming up behind them. "Take a break."

"Got any tobacco?" Postnikoff asked Andrew. "I'll pay you back."

The three of them stood in the barn door, far enough back to be out of the hot sun, and rolled their cigarettes. The guard moved further back into the barn to check on the other three men who were still forking manure onto a stoneboat. Postnikoff moved close to Andrew casually, as if he were only shifting his weight, and pushed some money into Andrew's hand.

"For tobacco," he said softly. Andrew said nothing, stared straight ahead at the row of guards' cottages, half-hidden behind the shrubs and poplars that stirred and rustled in the light summer breeze.

A woman stepped out onto the back porch of one of the cottages and began to hang wet clothes on the line. She was too far away for them to make out her face, but they could see that she was tall and big-breasted and big-hipped. The three of them squatted, smoking, and watched her as she bent to pick up a wet garment and stretched to hang it, the clothespins in her mouth. Andrew was the first to turn his head away, looking instead toward the main prison building where men in khaki-coloured uniforms that said 'Regina Gaol' across the back were working in the flower beds, cutting the grass, and trimming the lilacs and other shrubs whose names he didn't know, that decorated the grounds.

A prisoner came out of one of the small side doors in the prison and carried a cardboard box across to the pig barn.

"Christ, I'm glad I can work outside," Andrew said. Soon he and the others would be harnessing the horses and leading the teams out to work in the prison fields.

"City boys," Postnikoff said, watching the prisoner disappear inside the barn. "They like cooking in the kitchen, scared of the sun." Postnikoff's crime was some kind of petty theft, Andrew could never remember, among Postnikoff's endless stories, which one he was doing six months for.

"Bunch of fucking hopheads," Sawrenko said. "Us farm boys stick together, eh?" Sawrenko was from Yorkton. Drunk, he had gotten into a fight and put two men in the hospital. He was serving his three months with cheerful calm. He lowered his bulk to the ground, and as he did so his powerful muscles bulged and stretched his khaki prisoner's shirt. He yawned and squinted up at the sky beyond the overhang of the barn's roof. They could hear the guard coming back up the barn aisle, walking slowly, his boots squeaking on the clean cement floor.

"Not a bad day, is it, boys?" he said to them.

"Not bad," they said. "Kind of hot, but it could be worse." The woman across the way had gone back inside again. Sawrenko was watching the closed door. The clothes she had hung flapped sadly now and then as the light wind caught, then dropped them.

"Well, back to work," he said good-naturedly. They took their time butting their cigarettes and standing, but the guard made no effort to hurry them. He was nearing retirement and was no longer interested in flexing his power over minor things.

"Samson," he said, "time to shoe that stallion again." Andrew groaned. The horse was a Percheron, dappled grey, weighing a ton and a half. When Andrew picked up a foot, the horse leaned on him with all his weight, but still, Andrew was proud of being picked to handle the horse. And in the spring he had been the one to look after the hand-breeding of the prison's mares.

"That mean sonofabitch," Andrew said, thoughtfully, without much rancour. The guard laughed.

"Well, he's only got four feet," the guard said. "Be glad of that."

The guard handing out the mail came down the row of cells, mumbling the name of the occupant of each cell as he thrust the letters toward the interior. It was evening, the day's work was done, supper was over, and the cell doors stood open for the evening's recreation. Andrew paid no attention to the mailman, whose footsteps he could hear coming down the tier. He lay on his bunk, smoking, feeling the deep ache in his back and arms from his day's work in the field.

"Samson," the guard said, and held a letter out toward him. He waited patiently, studying the other letters in his hand while Andrew, immobilized by surprise, took a second to get up from his bunk and cross the short space of his cell to reach out for the letter.

A letter. He couldn't control the trembling in his fingers as he took it. But who would write to him? He tore back the flap, lifted out the letter, allowing the envelope to drop onto his table while he turned quickly to the signature on the back of the page.

It was from Karen. So she had found him. Her face, her eyes, the things they had said to one another came flooding over him. For a moment he couldn't bring himself to read what she might have to say to him. Then he turned the page over to the beginning and began to read, a quick perusal first, searching for what frightening possibility he didn't know, then a measured read-through, forcing himself to concentrate on each word she had written in her firm, even hand on both sides of the page.

"Andrew, why didn't you tell me what happened? At first I thought you had changed your mind about us. Then I thought you might be sick or in trouble or unable to leave your place. Finally, I asked around and after a month, I found out what had happened. For a long time I didn't write, thinking that your not telling me you were in trouble might mean you didn't want me to. But finally I had to write. Andrew, how will I do without you for two whole years?"

When he had finished reading it a second time, he folded the letter carefully and put it in the pocket of his shirt. Then he stretched out on his bunk, rolled another cigarette and lit it, then lay staring up at the grey concrete ceiling above him. He could hear the guard climbing the stairs at the end of the row of cells on his way up to the next tier. His boots rang on the iron steps, and the sound echoed and re-echoed till it became a meaningless din.

She would wait for him, she said. She would be there for him if he wanted her when his sentence was up. He didn't know whether to laugh or cry, after all the days and nights of swearing not to think about her, yet knowing that she had become a part of his body, that he could never forget her no matter how hard he tried, because this feeling for her was beyond his control. He thought of why he hadn't written to her: shame, and a sense of the hopelessness of their situation.

He tossed his cigarette butt into the toilet and sat up, looking around his cell at the rough brick walls, the bars, the open toilet, his bunk, the mean little table and chair. A feeling of pure, distilled anguish was spreading upward from his gut, through his chest, into his head. He sat on the edge of his bunk and held his head in his hands. To have her back again, to hold her against him.

"Who was it from?" a voice asked. He lowered his hands.

"What?" he asked. Archer, who lived in the next cell, was standing in the doorway of Andrew's cell. Andrew could tell by something empty about his hands, by the look in his eyes that Archer had once again received no mail.

"Who was your letter from?" he repeated. He glanced over his shoulder in a nonchalant way as if the answer meant nothing to him, then frowned, and looked back into Andrew's face.

"My girlfriend," Andrew said, hardly pausing between the two words.

"She don't write too often," Archer remarked, then drew on his cigarette. In the poor light from the dim, unshaded bulb, the tip of his cigarette glowed red, a tiny fire. "Sonofabitching censors cut out all the good stuff anyway." He laughed harshly. Behind him, men moved up and down the tier, in no hurry, visiting, strolling nowhere.

"Yeah," Andrew said.

The next morning he woke with the buzzer in the cold dawn, turning, feeling different somehow even before his eyes were open. What was it that made this dawn different? Today I take the pigs to market, he remembered, but that was a twice-weekly event, a relief from the daily monotony, but it couldn't account for this unexpected bouyancy. Then he remembered. Karen had written, had said she was waiting for him.

All the endless black and lonely days lay before him. He had held on this long without her, would have made it to the end without her, if only because he had no choice, and because, like it or not, he knew himself to be strong; stronger than he wanted to be, with a path laid out before him that he could walk if he kept himself drawn in, his eyes on the ground in front of him through the dull, hopeless days. Now she had said she was waiting and he was forced to think about that. For an instant he was angry that she had broken his solitude with her promise, had made him agitated, so that he forgot his way, had disrupted it and given no clear, new way.

Then he thought of her beauty, the softness of her skin, her clear, dark eyes, the huskiness of her voice, the way she gave her body to him, and he thought, maybe this is better.

He was standing behind Postnikoff in the breakfast lineup, holding his empty tray, when he felt a hand slide into his pocket.

"Leopold, tobacco," a voice murmured near his ear and without Andrew having seen him, the prisoner who had slipped the money in his pocket passed on by in the line of those who had had their trays filled.

"Sonofabitch," Postnikoff said. "Goddamn black molasses. Makes me sick to look at it." The molasses sat, gleaming and turgid, in the small bowl the cook's helpers placed on each tray as the men filed past. It was all they had to use as jam on their toast, or syrup on their pancakes, or sugar on their porridge. Andrew had simply accepted it as a part of his lot, but this morning he said, "It makes me sick, too," and was surprised at what he had said, although it was true.

As he walked back to his cell carrying his tray of food, a prisoner returning his tray and empty dishes said to Andrew, "You going out today?" Andrew glanced over to the guard who stood along the railing, watching the men come and go. He was looking the other way. Andrew nodded.

"Here," the prisoner set money on Andrew's tray and moved on.

After breakfast Andrew and Sawrenko hitched four horses to the pig-wagon, backed the hitch up to the pig barn, loaded the wagon with pigs, and Andrew set out for the nearby city. He enjoyed the solitary drive in the quiet of the early morning. They never sent a guard with him, knowing he could be trusted to do his job and return on time. He never once seriously considered driving on through the city and striking out for home or somewhere he thought he might not be found. There was no such place. All he wanted was to do his time and get out of prison, go home, be free again, so he set his mind on the job before him and did it.

The day was beginning to grow hot as the horses clopped down the dusty streets of the city. People began to appear on the sidewalks, hurrying to their jobs, and here and there a storekeeper unlocked his doors and began to sweep the sidewalk or wash a window. The city interested Andrew. He had never been in one this big before, he didn't count the one he was born in because he couldn't remember it, and as he swayed along he watched the people, thought about their lives, and pitied them. His own life on the prairie appeared vastly richer to him, and he thought these city people must be missing some kind of basic happiness that had been his ever since he had come to the West as a child. That he was a prisoner and they were not, didn't always occur to him. He tried to imagine himself scurrying down the grey sidewalks past building after building on his way to a job locked inside such a building. He thought of riding all day in the blazing sun or in the winter when it was twenty below. He thought of all the hard labour he had done in his life, the times he had wanted to give up; he thought of the things he had seen—wild animals, cattle and horses, children, and crocuses and cactus blossoms. And all these people he saw beside him had seen nothing, knew nothing, for how could they? Their lives constricted by the city limits. They couldn't even see the sky.

His thoughts turned to the way things were when he left them a few months before: no significant rain for years, the fields turning to drifting sandpiles, no crops, no feed for the animals, no money. And him caught in a limbo that was neither life nor death. He regretted with all his heart being where he was now, although he couldn't see how he could have lived his life any differently.

At the Burns plant he had to wait in line before he could unload the pigs. Once he had done that, he turned the wagon around and started back the way he had come. At the sidestreet café he went to twice every week, he pulled the horses up, unhitched them, tied them to the wagonbox, slipped on feed bags, and went inside, glad to get out of the hot noon sun. He had a voucher for a meal here. After a few months of coming to the café he had grown used to people staring at his prison uniform, to the careful way the waitresses treated him. He always ate quickly and left at once without bothering to smoke a cigarette.

He'd had a little trouble at first getting the horses, who had been walking the same route for years, to take the detour he wanted them to take, but now they did it without reluctance. He pulled the horses up in front of a small confectionery a block off the route to the prison, jumped down from the wagon, and went inside. The girl was waiting at the counter for him with the tobacco already on the counter in front of her. Quickly he tossed the men's money onto the counter, swept up the packages, and hurried out again. If he ate fast enough at the café and she had the tobacco ready for him, he was not late getting back.

He shifted the reins to his left hand and unbuttoned his shirt with his right, placing the packages next to his skin from his waist to his chest. Then he buttoned his shirt up again. Now everything depended on which guard searched him at the prison door.

Today he saw with relief that it was Powell. Powell was another bored, older man, close to retirement, with a naturally cheerful disposition and a surprisingly unsuspicious attitude, which came, Andrew realized, from not wanting the trouble that such suspicion might bring. When Andrew had unhitched the horses at the barn, he had made sure the packages were as flat as he could press them. Now he stood, trying to look nonchalant, and waited for Powell to get up off his stool and search him.

"Any trouble today?" Powell asked, not really interested in the answer.

"Nope," Andrew said. Powell stood in front of him. "Look, Powell," he said. "Don't search me too close, okay?" He grinned at the guard, who hesitated, then, a slow smile appearing on his face, he patted Andrew's chest once perfunctorily, shrugged, and waved Andrew past, shaking his head.

In the evening as Andrew and the rest of the farm crew filed into the cell block, Andrew was surprised by the abnormally high noise level, and by the number of men leaning against cell bars and talking down the rows or tiers to one another. There was an air of excitement. New prisoners, Andrew realized, and a lot of them.

Postnikoff, walking beside him, said, "Look at all the new boys. I wonder where they found them." Andrew's cell was between Postnikoff and Archer's but now in Archer's cell a young, sunburned man leaned, grinning out at Andrew. He had a black bruise on one cheek and a trickle of dried blood streaked the temple and one cheekbone. The guard waited for Andrew to enter his cell, then went on by.

"What's going on?" he asked the newcomer. "What are you all in for?"

"We're the On-To-Ottawa Trekkers!" the young man said loudly, eagerly. "Ain't you heard of us?" It seemed impossible to him that they had not been heard of.

"Don't hear much in here," Andrew said. "Got no radios, never see a newspaper."

"You don't say!" the young man said, astonished. He scratched at the dried blood on his cheek. "Maybe we can do something about that!" Andrew couldn't help but laugh. "Look," the young prisoner went on. "We been here in Regina for three weeks. We been on the road a month since we left Vancouver. And you ain't even heard of us! We're the strikers!"

"Strikers?" Andrew didn't understand.

"Hey, boys!" the prisoner shouted suddenly. "Hey, Art! This guy never heard of us! These guys don't know what we're here for!" Voices rose along the rows of cells and tiers.

"Tell them, Slim!" The rest of their shouts blended into a general uproar.

"Quiet! Quiet! Let Slim talk!" The voices died one by one, the last one echoing hollowly, bouncing off the cement and steel. The place grew quiet, the old prisoners listening and watching with curiosity, the new ones eager and proud. Then Andrew saw that all eyes seemed to be on the occupant of a cell across the tier from where he stood.

He was a tall, thin man, and his prisoner's clothes hung loosely on him. Andrew was reminded of the schoolhouse speaker of a year or so before. The man stood in the open door of his cell and raised his big, brown hands. His face was lean and brown too, even from where Andrew stood many feet away, he could see the man's blue eyes flash.

"Boys," he called, and then paused, as his voice bounced off the brick and iron, repeated itself, and repeated itself. He waited until the last echo died away. The cell block was silent, listening.

"We rode the trains from Vancouver, picking up men as we came, on our way to talk to the government in Ottawa, determined to tell old Iron Heel Bennett himself that we won't stay in the Relief Camps. We want to tell him ourselves that we want jobs! And we want decent wages!" As he said this last, his voice rising toward the end, he paused, stepped back momentarily as his men shouted their agreement from cells scattered beyond his, above and below, to his left and his right.

"Work and wages!" they shouted. "Work and wages!" Their voices swelled and mingled into a meaningless roar that slowly died away. The tall prisoner stepped forward again, setting his gaze upward.

"You prisoners been locked in this capitalist prison, they don't even let you know what happened, because if you did, they know you would rise up and join us!" There were loud mutters of agreement around the tiers.

"Bennett's cossacks jumped us the day before yesterday! We were holding a peaceful meeting . . ."

"Most of us weren't even there!" the young man in the cell next to Andrew's shouted, hysteria creeping into his voice.

". . . and they fired into our crowd, ran into that peaceful assembly with clubs, clubbed down women and children, shot at least a dozen of our men . . ."

"The fucking hospitals are full of our boys!" another, deeper voice above Andrew's cell shouted.

"So here we are!" the tall prisoner said in a quieter voice. "That's what kind of a government we got! That's how this country of ours is run! Nothing for the working man! Nothing but bullets and prison!" His voice had risen to a shout and from every corner of the cell block voices were raised over his, but he had stopped talking, had retreated into the shadows of his cell.

"Communist bastards!" Postnikoff shouted. "I know Commies when I hear them! Why don't you all go on back to Russia!" The guards had come running now, they were shouting for quiet, moving up and down the rows, threatening. The noise died down gradually. The tall prisoner had decided to say one last thing.

"We'll take it easy tonight, boys," he called. "I've got a call in to Gardiner, and we'll lay down some conditions when we see him. There's lawyers working on this, boys, so get some sleep and I'll call a meeting tomorrow."

At breakfast the next morning there was a lot of grumbling about the food. The new prisoners complained especially about the molasses they were given for their pancakes.

"You get used to it," an old prisoner said to one of the new ones.

"Sure, the slave gets used to being a slave," the prisoner said, his voice full of sarcasm. "It's swill for pigs!" Disgustedly he took the bowl of molasses off his tray and thrust it back to the kitchen worker, who shrugged and accepted it.

There were more guards than usual on duty this morning, patrolling up and down the line. Two of them passed Andrew and Postnikoff, heading toward the back of the line. A dozen men back, the guards stopped and singled out a prisoner. When the man stepped out of the line and followed them, Andrew saw that it was the man who had shouted his speech to them the night before.

"That's the last we'll see of that sonofabitch!" Postnikoff said to Andrew. A young striker ahead of them in the line, turned back to them and said, "That's Art and he's gone to negotiate for us. We'll be out of here by tomorrow"

"Yeah, sure!" Postnikoff taunted him. "So will I!" A guard stepped up.

"Shut up, Postnikoff," he said, "or you'll do a stretch all by yourself." Postnikoff subsided.

In the evening the guards announced that there would be a meeting in the prison chapel and anybody who wanted to go, could. Andrew, out of a mixture of boredom and curiosity, followed the line of men to the chapel on the top floor of the prison.

A minister stood at the front of the small chapel and beside him, the tall man with the bright eyes stood quietly, watching the men intently as they filed in. On the minister's other side stood another man. He was wearing prisoner's clothes, too, and his hands and face were sunburned so it was evident he was a striker, too. When all the seats were filled and the rest of the men were leaning along the walls down the side of the room and across the back, the minister climbed into the pulpit and began to speak. Immediately, the shuffling and conversations stopped.

"My name is East," he said, "and this man here, for those of you who don't know him, is Arthur Evans, Slim to those of us lucky enough to call him friend. And this is Mr. Cosgrove." Strikers sitting in the pews or leaning against the wall cheered loudly. The minister waited till the hubbub subsided, then went on. "I've come here today because I want to show my solidarity with the working men and women of Canada." The strikers cheered again.

"Shut up! Pipe down!" the other prisoners shouted, twisting in their seats to see who was making the noise.

"Some of you boys have come here from as far as Vancouver. All you were asking for was jobs, and for that, you've been hounded by the police, you've been stopped from travelling on the Canadian highway, you've been attacked, shot at, and now you've been thrown in jail." He paused, his lips drawn into a thin line, his face pale. His hands gripped the edge of the pulpit so fiercely that his knuckles were white. He waited for the strikers to settle down again. He seemed prepared to wait forever, not taking his eyes off them, but eventually the men grew silent.

"I can't stand by as a minister of the Christian Church and do nothing when I see men going hungry, when I see this kind of political oppression taking place. And that is why I have come here tonight. I want you men to know that I will do everything within my power to see that those of you who are guilty of no crime are released at once, and that while you are here, you are well treated." The strikers shouted again and then began to call for Evans to speak to them.

"Art! Give us a talk, Art!"

"What's going on, Slim?"

The minister stepped down from the pulpit and went to stand by Cosgrove. The two of them led the clapping as Evans walked past them, climbed the steps of the pulpit, and turned to face his audience. There were shouts of greeting and praise from the forty or so striking prisoners and boos from the other prisoners. The noise grew and grew instead of subsiding, until the few guards stationed inside the room began to move restlessly. Evans put up his hand and the noise dropped at once.

"You tell 'em, Slim," the young boy with the bruised cheek called into the quiet. Evans smiled briefly, without warmth, and his piercing eyes swept over his audience.

"The workers of Canada will be told about this," he said. "We'll have support from workers all across Canada, and the true nature of this Fascist regime will be shown for what it is!" The strikers started cheering again and the men in the pews and leaning against the walls who weren't strikers shouted back at them. Postnikoff, who was sitting beside Andrew, stood up and yelled, "You Communist bastard! Go back to Russia!" Other inmates shouted with him, "Yeah, go back to Russia!"

"Quiet! Let him talk!" Andrew was surprised to see that some of the prisoners who were shouting for quiet were not strikers. He couldn't understand this. The speakers were Communists! Couldn't they see it?

"Striker, labourer, or petty criminal," Evans shouted. "We're all in this prison together. We're all behind these Fascist bars! We all eat the same stinking food! But we don't have to put up with it! Haven't we proved that?" He leaned over the pulpit toward them. "If we organize, we can change our living conditions, even here. We can force them to feed us decent grub."

"We're locked up!" a prisoner shouted, "And they got the keys!" There were roars of laughter at this.

"Shut up!" "Let him talk!" "Dirty Red!"

"We can strike," Evans said. "We can refuse to eat what they give us. We can refuse to work. We can send our emissaries, like Mr. East here, out into the world to tell our supporters and our friends how bad conditions are in here. We can send them to tell the world that we're guilty of no crime, that we don't belong in here."

When he had finished speaking, Cosgrove spoke and then East again. Gradually the pieces of story came together. They had ridden the trains from Vancouver, picking up men along the way, there had been a public meeting in a blind street in Regina, and something had happened to make the police fire on them. Then they had rushed the police and many of them had been hurt and sent either to hospital or jail. Andrew kept his face impassive, anxious not to give away his bewilderment. It was an incredible story, he had trouble believing it, yet it carried the ring of truth.

When the speeches were over the men filed back to their cells and were locked in for the night. Andrew lay awake, staring at the ceiling. There was always a dim light from the bulbs along the tiers so that even at night the men didn't have complete darkness. Tonight the prisoners were restless.

They talked to one another and now and then had loud arguments through the cell bars. He lay and listened to them.

Sometimes it would come to him suddenly that he was a prisoner, that he couldn't get up and walk away. During the day he could become absorbed in the small details of his prison life. But sometimes at night, lying awake in the shadows of his cell, he would feel his bondage, his prisoner-hood. The knowledge would seep into him, he would lie rigid on his bunk, sweat oozing down his back and groin and chest, and he would think that he couldn't endure it. It was too much for any man to bear. Then, slowly, the terror would loosen its hold on him, the tension in his muscles would relax, the sweat would dry, and he would be lying quietly on his bunk in the shadows, the cell only a cell again, the bars only bars. But he would lie awake for hours listening to the prison silence broken by snores, or some-times by a moan or a shout from someone wrestling demons in his sleep.

In the morning it began. Half the men had taken their breakfasts to their cells and sat eating them, their cell doors standing open. The other half were still in the lineup to the opening into the kitchen where the food was handed out. Andrew was almost at the opening when some of the men began shouting.

"No more garbage!" the man at the front of the line shouted. He took his bowl of molasses and dumped it on the floor beside him, slowly and with elaborate care. The next man did the same. Behind Andrew men were shouting too, "We want syrup!" and from the tiers above there was the sound of dishes breaking. The men who had already been served their breakfasts were coming out of their cells, joining in the shouting and the dumping of the little bowls of molasses.

"Syrup! We want syrup! Give us syrup!" The cries echoed around the cells and passageways. Guards came running, shoving prisoners back into their cells and slamming cell doors, locking them in. Even then the noise didn't stop. The shouting went on behind the barred doors, getting louder, and they began banging on the bars.

Andrew was swept along by the guards back to his cell, all of them slipping or sticking in the molasses that had been smeared everywhere. Across the way from his cell Andrew saw Evans and Cosgrove walking down the alley between two guards. They went down the stairs and disappeared through the door that led into the passage to the warden's office.

After a while the shouting and pounding quieted a little. A pair of guards appeared and released Andrew, Postnikoff, Sawrenko, Fraser and Welsh.

"Nobody else coming?" Sawrenko asked as they were led briskly outside toward the barns.

"Nope," the guard said. "You'll be doing the chores for the next few days." They could see that they had been picked because they were all farm boys, all knew what to do without being told.

They did not go back to the cell block the rest of the day, even eating their hurried meals in the kitchen. With only five of them to do the work usually done by twenty men, they had to work quickly.

Andrew and Postnikoff took a break under a guard's eye in the shade of the pig barn.

"Christ! Can you figure it? Bunch of Commie bastards," Postnikoff said, although neither of them had been talking about the strikers.

"It's kind of interesting," Andrew remarked, having just realized this. "Breaks the monotony. I don't remember ever seeing so much excitement, except maybe during a roundup." Thinking of the life he had come from reminded him of Karen and he was glad she had no way of knowing what was happening. He thought of the steadiness of her eyes, and disgust at his situation rose up in him. He tossed down his half-finished cigarette and stepped hard on it.

"Yeah," Postnikoff said. "A man wishes for home sometimes."

"You got a wife?" Andrew asked, surprised at Postnikoff's understanding what he was feeling.

"Left her years ago, we couldn't get along."

"Kids?"

"Yeah," he said. "She moved them in with her brother, he's a bachelor. They don't let me near the place." Andrew glanced at him. He was staring straight ahead with a bitter expression on his face. "Ah, hell" he said. "I couldn't feed 'em, anyway. Her brother's got a big farm."

"I may be getting married," Andrew said, almost to himself. "If I ever get out of here." The length of his sentence stretched out before him into infinity. Would he ever be free again?

"Three weeks," Postnikoff said. "And I go out. Don't know where I'll go this time."

The ground beneath their feet seemed hard and unrelenting, the sky remote and alien. The prison buildings sat heavily around them and the long day was only another day in a procession of days from birth to death. His former life seemed idyllic, but just as impossible as the prison life he found himself caught in now. Life sat heavily on his chest now, like a dead weight. The struggle of the men inside the prison seemed far away and trivial.

In the evening, when they were marched back into the cell block, they saw that the molasses had been cleaned up and they could walk without having their boots stick to the floor. It was surprisingly quiet, too.

After everyone had eaten and the cell doors stood open for the evening, Andrew said to the striker leaning on the railing in front of his cell, "How come they're letting us have our recreation time? I thought they'd keep us locked up.

"You were lucky," the boy said. His bruises were fading. "You got out, we been locked up all the goddamn day. We quieted down, so they'd let us out!" He grinned, his rotten teeth showing.

"You from Vancouver?" Andrew asked.

"Raised there," the boy said. "My old man worked on the docks." He stared down at the men moving around below. "Me, I ain't never had a job." He raised his eyes to Andrew's and Andrew saw how wild they were, like a coyote's, both sly and fierce. "I spent the last year in a Relief Camp in the interior."

"Did they feed you good?" Andrew asked. The boy was thin, the skin that showed where his shirt buttons were undone was pale and hairless.

"Are you kidding?" he asked. "Mush for breakfast, stew for supper. Who knows what they put in the stew. Men said it was saltpetre." He laughed, showing his rotten teeth again. While they had been talking, a fight had broken out at the end of the tier and men were yelling at them. The boy's eyes lit up with a kind of yellow light, he seemed to forget Andrew, and hurried away down the passage to see what was going on.

The banging on the bars had begun again, and somewhere above him there was a steady pounding and a crunch of cement giving away. Down the tier the crashing picked up, and across the way it was taken up too, accompanied by the sound of wood splintering and the clanging of steel against steel.

Andrew could see into the cells across from him. The prisoners were smashing their toilets, using pieces of angle iron they had broken off their beds. Postnikoff crowded up behind Andrew.

"Those crazy fucking bastards!" he shouted. Water was running out of some cells now and dripping down from the passageway above them. The sound of porcelain cracking and breaking echoed down the passageways, backed up by the banging on the bars. There was a loud crash directly behind Andrew. He spun around just in time to see that the kid from the next cell had rushed into his, smashed his toilet and was rushing out again, brandishing a piece of iron. Water flowed across the floor, and Andrew, trying to catch the kid, slipped in it and almost fell. While he was still trying to right himself, a guard shoved him hard into his cell, knocking him down and slamming the door shut, locking him in. Postnikoff was already in his cell, standing sideways trying to see what was going on further down the row.

Cell doors were slamming shut all up and down the tiers, above and below them. Guards were shouting. Across the way the crunch of brick and cement could still be heard.

"Jesus Christ! Andy!" Postnikoff yelled to him. "Look!" In a cell directly across from them a striker, using an angle iron for a tool, had smashed clean through the wall of his cell and had climbed through the hole and stood grinning with the prisoner in the next cell. Andrew thought, this is madness!

The guards had everybody locked in now. Andrew had never seen so many guards patrolling up and down the passageways in front of the cells, threatening noisy inmates. Across the way, where the two men stood triumphantly in one cell, four guards came pounding down the passage, unlocked the door, and before either prisoner could retreat, had seized them. The prisoner who had smashed the hole in the wall cursed and struggled with the two guards who were trying to hold him. He managed to free one arm and he swung hard, catching one of the guards full in the face. The guard went down and one of the two who held the second prisoner let him go and sprang onto the first prisoner.

The three guards and one prisoner fought their way out of the cell, the fourth guard clanged the cell door shut behind them, and the guards and their screaming, struggling prisoner made their way slowly to the end of the tier and stopped. For a long moment Andrew couldn't see anything but the guards' blue-coated backs. A peaked cap went over the railing and fell slowly through the air to the floor below. Then the guards stepped back.

The prisoner hung by his handcuffed wrists from a pipe that ran along the tier just above their heads. His toes barely touched the cement floor. The men in the cells, seeing this, grew suddenly silent.

"When you settle down, we'll let you go!" a guard shouted.

"Fuck off, you lousy cop bastard!" the prisoner screamed. His voice was thick, and deep, his words barely coherent. The guards turned away, straightened their jackets, replaced their caps.

"I'll hang here forever, before . . ." his words grew unintelligible. After the guards had walked grimly away, a few voices shouted encouragement to the prisoner.

Andrew turned away, sickened. He sat down on his bunk, his feet in the pooled water, staring at his wrecked toilet, and tried to think while his heart pounded in his chest. He stared at his wrists, so thick and strong-looking. In the cell next door Postnikoff was, for once, silent.

Hours later the guards began to let out two prisoners at a time, to use the toilets in the shower rooms. Powell escorted Andrew and Postnikoff.

"It's a helluva mess, boys," he said mournfully to them when they were inside the shower room. "And me only six months from retirement." Neither of them said anything. "Had to call in the RCMP."

"The Mounties?" Postnikoff said in surprise.

"You better believe it," Powell said, nodding comfortably. "They're all around the place. Got their guns ready."

"They figure some of them Commies is going to try to break out?"

"Could be," Powell said. "They aren't taking any chances, anyway. I'll tell you boys . . ." He hesitated, looking over his shoulder as if he half-expected to find somebody in the deserted shower room. "They got machine guns. They're surrounding the place." He nodded once, firmly, watching them for their reactions.

"Holy Jesus!" Postnikoff said. "You hear that, Andy?" He whistled through his teeth.

"I heard," Andrew said heavily. As if what had already happened weren't enough. A shiver ran down his back, but he was careful to show nothing to the guard or Postnikoff.

Nobody slept much that night, judging by the coughing, and the squeaking of bedsprings. About midnight Andrew heard footsteps going down the tier, louder than the ones of the patrolling guards. He got up from his bunk and went to the door to see.

At the end of the tier and across from him, the handcuffed prisoner still hung, his head fallen forward, his black hair hanging over his eyes. He looked asleep or dead. Blood had run down his arms from his wrists to his elbows. One of the two guards spoke to him. Andrew could hear his voice rumbling softly down the passage. The prisoner didn't move or seem to reply. One guard lifted him while the other reached up and unlocked the handcuffs. His arms fell loosely, like packages to his sides. The guards each lifted one of his arms and draped it over their shoulders, then, supporting him on each side, they dragged him away.

The next day Andrew and the same four men were led out to do the farmwork. None of them had recovered from the previous day's labour, nor from their sleepless night. By evening, they were exhausted, almost too tired to care if they ate or not.

Andrew was lined up for supper with the other men when suddenly, without warning, something struck him hard on the head. He felt the blow, the pain, and something hot trickling down his face. At the same time, as his hand instinctively reached up to touch the place he'd been struck, he saw broken pieces of crockery falling around him, landing on the hard floor beside his feet.

"Up there," the man behind him said, and pointed up. There was blood on Andrew's hand where he had touched his forehead. One tier up, one of the strikers was leaning over the rail grinning down at him. "He dropped his teacup," the prisoner behind him said. Andrew wiped his face again and saw more blood on his hand from a cut above his eye. He looked up again and slowly counted from the first cell in the row to the one where the striker was sauntering back inside. He waited in line without saying a word.

When his tray was filled, he carried it back upstairs to his own cell, set it carefully on the table, noticing that his hands were trembling, walked out of his cell, stood counting the cell doors till he found the right one, and walked down the passage, past the men coming or going, till he reached it.

As Andrew stepped inside the cell, the striker, who was sitting at his table, started to rise and opened his mouth as if to say something. But Andrew had already slammed the cell door shut behind him, locking them both in. In the same motion he threw himself forward, catching the striker by the throat.

They grappled, smashing up against the brick walls, falling against the bed, which collapsed under them, sending the food on the table flying across the cement floor. The other man was strong, but Andrew was propelled by rage and he forced the other man forward, caught him with one foot, knocking him to his knees, and pushed his head over the toilet bowl. He shoved his head down and held it while he flushed the toilet.

Behind them, guards were shouting. The other man struggled free and hit Andrew in the jaw, smashing his head back against the wall. Andrew caught him with his fist, felt the satisfying crack and saw the blood well from the other man's nose.

But that was all. The guards had the door open and fell on them, pulling them apart. In seconds they were handcuffed and being shoved down the passage in front of the other inmates, down the iron stairs, stumbling and falling, being dragged up again, and down more stairs.

They were in the prison basement. Ahead of them were two steel doors facing two more identical doors, all without windows, only sliding panels inches long at the bottom. Solitary. The hole. A door on each side was opened, the handcuffs came off, each man was shoved hard inside one of the doors, which clanged shut behind them, and then there was only blackness.

Andrew's rage left him as suddenly and completely as it had come. His heart pounded in his chest and throat, and with each beat he felt his body quiver. He couldn't seem to catch his breath; sweat poured off him. He gasped for air. There was not a fragment of light around him, not a sliver.

He felt in the darkness for the door which he knew was behind him. He leaned against it, facing it, his head on one arm, exploring the cold sheet metal with his other hand. The metal grew cool against his face, calming him.

It was very quiet. Only the breathless humming of the blackness that might be inside him or outside, a part of the air.

Now he could feel the pain in the back of his head where he had hit it against the cell wall. He moved his jaw and winced at the pain. One shoulder felt as if it might be sprained. His face stung and he knew it must be a mess of scrapes and bruises. He thought of the man he had fought with and couldn't remember why he had been so angry, why he had tried to kill him.

He had tried to kill him. That was what was in his mind when he slammed the cell door shut and dove for the man's throat. If the other man hadn't been so unexpectedly strong, he would have killed him before the guards could have stopped him. Out loud he said, "I would have killed him."

It was as if he hadn't spoken. His words died in the air. I tried to kill him. I would have killed him.

He began to shiver, crossing his arms on his chest, hugging himself. He turned his back to the door and slid down the cold steel till he reached the floor, where he squatted.

He began to cry, sobs catching in his throat, choking him. He didn't know why he was crying, he didn't know what it was inside him that cried, but he felt a desolation he had been harbouring for years. He cried for all the things he hadn't done, and for all the things he had.

PART THREE

CHAPTER ONE

His son had wakened and cried sleepily for a moment when he stirred the fire and put wood on it, but the boy was asleep again before Karen was even out of bed. There wasn't time to wait for the room to warm, so Andrew dressed rapidly, pulling on his chilly clothes and sliding his feet into the cold leather of his boots. Only a few more weeks of this and they wouldn't need a fire, even at night. He lit the lantern, picked up the milk pail, and went outside.

The stars were out, high and bright in the indigo sky. Andrew watched them as he stood urinating in the limp, damp grass, thin and faded from its winter under the snow, the new green not yet started. The stars shone remotely, silently, an aeon away. His shoulders ached and he worked them slowly under his jacket. The small of his back had an ache in it too, and there was grit behind his eyelids from never getting enough sleep. He zipped up his pants and turned toward the barn.

The night's frost was still on the ground but his footsteps were silent, the pail brushing softly against his pantleg. It was still too dark to see but

177

he knew there was barely any snow left except in the bottom of the deep coulees and in places where it had banked up against buildings during the long winter. The air, too, was growing soft with spring and he breathed it deeply and felt himself begin to waken with it.

He slid open the barn door, lifting the lantern to find the handle, and picked a bridle off a nail on the wall more by feel than with the aid of the light.

"Here boy, here boy," he called softly. His saddlehorse came up behind him and nuzzled his shoulder. Andrew lifted his arm, the pungent, welcome smell of horse strong in his nostrils, and reached around the horse's neck. Prince stood still while Andrew bridled him, then led him into the barn. He would have to turn him out, chase in another saddlehorse. It didn't do to keep one in too long. It made them mean. When he threw the cold saddle onto his back, Prince shivered, then stood motionless.

Andrew sensed the horse's eagerness to go, and a longing to mount and ride with no destination in mind, the wind and the feel of his horse the only reality, swept over him. He laid his forehead against the leather of the saddle and closed his eyes. He saw the wild horses of his childhood sweeping past, heard the sighing of the herd in his ears. As if seeing the same thoughts, the horse lifted his head and pranced.

Andrew's throat constricted. He whispered, "Not today, boy." He ran his hand down the horse's silky throat, blew out the lantern, then swung into the saddle.

He rode through the corral and toward the wrangle pasture at a trot, dismounting to open the gate and then mounting again. The night was so still he knew that the creak of his saddle, his horse's hooves, even his own breathing could be heard far across the hills, if there had been anyone to hear. Once he looked back over his shoulder and knew by the yellow light in the kitchen that Karen was up, would be feeding their son, changing him, washing his chubby face and hands. He pulled his horse to a stop, both of them silent and listening in the darkness. Faintly, off to the northeast, he thought he heard a bell. He strained to hear. Yes, that was it. The mare would be bending to graze. He started out in the direction of the sound, riding slowly, he and his horse picking their way with care. He found them over the first rise, not too far away, and he was grateful. Even in the darkness he had no trouble picking out the lead mare, a white horse picked for her colour, and gradually he was able to make out the dark blot that was the rest of the herd. He started them back toward the gate. When they descended into a low spot he could make out only the white lead mare, but when they topped a rise, he saw their outlines clearly against the sky: a dozen and a half of them, six saddle horses, the rest workhorses. He pushed them across the field and through the gate toward the corrals.

Some mornings it was ten o'clock before he managed, working alone, to get them into the corral, the day half gone and the work not even started. They must be hungry, he thought. There was no grass left in the fields and he had only a few oat bundles left for feed. One by one he caught the six horses he would use today, and curried each one, feeling carefully to make sure there were no lumps or raw spots on the shoulders where the collar would go. Then he harnessed each horse and led it to its stall, tied it, and filled its manger with a small amount of oats.

As he led the last horse into the barn, a glow was spreading along the eastern horizon. He tied the horse and went back to look. Where the blackness of the shadowed prairie met the sky there was no colour at all, only space. He found it hard to look at that emptiness, yet some urgent unquenchable yearning brought him each morning to stare into it as if he expected to find something there. It was as if the world had been abandoned. He glanced again, and saw that the space was now tinged faintly green; above it, faintly yellow; then a deeper blue which gradually shaded into the indigo of night. The stars were pale, and the darkness at last was lifting.

He mounted Prince again and rode back out to the wrangle pasture, found the milk cow, chased her into the corral, then tied her in the barn and sat down to milk her.

He did not think of anything, watching the milk, bluish-white, foaming up the sides of the pail. He lay his forehead against the cow's warm flank. The horses chewed, their harnesses now and then clinking, their great hooves scraping the straw scattered on the barn floor. He could smell the fresh manure, hear it plopping now and then onto the wooden floor. He breathed in the smell of milk and cow, and his hands and wrists moved of their own volition.

When he was finished milking it was light enough to make out his fifty head of cows moving about on the slope of the land to the west and south. He would ride out as soon as he could and check the new calves, see if any of the cows were having trouble calving. His stomach tensed as he thought of it, so much work to be done, the sky lifting, soon to be filled with light. The day would whip by, in no time it would be dark again and not enough done. Never enough done, no matter how hard he worked.

Karen took the pail from him without speaking. He hung his jacket by the door, tossed his cap onto the nail beside it, washed his hands in the basin of water set out for him, and then drank a long drink of water. "I'll be out of water by night," she said, her back to him at the stove. Andrew smoothed down Alan's fine baby hair and touched his cheek before he sat down at the table. The baby lifted his arm and waved it, chanting happily to himself.

"Dada, dada." Andrew smiled, contentment flooding him.

"I'll bring more in before I go out to the field," he said to Karen. "There's no hurry," she said. "Noon or even tonight is soon enough." She turned to him, a mug of steaming coffee in one hand and his plate of hot food in the other.

"How's the firewood?"

"I'll look after that," she said. He glanced at her stomach pushing out her neat white apron.

"No chopping wood when you're expecting," he said. "I'll chop some before I go to the field."

"You'd think I was made out of glass," she said, without rancour. She lifted Alan down from his high chair, smoothed his hair, and let him go.

"Just common sense," he said gruffly. "You gotta save your strength." She had had a hard labour with Alan. They were both afraid of what might be coming this time. He would take her to town, where there was a doctor, at least a week before she was due. She would be too scared to protest then. Andrew watched Karen in the corner of the room, straining the milk, with Alan at her feet, playing with some toy horses Andrew had bought for him.

When he had finished eating and drained the last of his coffee, Andrew stood, put on his jacket and his hat, and went to the door. Karen followed him. He bent to kiss her hair, but she lifted her face to his and their mouths met and held. He sensed the softness of her breasts and the smooth mound of her belly through the heavy canvas of his jacket. She lifted her arms and held him. Involuntarily he moved against her, then pulled away.

"Got work to do," he reminded her, his voice husky. Her cheeks were flushed and her dark eyes shone softly at him. He almost relented, but no, maybe tonight, if he wasn't too tired.

He kissed her cheek, and went out the door and around to the wood-pile. The heat and goodness of her body stayed with him and his feet were uncertain on the rough ground. The prairie seemed to lift to meet the morning light and meadowlarks had begun to call. He tried to think of his coming together with Karen, but could remember none of it. With other women, when he rode away from them, his mind had been filled with what they had done and said, and how, but with Karen it had never been that way. When he entered her, he entered another world, and he could never remember her body after, only that dark and resonating world they went into gratefully together.

He had chopped enough wood to last her till he came in at noon. On the nearby prairie the cattle were beginning to bawl, looking for feed, but the last of the Russian thistle was gone. Soon the new grass would start and they would wander again, ranging four or five miles beyond the buildings.

The horses he had harnessed were waiting for him, their feed all gone. He led them out and hitched them together. Then he gathered the reins and began the half mile walk out to the field. As he walked, he tried to think of ways to raise a little cash. Tomorrow he would harness a bronc into the middle of the team, that was one way to break them, so he would have a few to sell. As soon as he was done seeding, he'd halter-break a few more young horses from his big herd, so they would be ready to break as soon as he could find the time.

But underneath this stream of rapid, industrious ideas, another part of him flowed silently. It was a stream which he never articulated, rarely even listened to, except maybe when he was drunk, or too tired to suppress it. It ran deep and it said, I am a man. A man. Everything depends on me. And then the question he didn't want to think about. What is life for? But when it came too close, he pushed it away with thoughts of ground to be broken, harness to repair, horses to be doctored, or he thought of the war some of his neighbours were going to.

He hitched the team to the drill, backing them up and edging them forward till he had them right. They made an even start at his command and he resolved that tomorrow for sure he would start a couple of broncs since these were all well-broken now. Most of his income still came from his horse sales; he had to keep working at breaking his herd. He should have ridden out last night and chased them in but it might have meant twenty miles on horseback by the time he was done and he'd been too tired after a long day riding the drill.

Over twenty acres he'd done yesterday, he estimated. He looked out over the field. Another seventy acres broken. With feed in such short supply the calves were none too good, but if there was any moisture this year, a hundred and fifty acres of spring wheat would go a long way to paying off his bank loan.

He didn't like farming. It was boring, dirty, hard work with none of the compensations of ranching. With cattle you had the pleasure of working with living creatures every day, of watching them grow and change and act the way that animals did. You could run with the antelope if the spirit moved you, or you could rest on a hillside, your hat over your face, while they grazed around you. Machinery was ugly, noisy, full of sharp corners and edges waiting to tear your clothes, to cut and bruise you, and as if that weren't enough, it was always breaking down. He farmed because he had to for survival, but he begrudged every inch of grazing land he'd already broken and he swore he wouldn't break another inch.

The seed drill hit another rock but he was braced for it this time, and hardly felt the jolt. The drill lifted and fell again, and he swayed with its movement. The horses plodded on, swishing their tails. A hawk looking for mice circled above them. Every once in a while Andrew looked out beyond the pale field he was seeding to the prairie beyond, soothing his eyes with the serene beauty of the grassland. When he was better established he would let his farmland go back to grass.

At noon, he unhitched the horses, drove them back to the barn, took their harnesses off and chased them out to graze. He had no feed left and they weren't strong enough to work a full day without a good rest. He would use the time to check his cows.

The noon meal was ready when he entered the house. Karen had seen him working in the corral and was waiting for him at the door.

"You look tired," she said. He nodded and hung his hat on the hook by the door and then took off his jacket.

"I think I'll lie down for a minute before dinner," he said.

"Good," she said, and went to the stove. He went into the living room and lay down on the couch. In a second he was asleep, dreaming of horses with manes so long they touched the ground, fields thick with green grass. He descended further into sleep and did not dream at all.

"It's ready, Andy." Karen was bending awkwardly over him, shaking his shoulder, resting one warm hand on his cheek. For a minute he didn't know where he was.

"How long have I . . ." he asked, rising so quickly that she had to jump back to avoid being struck by his head.

"It's all right," she said quickly. "Only fifteen minutes." He fell back to a sitting position on the couch again, his hands over his face. A pain had settled into the small of his back, and his shoulders and arms ached from pulling on the reins. He wanted to stay where he was, never move again. In the kitchen Alan was banging his spoon against his plate and singing cheerfully to himself. Karen bent forward and kissed his hands, which still covered his face. He dropped them and caught one of hers and held it for a second before letting it go. She watched him, her eyes worried.

"You okay?" she asked. He nodded, rising. She turned without waiting for him to say anything more and went into the kitchen.

When he reached the door, he leaned against it, his eyes closed. The temptation to quit, to give up, was almost overpowering. He wanted to sink to the floor and sleep forever, but the door frame held him, he could hear his child cooing softly in the other room, he could smell his dinner cooking, and he remembered Karen waiting for him, depending on him, another child coming.

Anger rose in him. It pushed him away from the door and he strode to the basin which she had filled with water for him and splashed it up onto his hands and face and the back of his neck. Then he took the towel she offered him and scrubbed his face till it felt hot and raw. He stood for a minute till he felt the anger subsiding enough that he thought he could eat without his hands shaking.

When he lifted his head, Karen was coming toward him, her eyes on the platter of meat she was carrying carefully, using a cloth to protect her hands from the heat. He wondered if she had let him sleep longer than fifteen minutes. He was angry again, but love for her welled up in him, and he couldn't help smiling.

"You feeling all right?" he asked her.

"I feel fine," she said, surprised. He remembered suddenly the day he returned from prison, climbing down from the train, how despairing he had felt, all alone in the world, and she was waiting for him, came running with her arms open. He would love her forever, he would never stop loving her, for that alone.

After he had finished eating he went back to the barn, mounted Prince and rode him out to the field to check the cows. They were calving wherever they could find a dry spot where the sun would warm them. It had been a hard winter and they were weak from that and from the poor feed. He hoped not too many of them had slipped their calves after suffering through a blizzard or a stretch of forty below weather. He decided to head north and work his way back.

Prince soon stretched out and Andrew, knowing better, let him go anyway. The sun was at its zenith now and it warmed him and brought the smell of spring to his nostrils. They ran across the drying prairie, through the faded dead grass, up and down the hillsides, skirting rocks and badger holes and patches of cactus. Andrew felt briefly young again and carefree.

But then they topped a rise, he rose in his stirrups to look around and saw to the west a dark spot on the hillside. A cow. He rode at a trot toward it, gophers scrambling out of his way and a flock of horned larks lifting in front of him. Far to the north a pair of hawks were circling, their piercing cries carried to him on the wind.

For a minute he thought the cow was dead, but when they were a hundred yards away she began to struggle, tryhing to rise, and he slowed Prince to a walk so as not to alarm her. At her side, he dismounted and walked around her slowly, studying her condition.

An older cow, one that had done worse than most over the winter. He could have counted every rib. She was dilated and he could see one small hoof protruding. She was so weak she could not get up. The calf was sure to be dead.

He swore out loud. He should have quit seeding sooner and checked the cows earlier, at daylight. Now he had a mess on his hands; a dead calf, a cow that might die, too. All the things he had to do, all his responsibilities came into his mind, and he felt overwhelmed, doubted he could handle all of them. He thought of Karen and his child, the child about to come, the ranch he was struggling to build, and all his wasted youth that lay behind him.

He went to his horse and unfastened the light, strong rope that hung on his saddle opposite his lariat. As he approached the cow she tried to rise again but couldn't, and he fastened the rope around the small hoof. He took off his jacket and rolled his right shirt sleeve above his elbow. The cow mooed and broke off in mid-sound, expelling air soundlessly. Her head fell back. He felt inside her.

The calf was turned the wrong way and it was dead. He tried to find the other leg. A contraction seized his arm, almost paralyzing it. As it subsided he found he couldn't move his arm. He waited and gradually the strength returned. He closed his eyes and tried to get a picture of what he was feeling with his arm and hand inside that tight space.

At last he found the other back leg and began to work it to the opening. It took him a good five minutes but he managed to bring it around and out so that a pair of hooves protruded now. At least it hadn't been dead long enough to smell.

He loosened the loop on the end of the rope and expanded it so that it enclosed both hooves, and pulled it tight. He stood up and started backing away, playing the rope through his hands till he judged the length was right for the most effective pull. He wrapped the rope around his waist, then around his hands, and began to pull slowly, gradually exerting more pressure. He was not able to move the calf at all. He'd have to use his horse.

He dropped the light rope and went to Prince, untied the lariat, fastened one end to the saddle horn and the other to the end of the calf-pulling rope. Then he backed Prince up till the long rope was stretched taut between the cow and the horse. He leaned hard on the rope, trying to force the calf out. Prince backed away, trying to keep the rope tight, but the cow dragged toward him as he pulled.

"Whoa, boy." Prince stood quietly, letting the rope fall slack. Andrew patted his neck absently, studying the situation. A flicker of movement caught his eye and he looked over his shoulder. A coyote sat on the hillside fifty feet away. Andrew searched the horizon all around him. There'd be a mate somewhere. He sighed. He'd have to cut the calf out. There was no other way.

He looked up at the sky, growing paler every day now with the approaching summer. He looked down at his boots, shabby and covered with dust even though it was still only early April. Another dry year. Would it never rain again?

On the ground in front of him was a dying cow and a dead calf that he would have to cut into pieces inside her, trying not to cut her uterus or himself. He would have to bring out the pieces one by one. He remembered the stench of the last one he had cut out of a cow. Dead three days. When he had tried to cut off a leg it had pulled off in his hand, still inside the cow. Nausea choked him and he retched onto the dead yellow grass, then straightened, disgusted with himself. He had only fifty cows, he couldn't afford to lose even one.

He reached into his pocket for his knife, brought it out, and slowly pulled out the blade. He knelt behind the cow on the damp grass, the knife-blade open, the little hooves near his hand. Behind him the coyote yipped, then began to howl.

When it was done, he walked a few feet down the hillside to a burnout filled with melting snow and washed his arm and hands in the freezing water. It was mid-afternoon and he had seeded maybe eight acres. He splashed more cold water onto his arm and scrubbed with his fingers till it was clean. Then he rolled his sleeve down and buttoned the cuff. He wiped the blade of his knife on the clean grass, then swished it through the bloodied water and dried it on his neck scarf.

The cow was moving again, trying to rise. Give her an hour, he thought, and she'll be up, looking for water and feed. He studied her with grim satisfaction. She'd be all right. He looked up at the sun again. Three o'clock and he still had to check the rest of the herd.

He rode for another hour through the herd, but everything seemed all right, all the pairs matched, and none of the cows having trouble delivering. Instead of stopping at the barn and leaving Prince there, he rode out to where the workhorses had been grazing while he was riding, chased them into the corral, dismounted, leaving Prince tied in the barn, harnessed the six horses and hitched them together again, walked them out to the field, and hitched them back to the drill.

He gathered the reins, mounted the drill, and slapped the team into motion. The jolting began again, and the long ride up and down the field through the turning earth, the dust beginning to rise in the light breeze, and the day cooling as the sun dropped lower. He hunched into his jacket and swayed with the contours of the earth as the seeder moved over it.

He thought of the calf he had just cut into pieces. The smell of its blood hung on him. The horses plodded on. He would have to sell his calves again this year. There was no hope of keeping even some of the bull calves in order to switch to the more profitable business of selling two-year-old steers. There were land taxes to pay, as well as the banker. If he missed them, he would lose everything. He had seen too many neighbours lose their land during the last ten years because they couldn't even pay their taxes, small as they were.

The day wore on. He was hungry and the pain had settled like an iron bar across his back. He set his jaw and kept going.

His mind slipped from active thought and worry into a dreaming state. He forgot he was riding the seeder, forgot the flies, the pain across his back, forgot even his hunger. He thought about his life in a long series of silent, but magically clear pictures. He saw the women he had known rising before him, felt their breath on him, their warmth warming him, their eyes clear and distant staring beyond him. He thought of their monthly bleeding, silent as the moon; he thought of their pain in childbirth, and wondered why it should be their lot and not his. He thought of the power of their love.

How he had loved women. For a long time the meeting of his flesh with theirs had seemed to him to be what his life was for. He had gone from one to another, their lovely flesh pulling at him, his own body pulling along an inner him in a bewildered fashion, without agreement. He had been insatiable. Now he no longer knew why he'd done it, or what he had thought he would eventually find with them.

He had found Karen, he told himself. And something had grown between them so that one day he found that his old need had been cast off and left behind, outgrown. Gradually he came back to the jolting of the seeder, to the nose flies and deerflies tormenting the horses. The sky still sang above him, pale and high and vast. The earth lay below, a pale brown, moist, its faint odour rising to him. He felt the reins in his hands, heard the rattle of the chain and the squeak of leather.

He remembered that he still had to chase the horses in so that he could cut out some broncs and break them, also remembered that Karen needed water and that he still had to chop wood. The sun was low in the sky behind him now. If he didn't leave the field right now, it would be too dark to find his herd and chase them in.

He climbed off the drill and began methodically to unhitch the horses. They were tired, although they'd only put in a short day, and they wouldn't go any faster than a plodding walk on the way back to the barn. By the time he arrived in the barn it was nearly seven.

Karen came out of the house as he was taking off their harnesses, and called to him.

"Andy? Are you coming in?" He shouted over his shoulder, "After I chase in the horses."

"Come and eat first," she called, starting across the yard toward the corral where he was.

"Haven't got time," he called back. She was leaning against the railing now across the corral from him. "I have to get them in before it gets dark." She watched him silently for a moment as he finished taking the harness off the last horse.

"You'll kill yourself," she said. He laughed. "Please Andy," she said. He didn't turn his head, didn't answer her. He went into the barn, took a few of the last of the oat bundles and scattered them in the feed trough. She was still watching him from the railing.

"Go on," he said. "Alan'll be getting into some trouble." She didn't move. At last he looked over at her and saw the stubborn chin, the worry in her dark eyes. "I'm not going to kill myself," he said, filled with impatience. "Anyway, you know what has to be done." He had stopped working and was looking fiercely at her from across the corral. Some of the tension left her face.

"Yes," she said slowly, turning her head to look back at the house. "It's only that I love you," she added, looking back at him.

"I know that," he said. Then, "I love you, too." They looked at each other for a long moment. "Seeding'll soon be finished," he said, "calving, too." She nodded, and without speaking again, left him there. He watched her cross the yard and go into the house. He remembered the water again, and the wood that still had to be chopped.

The horses had cleaned up the oat bundles in minutes. He chased them out into the wrangle pasture for the night and, leaving the corral gate open, rode Prince out to the far field where his herd of horses was kept. He hoped they wouldn't be too hard to find since he had only an hour of daylight left and they could be hard to chase. He really needed a couple of men to help him, but he couldn't afford to hire anybody and all his neighbours were busy now with their own work. He rode on, the fading, bluish light distorting distances, making the thin grass look white and grey.

They were grazing along the fenceline on the north side of the field. He came on them suddenly, his mind elsewhere. He was very tired, might even have fallen asleep in the saddle, when suddenly, there they were, their ears up, already starting to mill.

The lead horse of one of the bunches whinnied, raising her head, and they started to move, slowly at first, then gathering speed. He urged Prince, who needed no telling, and they were off, trying to cut off one bunch and direct them toward the open gate. The mare in the lead was an old horse, one who had been through this many times before and knew what was expected of her. For once it looked like she was going to do it. She thinks I've got feed, Andrew thought, and wished for the thousandth time that spring that he had.

There were about twenty horses in this bunch, enough to find what he needed and he made no attempt to cut out any more. He followed them as they raced up the hillsides and down. As they approached the gate, they slowed, and for one heart-stopping minute he thought they might veer off before entering. But no, the mare hesitated, then raced on through, the bunch following her. He urged Prince to his top speed, afraid that he might lose them between this gate and the corrals further on ahead.

But even this went right. The mare led them straight across the small field, through the open gate, and into the corral. He raced behind them, anxious to close the gate on them before something startled them. It was twilight now, the sky to the west blazing with creamy yellow light, turning everything an even darker hue, and spreading long shadows out over the ground inside the corrals. He dismounted and led Prince to the second gate, opening into the smaller pen where he would do his cutting. As he opened the gate, Karen came up behind him.

"What are you doing out here?" he asked, surprised.

"Alan's asleep," she said. "I came to help."

You shouldn't be in the corral with these rangy-tangs," he said. "You can't move fast enough anymore." She had tied a red scarf over her dark hair. In the twilight, he could see her eyes glowing.

"Nuts," she said, and he had to laugh. She turned away and walked to the far end of the corral where the horses were clustered. She walked the herd up toward him and the open gate. He fastened the gate open, mounted, and followed her.

"I want that dark one," he called to her, "and that bay." She looked the horses over, following his pointing finger, then nodded, her bright scarf catching what was left of the light. A deep rose was bleeding along the horizon to the west now, and pigeons started up from the roof of the barn, cooing noisily.

Together they chased a half dozen of the horses into the small pen and closed the gate. Andrew stayed on the inside, unfurling his rope, while Karen leaned on the fence to watch him work. It was almost dark.

"You go in," he called to her. "I don't want you out here in the dark. I'll cut them two out, throw 'em a little feed, do a couple of chores, and then I'll be in." Reluctantly, she left him. He watched her open and close the gate into the corral instead of climbing it as she usually did. He thought of her coming labour, his horse stepping under him so that his back swayed and he had to tighten his legs. If he lost her. But the thought was gone that quickly because he had to cut out the two horses he wanted right away before all the light was gone and since he had no feed he also had to chase the remaining horses back out to their field.

He did his cutting surely and precisely, then dismounted to open the gate, remounted and prepared to chase the rest of the herd out. But they needed no urging, were through the open gate at once and streaming out toward the open fields. He rode in a loop out around them, turning them so they would head for the gate he had brought them in through.

So yesterday had been, so tomorrow would be. He had lost count of the days and of the years that he had been working. He leaned against the corral and looked for the moon, but it had not yet risen, and the night was growing cold. He shivered, then stretched to relieve the muscles in his back. There was still the firewood to cut.

He picked up the lantern he had left in the barn, felt in his pocket for matches, and lit the lantern. It flared up, lighting a small corner of the barn warmly, the smell of horses and straw filling his senses, and he wanted to lie down on the floor and sleep till the morning light woke him.

But instead, carrying the lantern, he walked out of the barn, through the corral and around to the side of the house, where a square of light from the kitchen window fell on the woodpile. He set the lantern down, jerked the axe free from the chopping block and began to split the wood, old fenceposts, mostly.

The axe rose and fell, its blade glinting in the yellow light. He raised his numbed arms, steadying the chunk of wood with one hand, then withdrew it, and dropped the axe with a practised motion. The wood split, he threw the pieces aside onto the pile growing in the shadow against the house, found another, lifted his axe, and let it fall.

The sound of the axe on the wood rang in the cold still air. He could see his breath now when he bent over to pick up another chunk. At some point he seemed to wake, as though he had been sleeping as he chopped, and saw that he had enough wood to last through the night and well into the next morning.

Wearied beyond words or feeling, he dropped the axe, then picked it up again and replaced it in the split in the chopping block. He gathered an armload of wood and carried it around the house to the door which Karen held open for him as he approached.

When he had dropped his armload into the woodbox, she helped him take off his cap and then his jacket, and pulled out a chair for him to collapse into. She tried to kneel to help him pull off his boots.

"No," he said softly, touching her face with the palm of one hand. She rose clumsily, smiling shyly, and kissed his forehead. Slowly he pulled off his boots while she went to the stove and opened the oven door. The smell of roasting beef rushed out at him, and his hunger returned, even through his exhaustion. Alan, sleeping in his crib in their bedroom, the room that had been Andrew's since he was a child, turned and fretted in his sleep, then grew silent.

"God, I'm tired," he said. She set his plate in front of him, then sat down across from him, rising now and then to get him coffee or more bread.

"Are you feeling okay?" he asked her.

"I'm fine," she said at once. He frowned, studying her and she blushed and lowered her eyes. He remembered then that she needed water and half-rose as though to go and get it at once. She touched his arm to stop him.

"I brought in a couple of pails," she said. "I was careful," before he could protest.

192

"That's my job, he said gruffly, embarrassed.

"Maybe it'll rain soon," she said softly. He grunted.

"What time is it?"

"Nearly ten," she replied. He yawned, could hardly keep his eyes open. It seemed to him that at this moment he was happy. They sat in silence across from each other, their child sleeping in the other room. He felt peace permeating the room, the small house. It seemed to seep in from the darkened hills and fields that stretched endlessly outside their door.

Somewhere out there, only the eagles were awake, flying, formidable and black, like prehistoric birds, with a rush of wind over the earth. But he and his woman and his child were safe together, here in the house of his childhood and his future.

CHAPTER TWO

The sun was tinting the eastern horizon yellow when they arrived in the pasture to begin rounding up. The morning was cool, they always were in early October, the sky cloudless. They rode in darkness, the long shadows meeting around them. High above them the sky was still dark, a glittering dome that descended on all sides but the east to contain the grassy plain across which they rode. In this moment between night and day the air had a crystalline texture, so pure that Andrew felt transformed by it, as if he had left the house that morning and, without design, had ridden into a vast and holy temple. He could not recognize himself in it.

Beside him Alan rode silently on his pony, a silhouette, still half-asleep. Andrew remembered himself at eight, riding alone to the big fall roundups. On his other side, just as silently, rode Frank Philipow, a neighbour Andrew had hired to help trail the cattle to the railroad.

Gathering the forty-five head was easy work. Andrew had done the hard work himself the previous two days, finding and cutting out from the main herd the twenty-five steers and the dozen heifers he wanted to market, then filling out the load with culled cows and chasing them into this field separate from the rest of his cattle. Now all they had to do was trail them cross-country to the town twenty-five miles to the north where the train stopped and where they would be weighed, loaded, and shipped out for slaughter.

Full morning was on them as, pushing the herd ahead of them, they reached the gate at the northern edge of the field. When they were through and the gate closed behind them, Andrew said to Alan, pointing to the north, "We're heading that way, son. Frank and I will take the flanks—and you ride along the back. Keep 'em moving." Alan nodded. He looked up at Andrew with wide eyes, his lips tightened. Something in his face made Andrew suspect that in their tiny house Alan had heard his argument with Karen the night before.

He hesitated, wanting to say something to reassure the boy, but couldn't find the right words. He re-mounted.

"Push 'em easy," he said. "Don't want 'em moving too fast, losing weight. We got a long way to go."

In a moment the herd was re-grouped and moving in roughly the right direction. While he was riding, out of the corner of his eyes, Andrew watched Alan. The boy knew what to do and his small horse worked well for him, Andrew wouldn't keep a horse that wouldn't work, and he saw too that the boy was like a leech in the saddle. Like I was, he thought. He smiled to himself. Still, Alan didn't have nearly the experience he'd had at the same age.

He lifted his head and looked across the field to the pale, even hills they would have to pass through. A herd of antelope, at least a hundred of them, were grazing to the northwest, their white rumps clearly defined against the yellow-grey hills. "Alan," he called, his barely-lifted voice carrying easily over the distance between them, and pointed. The boy turned his head and as they watched, the herd stood motionless, heads up and turned toward them, began slowly to move, then gathered speed and flowed out of sight around a hill. On the far side Frank took off his hat, smoothed his short, grey hair and replaced the hat securely. "They always gather in the fall," Andrew called, his eyes still on the spot where they had vanished. When he was young he had kept up with them, even passed them on a good horse, and left them behind. This was one of the reasons he wanted his son with him, but he had been unable to explain this to Karen.

"He's too young to ride for two whole days," she had pleaded. "Andy, he's only eight. He's a little boy."

"When I was eight," he had said, "I was riding in roundups at the Willow Creek post eight miles before daylight, and by myself. At least he'll have me with him."

"That was different," she said, "and besides, he should be in school."

"No, it's not different," he insisted, still trying to convince her by argument. He ignored her remark about school. It wasn't worth replying to. "He's going to be a man soon," he said. "He's got to learn. He's got to get hardened in. I can't have him soft."

"Soft!" she had exclaimed, colour rising in her face. "He's eight years old!"

"You don't understand," he said. Then, "I'm taking him." There was a silence.

"Oh, Andy," she said, reverting to pleading. "Can't you see that the hard childhood you had isn't necessary for our kids? Don't you want their lives to be better than ours were?" He stared at her, surprised. Was that what she thought?

"It wasn't hard!" he said. "My god, Karen, I loved it!"

"But Alan isn't you . . ."

"If I just could get the chance to show him . . ."

"Andy, he's too young."

"He's coming with me."

There had been more, neither of them submitting to the other. They had gone to their bed in his mother's parlour in silence, undressing on opposite sides of the room, then lying stiffly beside each other. Finally, in the darkness he had said, "You've got three more to look after. I'll be taking one of 'em off your hands for a few days."

"I know," she said after a long pause. Her voice was muffled by the darkness and filled with what he thought he recognized as sadness. It echoed in his own inner being and he reached under the feather quilt and the rough sheets and found her plump arm.

"And none but Alan even in school yet," he said softly. She had turned to him then and clung to him and he had wakened and met her loneliness with his own.

But, he thought, spurring his horse to head a rebellious steer back into the herd, she still thinks I'm wrong. Settling into his saddle again he looked back to Alan. The boy was turning his horse in a tight circle, leaning over the side staring down at the ground. He lifted his head.

"Look, Dad, buffalo horns. Can I pick them up?"

"Nope," Andrew called back. "Got no place to carry 'em. You'll see plenty of 'em."

In the late morning when they were deep in the grassy, rolling hills, the cattle found an untouched patch of thick grass, immediately stopped and spread out to graze. The riders tried to get them moving, but as they prodded one animal into taking a few steps, then left him to chase another one, the one they had left would stop and go back to grazing.

"I guess we'll have to let 'em fill up," Andrew said, after a few tries. The three of them sat together on horseback and watched the cattle. They were grazing in a dried-up slough bottom and up the slopes of the hills that surrounded it.

"No sign of water," Frank remarked. He and Andrew had hardly spoken all morning. Each had settled in for a long chase and rode easy and quiet, dreaming in the saddle, hour after hour, while Alan trotted, turned, hummed to himself, went off to run in the hills by himself, then came back again. Andrew was counting on finding water somewhere along the way, but there were no guarantees, you never knew if you would or not.

"Hey, look," Alan said, such excitement in his voice that Andrew had to smile. Both men looked in time to see a tiny buff-coloured owl disappear down a gopher hole. "What was that?"

"Burrowing owl, boy," Andrew said. "You won't see many of them." As if in reply a gopher across the slough set up a long whistle that floated across the pocked, grassy slough-bottom to where they sat.

"She's good grass here," Frank remarked. "Whose land are we on?"

"Jake St. Clair's, I think," Andrew said. "Thought he lost all this during the Depression." The day was still, the sky the deep blue of late fall.

There was no sound now but the rustle of the cattle moving slowly through the short dry grass, their heads down. High above them a pair of hawks circled soundlessly and a jackrabbit, his coat already partly turned for winter, bounded by, paused motionless only a few feet from them with his ears up, then leaped away.

"Worked off the taxes, I heard, building road over at Chinook."

"Oh," Frank said. He was a short, heavily-muscled man with broad shoulders and a face deformed by the kick of a horse. He dismounted now, slowly. "I did that myself," he said. "Had to bring your own team and wagon, your own fresno and feed for your horses and yourself and they gave you six bucks a day for your trouble."

"Dad, I'm thirsty," Alan said, bored by their conversation. Andrew and Frank laughed.

"Thirsty are you, sonny?" Frank said, his caved-in cheekbone more obvious with his hat off. "It ain't even a hot day." Alan waited, looking from one man to the other. Andrew got down off his horse and began to lead him away up a low hill. There was no wind, they'd wait up where they could see all of the herd and where the ground was sure to be dry. The other two followed, Alan sliding down off his pony when they reached the top. They sat down on the grass, holding the reins loosely, their horses' heads just above them.

"There'll be cattle up ahead then," Frank said, spitting a yellow gob against a clump of sage. "Have to push 'em out of the way before we bring ours by."

"Dad? Can I have a drink?"

"No water, son," Andrew said. The boy was silent, staring up at him.

"How're we gonna carry water?" Andrew asked him, not looking for a reply. Alan looked down at his boots, his small hands resting in the grass on each side of his thighs.

"Never carry water," Frank said. "Have to learn to ride without it. It's worse in the summer.' He lay back, tilting his hat over his face.

"Gee," Alan said after a minute. His voice broke a little in the middle of the word, but he said nothing more. Andrew was proud of him, relented a little.

"Maybe we'll find some good water along the way. Anyway, we got food." Frank sat up again, replacing his hat on his head and sniffing, then spitting once more. Andrew went to his horse and took a loaf of Karen's good bread out of his saddlebags, and a chunk of salt pork. Frank already had his knife out. Karen had wanted him to take an apple for Alan but he had refused.

They half-cut, half-pulled off chunks of the bread and ate it with chewy pieces of smoked, salted pork. Below them the cattle grazed peacefully under the warm midday sun. A distant coyote howled morosely and another from some far-off point in the hills answered him. Frank had fallen asleep and Alan lay beside Andrew on his side, one knee pulled up, sound asleep too. He smiled down at him. My son, he thought. Karen was wrong to try to baby him.

But still, he felt badly when he thought about her. It was a hard life for her. Tomorrow night was the community fowl supper and they would miss it and the dance that followed. It was the biggest event of the fall.

"Couldn't you wait?" she had asked him, her voice wistful, when he had said they would be trailing cattle the coming week.

"How can I wait?" he had asked, guilt making him angry. "The buyer's been here, he wants 'em, and besides, the weather might not hold. I've got to get 'em out." She hadn't said anything. She never complained when he disappointed her like this. Sometimes he thought he would feel better about it if she would shout at him and complain. But she had only turned from her work at the counter to stare absently out the window.

"I was going to make raisin pies this year," she had murmured. "Maybe one apple." Her tone of voice, the way she turned away, scared him. He would have to try harder to get her out more before she turned funny on him like so many of the women did. At least she didn't cry, he thought. He wouldn't stand a chance if she cried.

There was no way they could get back in time for the fowl supper. The train they were loading the cattle on wouldn't even arrive before noon the day after next and it would take them the better part of a day to get home again.

Well, the cattle came first. She knew that. Maybe next year things would work out better. And in another year or two John would be old enough to come and in another six or so Kevin would come too. He lay back and looked up at the sky, his hat tilted forward to shade his eyes. The sky was so vast, so distant, would it never speak to him?

By evening they had reached Ernie Turquotte's. They left the cattle in a nearby field and rode up to Ernie's bachelor shack. It was the same one he had built when he came forty years ago. Smoke rose from the shaky chimney, and the woody odour, carried to them on the crisp evening air, smelled of warmth and comfort.

Ernie opened his door and came out in his stocking feet, stooping to avoid hitting his head on the doorframe. He looked up at them sitting on their horses, rubbed his grizzled chin, a lock of dirty, grey hair falling in one eye. When he grinned they saw he had no teeth.

"Evenin'," he said.

"Nice evening," Andrew said, leaning on his saddlehorn. The western sky blazed red behind the shack, casting it in shadow.

"No snow yet," Ernie remarked.

"Don't even feel it on the air," Frank said. But this was not true. The evening was chilly. They had begun to see their white breaths in the air in front of them.

"You comin' through with cattle?" Ernie asked, lifting one arm to lean it against the doorframe. He thrust the other hand through one of his frayed suspenders and rested it on his belly.

"That's right," Andrew said. "Trying to make the train on Thursday."

"Where'd you leave 'em?" Ernie asked. Andrew nodded toward the southeast. "They'll be good there," Ernie said. "You boys better come in, have some grub, stay the night."

"They ain't had water all day," Andrew said.

"There's a slough in that field. Good water in it," Ernie said. "It's toward the middle." There was a pause while Andrew debated.

"I'd better chase them down there. Strange field, they might not find it."

He nodded to Frank and Alan. "You two go ahead with Ernie. I'll only be a minute." Frank protested that he would go, but only half-heartedly. He was more than ten years older than Andrew, and Andrew knew he would be feeling a full day in the saddle and there were a couple more to come.

"That your boy?" Ernie asked, thrusting his chin toward Alan, who sat motionless and silent.

"That's right," Andrew said. "My oldest."

"First time chasing cows, eh?" he said. "Never figured you for a family man." He cackled, tobacco juice oozing out the corner of his mouth and trickling down his chin. Andrew grinned.

"Never did either," he said.

He left Alan and Frank following Ernie to the ramshackle barn where they would feed, water, and stable their horses for the night, while he back-tracked at a lope, he was rapidly losing light, to the field where they had left his cattle. He roused them from where they were grazing or where they lay resting on the grass, and moved them toward the slough. When the lead cows were drinking, he rode through the October night back to the shelter and warmth of the shack.

In the morning they were on the trail again. Alan had eaten a huge breakfast. He had been so tired when they had arrived at the shack that he fell asleep immediately and Andrew couldn't even rouse him to eat supper.

"All he asked for was water," Ernie said, laughing. "As soon as he got it, he fell asleep." Andrew watched the boy surreptitiously. He looked rested enough. For a moment Andrew had been worried, what would Karen say if he brought Alan home sick? What if the boy wasn't as strong as he was at that age? Then he shrugged his shoulders, irritated with himself and with her. Since the measles at four Alan hadn't been sick a day that Andrew could remember, and he'd always had good food, better than Andrew had when he was a boy. There wasn't a thing wrong with him but too much babying. A few trips like this would make a man of him.

By nightfall they had arrived at a field outside the town, not far from the stockyards. Again they locked the cattle in and rode into town in the dark. Alan was so tired he could no longer sit right in his saddle, his feet dangled uselessly in his stirrups and his back had long since lost its straightness.

They left their horses in one of the pens in the stockyard and Frank and Alan waited, squatting in the grass on the outside of the corrals while Andrew went to a nearby house. The Shillingtons milked a few cows, which they kept in their yard on the edge of town, and they were always willing to sell a little of their feed to the horsemen who came looking for it.

It was a cold night, colder than the one before and by the time they arrived at the Strauss house on the far side of town they were thoroughly chilled. They had walked through the dark, quiet streets, their boot heels clumping on the board sidewalks, their spurs jingling, dogs barking at them. Every once in a while Alan stumbled and almost fell. Andrew, without thinking, reached down and took the boy's hand. It was so unexpectedly small that he was shocked and overwhelmed by a tenderness that he had tried to stifle for years, since Alan was no longer a baby. He wanted to pick him up and cradle him in his arms. Instead he said, "The Strausses will put us up, Alan. They used to live near us years ago when your grandma was still alive." Alan murmured something which Andrew couldn't make out. The boy was asleep on his feet, his legs like rubber. "They starved out," he said. "It was too hard. Moved to town to live. Gus is a good mechanic." The boy stumbled again and Andrew said cheerfully, holding his hand more tightly, half-lifting him, "We're almost there."

Mrs. Strauss opened the door to Andrew's knock. When she saw who it was, she opened it wider.

"Bringing cattle in for the train tomorrow?" she asked, smiling broadly. "And who's this little man? Come in, come in." She stepped back to let them pass into the hall. "Where's your horses? At the stockyards? Gus is in the kitchen." But Gus was already behind her, welcoming them into the brightly-lit house.

"I was half-expectin' you," he said, his voice loud and hearty. "Thought it was about time for you to be coming through with steers. Sit down, sit down." He pulled out chairs and made room for them at the table. Silently Andrew poured a glass of water from the jug on the table and handed it to Alan. He was less thirsty tonight and drank it slowly.

"I'll never know why you boys don't take a canteen," Mrs. Strauss said, scolding. "You look a mite done-in," she said to Alan, smiling down at him. "I'll have some grub for you in a minute. You picked a good night to come through. I got a roast cooked already." She took a platter of meat out of the icebox, began to slice the meat and lay the thick pieces in a frying pan on the stove.

"This'll bring back your strength," Gus said. He went to the cupboard and brought out a full bottle of rye. Mrs. Strauss cast a glance over her shoulder but said nothing. He set the bottle in the middle of the table and brought out glasses which he filled. Gus, Frank and Andrew lifted their glasses to the light and Gus said, "To the end of the war. A few more weeks," then drank it all in one draft. While the beef sizzled in the pan and the gas lamp above the table hissed cheerfully, he filled the glasses again. Andrew, watching Frank down his second drink as quickly as the first, feeling the welcome glow spreading through his limbs, almost did the same. But his small son sat across from him, pale and tired, depending on him, and his wages for a year's hard labour waited in a field on the outskirts of town. He let the drink sit and sipped at it for the rest of the evening.

"It's the only way to take the ache out of your bones," Frank said, seeing this. Even his bent, off-centre nose was reddening. "You get to be my age," he warned Andrew, "you feel every broken bone you ever had, every sprain, every time a goddamn cow or horse let you have it." He rubbed his flattened cheekbone and took another drink. "And they all hurt at once."

Alan's head dropped every once in a while as he waited for his supper.

"Honey," Mrs. Strauss said, "the first piece is for you, and here's some potatoes. Now you eat up and I'm sending you straight to bed. You look wore out." The men said nothing, smiling benevolently at the boy, relaxed because there was a woman looking after him. Before even finishing his supper, Alan was asleep with his head lolling against the chairback. When Andrew said he would carry him to his bed, Mrs. Strauss objected. "A slip of a boy like that, I've carried heavier loads. I'll just put him in on the couch. You two can have the spare room upstairs." She was a big, muscled woman, almost bigger than her husband and she had lifted Alan out of his chair before she had finished speaking. When she turned with him his dark head fell back over her arm, his eyes not even opening.

In the morning they were up early. Eating breakfast in the kitchen, Frank was hung-over and morose, Andrew edgy and tense, anxious to be out of there, worrying about his cattle, thinking ahead to the weigh-scales and the loading.

"I hope the goddamn train's on time, Andrew said, forgetting Mrs. Strauss. She came to the table from the stove, a steaming frying pan in her hand.

"My daughter lives next door," she said, sliding eggs onto Andrew's plate. "She's got a boy just about his age. Why not let Alan stay with me? She can keep Harry home from school and he can play with Alan while you corral them cattle and load them." Andrew hesitated. He looked at his son. Did the boy look a little paler than usual? Alan looked eagerly back at him. Why, the boy didn't want to be left behind. He didn't need Alan for this, but if the boy wanted to come . . . .He turned to Mrs. Strauss and said, "Thanks anyway, Rose, but Alan's pretty keen to come with me. He ain't loaded cattle at stockyards before and he's gonna have to learn how. He's gonna be the boss one day. Mrs. Strauss turned quickly away but not before he saw something in her eyes that puzzled him.

She busied herself at the stove not relplying or turning again. Andrew looked back to Alan but Alan had lowered his eyes to his breakfast. Was he disappointed? Surely he hadn't misunderstood the eagerness in Alan's face. Surely Alan wanted to stay with the men. He dismissed his uncertainty. Of course he did.

"Eat up, Al," he said. "We got work to do today. You'll need something sticking to your ribs."

When they got to the stockyards another herd of steers had already arrived. They were driven in by old Parker, whom Andrew had once worked for and by two of his sons, men themselves now. Their shouts and whistles carried easily on the still, bright air. Parker had been the first to arrive so he drove his herd straight into the pens. The brand inspector was already leaning on the corral waiting for him, and a couple of big hats were bobbing above the railings at the far end of the pens where the scales were.

"Hey, there, Andy," Parker saluted him, as he passed the pen where Andrew, Frank and Alan were saddling their horses. His short white beard was neatly clipped and he looked as fresh and bright as if he had come by car; even the chilly fall air seemed to suit him. It brought a healthy, vital colour into his seamed face. Andrew was surprised to see him still riding so easily when he was well into his sixties.

"You set out with them this morning?" Andrew asked. He felt strange in front of Parker, and uncomfortable, remembering when he used to ride for him, how he raised hell in Havre whenever he could get away, and the agony of the mornings on his return. Often he had gone straight to work without even going to bed. Parker nodded. Behind him his big, range-fed Hereford steers were trotting down the alley. Mine look as good as his, Andrew thought, and they've been two days on the trail. Parker's big horse pranced and switched his tail and Parker's gloved hands pulled the reins tight.

"It ain't far," he said, laughing. His voice boomed over the clacking of his cattles' hooves and the shouts of his sons. "You ought to remember that, Andy, boy. Is that your son?"

"Yup," Andrew said. In the distance they could hear the faint long whistle of the approaching train and involuntarily they all looked to the east.

"You come all that way yourself on horseback?" Parker asked Alan, not unkindly. Alan nodded shyly, unused to the attention of strangers. "Gonna be a top cowboy, like your old man," Parker said, then he laughed, waved his hand, and rode up the alley behind his steers.

Andrew was doing up the cinch on his horse and as he glanced over his horse's back, he saw a thick, heavyset man wearing a clean black stetson and an expensive jacket striding along the far side of the corral. Eckberg, the buyer, in a hurry, as usual.

Just as Andrew, Frank and Alan rode out of the stockyards the train pulled in, its brakes squealing, rending the still morning as it chugged forward slowly, then with a groan and a screech, backed up till the right cattlecar was lined up with the wooden loading chute.

Once Andrew looked back and saw a low cloud of dust slowly approaching the stockyards from the west. He said to Frank, "More cattle coming." Frank turned in the saddle with what appeared to be a great effort. He had hardly spoken yet this morning. Now he wiped his nose with his arm, spat, then resettled himself in his saddle.

"Won't be enough room for all the cattle in them pens. We'll have to herd our bunch till they're ready for us." Andrew nodded, reflecting. They were in the field now, the gate open behind them.

"Listen, Frank," he said. Alan trotted nearby, listening too. "Eckberg's gonna be busy there. Let's sneak 'em down to the creek and water 'em before we bring 'em in." Frank only nodded, the morning's paleness accentuating the broken, awkward face, making it look even more grotesque than usual.

By the time they had watered the herd and chased them from the field to the grass at the back of the stockyards, the Parker herd was being weighed and the brand inspector was down in the corral checking the brands. Eckberg was standing by the weigh scale, his hands on his waist, his eyes narrowed and intent on the scale's face.

The second rancher, who had arrived with a carload of cattle while they were chasing their herd in, was a stranger to Andrew, but he knew one of his two hands. He and Andrew had worked together a few times in the days when Andrew had worked for other ranches. They reminisced on horseback, the fence between them, but Andrew, even while he laughed with the other men, could not truly feel any regrets over the passing of that time. He was proud to be running his own place now, and wondered why the other man was still working for somebdy else. At his age he would never do anything else and would wind up old and useless, tolerated on one of the ranches where he had once been a valued worker. He shuddered to think that that almost happened to him. Karen, he thought. If it hadn't been for Karen, would he ever have amounted to anything?

Soon Parker's cattle were being loaded, the train moved again to set another empty cattle car in position at the loading chute, the second rancher's cattle were being weighed and brand-inspected and Andrew, Frank and Alan were driving their herd into the pens.

When this was done, Andrew told Alan to dismount and tie his pony to a fencepost. Alan obeyed, then went down to the scales, where he climbed the corrals to watch. The morning was wearing on, the sun bright and high, sending down a thin warmth, and the air was full of the sound of cattle rubbing against each other and against the corrals, and with the dull clack of their hooves, punctuated by the occasional bellow and the laughter or shouts of the dozen or so men. Andrew began to relax. The job was almost done and it had gone without a hitch. He began to enjoy the fine day and the company of the other men.

He remembered the fowl supper that Karen had missed and regret stabbed at him. It was a hard life for women, no use pretending it wasn't and no wonder half of them turned strange. He vowed again to try harder to get Karen out more, to take her to town with him when he had to go, even if it was a nuisance waiting while she got all the kids ready and they slowed him on all his errands.

At last it was their turn. At the weigh scales Eckberg turned angrily to Andrew.

"You watered them sonsabitches, didn't you?"

"They were in a field with water," Andrew said in a reasonable tone.

"They just been watered, I can see they got their bellies full of water!" Eckberg insisted. "I didn't come here to buy a load of water."

"They been on the trail for two days," Andrew said. "Look how much weight they lost there, that's costing me money." Sitting across the corral listening, Parker was grinning behind Eckberg's back.

"Goddamnit!" Eckberg said. "You goddamn rachers are always pulling this stunt!" His face was growing redder by the minute. "I shoulda kept my eye on you." Andrew said, "They got a ten, twelve-hour train ride ahead of them. Nobody's gonna unload them before tomorrow morning. No food, no water. They'll be so shrunk by then . . ."

"Christ!" Eckberg said. "They're only going to slaughter!" He turned away angrily. Andrew allowed himself a quick grin directed to Frank. Eckberg might not like it, but it was too late for him to do anything about it.

When all the cattle were finally loaded and the train was pulling out, Eckberg gave each of the three ranchers a cheque. Then he shook hands with them, without meeting their eyes, got back in his car and drove away.

"Come and have a drink before you head home," Parker said to Andrew.

"I'm getting nervous about my stock," Frank said, turning to Andrew before Andrew could answer Parker.

"I'm hungry, Dad," Alan said from his perch on the rail. Andrew had completely forgotten the boy was there. He wanted a drink, could imagine the peace and camaraderie in the beer parlour. He studied his boy. No, he had to get home.

"I think maybe I better just feed the boy and get on the road home. Thanks anyway."

"You gonna ride all the way home?" Parker asked Alan. He shifted his eyes questioningly to Andrew.

"No other way home," Andrew pointed out, a little irritated by Parker's remark. "Unless we stay overnight and set out in the morning." Alan waited, looking from one man to the other.

"Well, no business of mine," Parker said, grinning. He put out his hand. "Drop by one of these days when you're in the country. Bring that family of yours." They shook hands and then he turned away and with his sons on either side of him set off walking down the dirt road into the village.

Andrew's plan was to ride straight home today and to be at the bank, which was twenty miles southeast of this town and almost twenty from home, the first thing next morning. He had had bad experiences with cheques, he needed to know if this one was any good or not.

"Do you think you can make it?" he asked Alan, knowing it wasn't a fair question. "We'll ride pretty fast," he cautioned. Alan nodded, without conviction. Karen, he knew, if she were there, would insist on waiting a day. But he had stock at home to look after, Frank did too, all the fall work was waiting, and he had to make sure the cheque was good. He didn't have a day to waste. Alan would have to ride back today.

They ate in the town's only café, then set out at once. Andrew kept the pace to a trot and a slow lope and by late afternoon they had covered ten of the twenty-five miles. Frank left them then and went on ahead at a faster pace. Alan was exhausted, even his pony was flagging. Andrew slowed their pace still more, worried about what Karen would say when she saw how tired he was. He let Alan dismount and rest every few miles.

The stars were out when they rode into the yard. For the last few miles Andrew had kept talking to Alan to keep him awake, but it had been quite a while since the boy gave a coherent reply. A mile back he had taken the reins and led Alan's pony so that all Alan had to do was hang on. Andrew began to feel the first real stirrings of guilt for pushing the boy so hard, he even wondered if he had made a mistake in bringing him, and he fought to subdue an irritation with the boy that he knew wasn't fair.

He rode up to the door, dismounted, and lifted Alan down out of his saddle. Karen was up and in the kitchen in her dressing gown. When she saw her son in Andrew's arms, her face went white, and she rushed to him.

"He's only asleep, Andrew said. Silently she touched the sleeping child's face with her palm. Andrew passed her and carried him into their one bedroom and set him on his bed beside John. None of the children stirred, except for Anne in her cot, who rubbed her nose violently, then subsided. Karen followed and began to pull off Alan's boots and then to undress him. She said nothing, but Andrew felt her rebuke in the tenderness with which she handled the sleeping boy. He left them and went back into the kitchen, feeling shut out and guilty, and angry too. He looked around the room once, then went quietly out into the night to see to the horses.

CHAPTER THREE

Andrew stood with his hands thrust deep in his trouser pockets, staring out the small kitchen window, beyond the corrals to the flat expanse of prairie that rose up into low, undulating hills.

Moira bounced up to him, thrust both arms around his thigh and hung from him, her face turned up to his. He looked down at her freckled nose and reddish curls without really seeing her, bent to pick her up and set her on his hip.

"Whatcha looking at, Daddy?" she asked, her bright eyes following his, straining to see what he saw.

"Nothing," he said, and laughed a short, mirthless laugh. On his left Karen was at the stove cooking breakfast. The door on his right at the other end of the room opened and Kevin came in, barely visible behind the armload of wood he was carrying. Without kicking off his rubbers he tramped down the room, skirting the table on the opposite side from Andrew. A piece of wood fell off and clattered to the floor, the whole load threatened to go at any minute, but he made it to the woodbox by the stove and dropped his load noisily into it. Behind him Andrew had reached out and shoved the door shut.

"Thank you, Kevin," Karen said solemnly. Andrew had to smile. Her way of teaching the kids manners. He didn't think his mother had ever said thank you to him. Kevin's cap had been knocked askew and he smiled up at his mother with a face that glowed from the early morning air that was still chilly despite the fact that it was almost May.

"Have to split some more, Daddy," Kevin said to him. "It's almost gone." Andrew nodded. Kevin tramped back to the door, where he pulled off his outdoor clothes in his harum-scarum way that none of the other kids had, then disappeared into the bedroom. I'll do it after breakfast, Andrew told himself, and the thought cheered him. But no, he had declared that the job of keeping a supply of split wood for the cookstove belonged to Alan.

Andrew felt that there was something wrong. The feeling had been growing on him all winter, he'd thought it would go with spring, but it was still with him and he couldn't name it. This morning he'd gone out with the kids like he always did and while John milked and Anne fed the chickens and Alan carried water to the house, he'd forked some hay to a few penned cows and calves and helped a couple of orphan calves suck their borrowed mothers. But then a sort of weary disgust overcame him and he locked the calves in their separate pens to keep them safe from the cows, who would kick them or bunt them if they tried to nurse, and went into the house without saying anything, leaving the children to finish up.

He couldn't say what it was. Only that there seemed to be less and less urgency about his work and less and less pleasure in doing it. It scared him. He set Moira down so abruptly that she stepped back and looked up at him, puzzled, before she ran into the bedroom where Kevin had gone. He rubbed the back of his neck fiercely.

Barn chores were nothing anymore with Alan fifteen years old and the other three to take up the slack. Time was when he had spent two hours in the barn before breakfast, did a half day's work before daylight. How he had worked, and never really minded it. Things were too easy now. He had never longed for a life of luxury and ease, he had kept his nose to the grindstone and worked for the few reasons he could see in front of him.

Now things were changing. He sighed to himself, he was careful not to show anything on the outside, and turned from the window. Karen bustled past him, in a hurry. Wryly he thought, she speeds up while I slow down. He pulled out his chair and sat in his place out of her way and watched her. Sometimes he could still see in the plump, busy matron she was now, the slender, steady girl he had married. She was wearing her usual cotton house dress, this one a greenish colour with some pattern on it he couldn't make out. A clean apron over that. Her beautiful dark hair that he had loved to finger and that used to rest loose on her shoulders was pulled back from her face and fastened with hairpins. It hurt him to look at her and to have to search for her former beauty. It hurt him that she had lost it in the service of some halfspoken dream of theirs that he was no longer sure of. She had her children, her life from sunrise till well after sunset was devoted to them. She had no time left for beauty. They could hear the kids coming across the yard, their chores finished.

"Here, Andy," Karen said. "You might as well start." She took his plate to the stove to fill it as they came in, Anne first, then John, who at twelve was already almost as tall as Alan, who entered last. They came in behind Andrew, kicked off their boots, hung up their jackets, washed their hands in the basin one by one, while Karen, after taking the pail of milk from John, dodged them to put food on the table. They squeezed into their places around the table. Kevin and Moira came from where they had been playing in the bedroom and sat down too.

"What are we gonna do today, Dad?" John asked when they were all seated and eating. The daily question. But today Andrew didn't feel like thinking about it. Time was when you had to ask, what can wait till tomorrow? since there was always too much work for one day. But even that he hadn't minded.

Instead of answering John he said, "I been thinking of putting in a dam in that southwest field. Can't depend on the water supply there and the field's no good for cattle without water."

"They can water like they always have in the dam in the next field, if you leave the gate open," Karen said, surprised.

"I been thinking of putting in a dam there for a long time," Andrew said flatly. Karen laughed. She looked down the table at him, her dark eyes amused and gentle, as if he were one of her children.

"You're just looking for work," she said. Then, "If it's work you want, you can build me a house."

He looked around the kitchen. The house was old. The floor creaked under the new linoleum he and Alan had laid, the window frames were worn-out and leaked rain in the summer and had to be stuffed with rags in the winter to keep out the wind. There was no room for anything. They were so cramped that now Alan and John were grown they slept in a bunkhouse Andrew had fixed for them, only moving into the house during stretches of forty-below weather. Anne was growing up and wanted a room of her own, and he knew Karen longed for a new kitchen, for running water and a generator so they could have electricity, and for a real bedroom for the two of them. It wa true. She needed a new house. God knows, he thought, she deserves it.

"Mike Mahoney has a Cat," Alan said. "He just bought it. We could hire him to build the dam for us—or even better, why don't we rent it from him? I'd sure like to learn how to run one of them things."

A bulldozer? Andrew hadn't thought of such a thing. He had pictured himself out in the field working with a fresno and team as he had done when he built the other dams on the place. He saw the Cat tearing up the grass, heard its roar, smelled its exhaust.

"I'll build it myself," he said. "With a team and fresno." There was a shocked silence.

"Are you kidding, Dad?" John asked. "Nobody does it that way anymore."

"The ground is just right for plowing," Andrew said. "No reason I can't start this morning." He concentrated on cutting his bacon, his family's silent disapproval hanging heavily in the air around him. He could see the earthen dam growing under his feet, he could hear the meadowlarks calling around him as he worked alone in the hills far from the house, he felt the fresno handle clutched in the crook of his arm and the pull he had to give on the rope to turn it over when he was dumping, and the ache in his back and legs from the miles of walking. He remembered how he fell into bed at night and was asleep instantly.

"I bet I walked a hundred miles a day," he said.

"A hundred miles!" Moira said, in the awestruck tone of a five-year-old. He came back to this family seated around the table looking at him and gave a short, self-conscious laugh, then grew angry.

"Old Matt Tookey," he said, "he built that dam on the Zimmer place with a wheelbarrow! He didn't even use horses!"

"He must have been crazy," Alan said mildly, reaching for the jam. Andrew grew angrier.

"You don't know anything about it," he said. "You never done a day's real work in your life. He was too poor to have horses." He put both hands on the edge of the table as if he were going to push himself away. His eyes met Karen's at the end of the table. There was a softness there he hadn't seen for a long time and for a second it silenced him. But then he went on.

"He looked around, that green Englishman, and he didn't even see the bald prairie with the sun burning it to a crisp every day. He saw English gardens, I guess, green grass and trees and flowers."

"What happened to him?" Anne asked into the silence. He smiled down the table at her. She was so like her mother.

"He went crazy," he said. "Worked himself half to death, couldn't even grow potatoes in that ground, and when his son came from the East to see him one spring, old Tookey, he was only forty, he had white hair and he didn't even know where he was anymore." Nobody spoke for a minute.

"Really, Daddy?" Kevin asked, his voice skeptical.

"I hope this means you've changed your mind," Karen said, her voice tart, "and that you'll hire the bulldozer to do it."

"No," he said. "It don't mean that.

"You really gonna use a fresno?" Alan asked. "And horses?"

"Yup," Andrew said.

"But why, Dad?" John asked.

Andrew didn't answer. He knew he was being stubborn. He even knew that in some way he was wrong, but he would build the dam the way he had always done it. He would do it that way because . . . because . . . he could not bear to see the way the past was vanishing without anybody even caring. His life. Each of them working their lives away like so many ants. It had to mean something. He lifted his head and met the eyes of each of his three sons in turn, and each of them dropped theirs.

"Because . . ." he began. They waited, but a heaviness seemed to fall on him, and all the words he might have used to explain to them what was in his heart, dissipated under its weight. He allowed Karen to pour him another cup of coffee. It was Saturday, nobody had school. When his children were ready to leave the table, he said, "There's a couple of cows in the northwest field got pink eye. Cut 'em out and bring 'em in. And that brockle-faced steer's lousy. Bring him in too. And make sure all them calves are matched up." His sons nodded. "And saddle Moira and Anne's horses and take them with you."

When they had all gone out Karen took her coffee cup and came and sat in Moira's place around the corner from him. There was such concern in her eyes that he leaned over and kissed her on the lips.

"Do you really have to do this?" she asked.

"Yes," he said.

"But why, Andy?"

"Why is everybody making such a fuss about it? It's a good way to do it. Those dams I put in years ago are still there.

"It's such hard work," she said. "You shouldn't have to work so hard anymore."

"I been thinking about a house for you," he said.

"Alan likes machines," she said, as though he hadn't spoken. "He was hoping to get to drive one of those big things."

"I hate machinery," he said. "Always breaking down, making a helluva racket. Did you hear what I said?"

"What?" she asked.

"I said I been thinking about building you a house." It had been in the back of his mind for a few years now, ever since he had started making a little money. He didn't know what made him finally commit himself today. He watched her as she straightened, her eyes on his, her face slowly changing.

"Really?" she asked him. "Do you mean that?" He nodded, grinning. "Can we afford it?" she asked. He shrugged.

215

"As well now as we'll ever be able to." She stared off into space, then began to look around the room from object to object as if she were finally seeing them as they really were. Abruptly she stood, turned away, and went to stand at the counter under the window with her back to him. Her shoulders rose and began to quiver. He was overcome with sorrow for the years she had spent in this shack, for the way she had never complained about it, for the way she had laboured to keep it clean, with all of them stuffed into it. Humbled by her courage, he rose from the table, went to her and put his hand on her shoulder. She began to cry in earnest, the sobs wrung out of her, even as she fought to keep them back. He took her by the shoulders, turned her, and pulled her toward him.

"I don't know how you stood it," he said. "It's a wonder it didn't drive you crazy." Her tears were getting his shirt wet. He held her close and laid his palm gently on the back of her neck under her tight bun of hair. She was not the lithe girl he had married, but he was no wild youth anymore, either. They had both lost something. And maybe gained something.

"I want to make it up to you," he said. She drew back, fumbling in her apron pocket till she found her hanky, wiped her eyes, and blew her nose. She didn't ask him what it was he wanted to make amends for.

"I'm sorry," she said. "I couldn't help it."

"No," he replied, filled with tenderness for her, and remorse. "I'm sorry." She laughed then, embarrassed. "You better start planning. We can start in June, be in it by Christmastime. Where do you want it?" As if he didn't know. Enough times on their way to town she had pointed out a spot in the basin of the hills to the west that she said would be a beautiful place for a house. "And the garden could go there, and the barn over there." He thought, it'll take me maybe three years to get everything built and arranged. It'll change everything. He didn't want to do it, but he pushed this thought back. He had to do it, for Karen's sake.

"It's such a lot of work," she said dubiously. "You have to build a new barn and new corrals—is there water there for the house and the stock?"

"I think so," he said. Always the problem of finding a supply of decent water. "I see a spot there that's wet sometimes when it hasn't rained. I wouldn't be surprised if we dug we'd find a spring. We'll get the well-drillers in. That'd please Alan." They both laughed and he remembered himself as a small boy watching the well-witcher working. For a second he thought Karen was going to start crying again.

"It doesn't have to be fancy," she said earnestly, and wiped her hands on her apron, trying to sound sensible and ordinary, and he pulled her against him again.

But when he was out in the yard, his mood changed. He stopped and looked around him as Karen had stared around her kitchen. Far off to the east the kids were black strokes against the yellow grass of the hills. He hoped Alan would keep them out a good long time and give Karen a break. He sighed. He liked it here at the old place, where there was nothing but the necessities. He liked the weathered buildings that looked as if they had grown there and were a part of the prairie. He was hardly inside except at mealtimes and to sleep. And before either of them knew it the kids would be grown up and what would they need a new house for then? But he had said he would build it and he would keep his word.

He walked around to the back of the house, past the plot where Karen had her garden, remembering that it would soon have to be plowed up again, and into a fenced-off area where he kept his few farming implements. The walking plow was still there, the blade a little rusty and nicked in a few places, but with lots of work left in it yet. He walked to the fresno. It lay where he had left it one spring a few years ago. He remembered that winter with a shudder. All his meagre supply of feed buried under mountains of snow from storm after storm. He had had to use the fresno to remove the snow piled high around the hay before he could get any out to feed his stock. Worked till midnight more than once with hungry horses and cattle standing by waiting to be fed. He stood looking down at it, then bent and picked up the long handle that was fastened to each side of the bucket. A simple tool, nothing to it really. A six-foot wide bucket with a handle. He pulled hard and righted it, then let it go. Nothing the matter with it either. He went away to the barn, caught his saddle horse, saddled him and rode out to chase in the workhorses.

When he had cut out the four horses he wanted, hitched them to the wagon and backed it up to the stoneboat, which lay in a corner by the barn, where the boys had left it after hauling manure, he hitched the stoneboat to the back of the wagon, then drove the team out to the yard where the plow and the fresno waited. He loaded the walking plow into the wagon, then dragged the fresno, which was bigger and heavier, onto the stoneboat.

When that was done, he climbed onto the wagon seat, drove the horses through the yard, past where he knew Karen was watching him through the kitchen window, past the corrals, and out of the house yard. He turned south down the trail, then after a few yards angled west across the prairie.

In half an hour he had reached the spot where the land drained and which, with a dam across one end, he hoped would allow the spring runoff and meagre rains to collect. He unloaded the plow, hitched the horses to it, and began to plow the bottom to a depth of about six inches. He would scrape the plowed earth off and use it for the dam, and at the same time would level the bottom. He had to keep stopping to throw aside rocks but in an hour he had enough ground plowed up to furnish the dirt for a day's work on the dam. He unhitched the horses from the plow then, unloaded the fresno, and hitched the horses, four across, to it.

He turned the fresno over so that the steel bucket was upright, tucked the long arm that was attached to each end between his right forearm and upper arm so that it protruded a couple of feet out behind him and, holding the reins with his left hand, clicked his tongue to get the horses going. He drove them down to the plowed bottom, lined them up, tipped the fresno enough to get the blade to dig into the turned earth, then hung on to the handle with his right arm and drove the team with his left. The bucket blade bit into the soft earth, the horses settled into the pull, moving faster as it filled and grew heavier, and Andrew wrestled to hold the handle down with his right arm so the bucket wouldn't tip and empty, and with his left arm fought to keep the team pulling evenly.

When the bucket was full he drove the hitch to the beginning of what would be his dam, let the arm rise so that the bucket tipped over, and dumped the load of earth. He was already sweating. He stood for a moment catching his breath, then pulled on the long rope attached to the

218

end of the handle to bring the arm down and right the bucket again. He left the rope to trail out behind him. Then he clucked the horses into motion again and went to pick up a second load.

It took him at least five loads before both he and the horses found the rhythm of the work and began to make a continuous circle; pick up fast, dump slowly but without stopping, move on, pick up again. The horses' feet tramped the loads down as they walked down the dam with each new load. Already Andrew's arms and shoulders were feeling the unaccustomed work, but he set his jaw, angry with himself, and worked that much harder.

He had been working a couple of hours when he became conscious of being watched. He called, 'Whoa,' to the horses and pulled on the reins till the horses stopped, then looked behind him. Alan and John sat on their horses looking down at him. When he saw their faces he was embarrassed, and being careful to hang on to the fresno arm and the reins, he straightened his back and his knees, wishing he could wipe off some of the mud he knew must be covering him, and called, "Hello."

"You forgot to come in for dinner, Dad," John said. "Mom sent us with a lunch. So that's how that thing works." He looked the fresno over with eager eyes. "Can I help?" Beside him Alan sat silently, his face revealing nothing. Andrew grinned at John.

"In a couple of years, Johnny," he said. He was conscious of the different tone in his voice when he spoke to John compared with when he spoke to Alan. He turned to him and tried to keep the same warmth in his voice. "But I could use you right now," he said. Alan didn't move. For a long moment Andrew thought Alan was going to disobey him and ride away. Then slowly he dismounted. "We'll eat first," Andrew decided. John dismounted then too and untied a sack from his saddle.

"We've already eaten," Alan said, his words clipped, his voice deep. John had already gone to find a dry spot. He sat down with the sack resting between his knees and waited while Andrew unhitched the team, took their harnesses off, tied them to the wagonbox and gave them each an oat bundle. Alan remained standing by the saddlehorses as if he were undecided whether he should stay or go.

"I'm starved," Andrew said when he was finished with the horses. "What did your mother send?" He climbed the slope slowly to sit by John. His legs ached with each step. He called to Alan, "You might as well sit down, boy," not smiling. "The horses need a break. It'll be a while before we go back to work." Reluctantly Alan dropped the reins of the two saddlehorses and came to sit down near John and his father. Andrew began to eat.

"I don't see why we have to do it this way," Alan said, staring down at the deepening track of dirt Andrew had laid below them. The horses tied to the wagon below them chewed their oats meditatively and a flock of horned larks swept by. Andrew sighed, trying to ignore his aching back.

"I don't want that goddamn machinery on my land," he said. "Ugliest damn stuff in all creation."

"I like it," Alan said, swinging his head to face his father. "I like what it can do," Alan said. "I like the . . ." he hesitated, searching for the words to express what fascinated him.

"I know what you mean," Andrew said. "But you're wrong." Andrew wished he could explain better to Alan what he felt. But what could he say? See the antelope over there? This morning on the way out here I saw a dozen prairie chickens, and I scared up a half-dozen whitetail deer out of that coulee bottom? What if he said, see the grass? See the hills, and the sky? When I was a boy there was nothing but clean prairie as far as the eye could see. He had never said out loud "the land is beautiful" and he knew he never could. But its beauty was so great at times—a winter sunrise, the line where horizon and sky met so pure that his chest hurt to look at it—that it had, after so many years, a lifetime of years, seeped inside him, he could no longer separate it clearly from himself. It was as if a plow cut into him, a Caterpillar gouged his soul. He remained silent, his eyes on the pale grass beneath his feet.

He wished that Alan would not fight him at every turn, would trust him a little. Things were not shaping up well between him and his oldest son and he didn't understand how they had gone wrong. Finally he said, "When the place is yours, you can do what you like."

After a while Andrew rose. John scrambled up beside him and Alan rose slowly. Andrew noticed that Alan was exactly the same height he was, and that John soon would be. It gave him a funny feeling. He turned to John.

"You go on back," he said. "Take Alan's horse with you." John picked up the sack and started for his horse. He mounted, took Alan's horse by the reins, and started to ride away. "Tell your mother to send us out some grub at suppertime," Andrew called to him. "I want to get as much done today as I can."

Alan helped him harness the horses and hitch them back to the fresno. Then he stood uncertainly beside the rig, frowning at it.

"What do I do?" he asked.

"I'll handle the horses," Andrew said. "You haven't got enough experience yet, and I'm not sure you're strong enough. Stand here." He pushed the fresno arm into position in Alan's arm. Surprised by the unexpected weight of the half-filled bucket, Alan let the arm ride up a few inches. Andrew grabbed it and pushed it down.

"Use both arms," he said. "I had to use the other one to run the hitch, but you can use both." Alan took a firm grip, using both hands. The blade dug in, the horses began to pull. "Hold it down," he warned Alan.

Alan tried to obey, his expression changing as he realized how hard this was going to be. He caught the rising arm and held it in place. Andrew was pleased, although he said nothing. The first time they dumped a load Andrew stopped the horses to show Alan how to do it but after that he kept them moving.

Another hour passed. He and Alan didn't talk, each concentrating on his job. Andrew was relieved to have Alan helping him, but he couldn't bring himself to say so. After being so obstinate about doing this, he couldn't admit that he found the work almost too hard.

Alan's face ran with sweat, he was breathing with his mouth open. The exertion showed in the muscles of his neck and face. He would soon need a break, Andrew saw, but he didn't suggest it right away. He wanted Alan to get the full flavour of the work, he wanted him to work the way he had worked. If he couldn't find the words to tell him about his life, then he would have to show him.

"Here, Alan," he said. "You try handling the horses." It was not an easier job, but it took different muscles, so it would ease Alan's back a bit. They switched jobs and Andrew gave Alan running instructions on how to handle the horses at the same time as he worked the fresno.

The afternoon wore on. They began to take breaks every half hour or so, standing wherever they stopped out of breath, on the long mound of packed earth that would be the dam, or on the plowed ground below it. One of them held the reins to keep the horses still and the other leaned on the fresno arm. Eventually John arrived with another lunch.

"It's seven o'clock Dad," he called from his perch on his horse. Andrew halted the horses and looked up. It was true, the light was fading. He had fallen into a reverie as he walked or half-ran to keep up with the horses. The work's rhythm had seeped into him and, exhausted as he was, he had stopped thinking about it, just kept working, seeing the turned brown soil, the dam slowly rising, the horses' feet packing load after load. He turned to Alan and was shocked to see how white the boy's face was when it should have been flushed with his effort. They should have stopped an hour ago. Why hadn't the boy said anything?

"I guess we better quit," he said quickly. "The horses are about played out." He realized now that his own knees were trembling. "Al," he said gently, "you go get the lunch from John and find a good place to sit." Alan let the fresno arm ride up and stumbled away as if, freed of the weight, he no longer had an anchor to hold him to the earth. Andrew cursed himself for keeping the boy at it so long. He hadn't thought about it, he hadn't meant to. He's young, he thought, he'll be fine in an hour. This relieved him a little and he began to unhitch the horses.

He took his time about it, working slowly, trying to give Alan as much time as possible to recover before they started back to the house. Out of the corner of his eye he saw the two boys on the dry grass above the dam, John sitting cross-legged, Alan sprawled out on his back. He hitched the horses to the wagon, called John to hold them while he went around to the back and unfastened the stoneboat, leaving it where it sat. When he looked over to Alan again, he was sitting up. This cheered him enough to call, "Climb in, Al, we might as well eat in the house." Slowly Alan rose and walked to the wagon. John went back to his horse, mounted, and started for home at a lope.

Andrew and Alan didn't talk to each other on the slow trip back, but Andrew saw that Alan's colour was better.

"Take something from the lunch," he suggested to him. "You don't have to wait to eat." Alan suddenly leaned over the side of the wagon and vomited onto the ground. Andrew was alarmed at this and tried to speed up the horses, but they were bone-tired too and although they moved faster for a few steps, they soon lapsed to a walk.

When they reached the yard Andrew pulled the horses up to the kitchen door and waited while Alan climbed down and went inside. Then he went on toward the corrals, unhitched the horses from the wagon outside, then drove the team into the corral, where he took their harnesses off, fed and watered them. He turned them out then, seeing that they were too tired to work the next day. In the morning he would chase in another four. He went to the house.

Karen turned from the stove when he entered the otherwise empty room.

"Where's Alan?" he asked.

"I sent him to bed," she said, and he knew by her tone that she was angry with him. He went to the basin, poured himself some water and scrubbed at his face and hands. "Why did you work him so hard?" she asked, her voice low and tight.

"He'll get over it," Andrew said. He wanted to tell her that he hadn't meant to, but the whole business suddenly seemed so trivial to him that he left it at that. "I'm pretty tired myself," he said. In fact, he thought if he didn't sit down, he might fall. His knees were weak, his back and legs ached with an intensity that was new even to him. Karen ignored the remark about himself.

"You're right, sure he'll get over his aches and pains. He's young, he'll recover from that. But don't you see what you're doing, Andy?" He sat down at his place at the table and put his face in his hands. All he wanted to do was lie down. He didn't want to hear any more about this. But she went on when he didn't reply. "You're going to make him hate you." He dropped his hands, surprised, and lifted his head to look at her.

"Hate me?" he said.

"Yes." She paused. "I don't know what you're trying to prove. It's like you're trying to punish him for not having to work as hard as you did, or something like that." She was frowning at him. "And you never give in to him. You never have. Everything he likes or wants to find out about you tell him is no good." He grew angry then.

"I'm too goddamn tired to listen to this," he said. "He's fifteen years old, what the hell does he know?" He got up and went into the parlour and sat down on the side of the bed which Karen had already made up. She followed him in, carrying the lamp.

"He's fine," Andrew said. "Tired out is all." Every one of his muscles ached, even his bones ached. "He'll recover faster than I will," he said ruefully.

"Will you hire the bulldozer to finish?" she asked. Her voice was soft now, the tautness gone.

"No," he said quickly, angry again. "Alan doesn't have to help anymore." They undressed, Karen blew out the lamp, they got into bed and lay down beside each other.

"At least he knows what work is now," Andrew said. But he took no satisfaction in this, a bitterness had lodged in his throat, and in sour disappointment he realized that the hard work had brought none of the old healing, none of the peace. And he didn't know why.

CHAPTER FOUR

Andrew stared down the table to Karen's empty chair at the other end. She was busy at the stove, doing something, he didn't know what. Alan, sitting to the right of her empty chair, was talking to Bud, the hired man, who sat beside him. He was speaking in an undertone, deliberately it seemed to Andrew, so he couldn't hear what was being said. When Alan laughed, Andrew said, too loudly, "What's on your mind, Alan?" The silence around the table grew tense and Karen, still at the stove, glanced over her shoulder at Andrew. He ignored her look.

"Just talking about Jim Stenson," Alan said, cutting his bacon vigorously, his voice loud, insolent in its very cheerfulness. He reached for the bread and began to butter a slice. Beside him Bud was looking uncomfortable. "He's breaking more land," Alan said, loud again.

Andrew bent his head over his food, feeling his jaw tighten and lips compress with anger. This morning everything made him angry. He knew it was because John was leaving, but even knowing this, he made little attempt to stifle the growing anger. Even though he wasn't hungry, he began to eat his bacon and eggs. The shot of whiskey he had drunk moments before coming to the table still burned in his gut, gave him back some of the fire he no longer felt. It was the only thing that could break through the dull heaviness that sat with him all the time these days.

Karen sat down heavily, sighing. She should lose some weight, he thought, not liking the high colour that was always in her face now.

"Pass the bread," he said gruffly, and Moira handed the plate to him, glancing at him with frightened eyes. She was eleven now, a redhead. He didn't know where the red hair had come from. He was sorry he had frightened her, but she was so easily frightened, it irritated him.

"Annie and Moira, no playing around after dishes," Karen said, in the abrupt way she had developed. "The whole garden's got to be done today, all the cornstalks pulled, the pea vines, everything." She slid more bacon onto her plate. Andrew watched, thinking, she ate four pieces already. How much does she need? That's more than I ate. He wished he could bring his bottle to the table. He needed another drink.

The door opened and Kevin came in, carrying a pail full of milk.

"What took you so long?" Andrew asked, angry again.

"She kicked me," Kevin said, and Andrew noticed that the boy had been crying.

"Looks like you'll live," he remarked.

"Where did she kick you?" Karen asked quickly. Kevin patted his thigh without speaking. He took off his cap and jacket and hung them up, set the pail of milk on the floor near the separator and went to wash his hands in the sink. "Honest, Andy," Karen said. "I don't like that cow, good milker or not. She's got a mean temper." Kevin came from the sink and sat down in his place on Andrew's left. He began to eat.

Karen rose again and picked up the coffee pot from the stove, turning off the burner. She began to fill the coffee cups, starting with Anne, who stood and took the pot from her mother, so that Karen returned to her chair. Anne was becoming more and more like Karen, the same dark hair, the same dark, steady eyes. A solemn, slow-moving, mature sixteen-year-old. He had no worries about her, although he had moments when he wished she would show a little more liveliness.

Anne came down to Andrew's end of the table and filled his cup, then went around to John, who sat on Andrew's right.

"No thanks," John said. "I gotta go or I'll miss the train." Everyone looked at Andrew, then away again.

"Wouldn't want you to miss the train," Andrew said, and laughed, then stopped.

"Who's driving you?" Karen asked.

"I'll drive him," Andrew said quickly over Alan's voice. "You've got work to do," he said to Alan gruffly.

"Well, don't make him late," Karen said. Andrew set his coffee cup down and stood, conscious that the whole family was watching him. He went into the bedroom, felt in his jacket pocket for his flask and drank a stiff drink from it. He looked around the room quickly, once, as if he might find something he was missing. But the room was silent and neat and held no answers. He took his jacket from the hook and went back into the kitchen.

"Ready?" he asked. John was already standing, reaching for his coat, which hung across a chairback at the wall behind him. His suitcase sat on the floor beside it. Chairs scraped around the table as the family rose to follow John and Andrew outside. They went through the porch and outside into the hard, chilly fall day.

Andrew tossed his son's suitcase into the truck box, went around and climbed into the driver's seat. Across from him John was bending to kiss his mother.

"Wish me luck," he said cheerfully to her, holding her hands as he drew back. Andrew knew there would be tears glinting in her eyes. John was shaking hands with Alan now, and then bending to kiss his sisters one by one, then tousling Kevin's curly hair. Andrew started the truck and John quickly climbed in beside him, waving and calling one last good-bye as he slammed the door shut. Andrew drove out of the yard. John looked back once for a long moment, then fixed his eyes on the road ahead.

After a while Andrew said, "You know I don't want you to go." John spread his hands on his knees in a nervous gesture. They were big hands, long-fingered and brown from the summer of hard work. John was too gentle. Andrew wanted to pull the truck over to the side of the narrow dirt road, lay his head on the steering wheel and cry. Where had it all gone wrong? Instead, he said, "I made too big a fuss. I shouldn't have. I'm sorry." He turned his head abruptly and looked at his second oldest son, sitting straight and slim beside him. Slowly the boy turned to meet his eyes with his own light brown ones. He smiled and Andrew, involuntarily, smiled back. "It's about time we got somebody educated around here," he said. John laughed. There was pure delight in the sound, and Andrew ached for his son's happiness, was filled with fear for him and a yearning for which there could be no expression. How he loved John.

"It's what I want, Dad," John said. "I don't know why. It's just something I've wanted for a long time." He paused, looking down at his hands. "Thanks for sending me. I know it costs a lot."

"We'll manage," Andrew said. "But if you're going to do it, you work hard. Don't let your mother down." "Anyway," John said, "you've still got Alan and Kevin." Andrew reached into his jacket pocket again, holding the steering wheel with one hand, pulled out the flask and put it to his mouth. The clear fluid burned all the way down and settled like fire in his stomach. He capped the flask and shoved it back in his pocket.

"A lawyer," he said. "You never did like ranching. I could always tell." He was getting angry again, the fire spreading through his limbs.

"Sure I did, Dad," John said. "Sure I like horses and . . . things, but I like books, too. I don't know why."

"It's from your mother," Andrew said. He sighed. "Well, one of you will make her happy."

He stepped on the gas and the truck jerked forward. Not so long ago he'd have driven John into town in a wagon. His hands ached for the feel of the reins. He turned his head and saw the plowed fields he was passing, pale in the weak fall light. A vast flock of blackbirds rose over it and swept away to the south. Nothing for them to eat on the plowed land, and nowhere to nest in the spring. They'd go south soon. He watched them mill and turn and rise, specks in the sky. The train had already pulled in when they drove up to the station. Farmers and ranchers and their wives stood in groups in front of their trucks, parked along the station platform, gossiping and watching the train. Andrew carried John's suitcase for him to the coach, nodding to men he knew, and handed it up to John as the boy climbed the steps. John had bought his ticket right after the day Karen came to talk to Andrew and told him he had to let John go or she would not forgive him.

The engine let out a steady stream of steam now, the whistle blew, and the train began to move slowly down the track. John grinned and waved to him as the passenger car, gaining speed, went by. Andrew lifted his hand, the train carrying his son away swept past him and was gone from the town. He dropped his hand slowly and stood looking down the track. He felt saddened and empty, the people around him like shadows, the colourless, silent day offering him nothing. He thought of the flask again, waiting in his pocket. He patted it absently, without noticing he was doing it, went back to the truck and took a long drink, emptying the flask. He started the truck and drove away.

He thought about his children. A certain eagerness, a kind of hope, shone in John's eyes. Alan's were veiled or hard, rarely meeting his, and Kevin, well, Kevin was still a child, but he was spoiled, cried too easily, wanted too much, couldn't stick with anything, had no time for his father. He thought about his daughters, but what was the use of thinking about them? They would get married and leave for good. Already they boarded in town to attend school and were only home on weekends and holidays. A man couldn't keep his daughters, anyway. Or his sons, he thought, his mind turning again to John. I love my kids, he thought, surprised. But what good does it do, in the end?

He thought again of Alan, the chubby, bright little boy who had grown into a man he didn't understand. He still didn't know what had gone wrong. He had always taken him riding with him, taught him to rope when he was still a small boy, taught him to halterbreak horses and then to break broncs. He'd taught him everything he knew about cattle—how to mark them mentally so that he would know beyond a doubt every single cow in his herd, how to cut them, how to chase them, how to doctor them for pink eye and cancer eye and foot rot and water belly and how to do Caesareans, even how to recognize a dozen different diseases they might get. He had taught him how to shoot them when they couldn't get up. There was nothing left to teach him.

And yet, somehow, even after he had lavished all this attention and knowledge on Alan, Alan only resented him. He couldn't understand it. Absently he reached for his flask, unscrewed the cap and put it to his lips, but it was empty.

Had he told Bud and Alan what to do today? He couldn't remember. There were a few cows in the corral that needed de-lousing, there was a broken gate to fix, a little doctoring on a horse or two. Before they knew it, it would be calf-weaning time, after they had rounded up the steers, cut them out, and trailed them to the stockyards in town.

On his right he passed a newly broken pasture and shook his head, watching it sourly till he had passed it. More land getting broken all the time. No wonder Alan was always after him to do the same. A few good crops and farming looked glamorous, profitable. The kid didn't know how dull farming was, how boring and how dirty, nothing like ranching on the clean, bright grass. There would be no farming on his place, he thought angrily. It had been years now since he had let that hundred and fifty acres he'd plowed up go back to grass. Now, gradually, he could see the native grass taking over, although it would be a long time and maybe those acres would never be the same. He thought with satisfaction how, when he was an old man, his whole place would be solid native grass, the way it had been when he first came here more than forty years before.

He turned down the dirt road that led into his place. To the east, on the other side of the hill, approached by another road, was his homestead. He remembered bringing Karen there over twenty years before. They had been happy there, it seemed to him. Maybe we aren't happy, he thought suddenly. The thought frightened him and he gripped the steering wheel harder, for something to hold onto.

He arrived in the yard and stopped the truck. For a moment he sat in front of the new house. Two stories, well-painted, windows, doors, rooms. He could see his two daughters working in the garden beside the house. Moira looked up and waved at him. He did not return her salute. Anne kept working without looking up. She would make some man a good wife.

He climbed out of the truck slowly, his body felt like lead. Far in the distance the hills were speckled with black strokes—his horses. It was time to get them in, start halterbreaking the year's batch of colts, break a dozen saddlehorses to sell in the spring, cut some of the young stallions. And no John, with his way with horses, to help. And Alan always impatient and angry with them. Alan doesn't love horses, Andrew thought heavily. He went slowly into the house. It was past noon.

"That you, Andy?" Karen called from one of the bedrooms. She started down the stairs. "Come and get something to eat."

"In a minute," Andrew said. He went into the bedroom, picked his bottle up from under the bed, took a drink from it, carefully refilled his flask, took another drink, then put the almost empty bottle back under the bed. Feeling a little better, he went into the kitchen.

Karen bent and took a plate of food out of the oven. She set it down at his place at the table. And he saw in a moment of suspended time, all the times she had done that, put a plate of steaming food in front of him. For what? he asked himself. What's the good of it after all?

"I'm not hungry," he said.

"Eat it anyway," she replied, brusquely. Angrily he caught her arm as she turned away. She stopped, surprised, and looked down at him. "What?" she asked. He let her arm go. They stared at each other for a long moment. Her eyes were still as dark as the night he first saw her, at the meeting in the schoolhouse. He remembered her skin, her mouth. He pulled her to him, bent his head, his hat fell off onto the floor and he let it go, and put his mouth over hers. She met him, then pulled back.

"Oh, Andy," she said softly. "I wish you wouldn't drink so much." He thought of how she used to wake in the night and caress him till he woke too.

"John's gone," he said. She touched his cheek, then dropped her hand. "He'll be all right," she said. But he saw the tears spring to her eyes again.

"I know he'll be all right," he said gruffly. "But I didn't want him to go." For a long moment neither of them spoke, till at last she turned back to the stove.

"Your food'll get cold," she said. He heard the catch in her voice. "Anyway," she went on, "you've still got Alan and Kevin. Alan's not interested in more school, and I don't think Kevin will be either. He's too . . . impatient." Andrew bent and picked his hat off the floor and tossed it onto the hook by the door and pulled off his jacket. Karen picked up the coffee pot and came and filled his cup as he sat down. He didn't want the food sitting in front of him. He reached back to his jacket for the flask.

"How long will this go on?" she said to him, not even reproaching him, only sad, her eyes gentle. He wished he knew; he wished it would end.

The door opened and Alan came in.

"What do you want us to do this afternoon?" he asked, not smiling or sitting down.

"Sit down," Andrew commanded, kicking a chair out for him. Reluctantly Alan sat. Andrew sipped his coffee. He had it in his mind to say something to Alan about what they would do now that John was gone, but he couldn't think exactly what it was he wanted to say. Alan moved restlessly.

"Your brother's gone," Andrew said. "He won't be back."

"I know," Alan said sharply. Andrew lifted his eyes and glared at him. Alan stared back, then lowered his eyes, as a flush crept up his neck. Andrew saw the blueness of his eyes, the thick black hair falling over his forehead. Surprised, he thought, he looks just like me, as though he hadn't known this, although everyone always said so.

"Now maybe you'll think about doing a little farming since we won't have as much help," Alan said in a carefully even tone. Andrew set his cup down abruptly. A little of the coffee slopped over onto the table. He reached for the flask and topped the coffee up with rye.

"Never," he said, simply, without meaning to. But then he said it again. "Never." There was a long silence. Then Alan said, slowly, in a determined, but quiet voice, "I want my own place." Andrew set his cup down in front of him. At the sink, Karen had turned to watch them. He saw the look on her face, not shocked or upset, only sad.

"How are you going to pull that off?" he asked, trying to hold down his rage. Alan was silent, then drew in a long breath and let it out.

"I hoped you'd give me some land. You got lots. And I always worked for you, since I was a kid. You owe me." Andrew couldn't speak, a hollow well of shock had opened deep inside him. He felt the loss of John's going so bitterly he couldn't speak. And now this. Alan stood, then strode across the kitchen and went outside, banging the door.

Andrew turned to Karen, who stood facing him, leaning against the sink.

"Did you hear that?" he asked, his disbelief in his voice.

"I heard," she said.

"This whole place'll be his," Andrew said, "if he could just wait." Karen turned back to the sink and began to wash the dishes.

"I never could understand him," Andrew said. "I never could."

It was getting colder out now. In the mornings there was sometimes a skiff of snow in the hollow places. It would be gone by noon, but any day they would have their first snowfall or their first blizzard. And still so much work to be done. They were riding in the hills, cutting out bunches of horses and bringing them in. Andrew paused, rising in his stirrups, then sitting again, while he looked over his land and his horses spread out around him. Their herd was up to five hundred head now, and Alan was complaining about what a nuisance they were and how the bottom had fallen out of horses. Horse ranching wasn't paying off any more, it was true, but Andrew could hardly bring himself to admit it. He wondered how many more years it would make sense to do this.

The bunch they were chasing was coming around the draw to his left and he spurred his horse, cutting the horses off so that they streamed out toward the south in the direction he wanted them to. When they got them into the corral, they cut out the ones they wanted to work with, pushed them into a smaller corral, then chased the others back out. This afternoon they were gelding young stallions.

On foot, they cut out the two-year-old Andrew had had his eye on since he was a foal. When they had him alone in a smaller corral, Andrew mounted and roped him. They tied the rope to the snubbing post, snugged it, threw the horse, and tied its legs. Bud sat on the young horse's head.

Andrew brought the pail of disinfected water and the tools and set them down beside the trussed horse. The branding fire in the corner, which Alan had started, crackled with a dull sound. The branding irons were still sitting in it although they had finished branding for the day.

Andrew decided it was time to let Alan cut. He had been thinking about it all fall. Now Alan was waiting, crouched patiently in the hard-packed dusty corral.

"You do it," Andrew said to him, gruffly, without meaning to. Alan looked at him, surprised. "Go ahead," Andrew said and nodded toward the horse. Alan rose, went to the pail of tools, reached for the knife, shook the blade dry, crouched, then hesitated, holding it above the horse's genitals. "Go ahead," Andrew said again, impatiently. He wanted the knife in his own hands, could feel the skin give as he made a clean, quick slice, anticipated already the horse's quivering. Still, Alan hesitated. "For Christ sake!" Andrew said, and had to restrain himself from taking the knife out of Alan's hand and doing it himself.

Abruptly Alan slit the sack, a ragged, too-deep cut. Blood seeped out. The horse jerked and Alan jumped back, lost his balance, then knelt again. Andrew almost shoved him aside, but held back. If Alan was scared, he would mess up the job for sure.

Now Alan was reaching for a testicle, struggling to keep it pulled up while the horse fought him, using his powerful muscles to keep them pulled up inside his body. Andrew wasn't sure his son was strong enough. The horse jerked and Bud had to fight to stay on his head. Alan jumped too, and Andrew wanted to yell at him to keep still. The horse was tied, it wasn't likely he could get up and Alan should know that.

Then Andrew saw how Alan's hands were shaking. He was just about to reach for the knife when Alan caught hold of the testicle and gripped it firmly. Andrew relaxed a little. He had the wood clamp in his hand, ready for Alan to take it from him. The horse struggled again and Alan let go and rose to a crouch.

"For Christ sake!" Andrew shouted. Without paying any attention to him, Alan bent over the horse again, grabbed for the testicle again in that rough, ruthless way he had, caught it, brought the knife around to slice the membrane that covered it, to peel it back. He cut quickly, too hard, the muscles of his upper arm and shoulder jerking once, then bulging. Blood spurted. He had cut the artery.

The horse gathered himself and gave a massive leap that threw Bud off his head. Alan leaped back, but the ropes binding the horse held. For a moment, as the horse subsided, nobody said anything. Blood was coming thick and fast, a bright colour that stained its dark flanks, and spread toward the ground.

Slowly Andrew loosened the ropes that held the horse and pulled them away. Bud looked at him uncertainly, then picked his hat up off the ground and went into the barn.

Alan had lost his nerve. That was what had happened. And this slender, perfect horse would die, was dying now.

Andrew looked at his son who hadn't moved since the horse had struggled to its feet, and then looked back to the horse which stood trembling in the corner of the corral. A stream of blood poured down the inside of his legs. Red. It was as red as anything he had ever seen. He looked at the horse's finely-shaped head, at its quivering nostrils, its long black mane, and its graceful shoulders covered with corral dust.

Alan walked away and climbed the corral, then leaned on the other side with his back to Andrew, as if he hadn't the strength to go any further. Andrew wanted to cry, then rage welled up in him as he watched the colt's life bleeding away.

He climbed the corral and went past Alan to the house. When Karen saw his face and then the blood on his hands and his clothes, she said, "What happened?" He pushed past her and went to the wall where his rifles hung in a rack. He took one down, sliding the bolt and checking it to see if it was clean.

"The kid botched the cutting," he said. "I've got to shoot the horse."

"Oh, Andy," she said, then stood still as though she were trying to decide what she could do, or what she could say.

"Forget it," he said angrily, and went outside, slamming the door. He strode toward the corral, feeling in his pocket for shells. Alan straightened as he approached, and Andrew was ready to thrust the gun at him and say,

"You do it, you finish the job." But when he saw Alan's face, he almost dropped the gun and instead of giving it to him, he kept on going past him.

He went into the pen where they had been working. The colt was still standing in the corner of the corral, his head down, the blood still streaming down his flanks. Andrew raised the rifle to his shoulder and sighted down it, but his eyes blurred; he saw again the look on Alan's face, tried to erase it, came back to the job in front of him and sighted again. He was trembling, he couldn't believe it. He lowered the gun, then took a firm stance, a deep breath, raised it again, and fired, once. The horse fell.

He turned, went out through the gate, leaving it swinging, crossed the main corral, calling to Alan or Bud or whoever was listening, "Haul it out of there." Then he got into his truck, and started it.

He sat for a moment, hunched over the wheel, and let what he had seen in Alan's eyes flood over him. He had seen simple hatred. His own son hated him. It was a revelation too harsh to be borne.

"Don't expect so much," Karen had said, more than once, but he hadn't listened. Suddenly he thought that he still might go to Alan, talk to him, maybe they could still reach some kind of understanding. He almost got out of the truck again. Then he remembered Alan's eyes and he knew beyond a doubt that it was no use. Things had gone too far.

Despair washed over him. Now he knew that for years he had been building and working with Alan's eventual inheritance in his mind. He didn't know when he had started to think this way, it had crept up on him without his even realizing it, and now, now he knew it, and it was too late. Alan would never take over the ranch, unless Andrew was dead. All his years of work washed over him. Had it all been for nothing?

He drove out of the yard, spinning the tires in the dirt.

CHAPTER FIVE

Winter came and passed again. It seemed increasingly to Andrew that the most amazing thing about life was the way it kept on going, year after year after year, in spite of the most cataclysmic things that happened in a season. Here it was, spring again, almost summer, another crop of calves were ready for branding.

At dawn he stood on the steps and saw that it looked like rain; purple clouds were banked in the west, reflecting the sunrise so that they took on a rosy glow. The wind was whipping the poplars Karen had planted when they first moved here. He couldn't help thinking of all the sunrises he had seen from the door of the shack that was just over the hill, unimpeded by the branches of trees or other buildings. Sunrises were a part of him, he saw them with his soul, his heart rose with the sun. He had felt the clean prairie, vast and bright, in the early light lying around him like a gift.

But this morning he looked without affection at Karen's neat flowerbeds, at the lawn always parched for water and the border of white-washed rocks down the drive. Without affection and uneasily, and yet with satisfaction. He had started with nothing, it was true, and he had built this place. The house loomed up behind him, a presence he could not help but feel menaced him, and behind it lay the barn, the shop, and all the corrals. A man's life, he thought, you measured it by buildings.

Cows and calves, driven in the night before, were bawling in the wrangle pasture. He and the boys had to get out at once, push them into the corrals, and start the sorting so that when the neighbours arrived to help they could begin branding right away. He looked at the western sky again, trying to judge whether it would rain or not, then turned and went inside through the hall to the kitchen where Karen was already at work.

As he sat down Bud entered through the outside door, in from the bunkhouse. He sat down too just as Anne came quietly in, tying on her apron. She stood, rubbed her eyes, then took the coffee pot from the stove and poured coffee for Bud and Andrew.

Karen was rearranging the dozen pies she had baked that were sitting on one counter, trying to make room for something she was working at in a big mixing bowl. Alan and Kevin came in together from upstairs and sat down at the table. The bacon sizzled in the frying pan on the stove and Anne hurried to turn it. They sat quietly, barely awake, sipping coffee and smelling the food cooking. Red-winged blackbirds competed noisily with the magpies in the trees outside the windows. The cattle bawled distantly.

"Wind's died down," Andrew said, listening.

"Them clouds are going on by," Bud said. "Nothing to worry about."

Andrew watched Anne as she cracked eggs into a skillet. She moved slowly, quietly, with assurance. She would graduate from high school in a few days. She planned to be married in late July to the son of a farmer who lived away to the east. She was so sensible, so steady. He felt as if he didn't know her at all.

Moira bounced into the room, her red hair flaring.

"You didn't wake me up," she complained to Anne.

"Yes, I did," Anne said.

"Look after that toast, Moira," Karen said over her shoulder. Already Karen's face was flushed. Today she would feed twenty-five men. The kitchen would be full of women; the yard, the house, the barn would be overrun with running, giggling, fighting, squalling kids. It would be dark before any of them had a moment of peace. Still, it was a good time, a happy time. Andrew looked forward to it.

By nine all the cows were separated from the calves, Alan had two branding fires going, and the neighbours had arrived, some of them unloading saddled horses from their stocktrailers.

Alan and Kevin were sitting in the corral on horseback, coiling their ropes, ready to begin heeling.

"Need some more heelers," Andrew called. The men in the corral milled around, sorting themselves out. "You two vaccinate?" Andrew asked two of them. He pointed to the vaccine guns and the vials of vaccine that sat in a box by the branding fire Bud was tending. The two men walked toward the box. "Bill, can I get you to castrate?" He had picked an older man, a neighbour whose know-how he trusted, before some greenhorn who would botch the job and kill calves on him, could volunteer. He handed Bill a castrating knife. He would use the other one himself.

Already Alan was dragging a calf from the pen, his rope caught around its back legs. It bawled as it slid across the ground.

"Need some wrestlers," he shouted as he halted his horse past the fire so that the calf lay in just the right spot. In the pen Kevin's rope was still whirling. Needs more practice, that boy, Andrew thought to himself.

Bring 'em out," he shouted, and one of the neighbour's rope caught and his horse started the slow walk, pulling the calf across the corral toward the second branding fire where Andrew stood, the knife in his hand.

Already a row of young girls sat on the corral in the morning sun, watching the men work. Small boys tried to help, running errands and sitting on the calves' heads and getting thrown off. Smoke rose from the branding fires, the smell of searing hide and flesh filled the air, cows bawled, calves bleated and cried, men's voices rose in shouts and laughter. In pails held by boys at each branding fire the pile of testicles grew, and the dogs had to be chased away. The day wore on, clear and bright, a perfect late June day.

They were running low on vaccine. Andrew tried to remember if he had brought it from the house or left it in the far corral early in the morning when he had gone there on some errand or other. He decided to check the corral rather than brave the kitchen unless he had to. He hopped the railing into the alley, climbed the fence and was in a smaller corral off which several others branched.

He climbed another fence, moving more slowly now, then stopped. The noise and dust faded behind him. He turned, leaned on the fence and looked across the railings to the big corral. He could see the hats of the men on horseback bobbing, the horses' heads jerking, the silhouettes of the girls sitting on the far railing, and the little boys sitting on the barn roof. A haze of dust and smoke hung in the air above their heads.

It was as though he was there and yet not there. An impassable distance lay between him and the people and the animals in the corral. Behind and beyond the crowd, beyond the yard full of parked cars and trucks, the house and fences and the trees, lay the prairie.

It did not seem so long since he had been a small boy himself at brandings, sneaking into the pens to ride the calves. He remembered all the roundups, brandings, and cattle drives he had been on. A quiet settled on him, a measured sadness. He saw as clearly as if it had been written on the weathered fenceposts in front of him that this was over. That something had been finished. He felt old, although he was not yet sixty, and filled with sorrow.

He lifted his eyes and stared at the bright, summery day. He could hardly believe what he saw. A small plane was flying over the yard and the corrals, so low that he could read the writing on its wings. It was the kind of airplane people paid for rides in at fairs, and the sight of it, a phantom, sudden and silent, over the unwitting heads of the ranching people in the corral struck him in the heart like an arrow. Spellbound, he watched its silver wings and belly catching the sun and flashing light as it passed by. Only as it vanished into a speck above the hills, did he hear its roar, a distant humming that grew quieter, then disappeared too. In the corral the branding went on, the plane's approach and departure unnoticed.

In late afternoon they finished the branding. Andrew, Alan, Bud and Kevin mounted and drove the cows and their bleating stunned calves back out to the wrangle pasture, then went back, opened a pen and drove the bull out into the pasture with them. The next day the three of them and Bud would do the mothering-up. Then everyone went to the house to wash up and eat the second huge meal that Karen and the women had prepared for them.

But the branding wasn't over yet. As soon as the men had eaten they went back out to the corral. Andrew stoked one of the branding fires, Alan brought more wood and when it was blazing well, Andrew and Bill took the pails of testicles to the pump just outside the corral and began to wash them. Behind them the other men were drinking the beer that Andrew had provided, squatting in the dirt and laughing together.

After a cursory washing they brought the pails of testicles back to the fire and Andrew and Bill began to peel the membrane off each one and to split them. As they finished preparing one, they handed it to one of the waiting men, who, using a green willow stick that had been used at quite a few brandings, speared it, singed it black on the fire, and ate it, washing it down with the beer.

Small boys watched hopefully from the sidelines.

"Here," Andrew said, and handed one to a boy of about ten. The child took it proudly and looked up at his father, who was leaning against the railing beside him. It was a quiet evening except for the wailing from the nearby pasture. At ten o'clock it would still be light. "Eat it," Andrew said, grinning. The boy's father offered his son his roasting stick. The child took it, and awkwardly thrust the testicle onto it. "You ain't a man till you've ate prairie oysters," Andrew said to the boy, laughing.

The child thrust the stick into the fire and waited. Alan said, "You guys feel like a little excitement?" The young men rose, leaned their sticks against the corral. Alan pointed to one of the pens. "Got a few cows left in and Josh brought his bull-rope." He started toward the smaller pen and the others, slapping the dust off their pants and pulling their hats on more securely, followed him.

The child pulled the stick out of the fire. The testicle was blackened.

He pulled it off gingerly, put it into his mouth and chewed thoughtfully. A peculiar look crossed his face.

"Here, his father said, and over the guffaws of the men, handed the boy his bottle of beer.

There were shouts coming from the pen now as the younger men drove a cow into the chute at the end of the alley. The pails were empty, the testicles all gone. Andrew rose slowly, his knee joints cracking.

"Christ, I'm getting old," he said to Bill.

"Remember when we used to ride in stampedes?" Bill asked, watching Alan and another man fixing the rigging on the big horned cow they had in the chute. Bill's boy, Josh, was preparing to ride her.

"Never did do much of that," Andrew said, "not in an arena, anyway."

The cow was out in the corral now, bucking as hard as any bull, raising her twelve hundred pounds into the air and coming down with a twist that hurt Andrew's back to watch. The men perched on the railings waved their hats and shouted encouragement. Laughter rang on the still air. The bell under the cow's belly jangled crazily and was drowned out by her furious bellowing. She jerked and suddenly Josh was dumped into the rolling dust and running hard for the corral with the cow after him. Out of the corner of his eye Andrew noticed the boy who had eaten the testicle bragging to a group of boys smaller than himself.

"I better check them calves over," he said to Bill. He tossed his empty beer bottle into one of the rapidly emptying boxes and went to the barn. He led his saddlehorse out, mounted him, and rode out into the wrangle pasture. You never knew when one of them might keep on bleeding.

He was glad of the excuse to get away if only for a few minutes. The good-natured shouts and laughter of the young men riding the cows reached him clearly where he rode in the nearby field. In the west the sun was sinking lower, colouring the sky yellow and red. He thought of Karen and his daughters at work in the house, and of the wedding approaching at the end of the month. It seemed incredible to him that he had somehow spun this web of lives when he had come alone into the world. Daughters who fell in love, sons who wanted, his own and his wife's desires. It was not even all the buildings and the corrals that surprised him now. He knew the prairie well enough to know that all his buildings were nothing, barely a speck on the face of the land. They could vanish overnight as he'd seen so many buildings vanish over the years. But this web of emotions inside of which all of them lived, usually, it seemed to him, at cross-purposes, was there no escaping it? No living free of it?

He rode slowly, studying each calf. The light was fading, the grass he was riding through turned pink in the last rays of light, the noises behind him died slowly. His unease settled some, he felt a weary contentment seeping through him. There was nothing more he could do here tonight. He turned his horse back toward the yard.

It was midnight when the last of the neighbours pulled out of the yard. Karen and Andrew stood on the steps and waved good-bye to the last truck as it backed out, its headlights lighting up the house and yard, then sweeping across the fields and slowly disappearing down the road into the purple-blue of the night. They went inside to the kitchen.

Karen stood in the doorway, still wearing her apron, and looked around as though there should be something more to do before she went to bed, but the women hadn't left until every last pot and dish was scrubbed and shiny and put away, till the tabletops and counters shone with wiping and the floor was cleaner than it had been when they arrived.

"Well," she said, sounding lost, "we might as well go to bed." Andrew had sat down at his place at the table, a last drink in front of him, every muscle aching. The big house was still.

"Christ, I must be getting old," he said. "I hurt everywhere." Karen stopped her uncertain glancing around the room and focused on him, her eyes gradually darkening, seeing him.

"We're neither of us as young as we used to be," she said, as though she was informing him of something he would do well to pay attention to.

Alan came in and stopped in the doorway. They turned to look at him. His expression was determined, his mouth set in a tight line. Andrew looked at him as though he was seeing him for the first time, noticing how tall he was, taller than Andrew himself, how fine-grained his skin was, like his mother's, and how there was none of the boy left in him.

Before Alan could speak, Andrew said, "I want to talk to you. Sit down." Alan hesitated, then came in, sat down across from Andrew and waited. Karen didn't move. "Get him a glass," Andrew said to her. She brought one and Andrew filled it from the bottle that sat on the table in front of him. He raised his glass, made a motion toward Alan, and drank. A second passed, then Alan drank too. Andrew sighed heavily, and rubbed his hand across his forehead.

"You want your own place, you can have it," he said, letting the empty glass rest on the oilcloth in front of him. Karen drew in her breath, then pulled out a chair and sat down. Alan didn't move. He raised his eyes to Andrew's.

"You mean that?" he asked. He had hardly spoken to Andrew since the gelding incident the fall before. It was as though they were not father and son anymore, but only two men who happened to live in the same house.

"I'll give you that half a section on the east side, across from the homestead. I'll give you . . . twenty cows. You've already got thirty head." Alan raised his hands as if to do something with them, then lowered them onto the tabletop.

"No," he said. "I don't want the cows. Would you buy mine from me?" Andrew stared at him.

"How the hell are you going to survive?" he asked.

"Il manage," Alan said. "Will you buy my cows from me, or do I have to put them through the sale ring?" Andrew thought for a minute.

"You're making a mistake," he said. "Think about it first. You'll need them." Alan's eyes moved from Andrew's face to a spot in the distance. He thought for a moment, then said, "All right. When do I get the deed?" Anger rose in Andrew and he shifted in his chair, leaning forward. He grasped the glass, then let it go, setting it down with a crack. He would have said something, but what was there to say?

"We can see the lawyer on Monday." He pushed his chair back angrily, stood, shoving it into the table as he turned away and left the room.

On Monday he drove to the lawyer's office with Alan following behind in his own truck. Together they walked up the wooden stairs to the lawyer's office and went inside.

He signed the deed over to Alan. Alan picked the papers up from the desk and studied them closely, holding them up to the light as if to make sure they really said the land was his. After a moment he set the papers down and shook the lawyer's hand. He didn't seem to notice his father's outstretched hand. Andrew stood then and put on his hat. Then the two of them left the office and went down the stairs, Andrew ahead, Alan following.

They stood for a moment in front of the lawyer's office on the board sidewalk and were careful not to look at each other. Andrew had the feeling that the lawyer was watching them from his window above. Andrew didn't ask Alan what he meant to do with a half section of grassland if he didn't want the cows, his own, or the ones Andrew had offered him. Without cows the land was only good for speculation, or else, and here Andrew had to pause in his thinking, Alan wanted to plow up the land and farm it.

"You'll be moving out then?" Andrew asked, staring at the clouds that were racing past, low in the sky. The day was warm, with a strong, hot wind. He pushed his hat back from his forehead and allowed himself a glimpse of Alan's face. His son was staring across the street to the grocery store as if it held some fascination for him.

"Yup," he said. "I'll find a place in town till I can decide whether to build on the place or not."

"There's water there," Andrew offered. "I can show you the place. I'm sure if you dug you'd hit good water."

"Yeah," Alan said, his tone noncommittal.

"The cows?" Andrew ventured, finally.

"I'll let you know." Alan turned away, but not without Andrew seeing what he thought was the hint of a smile. "See you later," and Alan was gone, striding down the street toward the stockyards. Andrew watched him go, stepping back into the shade cast by the building. He thought of going to the bar for a drink, but decided against it. For some reason, he didn't want to go home. He thought briefly of John who would graduate from law school next spring. And Anne would be gone soon. Only Moira would be home for the summer, and there was still Kevin. He found his back was aching in a low, persistent way and he pushed away from the wall, crossed the sidewalk, and got into his truck.

When he reached home, instead of driving into the yard, he turned the truck north and headed out across the prairie toward the field where his herd of horses were. He followed the trail that had once been the wagon trail to the larger town twenty-five miles to the north.

He stopped, opened the gate, drove through, stopped again, got out and closed it. When he put his hand on the sun-warmed wood of the fencepost, he saw in his mind's eye a picture of a horse he had once owned, a jumper. He never had to open a gate as long as he rode him.

He got back in the truck and drove down a faint trail across the field to the highest hill. The truck climbed slowly to the top. He parked, got out, and stood leaning against the hood as he surveyed the horses spread out in bunches below him.

The day was growing warmer, the sun blazing down as it always did at this time of year. Here on the hilltop he felt the full brunt of the wind that always blew, hard or gently, and he welcomed its singing in his ears. He listened to its moan as it swept through the grass and whistled around the truck.

Far to the north he could make out the elevators, shimmering like sails on the horizon. To the east, to the west, and to the south beyond his ranch he saw squares of green wheat crops, interspersed with squares of beige summerfallow, and squares of pale native grass. He wondered how long it would be before he would look out from this hilltop and see no native grass at all.

He sighed and turned his attention to the horses. With tractors and trucks being used more all the time there was less and less call for horses. Especially for a mixed, wild herd like his. He squinted in the brilliant light as he watched them grazing. Below him, near the bottom of the hill he had parked on, a curious bunch had gathered and stood, their tails and manes blowing in the wind, their ears pointed. If he moved, they would run.

He would have to sell them. Such bitterness rose in his throat that he thought he might choke. Abruptly he straightened, threw his arms out and shouted, "Go on, you bastards! Get out of here!" The horses turned as one and raced across the draw, rounded a dried-up slough, their tails streaming out behind them, and were gone around the base of the next hill, out of sight. When they had vanished, he got back in the truck and eased his way down the hill.

Alan arrived home in time for supper. When he came in, the others were seated at the table—Andrew, Bud, Kevin—and Karen was at the sink draining a steaming pot of vegetables. Alan banged the door behind him, his blue-eyed glance swept the table, he went to his mother and hugged her with one arm while he pulled his hat off with the other hand. She looked up, surprised. A kind of energy seemed to burst from him, he bristled with it, as though he could barely contain himself. Andrew lowered his eyes. Alan pulled his chair out with a clatter and sat down.

"I'm starved" he said. "Pass everything." Kevin laughed out loud. He watched his brother with admiring eyes.

"What's up, Al?" he asked, grinning. Alan piled some mashed potatoes onto his plate, began to ladle gravy over them.

"Sold my cows, found a place to live today."

"Ohhh," Karen said, then set the vegetables on the table. Nobody else said anything. Alan reached for the platter of meat, forked some onto his plate, but he couldn't help shooting one quick glance at Andrew. Andrew met it, then both of them looked quickly away again. But not so quickly that Andrew didn't see the triumph in Alan's eyes. A longing for his horses running in the hills touched Andrew so strongly that he could almost taste it.

"Why did you sell the cows?" Karen asked, perplexed. "Are you going into purebreds? Into registered cattle?" Alan said, "I'm going to be living in that old place of Switzer's, that small house by the post office, till I can get my own house built."

"Oh," Karen said. "You sold them to buy building materials." Alan didn't answer her. How can she be so stupid, Andrew wondered. Doesn't she see he's going to plow up my land? Doesn't she see he's going to use the money to buy farm machinery?

"Kevin," Alan said. "You going to help me cut out my cows tomorrow? I got a truck coming for them in the afternoon."

"Sure, Al," Kevin said.

Andrew said, as naturally as possible, "I'll give you a hand too. What time's the truck coming?" He smiled, and at the other end of the now too-big table, he could feel Karen relaxing.

"Thought you might come and work for me this summer, Kevin," Alan went on, with such firm deliberation that Andrew almost rose and struck him. He held himself in and took another forkful of potatoes. They tasted like cardboard, but he swallowed them.

"Alan!" Karen said. "Don't be ridiculous! There are plenty of men in town you can hire. Your father needs Kevin."

"What do you think, Kevin?" Alan persisted, half-smiling, looking at his youngest brother. Kevin had set his fork down in surprise. He looked at Alan and then at his father with an expression that was almost frightened.

"Gee, Al, I can't . . ." his voice trailed off. Andrew couldn't hold back his rage any longer.

"Go with him," he said. "Work for him if you want to." Karen intervened.

"Don't . . ." she said. But he had already stopped. What was the point of it. He had never even struck Alan, not once, since the day he was born. He had made him ride, sure, rain or shine, long after the boy was bone-weary, but that was what cowboying was. He had to teach him that. He had taught him all that he knew, everything. I never had a father, he wanted to say, you don't know what it's like to try to be a father when you never had one yourself. But he kept his head down, kept silent, forced himself to eat what was on his plate.

As soon as he decently could, he left the table and went outside. Force of habit drew him to the barn, where Nugget still stood in his stall waiting for someone to ride him or turn him out. The horse turned his head and whinnied when Andrew entered. Abruptly he slid his saddle off the rack and threw it onto the horse's back. He bridled him, led him out into the corral and mounted him. He decided to have one last look at his land before Alan had it broken.

He rode slowly, the horse's hooves swishing in the grass, his saddle leather creaking. He tried not to think, tried to just ride, concentrating on the feel of the horse, as if he were a green bronc. Behind him the sky was growing brighter with that last blaze of light before twilight and then nightfall. He felt the warm soft air on the backs of his hands and on his face. He could hear the hills whispering to him. He felt as though he had been riding forever across the prairie, across the pale and fading land.

It was dark when he returned, and the only light on in the house was in the living room. He dismounted, turned Nugget out, and went into the house.

Karen was sitting in her easy chair in the living room, knitting, the lamp beside her casting a warm yellow light over her. Her needles clicked and flashed. He sat down heavily across from her in his own easy chair. "Kevin gone to bed?" he asked. It was in his mind to talk with Kevin, but it seemed now like more than he could bring himself to do. He hadn't the heart for it. She nodded, yes, but kept on knitting: "What are you making?" he asked. She looked up briefly, surprised.

"A sweater for John's baby," she said. He had forgotten that John was married, that there was a baby coming. He lit a cigarette and leaned back in his chair. He was very tired. For no reason, he remembered the Montana outlaw he had known as a boy, remembered seeing him cornered and a prisoner in the badlands near the border, one hot summer day, a long time ago.

"Are you all right, dear?" Karen asked. He nodded, flicked the ashes off his cigarette. "Don't be too upset about Alan," she said.

"I don't want to talk about it," he said.

"All right," she replied. Her voice was soft. He remembered her as a girl. He rose awkwardly, went to her, bent, and kissed her forehead clumsily, then patted her cheek. She looked up and smiled and he could see tears in her eyes. "Things are never as bad as they seem," she said to him.

"Oh, yes, they are," he said. He went back to his chair and sank back into it.

They sat for a long time like that, Karen knitting, Andrew smoking, until they heard far off in the night the howling of coyotes coming faintly to them through the melancholy air. The dogs responded howling till their voices broke.

249

CHAPTER SIX

Something was the matter with Karen. She didn't hear him when he spoke, she never went out, when he came around the corner of the house he would hear her talking to herself as she worked in her garden staking her tomato plants or pulling weeds, or hoeing. He decided to talk to her about it.

He was reading his paper, sitting in his easy chair in the kitchen when she came in from outside, breathing heavily from exertion and from her weight, and unfastening her sun hat with fingers sticky with dirt from her garden. She ran water into the sink, scrubbing the dirt away. He watched her. At last he said, "You okay?"

She stopped what she was doing, turned the water off and wiped her hands vigorously.

"I suppose not," she said. "I suppose you could say not." He lowered his paper.

"What's the matter?" She let the towel hang from her hand, not even rubbing it absent-mindedly on the counter as she usually did.

I don't know," she said, staring at the floor in front of her. "It's . . . lonely," she said finally.

"Go and visit Anne and the kids, or Moira," he said. Mutely, she shook her head, then dabbed at her eyes with the towel. "Go out, go visiting," he said. "I'll drive you." She shook her head again, then suddenly pushed herself upright staring fiercely at him, her eyes dark and intense.

"We've gone wrong," she said. "We've failed." He let the paper fall to his knees. It slipped further and fell off onto the floor.

"What?" he asked incredulous, not bothering to retrieve it.

"Look around," she said. Involuntarily he turned his head to sweep the room.

"I am," he said, still astonished. She snorted angrily, her eyes still fastened on his. "Remember what we had when we started?" he asked her, angry too, now. "Remember . . ."

"You know what I mean," she said. In some deep part of him he did know, but he didn't want to think about it. He rose.

"I always loved you," he said. She stopped for a moment, her eyes changed and she saw him again.

"I know that," she said. She fiddled with her apron. "I can't even imagine ever loving anyone else." She grasped the towel in both hands, then began to fold it neatly in squares.

"I always worked," he said. "Always, even when I was drinking."

"Yes," she said.

"I don't know what else a man can do," he said, opening his hands as though to show her he held nothing back. She stared at his hands, then went to the stove, picked up the kettle, brought it back to the sink and ran water into it. He sat down again.

"So tell me what's the matter, what I can do." She put the lid back on the kettle, carried it to the stove, set it down, and turned the burner on.

"We aren't old yet," she said. "Not really. I'm only fifty-eight."

"I feel old," he said, although in his heart he didn't, even if he did in other ways.

"You always worked too hard," she said. "It's no wonder you feel old." "I had to work," he pointed out. She sighed. "You worked hard, too." She whirled suddenly, her skirt and apron swishing, to face him. "That's it," she said. "I mean, is that it? Is that what life is for? Just work?" He could not answer her, having wondered this a thousand times himself. "There's our kids," he said. "Our grandchildren." This seemed to calm her and she looked into the distance, seeing them, perhaps.

"Yes," she said, her voice distant and filled with pain. "There's that." He half-expected her to start talking to herself as though he wasn't there. She frowned, then said, "But . . ."

"But what?" he asked softly, when she didn't continue.

"But, no," she said, "because I was somebody's child once, and look at me." She looked at him with a puzzled expression. He couldn't answer this. "Your water's boiling," he said, finally. She looked at the stove, still frowning, then came to herself, said, "Oh," quickly, and turned off the burner. She took the lid off the teapot and made the tea.

Later that day he found her in the garden. She had been kneeling and had slumped forward and onto her side, into the border of nasturtiums and petunias she had always grown around the outer edge of the vegetable garden no matter how short the water supply was. Her hair, pulled back in a bun, had come unpinned and lay in a dark tangle over one shoulder. It had hardly greyed. He fell to his knees beside her, touched her face with the flat of his hand. Her eyes were closed, her mouth open. She looked more puzzled than surprised or afraid.

He did not know why he wasn't surprised, but he wasn't. A stroke, I suppose, he thought, humbly. She had grown so stout. He took her sun hat, that had tumbled away from her head and lay in the pea vines, and set it over her face. After a moment, he touched her hands, and straightened her body. Then he went into the house to make the phone calls.

When he was done he came back to her body. For some time now he had been suffering from spells of shortness of breath, and when one day, he had felt a severe pain in his chest that travelled down his arm, he had known that there was something wrong with his heart. He had told no one. He looked down at his dead wife lying among her flowers, the summer sun blazing down on her, and thought, I have to get her out of the heat. It seemed imperative to him to rescue her from the sun.

He bent and put one arm under her shoulders, the other under her knees. When he tried to rise with her, he couldn't. She was too heavy.

The old, familiar anger came boiling over him, so strong that suddenly he bent like a young man, braced his legs, and grasped her tightly. Sweat poured down his temples and the back of his neck. Slowly he raised her out of the crushed flowers, her head falling back and the hat he had so carefully placed over her face slipping off onto the ground. He let it go, turning slowly with his burden.

He staggered toward the house, almost fell, caught himself, still holding Karen, and took another step forward. His arms ached with her weight. He staggered forward another step. Sweat trickled from his hair into his eyes, stinging, but he couldn't let go to wipe it away.

His chest had begun to hurt, it was growing tighter by the second. He moved forward a few more steps. The kitchen door wasn't much further, he could make it. I have to get her out of the heat, he told himself. She never could stand the heat.

When he reached the house he thrust himself and her against the wall, balancing her with its help while he caught his breath. The pain in his chest was steady, not getting worse, not letting up. With one hand he managed to pull open the screen door, he eased her through it, feet first.

He would put her on their bed in their room off the kitchen. He did not want to set her down, but he thought he might have to rest her on the kitchen table. The pain had begun to grow worse; everything took on a red tinge. But he would not set her down. Haven't I carried her this far? he asked himself.

He lurched again, rounding the corner of the table, catching a chair somehow and hearing it crash to the floor behind him. She was his wife, he would lay her down on their bed.

As he set her onto the bed, he fell, sprawling out across her body. For a moment, smelling the scent of nasturtiums, he couldn't rise, the pain choked him, filled his chest, he couldn't get air. Then slowly, the pain easing a little, he pushed himself upright. He straightened her body, pulled down her dress and smoothed it, arranged her hair around her shoulders. He stood back and looked at her. He wished he could smooth the frown from her forehead.

So, it would end like this. He began to cry, the pain in his chest spreading to his arms and legs. He fell into the chair at the foot of their bed and let it wash over him.

By the time they began to arrive, he was calm again.

"I found her in the garden," he told them, and they all went out, one by one, to look at the spot, as if it might tell them something. He let them go without remarking. Alan came finally, and stood in the doorway.

"Dad," he said. Their eyes met and slid away. They had never said aloud to each other what needed to be said. The abyss was too wide now. They both felt it, and didn't try.

Anne arrived later that afternoon, and Moira in the evening, with her children.

"I'm sorry, Dad, but there was no one to leave them with."

"It's all right," he said. He did not ask her what had happened to her husband. There had been nothing but trouble there. Later he would give her some money. She looked as though she needed it. Karen had always been the one to tell him what was needed. He studied her little ones, a plump, dark-haired sleepy little boy, and a little girl with Moira's red hair.

"Where's Kevin?" she asked.

"Drilling in the Arctic," Alan said. "The funeral will be over before we reach him."

"All right everyone," Anne said. "Here's what I want you to do."

He woke in the night suddenly as though a weight had fallen on his chest. He couldn't make out what had wakened him, then remembered Karen was dead. He lay still, listening as though the night sounds might tell him something. The room was lit with a keen, blue light. A full moon. She had chosen to die when the moon was full. He rose from the bed and went to the window. An owl was hooting in the trees. He listened. The sound came to him clear as a bell: hoo-hoo, hoo-hoo, hoo-hoo. It repeated its question over and over again. When it fell silent at last, he turned away and went downstairs to the kitchen.

He sat down at his accustomed place at the head of the long, rectangular table. The moon shone in the window lighting the big room. He felt small, and alone. He looked down at his hands resting on the table. They were old hands, wrinkled and veined and scarred. Slowly he became aware of her presence there, with him. He felt her love for him glowing with a steady light all around him. She had come to say good-bye. He sat that way, not moving, until he could no longer feel her presence. Then he got up from the table, slowly, like an old man, and went back upstairs to the guest room.

When the funeral was over, the neighbours and his children gone, he felt the full weight of her loss. He felt it in the sound of his own footsteps crossing the carpeted floor, he felt it in the sight of her empty chair, her teapot sitting on the kitchen counter, he felt it in the weight of her frying pan in the morning.

He had never liked this house. He mistrusted it and what it stood for. It had always made him uneasy. And now it was empty. Empty and senseless.

One morning, two weeks after her death, after he had sent Anne back to her farmer-husband and her children, and Moira back to her typist's job in Calgary, he gathered a few things, walked ceremonially out the front door and closed it behind him. The latch was almost silent, but it seemed to him that he could hear the sound of the closing door echoing through the empty rooms behind him.

Her poplars sighed, rustled their shiny leaves. The short lawn grass was already dying without water. He felt immeasurably sorry for it, planted in a place it was never meant to grow, where it was doomed. The white rail fence he had built around the yard to please her had had its annual coat of paint. It gleamed boldly in the sun as if it would last forever. A couple of crows flapped out of the trees above him, black against the sky, cawing at him.

He went down the steps, got into his truck, and drove down the gravelled drive and out the gate.

PART FOUR

CHAPTER ONE

Morning had come again. Andrew stood on the steps in the blue pre-dawn shadows and watched the sun rise. It lifted rapidly over the edge of the earth, a molten gold, first one luminous, breathtaking ray, and a wafer gleaming above the dark horizon, then more rays striking him full in the face where he stood, so that he had to turn his head away. More light appeared and for a second Andrew had the sensation of the sun as an angry, exalted god hanging in the sky and of the earth he stood on spinning swiftly, wildly, inexorably toward it. The golden glow grew larger, took on curvature, then raced into view. Its light grew blinding, it poured over the land, erasing shadows, striking familiar objects and showing them for once precise, perfect and unreal.

He went inside his shack and shut the door. He moved slowly to the stove, crumpled an old paper, stuffed it into the bottom, found some kindling in the bottom of the woodbox, and set that carefully on top of the paper, and on top of that put a few small sticks of wood. He struck a match on the stove lid and threw it in. At once the fire blazed up. He was reminded of the sun rising outside, and he stared at the fire for a moment, thinking of this before he closed the lid.

He found his pipe where he had left it by his bed, walked back into the kitchen scraping out the bowl, filled it, tamped the tobacco down, and lit it. The room grew warmer. He sat down in the rocking chair that had been his mother's, stretched out his legs, and smoked while he waited for the fire to get hot enough to put in the big chunks of wood.

After a few minutes he rose and put more wood on the fire. When he was sure it would burn, he dipped his coffee pot full of water from the pail that sat on the counter, measured the coffee into it, and set it on the stove.

The small room was growing lighter now as the sun rose higher in the sky. Even in the middle of the day, though, the house was not very bright, because there were too few windows and they were too small. His mother had sometimes complained about that, but mostly during the daylight hours she was too busy working to notice how dim it was. When they had built that extra room on so long ago, she had a big window put in, but it was on the north wall so it hadn't helped much. And anyway, he reminded himself, she was never a person for the light. Except when she was dying. She had wanted light then.

He never went into the parlour now unless one of his children came. He had to laugh at the way they came in and perched gingerly on the dusty, horsehide sofa, looking around the room as if something might jump out and bite them. Thank God they hardly ever bothered him anymore, having figured out fairly early that trying to be nice to him wouldn't change whatever he had written in his will. He wondered if he was being fair to them.

None of them but Moira really needed his money, such as it was. He'd had to help her after Art finally left her for good, but now that the kids were older even she was doing all right. Alan's farming had paid off as he had said it would; he was a rich man, for as long as his land lasted, anyway. Anne's husband was a good farmer, although he had never tried to get big like Alan, and they were comfortable. John was still lawyering wherever he was. Somewhere in the East. Maybe working for the government. Andrew couldn't remember if somebody had told him this or if he'd made it up because it sounded so right. And Kevin, Kevin needed his money least of all. He'd gone off from Alan's place and worked on the oil rigs when he was still only a kid, had invested other people's money in his own drilling outfit and now, at thirty-eight or nine, or was it forty? Andrew couldn't remember, he was wealthier than his father or his brother had ever dreamt of being. And much good it would do him, much good it would do any of them, Andrew thought, amused. He didn't know whether to laugh or cry over what he knew. He said it out loud, softly. "I don't know whether to laugh or cry." It didn't sound any different than when he'd only thought it; the room was as still, the cobwebs hung indifferently in the window, the fire crackled. He couldn't tell anymore when he'd said something out loud or when he'd only thought it.

His coffee was boiling. He got up, poured himself a cupful, put sugar in it, and took it back to his chair. No, they hardly bothered him anymore. Anne with her brusque good sense understood he didn't want her, had said, "I love you, Dad," in Karen's voice, and gone away. He was no longer sure Alan existed, wondered if he'd been swallowed up by his ambition and all his land. John had been away so long that Andrew could hardly remember him as a man. And Kevin spent his time flying around the world. His children were remote from him, as, he thought, it was meant to be. He didn't miss them, nor did he have need of them. He thought of Karen lying dead among the flowers, and loneliness touched him, then passed. He had missed her from the moment she had left him, he would miss her till he saw her again.

When he had finished his coffee, he set the mug on the scarred wooden table and pulled himself to his feet. He put another chunk of wood on the fire so the room would be warm when he returned, put on his jacket, set his hat on his head, and went back outside.

Another spring had come, after so many springs. The snow was almost gone, the hills were bare and yellow, the sweep of prairie brushed here and there with the last of the snowdrifts. He stood on the step and looked far to the south, to the east, and to the north. The landscape lay unchanged, looking as it had when he had first seen it, in that far-away, dreamlike time of his childhood. He breathed deeply and felt calmed and comforted.

He took his walking stick from its place by the door, a weathered poplar branch from which he had chiseled the small branches and smoothed the surfaces, went down the two steps, and started for the corrals. They were silvered with age, collapsing into the ground, but still, every morning he walked through them. He poked at the poles with his stick, or paused to lean against a section that was still sturdy enough to hold him. He recalled clearly every detail of their construction, and all the repairs he had done to them, the changes he had made, as a boy, and as a man.

He watched the gophers rising and chirping, their paws held neatly to their small chests.

"Soon be green grass, boys," he told them. "Better go back in your holes till then." He walked slowly past the empty barn. Something on the far side rattled softly in the wind. A section of fence sang woodenly against a post. It had been a few years since he had sold his last cow and his last horse, but he could still smell manure and the dry, sweet scent of stored hay as he passed the open door. Pigeons and owls lived there now. "And welcome to it," he muttered. From his doorstep he could see them coming and going through the loft window or the holes in the roof. He liked to watch them. It didn't occur to him to feed them. He wouldn't have done it if he had thought of it.

He went out onto the prairie. From here he owned nearly all the land he could see. There were no roads on it since there was no call for any, and when the municipality had insisted on making fireguards he'd had no trouble persuading them to plow them on the perimeters where he couldn't see them.

When he was well out onto the grass and could feel the inevitable wind singing around him, he paused again, turned slowly in a full circle so as to look at things. The land he and his mother had plowed up over sixty years ago had long since gone back to grass, but the prairie was so fragile that he could still pick it out without difficulty. Once a plow touched this land it was ruined for the length of a man's life; there was no getting it back to the way it had been. Not enough rain, thin soil, drifting crop spray and other things setting back growth. He spat on the ground and looked back to his house.

After more than sixty years in the wind and rain and snow it leaned a little, this way and that. It was silvered too and looked now as if it had grown there and was a part of the landscape. The paint he had applied under his mother's stern eye had long since peeled off in the sun. Only once in a while coming around the house, he might find, unexpectedly, a fleck of ancient green paint still caught on the splintered wood. It always made his heart lurch when that happened. Once, he had flicked a piece of paint off onto the ground with his broad, stained thumbnail. Then he had been struck by the urge to stoop, to get down on his knees and scrabble in the dirt till he found it so that he could put it back where it belonged. He had stood there a long time, bent, staring down at the dust, but in the end he had straightened and gone away. Now, when he found bits of paint, he left them where they were.

He poked at the grass with his stick. The birds would be nesting soon. He raised his eyes to the sky and saw a jet stream, high, white and straight as an arrow move across the pale sky. He watched it soundlessly lengthen until its distant beginnings dispersed to irregular, falling puffs of cloud.

Soon there would be no sign that it had come at all, until another and then another jet came stinging across the sky leaving its boom behind to shake his house and to die away to an echo among the hills. He began to walk again.

Before long he sensed there was a coyote nearby. He did not look around, kept walking slowly, sliding his stick through the short grass, swishing it to and fro while he listened to the wind and the distant cry of a hawk hunting. He looked forward to finding the nests of meadowlark, horned lark and duck eggs and then to watching the young birds learning to fly.

When at last he turned to go back to his house, he saw the coyote sitting on the crest of a rise to his left. The animal was thin, but soon the prairie would scrabble with life, and mice and gophers would drop at his feet. As he walked he could feel the coyote trotting beside him a hundred yards away. When he reached the yard, he turned to watch the coyote leave him and trot away across the prairie. The sun was well up in the sky now. He could feel its thin March warmth on his face when he lifted it skyward.

He left his stick in its place by the door and went inside. He fried himself a little bacon and made a piece of toast by holding it on a fork over the open flame. He was out of bread now, although he could always make biscuits, but it would soon be time to make his monthly trip to town for supplies. He would pick up the mail too, not that there would be anything but a hurried note from Moira and a stilted, puzzling letter from John's wife signed by John. He sighed; he dreaded going to town. The village nearby that he had always gone to was a ghost town now, nothing but a few empty, leaning wooden buildings. It was twenty miles further to the nearest town and it was big and noisy and full of strangers.

He poured himself the last cup of coffee from the pot, and sat back to rest his legs and to ease the perpetual ache in the small of his back. The wind rattled the doorknob and the windowpane in a friendly, excited way. It whistled softly down the chimney, calling him.

Often it crossed his mind that he ought to be working, that he should fix the corrals, get himself some chickens and a few pigs, but he never did. Worked all my life, he said to himself, and where did it get me? But then, what else had he seen to do with it? He did not feel guilty because he wasn't working; he felt instead that the issue was remote from him, because he was old. Soon he fell asleep.

He dreamed a pale dream, a colourless dream, filled with a sense of the pale spring prairie, with the muted grass, and the soaring, endless sky. When he woke, it was afternoon.

This time he made tea. He drank it strong and hot and then went out again. He kept his old truck parked in the sun on the south side of the house where it would start more easily. He got in and turned the key and when the motor caught almost at once, he was not surprised. He gave it a moment to warm up, then drove slowly away from the shack, down the old trail he and his mother had started years before.

The tires crunched through the last of the icy snow, splashing in the wet spots, the truck lurching as it hit muddy patches, but he gassed it and it always went through. He rolled down his window and drove with his arm out, resting on the doorframe. After a short distance he turned east, off the deeper track that no number of years would erase, and headed down a fainter trail, bumping over rocks and rough patches and steering around the occasional badger hole or burnout or patch of cactus.

The smoke was still rising. He didn't want to look at it, but there was no avoiding it. The breeze was light this afternoon, and the black pall hung in a massive, flat cloud, low in the sky from a spot not far ahead of him where it billowed greasily upward. He climbed a low rise and its source came into view, the flames shooting red and blue, high into the air. Burning off gas from an oil well. This had been going on for months. The flame never went out, day or night, just kept burning, sending that ugly black smoke into the pure sky. He hated to look in that direction.

But on occasion he had seen the telltale smoke to the north and to the west as well. There was oil everywhere, they said. Under all this land, too, but he would never let them near it. That fire ahead was on Alan's land, and once, venturing farther than he ever had onto his son's land, he had come upon a whole sea of pumps moving relentlessly up and down. The sight had shaken him, for the oil patch was on a piece of land that had once been his, that he had signed over to Alan so long ago now that it too seemed like a fairytale. On an acre or so to one side, that the oil company had gravelled and fenced with a high, wire-mesh fence, there was a small steel building and a half dozen steel storage tanks.

Around the enclosure lay a summerfallow field, the grey earth ground to a powder that lifted in a fine haze with each breath of wind. Andrew hated to see the soil so overworked. You'd think he'd have something better to do, he thought, than to ride around on that tractor till he'd destroyed the soil under it. Andrew couldn't understand how a man could do that to the earth. In the end, what did a man have but the ground under his feet? He had studied the field, a strange, almost sick feeling in his chest, till he couldn't look at it anymore. It must be the power he likes, he had thought. And then, he won't farm long if he keeps that up.

Now he glanced in that direction at the flames shooting high in the air, at the dark shroud that hung motionless over the land, then turned the truck north.

He was driving on the border between his land and his son's. Since Andrew had stopped keeping cattle he didn't need fences, but it still alarmed and angered him the way Alan or his hired men had caught the fenceposts with their cultivator in their eagerness not to leave an inch of land unturned, knocking down sections of fence and dragging them down the field, whether on purpose or not, Andrew didn't know, and not bothering to fix them.

Here was the reason for Andrew's daily circling of his land, come spring. He drove his borders, watching the tractors work, letting Alan and his men know that he wouldn't tolerate Alan's cultivators slipping as much as a half an inch over onto his land. Wherever Alan could get away with it he plowed up the road allowances and farmed the ditches, and Andrew knew if he relaxed his vigilance for even a second the cultivators would stray one round onto his land and the next year it would be two rounds and on and on till there was no prairie left anywhere.

For long stretches, too, the old posts had rotted off with age and fallen so that the real fence between Alan and Andrew was not one you could see. From here on, even after the fireguard mercifully ended, Andrew travelled on his own grassland, which lay always to his left, and with Alan's cultivated land on his right, until he had completed the square and arrived back at his shack.

Now on his right there was a huge stubblefield, faded to white by the winter snows which had lain on it, tilting up to meet the sky. Alan had farmed hills so steep Andrew had thought they would be forever safe from the plow. They were hills you couldn't drive a half-ton up without spinning out, but Alan's new four-wheel drive tractor could climb anything.

Andrew drove slowly, staring morosely at his son's farmland. Soon Alan's men would be out again cultivating the stubble with their massive machinery, sending dust clouds a hundred feet into the air. They'd turn this yellow-white field to grey dirt again, and it would fade to the palest beige in the intense summer heat, the weeds barely poking their heads above the ground when the tractors would come again and turn it one more time, the land growing always finer and paler, till on windy days there would be a steady grey-brown haze hanging above it, discolouring the blue of the sky. He had read somewhere that during the previous summer, somewhere to the north, the dustclouds from cultivated fields had been so bad the Mounties had to close the highway. If he could help it Alan would never get the rest of his land. He would not let him turn it into a desert too.

He turned west in a hollow, still on the fireguard, avoided a clear pool of melting snow, climbed the hill and drove on past the long stretch of summerfallow on his right, which lay bare and still blackened from the snow that had melted on it. He noticed again that there wasn't a speck of snow left on the summerfallow. There never was. Turned earth has a warmer temperature than stubble, it melts snow faster, doesn't catch as much in the first place.

To rest his eyes he turned his head to look out the truck window to the long soothing stretch of prairie that lay on his left. He pulled the truck to a stop and for a long time looked out over the fading yellow grass, turning bluish in the distance, and far off to the soft green tones near the border. A half dozen antelope were grazing not far off and when they heard the sound of his motor, they lifted their heads, then ran off, the buck hanging back with his head up, assessing the danger. Andrew grinned to himself. Here at least the animals could still nest and feed and raise their young and live out their lives like they did when he first came. No swift foxes left though, hadn't seen one in more than twenty years. And fewer and fewer birds. Crop spray and insecticides had killed 'em off, he thought. But the sight of the prairie made him feel easier and he drove on west.

He steered the truck around a big patch of prickly-pears, climbed a slow rise and saw that at his favourite spot somebody was standing. A man. At first he was angry, then puzzled. Alan never got out of his vehicles, as far as Andrew knew, and nobody else ever came this way.

He was standing at the big flat rock on the northwest, the highest corner of Andrew's land. He must have walked in from somewhere because there was no horse or vehicle nearby. Andrew stopped the truck and got out. The stranger was painting at an easel, using the rock for both a table and a chair. A backpack in an aluminum frame was propped against the rock and a couple of cans containing paint brushes and pencils sat on the rock beside him. He was standing on an angle facing southeast, his small easel low in front of him. He turned and glanced at Andrew, and Andrew was struck by the brightness of his blue eyes in his windburned face. The painter turned back to his picture.

Andrew leaned against the hood of his truck and waited. After a long moment the man took a deep breath and expelled it slowly, pushed his straw hat back on his head and turned to Andrew.

"I heard you could see the Bear Paws from here," he said, "but I can't make them out." They both looked south again to the place where the sky should have met the land. The horizon had dissolved in a thick, blue haze.

"Forest fire smoke drifting in from B.C." Andrew said. "It's early in the year for that." He grunted, thinking more than he said. He went past the painter, moving slowly, the wind feeling with warm fingers inside his jacket, and sat down on the far end of the rock. It was a pale beige, a little yellowish, a huge, rectangular chunk of limestone left by the glaciers that had passed over so long ago. They had scraped away all but an inch or two of topsoil. It was the glaciers that had turned this land into ranching country, he often thought, not him. The stranger had a red scarf tied around his throat and its ends fluttered in the wind.

"You must be Samson," he said. Andrew didn't respond, just stared off to the south. "Okay if I paint here?" Andrew laughed, and looked down at the stranger's boots.

They were workboots, worn and cracked and covered with dust. They'd seen a lot of miles. There was an anthill off to the man's right, red ants scurrying over it and he was suddenly reminded of how when they were kids at school one of their games had been to put a stick into an anthill, catch a few ants on it, then take the stick over to a second anthill, thrust it in, and watch the ants fight. He laughed again, remembering. The painter had gone back to his easel. Now he had his back to Andrew and, when he stepped aside to study the scenery, Andrew thought to look at his painting. It was a picture of what lay before them, the soft yellow land billowing downward and outward, the land, brilliant with light, marked by ribbons of purple shadow lying across it. Andrew's small shack a speck down below, the larger house with the dead trees around it half-hidden behind a hill.

"Who lives there?" the painter asked, pointing to the big house.

"Nobody," Andrew said.

"Ahh," the painter said.

The sun had warmed the rock and in a shallow basin near the centre there was a pool of clear, melted snow water. He was reminded of how he used to lie on his belly on the damp ground in the spring and drink water from the pools of melting snow. When he was out riding, a long time ago. He closed his eyes.

"What's that?" the painter asked, pointing. Andrew looked. Far to the east and the north, a whirling white haze like smoke rose wildly into the sky. Andrew snorted, looked away.

"Alkali," he said. "Used to be a slough when I was a boy. Had ducks and geese on it. Wild swans sometimes, even cranes. Saw pelicans there once. Man owns that land drained the slough so he could plow it up and seed it. So all the salts came up and now it's good for nothing. It's just so much chalk."

The sun was moving farther to the west every day before it set. It hung now half-way beneath its zenith and the horizon far off to the southwest. It was too bright to look at, but at this time of the year he knew it had a cream-coloured corona, the centre would be the palest yellow, building up for the summer inferno. He warmed himself in its light. The painter worked at his easel. Andrew found he was not sorry he was there.

The country beyond his land was divided into squares of black and gold and the occasional square of a softer shade, grassland. It seemed to Andrew that when he looked each day there were fewer squares of grass than there had been the day before. He frowned and turned back to the painting.

The painter seated himself on the other end of the rock near his easel and wiped his paintbrush with a multicoloured rag that had been hanging from his back pocket. Together they scrutinized the picture. Then Andrew saw what had not quite registered before. The picture went on beyond his land, to the distant mountains, but nowhere had the painter put in farmland. He had painted it the way it was when Andrew first came. He turned, surprised, to the painter.

"I go farther every year," the painter said, not to him, looking into the haze where the mountains were hidden. "There's almost nowhere left to go." Andrew followed his eyes to the south.

269

"I never been nowhere much," Andrew said.

"Some people don't need to go," the painter replied, still squinting off into the distance. Andrew wondered what he saw. The breeze stirred the grass around them and a gopher scurried past, squeaking.

"I'm just kind of hunkered down here now," he said his eyes on the borders of his land. "When I go, so does this." Suddenly he wanted to cry. The tears bubbled up in him so unexpectedly that he had to wheeze to hold their hot presence down.

The painter didn't speak, just looked at the picture. Andrew dropped his head and stared at his hands lying loosely on his lap. How white they were, and how thin his thighs had become, concave where they had once swelled out with muscle, hard as iron. I go farther every year, the painter had said, and Andrew thought of all the long, dark journeys he had taken in his head, while life went on around him. Andrew heard paper rustle and when he looked he saw that the painter was drawing him.

"To tell the truth," Andrew said, "I've willed it to the Wildlife people." He chuckled, then grew sober. "I doubt they can hang onto it very long," he said, "but at least it'll slow them tractors up some."

They sat there together until the sun had reached its furthest point west and hung, a perfect fiery red circle above the edge of the earth. Then the painter cleaned his brushes, put away his easel and packed it, shrugged into his backpack, and with his wet painting held gingerly in front of him, turned to Andrew.

"May I come again?" he asked. The red light smoothed his weathered skin, made his eyes glow. The question surprised Andrew, and he thought for a moment, wondering why he was surprised.

"All my life," he said, "I thought this land belonged to me." He paused. Now I see that ain't right. It don't belong to nobody." They touched their hats to each other, then the painter was walking away with long strides and Andrew was climbing into his truck.

As he drove up to his shack, parked, and climbed out, he saw that there was another jet crossing the sky, so high he couldn't see the plane at all, only the jet stream pouring out behind it, coloured rose by the dying sun. He could not fathom such power, soaring high above the sun, the source of life, as if it were a god in its own right, and had no need of the old gods. Andrew watched the jetstream till it vanished high in the deepening sky, then he went inside.

He lit his fire, cooked himself an egg, made another cup of tea, and sank gratefully into his rocking chair. Another day gone by. He rocked and listened to the owl hooting on the ridge of the barn roof.

Sometimes at this time of day his mother came, but it had been so long since she had died that they had nothing to say to each other any more. When he first moved here Karen came often, scolding, and then, later, sitting with him silently, but for a long time even she had not come. Well, the time would come when he would die too; surely it was not far off.

He was ready to die. A man knows when he's lived long enough, he said to himself. A man knows when it's time. He thought about his life. He did not do this deliberately, he no longer had deliberate thoughts, but his life was there, inside his head, and it came flowing out, and he let it, couldn't have stopped it if he'd remembered how. Over the stream of images, the remembered voices, he thought how he had wondered over and over again, what it was all for, how he had thrashed around trying to discover a meaning, or to make one. For a moment he wished he'd gone to school, or read books, or known somebody wise. But even that desire washed away.

He was not afraid of death or of what he would find on the other side. He had not been a good man. He knew that, but this no longer troubled him. Better or worse than others—what did it matter? He felt it was all out of his hands, had probably always been out of his hands. He was a human, that was all. He had grown old, he would die soon.

CHAPTER TWO

Someone was coming. He heard a truck rumbling down the trail, but he didn't rise to see who it was, or if he had heard anything at all.

The door rasped inward, its hinges squeaking. Light flooded in around the figure in the open doorway. Andrew closed his eyes and waited. Would death come this way? Was he perhaps already a dead man?

"Mr. Samson?" a voice said. Cautiously he opened his eyes, but could make out nothing except a bulky masculine outline. The door closed, protesting noisily, the light died. He could hear the figure move to the table, pull out a chair, and sit down. He waited till he could see again.

"Who are you?" he asked. He was not afraid, not even curious.

"Brennan Adams," the man said. "I've come again." Gradually his vision cleared. It was the painter, sitting before him in his straw hat with a blue kerchief tied around his neck. Hadn't it been red?

"Eh?" Andrew said. "Thought it was Coyote maybe, come to see me."

"Does Coyote come often?" the painter asked. Andrew laughed. He struggled upright.

"It's time for tea," he said. "It must be."

The painter sat silent while Andrew filled the kettle with water, put another piece of wood in, set the kettle on the stove, and went back to his chair.

"I've been painting here for a week now," he said. "I haven't seen you around."

"Around?" Andrew asked. "I been here."

"I want to show you my pictures," the painter said. Andrew, using his stick, got up again and made tea. He set two cups on the table, put the teapot beside them, pulled out a chair, and sat down. He studied the painter, who was wearing a worn, paint-flecked denim jacket.

"I don't go too far anymore," Andrew said. "With my feet, anyway. Show me your pictures." The painter stood up.

"Didn't see you last year either," he said. He turned and went outside, the light billowing inward blindingly, then abruptly cut off. In the silence Andrew heard whispers but he couldn't make out what they were saying. Only the wind, he thought, and strained again to hear its message. He was bent that way, listening intently, when the light filled the room again, the painter entered, carrying a pile of things, and closed the door.

"This one is painted from the edge of your land looking this way." He held up a canvas. Slowly it came into focus, the dun-coloured prairie at the height of summer, heat waves distorting the distance, a blue mirage of cliffs lifted in a thin line between earth and sky, his own silver-grey shack sitting in the yellow grass under the high, hot sun. He felt a lassitude overtake him, things grew hazy, his limbs lost their energy. It was on him again.

"What is it?" the painter asked. Andrew sat, his head drooped forward, feeling the strength ebbing from his body. This time? He waited patiently, feeling the sun's heat on his arms and face. The wind was whispering to him again. Presently he lifted his head. The painter was watching him. Andrew felt the sapping languor slowly leave him. Not yet.

The painter set down the picture he'd been holding and picked up another one.

"This one," he said. His voice was deep and strong. The grassland in spring, a slough, the one in the southwest corner of his land, willets, killdeer, ducks, geese, a muskrat, antelope come for water. In the corner, a coyote, watching.

"Ahh," Andrew said. He felt himself there, listened for the clink of the bit as his horse bent to drink. He could smell the lifting, welcome scent of water carried on the air.

Silently the painter set the picture down and picked up another: Andrew chopping firewood in the moonlight, by the side of his shack, his lantern splashing yellow onto the blue-shadowed snow. He felt the falling weight of the axe in his biceps; his skin, where the flesh stretched thin across his high, hard cheekbones, burned in the cold.

"You were there," he said to the painter.

"A painter sees everything," the painter said, laughing softly.

"So does an old man," Andrew said. He could see into the painter's heart, he could count the ants in an anthill, or the stones in the yard.

The painter showed him picture after picture—the prairie in winter, in the summer, in fall and the spring. All the animals: badger, skunk, rabbit, snake, weasel, gopher, fox, antelope, deer, porcupine, coyote, bobcat, lynx; the birds: swallow, sparrow, crow, burrowing owl, great horned owl, snowy owl, Swainson's hawk, nighthawk, magpie, vulture, great blue heron, blackbird, sage hen, prairie chicken, partridge, meadowlark, horned lark, golden eagle; the plants: spear grass, needle and thread grass, blue grama grass, june grass, blue joint grass, winter fat, vetches, grease-wood, buckbrush, sagebrush, cactus, buffalo beans, club moss, locoweed, death camus, lichen.

The light in the room was growing brighter, but the pictures were clear, sharply delineated, and beautiful. His heart ached for the life that had been his. But then, he thought, how perfect it had been, how exact, and long, and detail-filled, how complete and beautiful. How beautiful.

The painter had come to the end of his pictures, but Andrew couldn't make him out, because the door was open again, and the light flooded the room, growing brighter at every second till it had melted the walls and the table before him, till the roof too, disappeared, so the light mingled with the blaze of sun, and he found himself dissolving, joyfully, into a universe of light.